GUNBOY

His left eyelid tore open, and sleep's fresh scab rolled down his cheek into the pit. The pitch darkness was as expansive as it was cold, cold enough to freeze the balls off a brass monkey, his father would say. No, not his father, Evan corrected himself. Dominic's father. This was Dominic's experience. Evan was reliving his thoughts, his entire digital being, and Dominic was exhausted. He stuck his tongue out of his mouth and licked his dry, cracked lips. He had no memory of drinking recently, no memory of arriving at this shared present.

"Where am I?" he asked with his own mouth, not Dominic's.

"Shall I just tell you how it ends?" Renner's voice sounded off. It wasn't in the same place as Dominic. It was elsewhere, BODILESS.

"No." He wanted to see it for himself.

GUNBOY

A Novel by Leighton Dean

GunBoy

First published in 2017 by Tickety Boo Press

This paperback edition was first published in 2023 by Leighton Dean

Copyright © 2017 by Leighton Dean
Edited by Leighton Dean & Gary Compton
Copy-edited by Siobhan Marshall-Jones
Cover Art by Leighton Dean
Book Design by Leighton Dean

For 'T'
my first fan.

"Before I express my gratitude, I must first offer an apology, something this office should have done long ago. We failed you. We believed the United Kingdom to be invincible, that we ourselves were invincible. And because of our arrogance—we are a kingdom, united no more."

Jonathan Reekes' Acceptance Speech 2030,
British Prime Minister.

PART ONE:
ZOMBIE

CHAPTER ONE
OFF THE RECORD

The sunrise banished the darkness, illuminating the aged satellite orbiting Earth, three hundred miles above England. Now a remnant of Heathrow's golden era, MI5 had repurposed the antiquated computer to monitor Britain's greatest embarrassment: the abandoned city of London.

Each night, the satellite scrutinised the prefabricated structures cluttering Heathrow's crumbling runways. Tonight, Pil tapped into the signal, watching the former airport—now a United Nations Aid Station—with eager anticipation. The crisp feed justified the money he'd spent, sent directly to his chipset and projected onto his contact lenses through digital wizardry.

It was a departure from his usual routine. Like many reporters, Pil had resorted to inflammatory accusations and opinions, vying for a share of the internet. However, his only recent story to gain traction was about Fray International's Human and Associated Networks Database (HAND). Despite exposing their 'lack of privacy policy' a month ago, they still considered him a harmless terrier.

Wisdom had escaped him as he aged, leaving behind regret. He'd made a living, affording a Rhondda Valley cottage, failed marriages, and state-of-the-art smart contact lenses. Crafted by Oakley, these lenses featured retina-projected HUD, 3D imaging, and recording synced to his chipset. They had earned him a fortune and refined his taste for vulgarity. Now, in his later years, he found himself lonely, without the comfort of self-respect.

But December 12th, 2038, would change everything—today held the promise of transformation.

Pil packed his Sony V-Slate and rushed to Heathrow. Although slightly outdated, the tablet connected to his skull chipset and held a charge. The scuffed edges and hairline crack were inconsequential—it worked. He pursued a real story this time, hoping to reclaim a part of himself he'd lost. Guided by a tip, he settled into Gate 5 Departure lounge and drowned himself in BullPhett.

He reached into his bag and pulled out another can.

For three nights, he scrutinised the satellite's green, glossy image, yielding nothing but a dull ache in his backside. One would think they could have upgraded the moulded plastic chairs. At 07:03 AM, after five hours, twenty-two minutes, and thirteen seconds of fruitless observation, he questioned his investment. Dismissing his HUD's time display and fading the satellite feed, the empty Gate Five lounge came back into focus.

The departure lounge remained deserted, save for the desk clerk, Alison. Pleasant enough, but Pil couldn't overlook her habit of licking her front teeth after every sentence to learn more about her. Nevertheless, she was twenty-seven, thirty years his junior, and Pil promised himself that if nothing happened within the next hour, he'd ask her out.

The Sat-feed HudAPP icon flickered twice, indicating movement.

A quick right-eye wink activated the chip in his brain, revealing the satellite's imagery. Nurses, volunteers, and soldiers poured through the camp.

He dismissed the feed as UN soldiers sprinted through the lounge, weaving past empty seats and Alison, disappearing through a door marked Authorised Personnel Only.

He rose, shook the numbness from his feet, slid the V-Slate into his bag, and trailed the UN soldiers, preparing his most charming grin.

Alison glanced up from her workstation. "No."

"This is it," Pil said.

"I can't let you in, so you may as well sit down."

"Alison, c'mon, it's me."

"I know." Her response stung like a slap.

His tongue pressed against sealed lips; what was her problem? She knew he'd been waiting to get on the ground floor.

"Don't." She cut him off before he could muster a solid argument.

Press freedom wasn't what it once was. Glancing at the vacant rows of plastic seats, he foresaw the end of his career.

2

Plan B led him outside, among doctors and nurses. His press pass still gave him some privileges. He snaked through the manic crowd; it was bedlam, resembling a January sale frenzy more than an organised response station. So packed, he lifted his satchel overhead to protect his V-Slate from the scurrying personnel. It hadn't been this busy since the '29 nuke threat.

The first major alert in nine years, and Pil found himself right in the centre. He couldn't help it; he felt twenty-five again. Grinning, he bounced between people, passing lightweight barriers and flashing amber lights toward the row of Red Cross helicopters.

Large hulking tactical transports with the weapon systems removed. They'd become common hand-me-downs from private firms. Soon to be scrapped, but today were being loaded with paramedics and supplies. Today they'd save lives, making history—and Pil would share their glory.

Pil dismissed his HUD's list of vehicle registrations, already spotting the aircraft he needed. Second in line, a dark-skinned Spaniard hoisted a crate into its belly. He lowered his satchel and called, "Tango!"

Tango squinted in the dim light, smiling in recognition. "A bit early for you, old man?"

"Sounds like a brush off."

"Depends if you're after smokes."

Tango slid a crate into the transport's belly and extended his right hand. "Quit," Pil said, grabbing it. "Insurance will kill you."

"Tell me about it."

"I'd rather you tell me about it," said Pil, nodding at the chaos.

"Off the record?" A question harkening back to a time before Tango was born. With modern recording options, upholding the old code had become a disadvantage. Pil was one of the few reporters who did, and Tango knew it from their past dealings.

"They won't know it's from you," Pil said.

Tango said nothing, but Pil, a keen observer of human behaviour, didn't need a HudAPP to recognise his twitching eyebrow as nervousness. "They won't know it came from you," he repeated.

"Alright," Tango said, "an SOS came in from behind the fence. Explosion or some shit, we're taking a couple of choppers out to provide help."

Pil's spider-sense tingled. "SOP?"

Special Operations Police had a series of bases beyond the fence, but they were privately funded with their own medical teams. If they needed help...

Tango shook his head. "Don't know. Just been told to kit up and move out."

The mystery deepened. An SOS from behind the fence. Someone besides the SOPs? His mind raced. There'd been no known negotiations with London. This was huge.

"You know what I'm going to ask," he said, masking desperation with a forced smile.

"You want to come with me?" Tango asked.

Pil nodded, grinning like an eight-year-old. "C'mon, think of it as an early Christmas present."

"The signal must be heard, huh?"

Pil laughed. "I've got three daughters from three wives, Tango. I need the cash." He locked eyes with Tango, silently imploring.

"Get aboard before someone spots you."

3

Within seven minutes, two Red Cross transports sped into Greater London, trailing their escort—an AW250 Lynx Wildcat, a remotely piloted weapons platform worth more than Heathrow's entire Red Cross fleet. This state-of-the-art killing machine eased any fears the paramedic team had about potential attacks.

Tango's transport held the middle position, co-piloted by Juarez, a slick fly-boy. Shorter than Tango, he seemed to compensate for his height with gym sessions. In the passenger hold with Pil were four paramedics. He considered interviewing them, but they were inexperienced, and he sought more than a fluffed-up editorial.

He craved the fabled scoop of a lifetime.

Thoughts consumed him; an SOS was unprecedented, at least publicly. London had become a violent, anarchic gangland. Danger lurked in every corner—drug factories, human trafficking, kidnapping, rape, murder; everything they could squeeze into the brochure, and he would see it first-hand. To prove or disprove, he didn't care. He was the first non-military, non-private militia to witness it in fourteen years. He silently dedicated his imagined Pulitzer to his children and ex-wives, without whom he wouldn't need to work.

Elated, he ignored the safety instructions, leaning as close as possible to the open side of the chopper. He closed his eyes, letting the wind whip through his silver hair, oblivious to the nervous chatter and questions directed at him.

Only when he felt a tug on his sleeve did he notice all four paramedics staring. He tapped the soft tissue behind his ear, switching to the local channel. "Sorry?"

"You're the reporter, Pil?" asked the nearest paramedic, sporting blond, tousled hair and a youthful face.

"Uh, huh?"

"I told you!" his friend exclaimed, grinning like a Cheshire cat.

The blond nodded. "Will you make us famous?"

"I hope so."

"What's going on?" asked Cheshire.

"No idea," Pil said, perhaps too curtly, as the crew nodded and fell silent. "We'll find out soon enough," he reassured them.

Blond shook his head but remained quiet. Pil returned to the door and observed the city below. What remained of it: grass replaced roads ran and trees climbed infiltrated and disfigured buildings. Yet, he recognised London—no city was as distinct, especially to those who'd grown up there.

Eight airborne minutes passed, and they were over Hounslow. Roofless homes and long-abandoned vehicles littered the landscape, making tales of a gangland city seem overstated. It was merely a ghost town.

Pil retreated inside the cabin, tapped the wall behind the cockpit, switched to the pilot's channel, and asked for updates. "Nothing since we left," Tango said. Pil sighed; if it was this dull, he might as well write. He activated record mode on his contact lenses, pulled out his V-Slate, and wrote the date and time: December 12th, 2038, 07:32. He pondered his opening—something dramatic, daring to captivate readers.

The cockpit alarm blared, and he cursed his own tempting of fate. Gripping the handrail, ignoring the paramedics' fearful expressions, he shouted, "Tango?" His voice vanished in the helicopter's thunderous roar. "Tango!" he tried again, but received no answer.

Pil leaned out the side, seeing no difference in the streets below. "Shit!" He spotted a jet-black smoke trail streaking towards him. Recognising it as an RPG, he banged on the cockpit door, shouting a warning. Three paramedics panicked, screaming in terror. Only Blond joined Pil at the edge, eyes widening at the approaching rocket. The craft banked hard, jerking them back inside.

Pil's hands found the tight orange straps securing the medical supplies, his arm locked in the net. Blond, less fortunate, screamed for his mother as he fell out the hatch, followed by the rocket and the medics' terrified cries.

Black smoke filled the cabin, scorching everyone's throats. But with burning eyes and blackened lungs, Pil felt exhilarated. Pity about Blond, but he'd remember to buy Tango a bottle of the good stuff for saving their lives.

Above the helicopter's roar, Pil heard the distinctive whine of the Wildcat's machine guns. He needed a better view. Ignoring Cheshire's question, he crawled over crates, wedging himself between Juarez and Tango in the cockpit. He watched the Wildcat pummel the buildings with gunfire, recording it all on his chipset.

"What are you doing?" Cheshire repeated his question, and again Pil didn't hear.

"Another bogie!" Juarez pointed at a second smoke trail approaching the Wildcat. Tango yanked back on the control stick, reversing their position. Too late—an RPG clipped the Wildcat's tail, exploding and showering their chopper with debris.

"Brace yourselves!" Tango ordered, forcing Pil back into the crew section. He locked his arm in the orange netting, stealing another glance through the cockpit doorway to see the spinning, out-of-control Wildcat heading their way.

Pil freed his hand and blinked a command to his chip. He would not let death stop him from receiving the Pulitzer. As Cheshire and the others hunkered down, he leapt from the transport. Mid-air, he saw the flaming Wildcat collide with the helicopter, a fireball lighting up the sky. Pil smiled; he was about to live forever.

CHAPTER TWO
THE LEADERSHIP

Under pressure from law enforcement, the British Government evacuated Whitehall when the third riot ran for eight consecutive days. As Police struggled to protect Downing Street, Cameron reluctantly moved his base of operations away from its two-thousand-year-old seat of power.

After the 2014 referendum, Edinburgh was off the table, making York the logical choice. Previously a defensive outpost against Scotland, it now sought to regain control of its southern territory. Greater London, Kent, and southern Essex had succumbed to economic strife and overpopulation from migrants fleeing a war started by England.

In 2018, the Provisional Parliamentary Building (PPB) was completed, transforming York into the heart of a new Britannia. Skyscrapers emerged around the city, towering so high they seemed to pierce the sky. British Press hailed them as symbols of England's triumph, while the international press saw them as compensation for a nation in chaos.

By 2038, international criticism against England persisted. Yet the development of Northern England generated significant income. Although some economists disagreed, the British consensus viewed the South's decline as a boon for the North.

The PPB consisted of five outer buildings arranged in a star pattern around a central sixth structure. Standing twelve storeys tall, with interconnecting bridges on the fourth and eighth floors, the design prioritised logistics and efficiency over architectural elegance. Each building was self-sufficient in power and water, and the central residential and commercial compound could be accessed via underground and air routes.

Oliver Trench seldom used staff quarters, opting to commute daily from his townhouse. Unsettled in his workplace, he attributed this discomfort to the 150 troops living and training in the basement or the impending invasion they prepared for.

After an extended, unscheduled day, he reluctantly retired to his quarters, finding sleep elusive due to faulty air conditioning and anxiety over sending two men, including his late friend's son Kyle, on a covert mission into London.

The decision was last minute, a Band-Aid for a gaping wound. Evan, a brilliant strategist but untested field agent, had been manipulated into volunteering by the Prime Minister. Oliver then felt compelled to involve Kyle.

With Evan off-site, Renner assumed control room responsibility. Though Oliver recognised Renner's technical skill, he lacked strategic prowess. Official channels would have provided options and contingencies, but the Prime Minister's paranoia narrowed their list to a few trusted names, which were dwindling.

At forty-seven, Oliver felt the impact of sleep deprivation when his chipset buzzed him awake at six. Groggy and irritable, he flung the sheets aside and stumbled to the bathroom. Relying on legal stimulants from his Medical App, his bloodshot eyes soon appeared as youthful and energetic as the Party's Chief Whip ought to be.

Oliver grabbed an Armani suit from the wardrobe and checked his Heads-Up Display for the day's itinerary, already aware that the first hour involved breakfast with the Prime Minister. He tied a full Windsor and prepared for work in under fifteen minutes. Satisfied with his appearance, he pressed behind his ear. "Lloyd?"

After a brief pause, the PM's personal secretary responded, "Morning, Oliver."

"Is he in yet?"

2

Oliver took a short walk through the commons, fetching two coffees before arriving at the Prime Minister's office. After brief pleasantries, he delved into the concerns that had troubled him throughout the night.

"Renner's running the show," Jonathan stated the obvious. Oliver knew the PM's perspective, as they had discussed at length since Dominic Fletcher's disappearance, but no better solution was apparent.

"Kyle will get him where he needs to go," Oliver reassured himself, though he hesitated to fully endorse their plan. Doubts lingered about dropping them into London without understanding Fletcher's disappearance, and he worried about rushing to contact Window in case it was a trap.

"Prime Minister, the Home Secretary is here to see you," Lloyd's sarcastic voice interrupted via the intercom. "She would very much like to join you both." Oliver easily pictured Antonia pressing urgent business on the man to push into the room sooner than he'd allow.

"Come in, Antonia," Jonathan beckoned.

Years prior, Antonia had introduced Oliver to Jonathan. From their first conversation, it was clear to Oliver she was smitten with Jonathan, but not romantically. They became inseparable, and she affectionately dubbed him her 'little poster boy,' captivated by his rugged rugby looks and intellectual prowess.

"Good morning, Prime Minister, Oliver," she said, unfolding a digital sheet and pressing it flat on the Prime Minister's onyx-topped desk.

Jonathan glanced up from his own document, eyebrows raised in anticipation. "Good morning, Toni."

Oliver leaned in for a better view of the document, quipping, "Brought us breakfast, have you?"

"Afraid not," she said, turning to Oliver, "an army AW250 Wildcat was shot down." Then back to Jonathan, "Along with a Red Cross transport. Seven dead."

Jonathan sighed, picking up an orange from the desk's fruit bowl. Oliver retrieved the abandoned document and began reading, quickly finding the distressing detail.

"Is this accurate?" he inquired, hoping for an error.

She glanced at the indicated spot. "Yes."

"What's the matter?" Jonathan asked, peeling his orange impatiently.

"An embedded journalist was with the Red Cross," Oliver said, lifting the digital paper to reveal Pil's face.

"Freelance journalist," Antonia corrected.

Oliver grasped the distinction and felt a sliver of relief. Had the journalist been affiliated with a media mogul, they would have already heard the news. He examined the time stamps; the information was fresh. The transport and its passengers likely still smouldered.

A tense silence enveloped the room as Oliver finished reading the document. He joined Antonia in watching Jonathan's face redden with contemplation before he finally uttered, "Bury it."

"Jon," Oliver interjected, unsure he'd heard correctly. Surely, Jonathan didn't believe they could cover this up? "I think we can leverage this—"

"And how do you propose to 'leverage' seven deaths?" Antonia asked, barely restraining a disapproving eyebrow raise.

"I'm sorry," Oliver feigned. "But you don't know—"

"I know," the Prime Minister interrupted.

"We need to show how desperate things are," Oliver said.

Jonathan tore a juicy segment from the orange, tossing it into his mouth. "Get it off the table."

"Sir, I must object," Antonia said, "You can't expect—"

"I don't care how you do it, Toni," Jonathan interrupted. "You were the spin doctor; now spin it."

Oliver winced at the command. Antonia hadn't been press secretary for nearly five years. Jonathan had exploited her previous role to belittle her, and her wavering eyes revealed its effectiveness. "Sir, I'm hardly able to—"

She halted when he raised his large hand, a gesture that ended all discussions.

"How many people know about this?" he inquired, signalling that he wouldn't accept delegating this task to someone uninformed.

"The Army," Oliver said.

"That means Rockwood, a handful of analysts." Jonathan paused, deep in thought. "Anyone else?"

Oliver finished reviewing the document and glanced at Antonia, who said, "The second Red Cross helicopter crew and myself." She paused. "And my secretary."

Ordering Rockwood and his analysts to stay silent would be simple. The second Red Cross chopper, with its six witnesses, posed a challenge. That didn't even account for the journalist who might have posted footage posthumously, or worse, survived.

"I want it off the table," Jonathan repeated, ending the argument.

"Yes, Prime Minister," she said.

Oliver didn't see how she would manage it—perhaps a couple of days, if they were fortunate. She'd received the thin end of the wedge, and he was relieved not to be tasked with making the news vanish. He couldn't let Antonia handle it alone. "I'll look into this Pil character."

"Don't be ridiculous, Oli," said Jonathan. "You're Chief Whip. Rockwood will assign an analyst for that. I need you to track down Toliver and Herman."

"Sir?" Antonia said. "Is there something I should know?"

Oliver glanced up from the paper, ready to interject. Clever Antonia. She'd been dealing with the Belfast bombing and had not been included in their extracurricular activities of late. She must have been curious about the PM's excellent mood that morning.

"Evan's on the ground," Jonathan said, "in London, as we speak."

On seeing her confusion, Oliver added, "Fletcher went dark two days ago. Evan stepped up."

"Yes, but he's not qualified, is he?" Her concern was sincere. "He won't—"

"He has company," Jonathan said, referring to Kyle. "So, as you'd expect, I'd prefer not to distract myself with the crash."

"It's really happening?" she asked.

"It's a long shot," Jonathan nodded, "but we've contacted this Window character and are getting him out. So, I need this off the table for a couple of days." He glanced at Oliver. "A week at most?"

It was a cautious estimate, but one Oliver reluctantly accepted. "A week at the most."

"Of course," Antonia said, relieved.

Oliver wondered if Jonathan had mentioned this earlier, whether Antonia would have consented to side-line the crash right away. He started thumbing through the document, stopping on the Wildcat's kill cam and tapped play. He watched it silently as it spiralled into the Red Cross helicopter.

"Aside from this room, three others know about the mission, and two of them are on the ground," Jonathan said. "So, get the attack off the table, understand?"

"I'll get on it right away."

Oliver observed as she left the room, waiting for the door to close behind her before asking Jonathan about his fruit intake. "A bit early for that, isn't it?"

Jonathan followed his gaze to the orange peels on his desk. "Vitamin C?"

"If you say so."

"Don't you have work to get on with?"

Oliver slid the paper onto Jonathan's desk and stood. It was, after all, his cue to leave, and he wanted to catch Antonia. "I'll see you later this morning?"

Jonathan picked up the document and read but didn't look up. "After the briefings, I imagine."

"I'll ask Doris to set something up with Lloyd?"

"As you see it."

Oliver sent his secretary the meeting request via his HUD and buttoned his blazer, smoothing the creases before exiting the room. Better to leave now than to say something he'd regret. "Loving your work," he said to Lloyd and hastened to the corridor, catching Antonia as she turned right toward the lift lobby.

"Hey," he said, grasping her elbow.

She turned. "Oliver."

He knew straight away she was annoyed, and rightly so. "I'm sorry."

"No need," she said, pressing the call button.

"We were going to tell you."

She stood her ground, not showing an iota of weakness, one of the many traits Oliver loved her for. "I'm fine, honestly."

That was that then. If he pushed any further, she'd think him condescending, and he'd have insulted two of his friends before nine o'clock.

"He's wrong."

"Oliver." She looked him in the eye. "What's on your mind?"

With a quiet ding, the elevator door opened, revealing an empty cab. They entered and pressed for the ground. "Don't wait," he said. "You're going to listen to him, but this thing is going to blow up in our faces."

"Were you in the same room?"

"He's been more erratic of late."

"If that's what you're calling it."

"He's still Jonathan," he said.

"He's still the Prime Minister."

"Which is why we need to help him. We need to give him all the information," Oliver said as the elevator doors opened to the ground floor lobby.

She touched his elbow, in the way she did whenever she wanted him to know that she trusted his judgement. "I'll ask MI5 to go over the information, see if they turn up anything that Rockwood's analyst doesn't find."

"Thank you," he answered, pressing for the third floor.

She walked out of the cab, ending the conversation over her shoulder. "But if he screams at me again, I'm telling him it was your idea."

CHAPTER THREE
JUNCTION TWO EASTBOUND

Several thick red wires, bound with blue cable ties, extended from the main interface hub. They disappeared under the flooring, re-emerging through a circular access hole and climbing the spine of the control chair before connecting to a socket in the mission controller's skull.

Cable is still the most secure form of data travel, declared a brass plate above the identification scanner to the left of the door. Like everything in the room, it had been positioned precisely as Renner wanted. He was a particular person with particular requirements. The brass plaque was just one of his idiosyncrasies. His striking ginger handlebar moustache was another, but without his quirks, he would be merely a stereotype.

A reformed black hat hacker, Renner now worked for the government—a true child of the millennium, understanding code better than reality. His nonchalant attitude shuffled him around the department, with few paying attention, except for Evan. He had recognised Renner's genius and enlisted him for his project.

Currently, Renner occupied the heart of his luminescent fantasy. His screens, keyboard, and mouse comprised pulsing white lines. In actuality, he was connected to the room's sole furnishing: his leather recliner. Everything else was a mere projection, visible only to him as the mission controller.

Twenty-seven screens fed him information every second; satellites, high-altitude drones, weather drones, local communications signals, and traffic reports poured their collective knowledge into his virtual domain.

One strand of particular interest was Window's pirate radio signal and was what prompted Evan to seek Renner out.

It was also the reason Evan had chosen the call sign 'Bluebird' and elected to cross the fence. Window was the man who would be king of London and Bluebird was on his way to meet him.

Renner extracted the dialogue strand from the mix, running it through a dictation program he had borrowed during his time at the BBC. He read the fervent monologue instead of listening to it, keeping his audio unoccupied and focused on the voices of Evan and Kyle. The latter had the designation 'Fallout.'

These two intrepid men were under his supervision, venturing into London while he remained in York. He had observed them casually for most of the night, but now they were approaching the off-ramp and entering the city. It was time to justify his salary.

"Next junction, fellas," Renner said.

2

"Copy that," whispered Evan, blinking to command his chipset to project his HUD onto his retina and display the relevant location details.

To their right, the shattered remains of the GlaxoSmithKline building loomed. The structure, like all others that stretched to the winter horizon, had long decayed. Evan had never visited London; he vaguely recalled his life in Kent, but the memories felt distant, almost belonging to someone else. Gazing over the crumbling vista, he couldn't help but feel an awesome foreboding bearing down on him.

Evan rubbed his hands together beneath his worn leather poncho as the morning chill lingered. A crisp, clear sky with the first winter sun rose on their right. It was serene, which unnerved him. No personalised advertisements or Starbucks discount offers filled the air. It was eerily quiet.

"I'm running one last check on your systems," announced Renner.

"Paranoid?" Kyle asked.

"You'd be too if your boss was strolling into hell."

"He is." Kyle looked back, ensuring Evan was still with him.

Evan's feet ached from the long walk from Heathrow. Envious of Kyle's enhancements, he knew his minimal cybernetics would make the mission a physical and mental challenge. Evan raised his fingerless gloved hand, giving a thumbs-up. He remained quiet, observing the surroundings and listening to Window's broadcast. There was no reason for concern. True, they were entering hell, but with a Secret Intelligence Service superstar by his side and enough firepower to devastate a small town, they at least had a chance. For a moment, they could stop worrying about him and focus on the task at hand.

"If you can help, please contact Han on the usual channel," announced Window, the voice of Free London.

They were still in the outskirts of the city, yet they had already seen his mark. The K and U, painted on the remains of billboards. K and U – Kingdom United, the name of Window's pirate radio station. "As always, our prayers are with those whose lives have been lost in the name of freedom."

An explosion had occurred.

Details were sparse, but at least fifteen had died. Window had been on the radio all morning, attempting to calm the animosity between gangs. No one claimed responsibility for the explosion, but according to Window, the Triad sought revenge.

So far all the information Evan had gleaned was from Window. There'd been none coming from base camp and the quiet gnawed at him like a persistent horsefly. London's infighting should have ceased months ago.

"Anything on the explosion?"

"Nothing on the channels," Renner said.

Evan frowned. There should be information about an explosion. In York or Cardiff, there would be coverage, or at least a mention on a blog or a teenager's HAND page.

"Guys." Renner's voice interrupted Evan's thoughts. He observed his surroundings, noticing Kyle had dropped to his knee and was sliding his assault rifle from under his scarred poncho, readying his aim.

"I've got, yes—uh—definitely," Renner continued. "Game on, fellas!"

"I can't see anything," Evan said.

"Welcoming committee," Kyle remarked, springing into action.

"Uploading positions in five, four..."

Evan followed Kyle's, shouldering his rifle, dropping to one knee and waiting. He scanned the landscape, spotting countless cover positions for snipers and rocketeers. If the new arrivals held any of them, they would be sitting ducks. Amid his rising anxiety, it still surprised him at how quickly they had been detected.

"Three, two, one..." Before Renner finished, red tags populated the two buildings to their left, each representing a heartbeat.

Evan darted to the hard shoulder, scanning the building and counting tags. "I've got seven."

"Eight, one north of the group." Renner's voice guided his scope to the roof of the neighbouring building, where a sniper aimed back at him.

The battle's first two shots echoed through the cityscape. Evan's shot replaced the sniper's skull with a pink wisp. The sniper's shot struck Evan's shoulder; his smart cloth undershirt tightened against the impact, preventing the bullet from piercing through. But the force of the .308 calibre knocked him off his feet, cracking his collarbone.

Evan's rifle clattered to the floor, followed by his own painful impact. The agony was unlike anything he had ever experienced, causing him to thrash and scream against the asphalt.

"Bluebird's down," Kyle's voice was faint amidst the gunfire, but Evan heard it. He latched onto his voice as if it were the rope to his drowning man, refusing to be downed within the first hour of the job.

"Bluebird's down," Fallout repeated.

Evan watched tracer bullets streak overhead.

Kyle crouched at a distance, too far to pull Evan into cover, leaving him sprawled across the tarmac like a rag doll. Exposed and uncertain, Evan called out, "Ky—" correcting himself. "Fallout."

"Stay down," Kyle said, returning fire.

Evan rolled to his good side, quickly discovering it was a mistake as bullets kicked up dirt around him. Heeding Kyle's advice, he stayed down, but resolved to help. Pulling up his HUD, he set commands in motion to address his wound. Once the pain subsided, he accessed Kyle's live feed, watching the battle through his eyes.

Kyle moved to a new position, guided by a vibrating navigation arrow. Amidst local temperature, wind speed, and distance data, Evan saw his own medical condition. Despite the clutter, Kyle managed the information with ease; he was a machine.

Kyle slid behind an overturned Nissan, fired two quick shots, and eliminated a target. He ducked as automatic fire peppered his cover. "Renner, I need a better position."

"Patience is a virtue."

"Shove virtue up your socket and find me a better position!" Kyle yelled as bullets sparked off the car.

"Guys?" Evan groaned.

"Stay down, damn it!" Kyle clearly lacked people skills.

A new navigation arrow appeared on Kyle's HUD, guiding him to a position behind the concrete hard shoulder. The report indicated 84% cover. "That's your best option," Renner said. "Optimum range and target options."

"Copy that," Kyle replied, dashing to the new position. He fired at their attackers as Renner updated enemy tags, marking yellow for good vantage points.

Evan disconnected from Kyle's feed, finding it too confusing. Eyes closed, he listened to the gunfire, the pain in his shoulder dulled by his body's augmented morphine production. He didn't hear "Bluebird?" until Kyle repeated it a third time.

"He's on meds," Renner answered for him.

Evan couldn't understand why it was funny, but he laughed just the same. "I'm good," Evan said, raising a hand and waving it above his face.

"Stay down!" Kyle ordered. "There's six across the way."

Then the air around the junction cracked like a giant's whip. "Fee fi, fo, thumb." Evan smirked, momentarily aware of his elevated state.

"Jesus. Where did that come from?" Kyle asked.

"Pass, but you're down to five targets," Renner said.

"That's comforting," Kyle said, his voice dripping with sarcasm.

Another crack resounded. "Wait, make that four. Someone else might be with you."

"Tell me something useful. Paint them up."

"I'm only seeing four contacts, plus you and Sickboy."

Kyle muttered something under his breath before asking if they were shooting each other.

"What?" Renner said, "Like a suicide squad?"

Evan chuckled at Renner's tone more than the joke itself, understanding less as time passed. The darkness comforted him, his heart rate slowed, and soon he slipped into unconsciousness.

3

Evan awoke to Kyle crouching over him. "You okay?"

"Fine," Evan replied, feeling a throbbing pain where intense heat once was. He checked his medical report on his HUD. His armour had stopped the .308

round, but the impact fractured his clavicle. Fortunately, nerves were intact, and the swelling wasn't worsening. His chipset administered morphine and nanobots to repair the damage.

He was lucky. Modern spec ammo, or better aim, and Kyle would be hauling his corpse back to York.

"Popped your cherry?" Kyle asked.

Evan grinned. Twice in his life, he was no longer a virgin. He tried to move but winced, remembering the pain's dominance. He lay still, gazing skyward. "Did you get them?"

"Not exactly. A sniper joined in, took most of them out." Kyle leaned against the bullet-riddled Micra, peeking around the edge. "Determined the origin yet?"

"Can't be certain," Renner said. "I have several possibilities."

Renner's choices appeared on Kyle's HUD, synced with Evan's. "Six trajectories," Kyle remarked on the imprecise assessment. All originated from the Glaxo building.

"I told you, I can't see him," Renner said. "It's my best guess."

"Guesses," Kyle corrected.

Evan examined the lines. "There could be more than one."

"Now that's a scary thought," Kyle admitted.

"Guardian Angels?" Evan whispered.

"Or the Ghost of Lee Harvey—" Renner began as Kyle stood up. "Jesus, stop!"

Too late. Kyle already stood, stepping out from behind the car and saluting the GlaxoSmithKline building.

CHAPTER FOUR
CERBERUS

Evan watched the dog run off, their sole encounter for over an hour, but neither he nor Kyle complained. The surprise motorway attack left an uneasy knot in his stomach. The area should have been sparsely populated.

They walked along the derelict street Evan had expected. No-man's-land, a three-mile band along the Orbital, housed smugglers, deviants, and those foolish enough to confront the Special Operations Police force. This was their domain, encircling as much of London by following the M25 Orbital as possible. London itself, deep in lost England, was likened to Cold War Berlin by scholars. All the King's land in London received supplies from Heathrow aid station. Maintaining a foothold was crucial, agreed upon by all political parties, until they found a solution.

The SOP's mandate: keep the foothold at any cost.

Profiting from marijuana farms and narcotics kitchens, they focused on quelling violence. They were the first and last line holding onto London—an expensive, indefinite line the government couldn't afford. Despite their corruption, they reported to the MOD, and they turned a blind eye as long as peace was maintained and the SOP kept indiscretions away from the media.

While Bluebird and Fallout remained in the SOP zone, they should be relatively safe. Eventually, they would enter Greater London. Renner had prepared false identities for the checkpoint, Evan's initial concern before the unexpected attack. The memory of the event twisted his gut, and he tried to push it aside. Stay focused, he told himself, recalling it had only been five years since he left Cardiff University. Now he was on a James Bond mission behind the fence. He grinned. Evan Bell, twenty-eight. Codename: Bluebird.

His father, Howard Bell, a reunification supporter like Evan, questioned his son's involvement in the mission. "What the hell do you think you're doing?" His father's overprotective voice scolded him from a hundred miles away. The doubt returned, making Evan wonder if his father was right. The M4 bullet was all too real and too early in the mission.

Embarrassed, every pinch in his shoulder tightened his chest, reminding him he'd been shot before entering London. Kyle, thankfully, hadn't mentioned it, but Evan sensed his concern. Kyle's primary mission was to ensure Evan reached Window. They briefly discussed the attack, concluding they were unlucky, encountering local smugglers defending their turf. It was an easier pill to swallow than the alternative: their mission wasn't as secret as they'd hoped.

Evan's original plan went awry when Dominic Fletcher disappeared. Now he was on Plan B, with no Plan C. If their false identities failed, they would be detained, miss the rendezvous, and their journey would be in vain. The lack of information from Control made failure easier to dwell on. Renner's silence irked Evan, who couldn't help but tug on that cord of fear, the thread that could unravel the mission.

He and Kyle might be walking into a trap. He clenched his fists, trying to banish the thoughts. Concentrate on the second part of the mission: get past the SOP checkpoint, then a couple more hours to Notting Hill Underground to meet their contact. God willing, they would meet Window.

A green snap-flash blipped on his HUD, an alert from his Tactical Assist Program (TAP). His chip passively scanned for threats and found one. The alert appeared just before Evan saw Kyle drop to his knee. He followed suit, aiming his rifle in the warning's direction.

"It's gone," Kyle said.

"Did you see it?" Evan asked, replaying the visual recording but finding no answer. Whatever it was, it was fast. He linked with Renner for cover positions, which quickly appeared on his HUD, including a tactical vantage point from a second-floor window across the road. "Thanks."

"It was a sound. No heartbeat." Kyle's words reminded Evan of the sniper—no heartbeat... "Anything else, Ren?"

"Nada," replied Renner.

"Checking it out," Kyle said, leaving his position. He followed the path on Evan's HUD, past the overgrown garden bush, toward the crumbling derelict house.

Evan stayed put, covering Kyle's approach. When Fallout stopped at the garden fence, Evan followed his display's advice, moving to a car parked on the opposite side of the road. In position, he signalled Kyle, who vanished behind the bush. Evan's tactical assist program (TAP) showed a 26% threat, switched to combat mode and flagged Kyle's position.

Evan's display bounced a thumbnail on its dock, which he expanded to a partial view. The image filled his right eye's field of vision, dividing his concentration. His left eye scanned the surroundings while his right eye watched Kyle's live feed.

Kyle crept through the garden, treading on the stone and brick remains of the house. Rifle shouldered, aim steady, and reflexes ready, Evan observed from across the street, his own rifle trailing Kyle, waiting for TAP's alert.

The street turned eerily quiet. With TAP's help, Evan's ears searched for potential threats. Despite the computer's reassurance of safety, his instincts told him otherwise. Something or someone had been with them since the motorway attack.

As Kyle closed within a meter of the house, Evan's TAP reassessed the situation, offering a 22% threat warning. "You reading that?" he asked via their comms system.

"I'm checking it out." Kyle seemed unconvinced, but Evan wasn't sure if that was good or bad. They could be followed by dealers, SOPs, gangbangers, or a crazed lunatic—anything could fester in this forsaken place.

The alert pinged again; startled, Evan gripped his rifle and searched the garden where Kyle had stood, finding nothing.

"What," Kyle said, "are you doing?"

Evan's shoulders slumped as his mind caught up with his actions. He'd misread the alert; it wasn't a threat. TAP advised moving closer—Kyle was leaving effective cover range. "Moving up."

"You sure?" His sarcastic tone reminded him that Kyle probably was watching his live feed, too.

"Yes." He minimised Kyle's live feed, swapping it out for TAP's suggested position. "Now." He announced his first step, leaping to the nook between the two parked cars outside the garden's railings. He located Kyle, crouched and ready to enter the building before bringing back the live feed. "Go!"

Evan observed through Kyle's eyes as he explored the dust-covered interior. The second floor shared the same space as the first, and only a few paw prints marred the tomb-like silence.

Kyle adjusted his vision to the low light, allowing both of them to see in tinted green; the room was empty. "Checking the next room."

"You're wasting your time," Renner chimed in.

"I'm not so sure," Kyle said, echoing Evan's suspicions. He was certain they were being followed, that someone hid in the ruins. Yet there was nothing but dog prints in the dust. "Stop..." Evan halted Kyle.

Evan rewound the feed. "There." A crack in the far wall. A shadow masking a head's silhouette. Neither Kyle nor Renner said anything, and Evan counted the steps between Kyle and the crack. If Kyle stepped back, the shadow would know they had spotted it and would act.

"I'm going through the doorway and around." Kyle's message played in Evan's ear. He'd assessed the situation similarly. The back room provided cover for approaching, and he blinked his exact path for Evan to see.

"There's no one there," Renner's voice came in barely audible undertones. Evan doubted he intended for them to hear, but it didn't matter—

someone was there. Kyle would flush the shadow out, and Evan needed a flanking position. He blinked the request to his chip, which offered several choices, but none were useful if the shadow escaped through the house's rear.

"Stay where you are!" Kyle ordered.

"Copy that!" Evan replied, watching Kyle move from the main room into the former kitchen. The furnishings and plumbing had been removed, but the drainage and '90s laminate flooring remained. No sign of the shadow, just a boarded-up window and another door. As Kyle showed Evan his next move, they watched the corners for movement. Nothing. Not even the breeze Evan felt on his face. The house was dead.

"You're wasting your time," Renner said again, this time intending for them to hear.

"Shut it," Kyle snapped back.

"There's nothing here..."

"Ren," Evan interjected, "go grab a coffee."

"He can stay; I'll just mute him." Evan knew Kyle was grinning.

Kyle paused at the doorway, angling his gun through the gap first, connecting his sight with the scope to peer around the corner. Down the dank corridor to the crack in the wall, where they expected the shadow to be.

"Nothing!" Kyle called it.

"I fucking told you," Renner burst out.

"Wait!" Evan said, expecting Kyle to turn around and leave the house.

"There's no way someone could've slipped past you," Renner added, but neither paid attention to him. Kyle had entered the corridor, his scope low, aimed at the spot Evan had called out. On the floor, among the broken brick and red dust, lay a small footprint. Kyle's display scanned and measured it.

"Is that a... child's?" Evan couldn't believe his eyes.

"Think so," Kyle replied, checking his corners again. "Looks fresh too."

Renner, a man who trusted only his instruments and rational explanations, struggled with the idea of a child evading his tech. "Let me get this straight. You're chasing a killer... munchkin?"

"Well, we're not in Kansas anymore," Evan quipped, feeling more at ease now that the danger seemed to have passed. "Come on, we need to move." He stood up, feeling a sting in his collarbone. Instinctively, he reached for it with his spare hand and rotated his shoulder until the pain subsided.

"How is it?" Kyle asked as he emerged onto the street.

Evan's HUD informed him he was at 42% combat efficiency. "Okay."

"You know I have access to your medicals," Kyle reminded him.

"I'm fine," Evan insisted, arching an eyebrow, signalling Kyle to drop the subject.

Undeterred, Kyle continued, "Is that sitting-behind-a-desk fine or—"

Evan shot Kyle a look that warned him to stop or face consequences.

"Because I don't want to go through a SOP checkpoint with you at 42%." Evan realised his earlier look probably appeared silly to Kyle. The 42% wasn't the real reason Kyle wanted to avoid the checkpoint—it was just an excuse.

They had argued about the checkpoint twice already. The first time was in York when Evan had explained his plan to Kyle, and the second was en route to Heathrow. Kyle trusted Renner in tactical situations, but not in low-tech environments like Mozambique, Nicaragua, Afghanistan, or London. Relying on a hacker in a low-tech area never has good odds. It wasn't like the Mission Impossible series.

"This is mission impossible," Evan had replied forcefully, ending the argument—so he thought. But it seemed the issue was about to resurface.

"If Renner can do it."

"I'm right here," Renner interjected, sounding genuinely offended.

"He can't see who's following us," Kyle continued. "You've broken your collarbone; we should avoid the checkpoint." Belittling both Evan and Renner's plan. "There are plenty of gaps we can take advantage of."

He was right, and they all knew it. They could bypass the checkpoint and slip into London without fake papers. But Evan needed those passes, granting them access to any number of SOP safe houses and bases they might need in the next few days.

"We're sticking to the plan," Evan said.

Kyle disagreed. "Fine, but Renner better be as good as he claims."

"I'm still here, mate," Renner said with a huff. "Jesus, what's your problem?"

Evan looked at Kyle, remembering an earlier comment. "Do you still have Renner muted?"

Kyle's eyes rounded. "Apologies, but I've tumbled with SOPs before, and you better be shit-hot. I don't want to be caught in a crossfire clutching my stones."

"Fallout," Renner said. "I'm better."

Evan grinned, knowing Kyle enjoyed flaunting his arrogance in old mission control. His friend's choice of words for his family jewels also triggered a memory. Evan scanned the ground, found what he needed, and walked over. Kneeling by a crumbled kerbstone, he scooped up a handful of gravel and placed it in an empty cloth bag. He tightened the drawstring, securing his "precious stones" and noticed the silence in his head.

He rose, and Kyle was already heading toward the checkpoint. Time to put Renner's bravado to the test.

2

"There it is." Kyle didn't point, but subtly tilted his left shoulder toward the distant sniper tower, a cruel structure dominating the artificial horizon. Fifty feet of high-tensile steel encased in concrete, with three levels of platforms, plate steel armour, and razor wire up the intimidating mast. SOP checkpoint nineteen—their gateway into London.

On cue, Evan's TAP program alerted him to threats from the tower. He swallowed hard as four sniper rifles targeted him. They won't shoot unless they perceive a threat, he told himself, but knew the SOPs had TAP on them too.

The checkpoint's position worsened matters, standing at the end of the road, in the centre of a junction, funnelling anyone approaching it into the snipers' line of fire. Feeling exposed, Evan checked Kyle was still with him. They hadn't spoken since the derelict building. He wasn't sure if he was pouting; he didn't appear to be a man who would, but he toyed with the idea, anyway. It made him feel more masculine. Right now, however, on reading the updated display information, he felt like a child with three of the snipers aimed at him.

It was too late to turn around and, as his father always said, 'in for a penny, in for a pound.' It was time to call in the big guns. "Renner?"

"I'm here," Renner replied.

"You ready?"

"Always."

Evan patted the pouch of gravel in his pocket, reassuring himself. It's going to work. He pushed SOP rumours aside as they walked toward the tower, taking another twelve minutes according to the GPS widget. Yesterday, the plan seemed easy at Special Branch, just an inch on a map. Now, with the tower looming, he couldn't ignore the rumours of abuse and torture. Two snipers still aimed at him, the other two on Kyle. He envisioned their plan failing, the SOPs mocking and arresting them, dragging them into a nearby home for some waterboarding. Would Kyle let it go that far? Evan doubted it. Kyle seemed the type to fight back, even if it got them killed. He told himself to get a grip.

"Quit being a wuss," his father's voice echoed from the past, recalling his first swimming lesson. Standing poolside, staring at the water in terror. He'd despised the water, the chlorine's bite, and the resistance against his movements. Fear of drowning, not unlike the present situation. He had conquered the water, and he'd conquer this.

It will work. Renner's got this. The false IDs were foolproof, and the identities had valid reasons to enter the city. The plan was solid. Yet, he debated it in his head four times as they neared the checkpoint, feeling better and worse with each repetition. Unwilling to share his doubts, he refused to give Kyle the satisfaction of being right. The plan is solid, so quit being a wimp.

First came lightweight frames, warning cordons alerting anyone approaching that they were within assault rifle range. He'd already been in sniper range for over thirteen minutes—what were a few more guns? The frames lined the road, allowing only single-file walking. Vehicles had to wait for inspection.

Beyond the first line, more cheap frames slowed any approach. At the junction, four motorised barrier arms sealed each street, enclosing a mobile command centre with two adjacent Armoured Personnel Carriers.

Close enough for Evan's HUD to display the troops' full details. Registered personnel had access to each other's details under TAP's friendly fire prevention rules—rank and number hovering above each trooper's head. But it didn't work the other way; black ops remained hidden unless they chose to be seen, and Evan had no intention of being visible.

As they neared the gate, Evan's display counted and labelled all the troops: mainly privates, some sergeants, and a corporal. "Look for the Post Commander," Renner advised.

The SOPs wore sandy grey urban fatigues, reinforced chest cocoons, and all-encompassing helmets with facemasks, gas filters, and anti-flare mirror lenses. They carried automatic rifles or XP sub-machine guns and grenades. To Evan, they resembled Stormtroopers, but more menacing because they could shoot straight.

"That's him," Renner said as Evan's HUD beeped. The Post Commander descended the Mobile Command Post steps, not taller than his troops, distinguished only by red and yellow stripes on his forearms.

He swaggered toward them.

"You two look a little lost." His voice, like his facemask, stripped away his humanity. Evan raised his hand for the Commander to clasp, hoping silence would lend him an air of aloofness. "In a hurry?" The Commander didn't take his hand.

Instead, Evan was forced to stare at his own reflection in the Commander's anti-flares. Don't be a wuss.

Evan stared at his reflection in the Commander's anti-flares, thinking, Don't be a wuss. He sensed Kyle observing the mounting tension. The Commander remained silent and was yet to take his hand. And Evan grew more aware of the guns aimed at them and the foolishness of their ploy. It's going to work.

"Straight to business, huh?" The Commander finally broke the silence and clasped Evan's arm. As they grasped hands, the blue 'Human and Associated Networks Database' logo appeared and spun between them, visible only in their personal displays. A graphical interface for augmented reality and its appearance confirmed the connection of both the Commander's and Evan's chipsets. This marked the plan's beginning. The rest depended on Renner.

Evan's chip requested the Commander's details, Lt. Commander Dillon Meyer, and Dillon's chip made the same request. Instead of Evan's details, his chipset provided his new identity and the permits Renner prepared. Both Evan and Kyle's alter-egos were bounty hunters searching for Jonah Goldhagen, who had escaped the Asuka Corporation three days ago. It was a convincing cover story; Jonah was reported missing, and many seeking to escape corporate control fled through London, and its sprawling mass of black market connections. People found new identities and transport to the Continent for fresh starts. Corporations disliked losing their own, especially to competitors, so they sent bounty hunters after them.

The false identities and cover story, crafted meticulously by Renner, were the simple parts. The challenge came now, while Evan held the

Commander's arm. "I'm in," Renner announced, indicating his successful breach of the Commander's chipset via the HAND program.

Evan waited, skimming Dillon's details, trying to look natural and not dwell on Renner's infiltration or the possibility of the Commander's security detecting him. It's going to work. Evan studied Dillon's featureless face, seeking any hint of his thoughts.

After the longest nine seconds of Evan's life, Renner broke the silence. "That was embarrassingly easy. Someone should file a complaint with the MOD." Evan relaxed, now only waiting for Dillon to finish reviewing their fabricated papers.

"It's not over yet," Kyle reminded them.

"Don't jinx it," Renner quipped, his confidence overshadowing Kyle's doubt.

Evan felt the Commander's grip loosen. "We won't be over two days," he asserted, as confident as Renner.

Dillon's facemask stared at him a moment longer, revealing nothing. Evan expected him to release his arm, but the Commander tightened his grip, forcing Evan's reflection to struggle for composure. Seconds ticked by as the Commander scrutinised their forgeries.

Kyle shuffled behind Evan, surveying the troops, still unconvinced by Renner's genius. His doubt seeped into Evan, who blinked a request to his chipset and regretted it when TAP offered no solution if the forgeries or hack failed.

Without warning, Commander Meyer released Evan's arm. "There's a charge for entry, bounty hunter." Despite the mask, Evan detected contempt in his voice.

They knew about the customary payment—a fistful of diamonds. Evan reached into his pocket, pulling out a cloth bag and dropping it into the

Commander's open palm. "That should cover it," he said, watching the Commander reveal a heap of dust and gravel. Only Evan and Kyle saw the truth: inside Dillon's chip, a small virus identified the insulting payment as clear, uncut diamonds. The same virus spread through Dillon's squad via their local communication network.

"Are we good?" Evan inquired, confident they were.

"Oh, we're good," the Commander replied, contempt gone. "But you picked one hell of a day to go hunting."

"Why?" Kyle asked.

"The Triad have gone fuck-mook." He looked up from the diamonds, seeing both 'bounty hunters' staring at him. "They're tearing the city apart, knocked out two of our stations, and shot transports from the sky. It's chaos." He laughed, fingering the diamonds, and Evan felt the joke was on them.

Navigating London was difficult enough without the largest gang wreaking havoc. All factions, including the Triad, were supposed to be at peace. How had this happened in just a day? A chilling thought crossed Evan's mind: What had he got himself into? He forced a casual smile and asked, "Any reason for them going fuck-mook?" directing the question at both the Commander and the eavesdropping Renner.

Commander Meyer refilled the cloth bag and signalled a subordinate to open the gate. "No idea."

A moment later, Renner added, "I'll check it out."

The Commander stepped back, revealing a path to the gate. "Whatever it was, it happened this morning." The barrier behind him rose silently. "Welcome to Hell, boys."

CHAPTER FIVE
Welcome To the Jungle

Hell was no different to what they'd already seen; derelict homes, abandoned cars, and the tedium of monotony. Street after street, the only variation came from the gang tags scrawled on boarded-up windows and doors. The most widespread was the 'KU', a damn plague; sprayed over rivals' tags on cars. Even the damned streets.

The quiet couldn't last. Evan knew better, but savoured the peace while it persisted. Renner's intermittent chatter confirmed the Post Commander's warning. This realisation unsettled Evan, but he had resigned himself to the fact that today wouldn't go as planned. He could only rely on himself and Kyle to reach Notting Hill. As for the Triad attacks, Renner could only provide scraps. The Triad had hit several SOP stations and gangs. He gleaned intel on the first part by leaving a portal open—a digital peephole inside Commander Dillon Mayer's mind.

The latter was hearsay. Airwave chatter, nothing substantial. No solid evidence, no persuasive reason the Triad would or wouldn't cross their path. Anticipating the worst, Evan braced for their imminent arrival. Every turn, every alley led them closer to peril—but another hour passed without incident until they reached Goldhawk Road. A wide four-lane street leading to a shantytown. According to Dominic's map, they were ahead of schedule. Dominic should've been there. It was his mission, after all.

Did Evan blame himself for Dominic's disappearance, or did he blame Dominic? The answer left him uneasy. If Dominic hadn't vanished, Evan would've been back in Special Branch, not roasting in the Devil's playground, awaiting the next bullet. He lacked the training for this, unlike Dom, who'd spent months searching for Window. Maybe Dom was dead. It wasn't a stretch of the imagination. If so, it'd be on Evan—he was the mission leader who'd sent Dom here, alone. Witnessing this hellscape first-hand, Evan wondered if, given the chance, would he send Dom again?

"Heads up," Kyle said, having spotted her first, and transmitted the location to Evan's HUD.

About forty meters up the road, on the right, a young woman lounged on the open roof of a decaying home. As they neared, Evan saw her sipping bottled lager in the cold midday sun, eyeing them with morbid curiosity. She remained silent, even as they passed. Her dirty gold hair fluttered across her face, her gaze tracking them until she merged with the horizon.

After her, more people emerged, small clusters of threes and fives, and then more. To Evan's astonishment, the uninhabitable houses teemed with families—families too large for the buildings. They'd expanded with corrugated iron and scavenged materials, extending the structures forward, reducing the four lanes to two, sometimes just one. The transformation was jarring. It was difficult to believe this was a living community—a marvel to witness, but it raised a single, perplexing question: Why had they crammed on top of each other with all the empty homes?

"Bagdad hit London," Kyle said.

"With Rio," finished Evan. Neither looked at each other, instead scanning their surroundings. They'd read the reports; Evan even delved into the simulations, but nothing could have prepared him for the reality of these slums. People's clothes hung off their bodies, a few with enough weight to be considered well-fed, and the putrid smell of old sewage. Groups clustered around oil drum fires, while others walked purposefully. All stared at the travellers.

Evan's HUD flagged potential threats one by one. "They seem edgy."

"Watch your left flank." Renner's angelic voice directed their attention to five young men, the oldest around twenty, the youngest barely ten. All wore tattered yellow and brown striped football jerseys, all five watched them with a look in their eyes that Evan took an instant dislike to. Everyone else they'd passed had regarded them curiously. In some, Evan even recognised a little fear. But these boys, these teenagers, had nothing but murder in their eyes.

Evan didn't need to read the scans or zoom on their faces either. He recognised the telltale signs: incessant chewing, twitching fingers and eyes, and burn marks on their nostrils. You didn't see them in society because society had embraced the digital drug revolution. These were Outskirters, the ones the net warned you about. The ones that still took chemicals, Raid or Crack, judging by their physical deterioration. They were the poster kids for anarchy, and the slogan: Stick with us, or end up like this. 'Go back to bed, England. Your government is in control.' It worked. No one but the freaks took chemical drugs anymore.

"The five-a-side team?" Kyle said, adding, "Seriously?" in case no one had understood his sarcasm.

Evan glanced at Kyle, gave a quick grin, then refocused on the kids. His Tactical Assist Program highlighted their custom blades and homemade pistols. He swallowed his fear, having prepared for this. These kids were but a small part of the gang. They would be full of bravado, taunting, beating their chests, but wouldn't attack—no matter how horrifically violent and twitchy they looked. More importantly, they weren't Triad.

Two of the boys stepped forward, yelling in a pseudo-language born of the streets, a mesh of immigrant Indian, Polish, and English. City Speak, or one of its many dialects. Whatever it was, they were speaking too fast for Evan's chip to understand. While their articulation was poor, their yelling and threatening blades needed little translation. Evan gripped his rifle under his poncho, just in case.

Maintaining their pace, they gave the kids no reason to attack. Avoiding eye contact, Evan focused on their filthy blades instead.

"Stay calm." Kyle placed a hand on Evan's shoulder, a gesture that failed to reassure. Perhaps it was the way Evan's finger rested on the trigger guard that prompted Kyle's comment, or the bead of sweat running down past his left brow. Either way, the observation made him feel small and as young as the addicts encroaching on their personal space. It made him feel like a coward. He knew it wasn't intended. Kyle hadn't studied the area as much as Evan, but he'd been in many situations like this before. These weren't civilised augmented people; they were simpler, more erratic foes immune to simple brain hacks.

"New threat, guys," Renner announced, bringing more good news.

He didn't need to extrapolate. The low rumble of approaching engines signalled trouble. The atmosphere went from tense to critical. Everyone around them appeared calm, simply moving faster. People who had huddled around burning barrels dispersed into the corrugated shelters.

"What now?" Evan asked, ignored by everyone except the five-a-side team, the only ones remaining on the road. Unafraid or too high to notice, they stood their ground.

"Nine trucks are approaching from the north," Renner informed them. Kyle placed a hand on Evan's shoulder, pointing to a shanty hut on their right. Evan nodded and followed, monitoring the taunting kids, with Kyle doing the same.

"SOP?" asked Kyle.

"Not registered," Renner replied. All military equipment had transponders that pinged satellites; Renner would have identified them as SOPs if they were. These trucks were unidentified.

The kids remained ignorant of the engines, now loud enough for a trained ear to pick out the four-cylinder engines and the more telling, more worrying, rat-a-tatting automatic fire. The kids weren't scared: they may be high but there was no blasted way they couldn't hear the approaching war-band. "The rest of the gang?" Evan suggested, reasoning that the trucks, being non-SOP, could be backup for the kids' gang, ready to take out the two intruders.

Kyle's hand shot forward, pushing Evan into the corrugated hut as a rock narrowly missed his head. The makeshift projectile clanked against the iron sheet and landed on the ground. His assailant was one of the five-a-sides. Evan and Kyle's departure from the road must have been misconstrued as a sign of weakness. The dark-haired freak with a Bowie knife made crude hand gestures, leading his friends in a chorus of laughter at Evan's tumble to the ground.

Kyle readied his rifle under his poncho, anticipating their next move. "I don't think they like me much," Evan said, watching the kids' heartbeats quicken on his HUD. They were preparing to strike. Kyle stepped between Evan and the crew, urging him deeper into the hut and away from the road.

"The one on the right," Kyle said as the kid pulled a pistol from his waistband. A cumbersome, magazine-loaded pistol that on any other day Evan would have found amusing to see the kid shoot. But with the barrel aimed at his head, Evan didn't feel like laughing.

"You want to get off the road." Renner urged. "Now fellas!"

"We are," snapped Kyle, aiming his rifle at pistol-wielding little shit.

"I can see you standing at the side of the road."

Kyle kept his sights on the kid. "Renner, so help me—"

"Get off the fucking road!" Renner yelled as the convoy of trucks screeched around the corner. Kyle and the kids locked eyes, waiting for a distraction to gain the upper hand. Evan couldn't see the trucks, but he heard them speeding up the road, accompanied by automatic gunfire. Kyle stepped back, closer to Evan and into the shack. Bowie knife glanced to his left, eyes widening before raising his blade toward the oncoming vehicles.

Evan saw that everyone else had vanished from the street, except for the five-a-side kids. Kyle maintained his aim on the little shit, who was relentless in his taunting of them with his oversized pistol, and continued to do so until the first of the five broke formation. Panic-stricken, the youngest bolted from the street.

Bowie was second to run, then two more, leaving only Little-Shit, eyes wide in rage and focused on the approaching convoy. He stood his ground, laughing as he planted his feet wide, held his pistol toward the oncoming traffic with both hands, and yelled. His voice was lost under the loud roars of the engines.

The kid pulled the trigger, the pistol jerking upward, but he stood firm, determined to defend his turf. He fired again, recovering from the recoil faster and squeezing off one last shot before the first truck hit. What wasn't caught in the grille was flung back, then crushed under the wheels and spat out for the next truck, and the next...

Evan closed his eyes, unable to watch the kid's entrails being passed along the convoy. Kyle noticed the gang signs painted on the trucks. "Triads," he said, confirming the Post Commander's intel. Fortunately, the convoy passed without detecting them.

A bullet sliced through the corrugated roof, raising a dust cloud. It landed mere inches from Kyle, who grabbed Evan's shoulder and hauled him up before the second bullet struck the floor. They sprinted deeper into the shanty, dodging stacked boxes and leaping over bedrolls. The world raced by, crates tumbling and tin walls collapsing as a deadly hailstorm rained down around them.

Evan grazed an oil lamp, his eyes locked on Kyle's shoulder in front of him. Evan's HUD flickered, a counter climbing from zero to eight in under two seconds. Another bullet zipped between them, grazing Kyle's boot. Evan kept his eyes on Kyle's shoulder, the counter continuing to build. The numbers belonged to the residents stampeding behind them.

Another bullet tore through the roof and a chicken cage exploded into feathers. Evan squinted through the flurry, following Kyle's evasive manoeuvres until he collided with a baby's cot protruding from a doorway. He spread out his hands, catching the ground with his palms and preventing his fall. Smiling, he allowed himself a moment to catch his breath before hearing the stampede behind him. The approaching chaos jolted him back to reality. The impending doom of lead rain sent his thoughts into a frantic loop. He was going to die, and he was going to die on his knees. He shut his eyes and awaited the inevitable.

But it didn't come. Instead, Kyle's firm grip lifted him, carrying him toward a stone building. Evan managed a weak "Thanks" before Kyle flung him through the front door to safety.

He landed on the worn stone floor, adrenaline coursing through his veins. He ignored the scrolling data, Renner's voice, and the surrounding people. The dam wall he'd built with good old British stiff upper lip and 'don't be a wuss' was smashed. He'd been kidding himself. He was a desk jockey, not a field operative, and he had no business being in London. The realisation pinned him to the floor as tears welled up in his eyes, and he spat the taste of iron from his mouth.

"You alright?" Kyle asked, his voice familiar yet alien, as he crouched beside Evan with a hand on his back.

Evan couldn't speak, his voice and reason having deserted him. Instead, he shook his head.

"Of course he's alright," Renner interjected, misinterpreting Evan's elevated heart rate as adrenaline-fuelled excitement.

"No," Evan managed, "I'm not. I'm really not."

"Take a moment. We have some time," Kyle reassured him.

Evan surveyed his surroundings; the stairs seemed as good a spot as any. He stood, his legs shaky, and glanced at Kyle, silently urging him to keep his distance. Kyle obliged, and Evan cautiously approached the stairs. Grasping the banister, sturdy despite its worn appearance, he sat on the third step. It creaked in objection before taking his weight.

Kyle had followed him to the foot of the stairs and now he was looking around the room, his gaze turning faces away. There were at least thirty people in the house with them and more upstairs. None of whom Evan was aware of, despite his HUD's feeds. His thoughts were instead of his failure. The Triad would catch them; not now perhaps, but they would. He'd be killed before reaching the rendezvous—his body splashed across the grille of a 4x4, mowed down by automatic fire or having his face blown off by a close-range shotgun blast.

So engrossed in his morbid fantasies, he missed Renner's update about the Triads heading towards Dillon's checkpoint. "Let's go home..." he muttered, interrupting Renner's report.

Kyle moved closer, demanding, "Say again?"

Evan locked eyes with Kyle, feeling his face flush. "I can't do it. I thought I could, but I'm not cut out for this." He forced a nervous smile. Renner remained silent while Kyle stared at him with a calm, cold intensity that only worsened his unease. "You can't disagree."

"Why are you here?" Kyle asked, breaking the silence with a textbook question.

"Because Dom…" Evan started, but Kyle pressed a finger to his lips. Evan nodded, suddenly aware of the many spectators in the building. "I lost Dom Fletcher. I didn't have time to train someone else. There was no one else. I had to come."

"Why are you here?" Kyle repeated, and Evan's frustration grew.

"I just told you."

"That's how you got here. Not why." The soldier corrected him, forcing Evan to think beyond his panic.

Evan considered the reason behind his presence, why Jonathan Reekes had summoned him and why he'd agreed without hesitation. He exhaled sharply and grimaced, feeling like a child who had just cried himself silent. He understood. He no longer desired to retreat, but to push forward.

2

A Special Branch guard in black opened the door to the Cabinet Room, and Jonathan strode through, with Antonia following. Despite what was stamped on the bulletproof glass door, no one called it the Cabinet Room. They called it the War Room.

A massive onyx conference table dominated the long, unremarkable space, around which sat the twenty committee members, comprised of Cabinet and military staff. They addressed border patrol and related issues, like the fence, in this meeting preceding the actual cabinet meeting. All present stood as the Prime Minister entered the room.

Jonathan walked to the head of the table and sat. "Good morning."

The gathering echoed his greeting with varying enthusiasm. The Foreign Secretary Percy Browne, being one of the more zealous, lingered until the rest of the room sat before joining them.

Antonia settled into her seat across from Percy, with Harry Rockwood from the MOD two spots down from the Prime Minister and General Pike of His Majesty's Armed Forces opposite him. Reekes activated his personal display to reveal the meeting's agenda. "I know Birmingham was our intended starting point. However, the Triads broke their ceasefire this morning. It's a tragic scenario and will be a problem." He let his words settle before adding. "Antonia, would you do the brief?"

"Yes, of course." Placing her hand on the table, brought her report to the surface and with a flick of her wrist she sent it to every display. After bringing the group up to speed on the attack, she said, "MI5 informed me that a packet was transmitted from the location during the attack. We believe it was from Michael Ellis, better known as the blogger Pil. The packet's size suggests video footage, likely of the attack itself."

"You can't be sure of that," General Pike said.

"No," Antonia concurred, "but we've started proceedings to acquire the packet."

"The media exposure is covered in the last paragraph," added the PM.

Rockwood chimed in, "They took out two transports with an RPG. It's an isolated incident, sir. They were just posturing."

Jonathan's face conveyed his disdain. "You want to try that again?"

"Sir?"

"Posturing? Seven miles outside their territory?"

"Yes, sir. They're still just a street gang," Rockwood defended.

"Yet skilled enough to take out two transports with decades-old grenade launchers, including a multi-million-pound attack drone."

"I believe—" Percy attempted to interject, but Jonathan cut him off.

"I know what he meant. Thank you, Percy."

"I know what he meant," Jonathan cut in. "Thank you, Percy."

Antonia sensed the disbelief around the table, with no one coming to Percy's defence. Every man for himself, she thought, and stepped in. "MI5 assures me they will acquire the footage before the press."

"Not through official channels, I presume?" Pike asked.

"I didn't ask, but I'd believe they'll appropriate the server it's stored on," she said.

Rockwood pointed out, "That may not even be in the country. It could take them days—"

The Prime Minister slammed his fist on the table, silencing the room. "Enough with this squabbling." His eyes moved from Rockwood to Pike and finally rested on Antonia.

She had felt his icy gaze before, and none of those experiences had been pleasant. "I need to know the potential repercussions in Europe if this information becomes public," he said, his stare unwavering.

The room looked to Percy, who, noticing the silence, glanced up from the document. "You'll have a full report by three, but I can tell you one thing now. The sauerkraut will exploit this."

Antonia thought of Konrad Jaeger, the German Chancellor and unofficial King of Europe. Everyone at the table knew he'd seize any opportunity to make Reekes' administration appear weak. Britain was

Europe's problem child, constantly battling to maintain sanctions and enforce laws. No one at that table had a favourable word to say about the German leader.

"Then I look forward to reading your report," Jonathan quelled the murmurs of agreement. "I need a measured response that doesn't involve massacring civilians." He directed the remark at Rockwood and Pike, waiting for their nods before continuing. "Good. Now, I'd prefer to deal with just this – I don't want any more attacks."

"As I said, sir, this morning's attack was an isolated incident," Rockwood said.

"Posturing," Jonathan echoed.

"Yes, sir."

"Fine," Jonathan said. "I don't want any more posturing."

3

Since the drive-by, Renner had dropped some intelligence. His sources confirmed an explosion in Triad territory, killing their Dragon King, Sin Lao. Evan knew from his research that the lieutenants would now battle for the crown. However, it appeared the Triads were retaliating against the most likely provocateurs – the SOPs. Although it gave them a reason, Evan doubted the SOPs would willingly make an enemy of the Triad. Their mission hadn't changed in fifteen years: keep the peace, not provoke war.

As Renner guided them through the boroughs, Evan noticed Dominic Fletcher's reports had been superficial, so much so, it had to have been intentional. Many old department stores and hotels had become factories, producing cheap goods for the wealthy elsewhere. In the absence of watchdogs, underpaid workers and unsanctioned chemical trials operated freely, with profits funnelled through black markets.

Locals brandished weapons or bared their teeth as Evan and Kyle moved through the area. They were lightning rods in a storm. Fortunately, they hadn't encountered more Triads, and the locals seemed less inclined to attack them outright.

Evan had time to reflect on his moment of weakness and move past it. He wasn't a field operative but a 23-year-old tactician and problem solver. That was why he was here.

"You've been shortlisted," Parker Jones had said. He didn't like Evan, but then he didn't like any of the systems analysts under his charge. He wasn't suited for office duties. He was only there because his insurance hadn't covered the cost of a replacement foot. He walked with a decided limp, blaming the basic replacement, smashing it into the floor with each step.

"For what?" he had asked.

"Just get your ass over there." Evan had followed his limping commanding officer, hearing those uneven footfalls for the last time.

His stomach churned when first met Prime Minister Reekes' hand. The man's enormous hand easily enveloped Evan's, perhaps explaining Reekes' nickname in the house, Gorilla.

"So, you're the whiz kid," Reekes had said without authority, putting Evan at ease.

"That would probably depend on who you speak with," Evan had replied, deflecting the compliment while still not quite believing the situation.

Jonathan eyed Evan, grinning. "Tell me about Project Thorax."

Thorax had been a nine-month mission to crack Chinese counter-intelligence programs. "Any part in particular, sir?"

"The part that got you through my door."

Evan detailed his role in the operation. He wasn't a genius like Renner, but he thought practically. When logical steps failed, he thought outside the box. Chinese programs relied on three large private security companies. Evan targeted Mi Mi, the largest, simply because the CEO's daughter studied at Stanford, USA. Renner worked his magic on her chipset, allowing him to pass a virus to her father during a weekly chat. He then put the virus to work.

Renner had called it child's play. Evan and the rest of MI5 had recognised it as brilliance. He could count on one hand the number of coders who could sneak a virus into a Gen VIII chip.

From there, the virus infiltrated Mi Mi, providing access to the other two companies, and the algorithm needed to break the Chinese code.

Evan's summary was modest, but Reekes had heard enough. Evan had spotted Renner's talent, bringing him and five others onto the team—an eye for raw talent and the ability to manage insubordinate ankle-biters. Evan wondered if Jonathan had already decided or based it on Evan's account of events. "Evan, my boy, how'd you like to help me put this country back together?" To be part of this would make history, and that brought a smile to Evan's face.

To unite the broken kingdom—that was the reason he was here.

Jonathan explained that London's gang bosses were listening to Window, a mysterious entity on 92.2 FM. Window asked for peace among gangs and anonymity in return for truth. "The signal is constant, informing London of incidents and outbreaks of violence," Jonathan said. "Anyone requiring help contacts Window, and their request goes out to the city.

"Sounds like tripe, I know. But it's working. They haven't fought in over a month. The transmissions even warn of SOP movements, avoiding confrontation." Jonathan's voice trembled with excitement. "That's why I want you to find him. If Window has the slightest control over the gangs, if they trust his judgment, then he's the key to uniting the country under one flag."

Evan watched Jonathan's huge hands engulf his own, knowing he was in for the long haul. He couldn't see the end, but nobody could. He wondered if he would have said no if he'd known the future. Gazing at the shanty, the poverty, and the societal imbalance. He still breathed. He had Renner looking ahead and Kyle watching his back. No, he concluded. He wouldn't have changed his mind. There was still a slim chance he could be the linchpin.

Three days after meeting Reekes, Evan received his official orders by courier. His task was to select five names, and the Prime Minister would narrow it down to two—one field agent and one desk agent. Julian Renner topped Evan's list, and Reekes readily agreed.

Next, Evan wanted Lt. Dominic Fletcher. The man had an impeccable file but with one significant obstacle—he was Army, not Special Branch. Despite this, Evan wrote Fletcher's name on his pad. Evan had met him a few times and was impressed by Fletcher's rare talent—he could speak four dialects without relying on downloaded languages: French, Mandarin, Cantonese, and Punjabi. Three of those were spoken in Greater London, an area with scarce technology. Fletcher also had a knack for poker, leaving Evan with a lighter wallet on multiple occasions. Fletcher had the nerve and military skills to be the point man on the ground.

Reekes took some convincing, but Evan persisted. "You want Window? This is the guy," Evan said, pointing at Fletcher's profile. "We send him into the SOP ranks, and he can slip into London."

"He'll be hated," Reekes responded.

"He'll be disenfranchised, haunted by the actions of the SOP, and in need of something new to believe in. He'll be... awesome."

The team had come together after that, with Fletcher and Renner developing a mutual dislike. Fletcher began training for his cover as a time-served soldier fresh from a tour in Pakistan, looking to make easy money. His alias would be Daniel Blake or DB.

Evan and Renner worked on locating Window's transmission, which proved difficult. It was an old FM channel, coming in at 92.2, but triangulating it wasn't easy. Renner soon came to call it the little bastard. There had to be something else. It took a couple of days but he found it, apparently glaring him in the face all along. He'd taken the time to explain it and Evan was polite enough to pretend to understand, but he was just thankful he'd finally cracked it.

Eventually, they pinpointed a list of transmission towers accurate to within a mile. It was time for Fletcher to step up as DB and join the SOPs. Three weeks later, he found himself stopping vehicles at a checkpoint.

He had another hour before his shift ended, and he couldn't wait. It had been a hellish day—too hot to wear full combat armour. He drank as much as he could and sought shade near the APC.

Two neighbouring checkpoints had been attacked that morning, and though insurgents had been killed, more assaults were expected. Especially by Jordan Dale, the zealous soldier who hid his remorse behind bravado. Cocking his rifle, he said, "What do we do this for, if not for King and bloody country?"

The old Transit van pulled up, flywheel screaming as it neared. One man sat behind the steering wheel. DB approached and could see from the man's averted gaze he was hiding something. But he didn't expect it to be his family. No wonder he was sweating when Jordan slapped a hand on the driver's door. "Out!"

The man did just that. His eyes were rounded, darting across the masks of the surrounding soldiers. His hands were already up, but Jordan took delight in spinning the man around and planting his face against the side of the van. "What's your business?"

The man answered in Punjabi. "Visiting family." Fletcher didn't need the translation from his chip, but he was aware of the second delay from Jordan who was reading his.

"Where?" Jordan asked. By now, he would have scanned the back of the van. His chip would have told him, like it was telling Daniel Blake, that there were four hearts beating strong from inside it. None of the troop listened to the man's response. They were forming a firing solution around the van.

"Please, my family," the man pleaded, "my baby."

"Open it!" Jordan commanded, stepping back from the father but keeping his rifle aimed at him. "Open it!" he repeated.

Daniel Blake stood a few meters back, his rifle aimed at the van's side door as it slid open. The man's family huddled together inside, just as he had claimed. The SOPs breathed a little easier upon seeing them. Jordan shoved the father aside and stepped into the van, causing a battered leather football to roll out.

Jordan yanked the youngest girl from her mother's arms, dangling her by her wrist in front of her father, then raising her higher for his troops to see, reassuring them it was all okay. And it was. Until one soldier, Darrick, kicked the football.

The explosion incinerated his foot, and the blast threw him and two nearby SOPs through the air. More soldiers fell to the ground as Daniel and the others switched to heat vision, firing bullets into the van. Panic-stricken men with guns. The detonation threw several others to the ground, and Jordan into the van, dropping the girl. Amongst the kicked-up dust, Daniel and the others switched to heat vision, firing bullets into the van. Panic-stricken men with guns.

Sudden short-lived screams called out for help. Someone yelled, "Holy shit! Jordan's in the van." Blood dripped from the doors, pooling around the bodies of a father and daughter. Their family, along with Jordan Dale, Darrick Bevan, and two others DB barely knew, were dead.

The APC's long-barrelled gun screamed. Its shot hit the van square in the bonnet and threw it back at least six metres, sending it crashing into the unsteady wall of someone's old home.

The official report claimed a third checkpoint had been attacked that day. The team received time off to recover from the traumatic event. Jordan and the other casualties were honoured; the family was burned and forgotten. As for DB, he vanished, allowing Dominic Fletcher to move on with his cover story.

The Intel he provided helped to unveil London's criminal hierarchy, with Window maintaining order at the top. He provided their names, such as Sin Lao – the Dragon King of the Triads, Deep of the Tooty Nung, Carr of the Shadowkingz, or Blastarr of the

Bushwackers. These were the highest-ranking individuals of the largest and most violent gangs.

Then four weeks ago, he had met Window. Evan celebrated their progress, believing dialogue with the south was within reach. But then, three days ago, Fletcher disappeared and, in a sense, so had Jonathan Reekes.

Reekes was no longer the Prime Minister Evan had known. He'd transformed into a volatile creature, and Evan reconsidered the origin of his nickname 'Gorilla' during his verbal beating.

"I don't think that's a fair assessment, sir," Evan defended. "There was no warning."

"This was your op, your command. Your operative is missing. Three fucking days before negotiations are supposed to start! Am I wrong?" He wasn't.

"I think—"

"Don't think, do. You won't get fuck-all done by thinking," he continued to rage.

"We received a message," Evan replied, though it was an assumption. They had intercepted a broadcast the morning after Fletcher had gone missing. He connected with Reekes and played the recording.

"A friend has been lost, but the party will still go ahead." Window's voice came through the transmission, followed by his usual report and mention of his first meeting with DB. It was the rendezvous they were now headed toward.

"Get a team into London ASAP. Find Fletcher if you can, but the priority is Window," Reekes demanded, glaring at Evan. "Who can you trust with this?"

"Yes," Evan stumbled, scrambling for a name he could trust with the task. "You can trust this with me, sir."

While Evan had inwardly cursed himself for volunteering, Reekes looked him up and down before casting an eye to Oliver. "What do you think?"

Oliver only raised an eyebrow.

Reekes turned back. "Get it done."

With clearance from the PM's office, Evan's plan was initiated after two alterations. Instead of Timothy Lawson and Craig Chalmers, two highly skilled field agents of Evan's choosing, it had been Commander Kyle Ross who was selected to accompany him into the belly of the beast. And in the belly they were; the crowds alerted TAP so often there was an almost constant threat alert. He still felt the tug of fear, but like the timing between the lightning and thunder of a passing storm, it felt further away and easier to dismiss.

He trusted Kyle, not as a person: he had met him only a day before. He trusted his skill, and Oliver who had chosen Kyle to get them through London. Then this morning, Kyle had put himself in danger to bring Evan to safety. Evan took comfort in that, but also felt a little guilt. Because he couldn't say for certain whether he'd be able to do the same.

The back of his tongue curled up away from the sharp taste of adrenaline. Refocusing on their mission, Evan's HUD displayed a map showing Notting Hill Gate tube station just around the corner—the end of the first leg.

4

Kyle stopped at the alley's end. "How's it looking out there?" Evan moved up beside him.

"Area's clear," Renner reported.

Kyle glanced into the street, and Evan piggybacked his hardware to survey the scene. The road tapered out near Notting Hill station, creating a bottleneck for defence. The station itself was proudly decorated with SOP banners hanging over the roof, like tapestries.

"There." Kyle highlighted the nest on his HUD. "Machine guns." Indeed, three mounted guns sat inside the station, their barrels peeking out of the entrance.

Two SOP guards accompanied each gun—one spotter and one triggerman. "There'll be more inside," Renner warned.

"No doubt," Kyle agreed.

"Glad we have those papers," Evan remarked, aware of the heightened security at the station.

"You're most welcome," Renner replied.

"We going in?" Kyle asked, turning toward Evan.

Evan hesitated, weighing the advantages of being off the streets against the potential risks of navigating the underground tunnels. "We're early," he stated, "by two hours."

Kyle smiled. "And you're not happy because...?"

Evan acknowledged Kyle's point but worried about waiting blind with no escape plan. "Ren, can you see inside the station?"

"Foggier than a Hammer Horror, but you're better off going in," Renner advised.

Evan nodded at Kyle. "Keep an eye on our backs."

"Aye aye, Captain!"

"Then let's do this." Evan tapped Kyle on the shoulder, disconnected his HUD, and followed him into the street. His chip's tactical alarm sounded as it registered weapons aimed at them. Guards at the station and snipers on nearby buildings and roofs flanked them.

"This isn't your run-of-the-mill checkpoint," Kyle observed.

"It's the principal supply base for the postcode," Evan explained. "Food, livestock, and weapons. Fletcher acclimatised here before being posted."

"This is not a good place to meet."

Kyle's arrogance irked Evan. "Did you not read the mission briefing? Besides, there wasn't a war when I agreed to this place." Evan felt a small sense of victory in his argument when Kyle didn't respond. However, he couldn't deny that this was no longer the safest place to meet. Not by a long shot.

Underneath the street that they now walked was a subterranean hamlet, possibly even a small town. Numbers were difficult to quantify when people don't stand to be counted. Notting Hill was the largest SOP station in the region, the last bastion of neutrality and had been the optimal choice for a meeting, at least it had been yesterday.

He stepped up the mud and shit-crusted stairs to the doorway ahead of Kyle, greeting the approaching SOP. The Sergeant's credentials swiftly appeared on Evan's HUD followed closely by Renner's introduction. "Sergeant Tangeer."

Tangeer was a shorter man than Evan but far more intimidating. He'd uncoupled his facemask, and it hung to the side, revealing a stern unreasonable face. He showed no sign of the undercurrent of fear that ran amongst his troops. "Papers," he said, extending his hand.

"Expecting anyone?" Evan inquired, surveying the troops.

Tangeer didn't respond right away. Instead, he clasped Evan's hand, and their profiles appeared on the HAND interface. Tangeer read through the papers signed by Commander D Meyer and grimaced. "Triads," Tangeer finally said, studying the glowing data between them. "They've hit nine checkpoints, including Commander Meyer's."

"Did they hold them back?" Evan asked, hoping his presumption would be wrong.

Tangeer continued to read, not looking up. "Everything checks out," he said, releasing Evan's wrist but remaining focused elsewhere. "Just staying the night?"

"Just the night," Kyle interjected before Evan could weigh the decision. As bounty hunters staying one night, they would appear less threatening. If they seemed to stalk or be hunting their bounty, the SOPs might intervene, which was the last thing they needed.

The tense atmosphere suggested they all expected a deadly confrontation. "You mentioned the Triad... this is still Nung territory?" Evan asked, knowing they were within their borders.

"The Triads aren't picking a fight with the Tooty Nung today," Sergeant Tangeer divulged. "And as sure as I am that the Devil sleeps in Hell, they won't be lending us a hand."

The Tooty Nung were a resurgent gang from the last century, a violent splinter group of the Holy Smokes—Muslims who'd banded together to protect their neighbourhoods from racism and violence, who refused to let go of the power after they'd vanquished their enemies. They had no love for the Triad, and their battles were well recorded by the SOPs. But now, after Window?

"Is there going to be any trouble?" Tangeer asked.

"Not from us," Evan replied.

"Then get out of my killzone." If Tangeer meant it in jest, he made no sign of it.

The interior, though clean, showed signs of wear. Like the rest of London, new décor had been layered over the old. A security checkpoint scanner, an old plastic-cased model, stood just inside the door. Evan's display identified its age. Despite its antiquity, it remained in use, and why not—the 'Chipless' and 'Freemen' were the majority of London's population. Why anyone would want to disappear to a place like this Evan failed to comprehend.

The tiled floor needed replacing, with weeds only held in check by heavy foot traffic. A few had even flowered in the corners and against the wall where Evan stopped. Before him was the largest, most elaborate artwork he'd seen since the Bayeux tapestry. Smaller, but equally impressive and bloodthirsty.

"What's that?" Kyle inquired, noting it also.

It wasn't a crude daubing by any description. The detailed story unfolded before them, a testament to the skill and effort of multiple artists. Evan pointed to the blue football jerseys. "It's the station's history. These were the first owners, the Chelsea FC Head-hunters. They defended the neighbourhood against immigrants." His finger traced the dark faces, then the heads on sticks. "These are Mafiosi, displayed at their borders as a warning." The Head-hunters were depicted with large barrel chests, considerably larger than those they fought, and it was easy to presume they had endorsed the mural.

Kyle ran a hand over the wall. "Monet?"

With a wry smirk, Evan said, "He painted landscapes." This was London's gritty reality, where pre-existing gangs had swelled in numbers. The civilised inhabitants had turned to the football groups, the people they knew but avoided after a few pints. They had no choice after the crash – it was strength in numbers and those without numbers were swallowed up. Stories of beheadings, emasculation, and religious cleansing had saturated the headlines until the early twenties. It was these stories which had metamorphosed into the modern-day myth of how London operated.

He followed the mural to its inevitable conclusion; the artwork changed, character's eyes became larger, bodies thinned and their skin darkened. A new author continued the story, the Tooty Nung. They'd been in London since before the financial crash, but in much smaller numbers and the Head-hunters had forced them out at first – but when the refugee lines poured in, the immigrant-founded gang found limitless support.

The Nung were a brotherhood that matched their honour code with a brutality the FC gangs hadn't been prepared for. Some of the FC's remained today, but nowhere as prevalent as the early twenties. The Nung's attacks were bloodthirsty and precise, and the painting ended at their climax. The Nung's celebratory football match, where the gang had played with the severed heads of Chelsea FC.

Kyle whistled and leaned against the ticket-machine at the top of the escalator stairs. Evan, suddenly aware of the background noise, furrowed his brow. "Is that music?" he asked, struggling to discern whether the nightmarish drum and bass beating up the stairs qualified.

Kyle grinned. "Could be."

Reaching the top of the escalator and finally distinguishing a riff from the drums, Evan reluctantly agreed.

"After you," Kyle said, gesturing downstairs with a grin.

"Give me a second." Evan accessed his HUD and issued a command. Adjustable dampeners in his inner ear silenced the music. "Okay," he smiled at Kyle, "let's do this."

From the bottom of the escalator they had to walk single-file between stalls barely shoulder-width apart. Ramshackle vendors had planted themselves against the wall, with no uniformity or consideration of their cramped surroundings. In fact, the thin slip of a path they took had patrons coming the opposite way, and more often than not they were forced to shuffle sideways, squeezing past the locals.

They walked single file between narrow, ramshackle stalls at the escalator's bottom. Vendors occupied the cramped passage with no regard for uniformity, forcing Evan and Kyle to shuffle sideways past the locals. Fluorescent strip lamps hung overhead, some flickering, as the smell of sweat and cooking fat permeated the air. The heat from food stalls' stoves intensified the odour, prompting Evan to issue another command to his nostrils.

Stalls offered everything from scavenged machine parts and patched clothes to fresh vegetables and designer labels. A chaotic melting pot, Notting Hill Gate defied the odds, forming a community more accommodating than the five-a-side team's.

"Where are we meeting?" Kyle asked, snapping Evan from his thoughts.

"He'll find us."

"Hey, look." Kyle tapped Evan's shoulder and pointed to the tunnel's end, where it split in two. "I see a bar." There it was, with wooden frames and patio furniture. Barely space for three tables, but they'd managed.

"Good call." Evan agreed, squeezing past the last couple of stalls and ducking under a dangling foot. He looked forward to sitting down and resting. He didn't notice the foot's owner on the stall's roof or the man raising an open bottle of beer to the young hand reaching down.

5

"Save yourself the energy Paul, please. You know I'm right." Oliver was using his headmaster's voice, a tone honed over his years in politics. A punch of authority added to two pinches of panache with a spoonful of contempt. This man however, had earned himself a little more of that last ingredient. "Or would you prefer I read you these files?" he moved a finger around the document's icon waiting on his desk.

Oliver had, of course, read through the documents. Once was enough when you have a computer-maintained eidetic memory. Besides which the documents were a sickening read, and he did not wish to read them again, but he would; should he have to, but he was willing to bet Paul would fold first. In Oliver's experience, ugliness always retreated when forced to stare at itself in the mirror, especially when one's family were also invited to the vanity.

He'd confronted Paul Andrews with two options. Neither of them could have been considered the proverbial carrot. The first was to do as he was told and the second was a sure way to end one's career in politics. One should never fuck children and that rule goes double when you represent a constituency.

People don't care what sex the child was at that point, they don't care how pretty the child was, or whether they were asking for it. The image of a lurid limpet like Paul pinning a slight frame to the ground while his pustule-riddled tongue raped the child's innocence, overshadowed the fact it was a young boy, purposely grown for such acts in the Asian in vitro laboratories.

Oliver had nothing but contempt for Paul and the other nameless ministers who shared his lust. Yet, they served their purpose. Indiscretion was, after all, good for the party. As long as Oliver knew about it, he could keep their dicks in their trousers and their votes in line with the Prime Minister. So it had been the way of the Chief Whip and so it shall always be the way of the Chief Whip.

Every little perverted secret they possessed, Oliver cherished the photo album. Every underhand deal they worked on, he filed the receipts. Every cross-party delusion they fantasised over. Every skeleton they buried, he knew the GPS coordinates. A handful of these bottom feeders would guarantee the passing or failing of a Law while a majority would guarantee a unified government. Indiscretion was good for the party, it was not good however, for Paul Anderson's wife.

Jenny was truly the salt of the earth. As Oliver's father would say, in every sense of the phrase, she deserved better. Better than what this cretin Paul provided. Oliver knew that this outing of information, this jabbing of the bee's nest would cause him the greatest pain at home. For it would not only bring Jenny to tears but also the edge of their penthouse in Albert Dock.

"If I'd known..." The young fop trailed off, confounded by the situation that Oliver had put him in. The same situation that Oliver was thrilled to be a part of. He did so enjoy putting the screws on.

"You knew Paul," Oliver said. "You know who the party leader is, don't you? Big chap, grey hair, always impeccably dressed?"

"That's not what I meant."

No, of course not, Oliver. Paul meant if he'd known there was a photographer skulking around that whore house in Jakarta, he would have chosen another one. "I'm not without sympathy to your situation, Paul. You're a good man, I know that. Just as I know Jenny..." he watched as Paul squirmed in his chair, "would be devastated by this unfortunate, mistake."

Paul's eyes widened at the sudden shift in Oliver's tone, sensing a possible escape. "Yes, it was. It was a mistake, Oliver, a disgusting mistake. I'm so terribly sorry."

"Let's try to imagine a world where this didn't happen," Oliver said, resting his hand on the file. "One where you kept your position and leaked some information about a special project the PM approved for Harry Rockwood."

"The Prime Minister?" Paul asked, dumbfounded.

"Yes, the Prime Minister."

"I've nothing against the Prime Minister. I honestly thought he knew."

Oliver suppressed a raised eyebrow; Paul wasn't the first person to mention this. Conroy Tempers, a backbencher, had put Paul in Oliver's sights an hour ago.

"I thought it was legitimate!" Paul pleaded.

Two backbenchers knew about a secret project the Prime Minister had allegedly signed. This casual conversation wouldn't do, especially if connected to the helicopter attack. If Oliver had been suspicious someone was stirring the pot, this confirmed it. "I hear you, Paul," Oliver said, "but I don't understand what you're trying to tell me."

"I thought the Prime Minister knew about it, as you just said. I thought he'd signed off on it." Again, the same words as Conroy.

"Why do you think he doesn't know about it now?" Oliver asked.

Paul floundered, his mouth gaping. "I haven't said otherwise, have I?" Oliver knew he hadn't; he had merely questioned Conroy's claim. "I..." Paul stuttered. "I assumed that since you didn't know, the Prime Minister couldn't know."

"Then I must apologise," said Oliver, feigning humility. "I've misled you. I'm not trying to dismiss the claims. I want to learn what you know and how you found out." He smiled reassuringly, circling his fingers around the document.

"I'm on side. Wholeheartedly."

"That's good to hear, Paul. One must know who to trust."

"That's exactly what I'm saying, Oliver. You can trust me." It sounded almost rehearsed. "And I won't lie to you."

Oliver fixed his gaze on the man squirming in his seat, confident he would now tell the truth. "Good, because I understand you're the man to ask about it." Conroy had given him Paul, who supposedly had the operational name—a name Renner couldn't find in the Government database. It meant one of two things: first, it was hogwash; second, a far more intriguing and worrisome reason—it was buried so deep that not even Renner could find it.

He needed confirmation on the operational name. If Paul said it, he would pursue it despite the apparent lack of evidence. There was no need for Paul after this conversation either way; Paul was too small a fish. But with the proper motivation, he could point Oliver in the right direction.

"If I tell you," Paul said, eyeing the folder, "you'll make it disappear?"

Oliver considered himself fair, "Until next time." But he didn't want to give the wrong impression. He sat, patiently waiting for the one word, two syllables that Conroy had mentioned. The operation's name. "Are there other parties involved? Ones that have something on you too?"

"No," Paul replied, and Oliver believed him.

The pause implied something else; just how deep was Mr. Paul Anderson involved? "Then what's stopping you, Paul?"

"I don't know what it is. Well, not exactly..." Paul began. Not the start Oliver was hoping for, but it was something. "Operation Lockhead." Bingo. Oliver concealed his enthusiasm by leaning into his chair. "It's foreign-based, set to save us a lot of money, and put our military back on the map.

"Other than that, I know it's in the testing stage and that it's the Prime Minister's baby." He couldn't be sure if that was enough. "That's all I know. Please, Oliver."

Oliver studied Paul for a torturous second; a repulsive being, begging for the return of his life and still refusing to give a name. "Who told you, Paul?"

"I overheard—"

Overheard? "Don't give me that, Paul. You don't get near conversations like that. Someone is recruiting, and I want to know who."

Paul glanced at his file. "Yes." And Oliver knew by the man's pensive look that he didn't want to divulge more than he already had. "Faraday."

"Jack?" Jack Faraday wasn't the largest catch in the sea, but he was a sizeable fish in the pond. He wielded significant influence in the House of Commons and, because of his sister's marriage, in the House of Lords too.

Paul Anderson nodded in defeat. Good, Oliver thought. He was finally getting somewhere, and it had only taken him the effort to extort a drunkard and a child molester for information. "Thank you, Paul," he said, smiling. "I'll put this back in the drawer." He did so, eyeing the paederast as he attempted a smile. "I don't want to read this filth again."

"Thank you, Chief Whip." Paul leaned forward, offering his hand.

"Remember, Paul, loose lips sink ships." However, Oliver had no intention of shaking it. "Now get out of my sight, there's a good chap." He waved his hand dismissively, and Paul's hologram promptly vanished from his chair.

So Lockhead was an operation, or at least what two ministers believed to be one. An operation supposedly authorised by Jonathan himself. The thought troubled Oliver: Jonathan running a scheme without him didn't sit well. They'd been in politics too long and had been friends even longer. No, Jonathan couldn't be behind it. After all, his priority was finding Window and opening negotiations with London.

Whatever was happening aimed to undermine the Prime Minister. He wouldn't intentionally do that himself. Oliver would follow it up, speak with Faraday, and learn more. He blinked a message to his PA, Doris.

"You've space this afternoon – James Revell had to leave for Berlin. I just updated your calendar," her reassuringly authoritative voice replied.

"That was at two?" Oliver asked, recalling the meeting.

"Yes. If you want it sooner, you'll have to do it over lunch. You've Francesca Blake at one, and I'm not cancelling on her for you again."

Francesca represented the Whitby constituency, opposing fracking permissions. She was a good politician, and Oliver somewhat enjoyed their debates, but she was no Paul Anderson. She was squeaky clean. That gave him no leverage on her other than political knowledge, and in that area, she was too good for his liking.

Fracking, though favoured by its shareholders, wasn't popular with the country. The government had decided that it needed money more than popularity. That gave Oliver the doubly difficult task of arguing against Francesca's permissions to stop fracking when he privately agreed with her.

He wanted to reschedule her meeting, but this was politics: standing toe-to-toe and trying not to spit on each other, as his father would say. "Keep Francesca. I'll catch Faraday at the Pond. Tell him I'll be there for a spot of lunch."

"Done and done," Doris said, as she always did once the decision had been made.

"Can you patch me in with the PM?"

"Of course."

He waited until the word 'connected' flashed on his HUD. Then, before the Prime Minister's torso filled the area of Oliver's desk. "Prime Minister?" he said.

"Speak of the devil," Jonathan replied.

"Who's with you?" asked Oliver.

To Jonathan's left, Antonia faded in. "Oliver."

"That bad?"

"Worse. I'm getting the feeling the Forces are looking to usurp me." It was poor humour, and Oliver had to stifle his smile.

"Funny you should say that. I have an avenue of interest."

"Yes?" asked Jonathan.

Oliver sent him a private message. "Lockhead?"

"What is it?" Jonathan looked appropriately oblivious, but then one doesn't become Prime Minister without first learning to hide truths. "And shouldn't we be talking in person?"

Oliver, like Antonia, cared little for Jonathan's paranoid fixation on secure lines. They were, after all, secure. Entrusted to Renner so that all of their conversations were protected. Where Antonia and he differed was that Oliver enjoyed rattling Jonathan's cage once in a while. "I don't think it's worthy of a closed-door conversation yet. It's just hearsay at the moment."

"But you just said that it's an avenue of interest. It could be something. Could be something big."

"And it may be nothing but brandy-brewed gossip," Oliver reminded him. Besides, Oliver had gleaned what he needed from the Prime Minister already. Jonathan had denied knowledge of Lockhead point-blank. That was as solid to Oliver as the world was round. There was no more point discussing the rumour until after he had spoken to Faraday.

"If you're certain," said Jonathan.

"I am."

CHAPTER SIX

RENDEZVOUS

Evan tore the label from his lukewarm, half-empty lager bottle. He'd sat at the table for three hours, the beer had gone flat, and his taste for it had vanished. They were now an hour past the rendezvous time. As expected, they couldn't reach him through the subway station's walls. To speak with him, one of them had to walk up to the gate. So Kyle had ventured up to the SOP gate to find out if there was any news. If not from Renner, then from the SOPs.

They repeated this journey hourly, pinging each other every fifteen seconds, and each ping succeeded. The dialogue got choppy when Kyle reached the top floor, but their chipsets maintained contact. They could still monitor each other's vitals and the locator system ran as smooth as the factory settings. However, each trip yielded the same result: the SOPs stayed silent, and Renner had no new information. So, Evan peeled the Coors Light label from the bottle and flattened it on the table. He didn't anticipate Kyle's next trip would be any different. He folded the label in half and flattened it again.

In three hours, he'd had seen a lot of faces and any of them could have been the contact. He folded the label once more and flattened it. The contact might have seen them, got spooked, left, or anything. He didn't like that thought, but couldn't shake it. He hated the idea that the country's salvation could hinge on someone's impression of him.

Evan downed the last mouthful, took a coin from his pocket, and placed it on the table before signalling the barman for two more beers. Like Kyle, he could filter out alcohol if needed. They could blend in without truly indulging. The barman, a wiry man with greasy blond hair and a habit of excessively scratching the eczema on his face, brought two more bottles and snatched the coin with a grin.

Evan savoured the first cold, crisp mouthful, washing away the stale remnants. "Guess what?" Kyle said over the comm.

"Nothing?"

"Nada," came the confirmation.

"I've got another round in. We can finish these and head down a level?"

"We've tried that already."

"He could be underneath us."

"You don't know he's a he."

"I don't know anything," Evan admitted.

"Renner thought the contact could have been killed, you know, with the fighting outside."

Evan's eyes grew heavy, tempted to block out the world. It was entirely possible. They had faced heavy gunfire themselves—why not the contact? Anything could have happened. "What do you think?" he asked.

"It's possible, but I wouldn't write someone off for being a couple of hours late, especially in this climate. They could be playing it safe, moving slower. Might have seen us and making sure that we don't mean them harm—hang on a minute."

He was about to request a link to Kyle's eyes when the ceiling shook. His eyes snapped open, only to be filled with falling dust. He brushed his face and spat away what landed in his mouth. "Kyle?" He tried again. He had heard a loud slap when the ceiling shook.

2

"Kyle?" He wasn't ignoring Evan's call. He wasn't registering it, dialling Evan down to single digits as the immediate danger presented itself.

Kyle ducked behind the row of ticket-machines when the first flaming car raced toward the station. The mounted guns sang and his chipset instantly muffled the sound. The guns split the car in two, one half toppled forward, skidding a metre before stopping. The other side careened into a tin shed and the back seat bomb exploded short of its target.

The SOPs cheered, one even taunting the unseen foes. Sergeant Tangeer, however, stayed quiet and watchful, waiting. Kyle stood up, his rifle ready under his poncho, and skirted the mural to find a better vantage point. He looked out the gate past the silent SOPs, wondering what the next move would be.

The car wreck, flipped in the explosion, now lay right side up, continuing to burn. If there had been a driver, no sign remained, only black smoke from the upholstery and the scant fuel left. He blinked, and his vision altered, revealing the light blues, deep reds, and flaming yellows of infrared.

He was about to call it—mark it down to an outrageous prank—when he glimpsed the first. He stepped back when he saw the second. Two flaming masses of red and yellow raced toward him, followed by a third.

The mounted guns opened up again, aimed at the approaching vehicles, all rigged to explode and targeted at the front gate.

"Move!" he called to Evan.

"Kyle?"

3

"Move!" Kyle repeated his order, then again. "Move, now!"

Evan knocked over his chair as he stood. Old Chinese Guy scurried past him, heading down the stairs with a few others. He turned and saw Eczema Man leaving his bar unattended. It was as if everyone had heard Kyle's order.

It was chaos.

He reached under his poncho and found comfort in the hilt and trigger of his rifle. "I'm heading down a level. What's happening?"

"Triads," Kyle answered, causing Evan's knuckles to whiten around the rifle's grip. "Fucking lots of them. I'm on my way."

Evan pushed past the stairs, and the flow of people surged toward him before pitching down to the next level. He pulled into the stream, letting the current take him. With his trigger hand on the hilt and finger on the guard, he fell in behind Eczema Man.

He was pulled left, then right, and pushed further along. Everything looked the same, and his HUD showed only static—no map, no position. "Kyle?"

"Stuck on first."

The kid blindsided him, jolting him out of the flow. Evan barely caught a glint of metal against the fluorescent lights, but felt the force of the dull end pressed into his crotch. He caught his breath, jammed between two stalls.

The boy, no taller than five feet, possessed jaguar-like strength; lean, scarred muscles carved by a life of combat. A nano-crafted tattoo Raven fluttered its wings on his shaven head, a striking Native Indian design tattoo perched on his ear.

"Two plus two?" the kid rasped, his face scrunched in concentration as the current of people continued to rush down the tunnel.

"Is it happening?" Kyle asked.

Evan glanced down at the Desert Eagle pressing hard against his groin. Both the kid and his bird tattoo stared at him, waiting for an answer. The question was the code, picked by Fletcher, the Orwell fan. But who was this kid?

"I won't ask again." Impatient, the kid pressed the Eagle even closer.

"Five," Evan replied, perplexed.

The pistol slackened, and a second later, it was holstered, one of a pair hanging from the child's rough leather bandolier. "Move. We'll be trapped once they start the squealers."

Squealers... Fray shares had jumped four points that afternoon. The kid pointed to a loose ventilation grate, knee-high against the wall behind him. "Out of the way, princess," he said, shoving Evan aside as he yanked the grate from its fittings.

"What's happening?" Kyle's voice echoed again.

"Wait, we have to—"

"Move!" The kid cut in. "Have your friend meet us at platform five, south end."

"Copy that. Platform Fi-" Kyle's sentence ended in static.

The kid moved fast, producing two black plugs and inserting one into each ear. He dropped to his knees and crawled into a ventilation shaft. Evan followed; he was halfway through the opening when the abrasive pitch of white noise erupted.

He remembered the Squealer demonstrations—the anguish in their faces as they dropped, the entire crowd falling to their knees, clutching at their bleeding ears. On the bottom right of his HUD, the words 'Frequency Blocked' flashed, and the noise vanished.

Ahead, he could see the kid racing along the vent.

4

When Kyle confirmed the meet at Platform Five, his HUD informed him comms with Evan had ceased. His chip would continue to ping until a connection was made, but until then, the failing would be confirmed every fifteen seconds.

He gritted his teeth. The timing was impeccable. Two hours late and the contact decided to meet just as the Triads attacked the base. He shouldn't have left Evan. He was his mission, and leaving him was an error—one he would rectify. There was no point thinking about it anymore.

Kyle had made it halfway down the escalator steps when the squealers started. A slang term for pitch-oriented crowd control methods, causing anyone without ear augments or a way of muffling the sound to soon be running, panicked from pain attuned to their ears, herded like cattle or the kids of the sadistic Pied Piper, to wherever their shepherd or piper intended.

Whatever lay beneath him would be brutal. He counted his spare ammunition and felt grateful for his automatic pistol, six grenades of varying destructive capability, and an assortment of toys and gadgets. Blinking, his eyes switched to survival mode, blacked out with an iris of chrome, strong enough to ignore the burning environment.

His feet stepped into the smoke, hovering at the lower level's ceiling. He descended the escalator, disappearing into the thick, burning fog. His air filtration system kicked in, drawing oxygen from his liquid reserves. The timer flashed on his HUD—he had nine minutes until those reserves depleted.

His heat vision remained his primary visual. The smoke surrounding him was the only thing trying to escape toward the entrance. No one ran toward him, no red and yellow mass screaming for help or coughing and dying on the floor. Only smoke racing upward. He followed the tunnel to the source.

The ramshackle stalls now served as makeshift barricades, toppled and spanning the tunnel's width. Every other one burned. The Triads were still behind him, so it had to be a defensive tactic. The SOPs had breathers, the Triads did not. Simple and effective.

"Drop your weapon!" The order came from behind the stalls. He searched for the voice's origin. With all the fire, it was difficult to pinpoint, but with a little calibration to the infrared, he found them—seven SOPs crouched behind the old Chinese man's tipped stall. Special Operations Police in front of him, Triads coming up behind him.

Things were about to get ugly.

Kyle had picked up some scars in China and lost his legs in Afghanistan, yet he still fought tenaciously for his country. They patched him up each time, dropping him into another shit storm. Now, he was forty-two million quid's worth of a combat machine.

Things would get ugly, but not for him.

Black eye-shields slid down from Kyle's brow. Liquid filled his mouth from engineered glands, as thick as glue; it armoured his teeth and sealed his throat. Millions of nanobots raced to his spine, coating and strengthening his vertebrae. More bots spread over his ribcage, shielding his chest and the vital organs within.

Game on.

5

The battery chicken appeared no more distressed than usual. It tilted its head curiously when the nearby ventilation shuddered. Then the caged hen below clucked, and the top chicken followed suit. Soon, all fifty-eight cages were clucking.

The vent shot outward, and a size five boot appeared before disappearing back into the vent. Moments later, the kid crawled out onto Platform Five, with Evan right behind him, grateful to leave the grime-slicked tube.

With the kid already jumping down onto the tracks, Evan stood and surveyed the platform, noting the iron cages webbed against the walls. Poultry occupied the closer ones, while cattle were on the northern side of the tunnel. Welded rails bolted to the ceiling held empty chain harnesses. It was a slaughterhouse. Animals were kept on the platform and hung over the tracks to bleed.

Blood was everywhere—on the platform, splattered against the wall, and pooled on the tracks. Layers of dried blood from years past crusted the surfaces. His nostril filters had blocked the stagnant aroma long before he reached the ventilation grill, a minor victory.

He peered over the platform's edge, where discarded carcasses rested on red-stained tracks, stripped bare of unused flesh by the local rat population.

"Come on," the kid called up from the tracks.

"Wait." Evan wouldn't leave without Kyle. "We need to wait."

"Your friend is close. Come on."

"How do you know that?" Evan asked as locals sprinted from the platform entrance, jumping onto the tracks. They stumbled over one another, leaving the fallen behind, and ran toward the dark South Tunnel. All of them clutched their ears; the screamers still blared at full force, even on the deepest level.

The kid waved at him, both he and his raven tattoo expressing impatience. "Come on!"

Evan ignored him, unwilling to abandon the man who had saved his life twice. He turned his back on the kid and walked toward the platform entrance as more station dwellers hurried past. He reached for his sidearm, unclasped its holster, and drew it. It lacked the stopping power of his rifle, but he felt more comfortable using it at close range, not wanting to hit any bystanders.

Kyle had mentioned Triads attacking the station. The SOPs must have started the squealers to force the local population downward, out of harm's way. It was a crude and violent manoeuvre, but Evan understood the necessity. He couldn't say he'd make a different choice in Sergeant Tangeer's position. Any number of residents could be Triad. He might have been fighting the battle on two fronts. This way, he'd forced the population down here, to the safety of the tunnels.

"Princess!" the kid yelled, and Evan realised he'd been called princess earlier.

"Stay out of sight," Evan said, waving his free hand downward, showing to the child that he should duck down on the tracks. He would be safe there, at least until Evan could check out what was happening.

More civilians pushed past him. Then gunfire echoed through the tunnels. Not near him, but from above. A battle raged somewhere above, and Kyle, he hoped, was already somewhere in between. "Kyle." He sent his message, knowing it would fail. His ping hadn't been successful in eleven minutes. "Come on," he mouthed the words and brought his Browning sidearm up under his poncho. He estimated a one-minute trip to the end of the corridor. He'd still be in sight of the kid if something went wrong. From there, he could check the stairs. Check if Kyle was—

"Bluebird!" Evan stopped, utterly distracted. He turned away from the oncoming traffic and found the kid back on the platform, crouched on one knee with one of his Desert Eagles ready for some killing.

Bluebird, being his operational name, was privileged information. Only Kyle, Renner and the Prime Minister's Office knew it. "How do you—"

A sharp, sudden bump to his kidney threw him off balance. He felt his knees buckle and stumbled forward. One of the panicked civilians had blindsided him, crashing into him while screaming something about a 'fucking maniac.' As Evan struggled to find some grip on the blood-caked floor, the scrambler carried them off the platform.

He didn't see what followed. He only heard the gunshots. Automatic fire first, a quick three-second burst. Then a single shot before silence. He pushed the scrambler off him, using what felt like the last of his strength. Fresh shards of ceramic lie around him. He glanced around; the curved wall of the tunnel had been peppered with bullets. That accounted for the automatic fire. The kid had dropped next to him, his smoking pistol waving uncomfortably close to Evan's face. That accounted for the single shot.

"Get up," said the kid, as if it were the simplest of things to do.

Evan tried, but his legs wouldn't cooperate. He knew where they were. He was telling them to move, but they just weren't listening. All he could do was keep his hands at his side and rear, propping himself up. "I can't."

The kid looked anxious, more than annoyed. "Are you hurt?"

Evan wasn't sure. He couldn't feel anything except the throbbing inside his head. He called on his chip and felt his face drain of colour. His display didn't respond; it wasn't there. He had nothing. He blinked again, willing his medical documents as he had done a second ago. Nothing. He tried again, this time asking for a prescription. Something for the throbbing. Nothing. Not even an acknowledgement. Not even a fucking error message.

"Are you hurt?" The kid repeated. "Stop blinking!" The kid checked the corridor for any further trouble. When satisfied, he laid his DEagle on Evan's lap and used both his hands to check his shoulders, neck, and head. He stopped at the back of Evan's head, pulled his hand away, and paused.

"What?" Evan couldn't see what he was looking at. "What is it?"

The kid didn't answer. He picked up his pistol instead. Then he knelt next to Evan and raised the man's arm over his shoulder. "I'll help you," he said.

Evan raised his left hand to the back of his head. Amongst the hot, slick wet hair, he caught his finger on something that didn't belong. Something sharp. He looked at his hand, red with his own blood.

"Come on," the kid hurried him. "You're too heavy to carry by myself."

Evan refocused on the simple task of standing up. He could see his legs. They were the two ignorant bastards in front of him. He touched his thigh with his hand. He could feel them, too. They ached. So they didn't have any excuses. If he waited here any longer, the Triad would turn up. His left foot twitched, and he grimaced. His legs wanted to live too.

"Stop!" Kyle's voice boomed, echoing through the station. He stood at the platform's edge, eye shields down, skin a dark shade of grey, splattered with blood. If he intended to look a badass, he'd succeeded. He aimed his rifle downward, dead centre on the kid's face.

Evan raised his hand to Kyle, palm first. "Don't shoot."

Kyle remained still, his rifle trained on his target.

"We don't have time for this," the kid snarled.

"He's the contact," Evan said.

Kyle's finger relaxed from the hair trigger. "Really?"

"Yes, really." Evan's words were drowned out by Chinese war cries from the tunnels behind them. He hadn't noticed the squealers had stopped—or had they? Or was his chip still blocking them out? He sniffed the putrid smell of the slaughterhouse floor and gagged, no longer caring whether the squealers had stopped.

Kyle lowered his aim; the kid holstered his DEagle. "I don't suggest going back up."

"This way," the kid pointed to the south end. He took Evan's weight and started for the exit.

Kyle dropped onto the tracks, ignoring the filth he landed in. "Let me." He took Evan by the arm and lifted him over his shoulder. "Comfy?"

"You have a pillow?" Evan asked.

"No."

"Then I'm comfy."

Evan's world bounced as Kyle broke into a run, soon sprinting and keeping pace with the kid. They had a clear, uninterrupted path to the tunnel, but if they didn't move fast enough, the Triad could easily pick them off.

Civilians had stopped flooding the platform, and both gunfire and squealers' cries had fallen silent. Piecing things together, Evan figured the Triad had either been beaten back or run out of opposition. He doubted their luck would hold for the former, and Kyle's speed suggested he agreed.

Evan felt the urgency more intensely because of his inverted position, slung over Kyle's shoulder, watching their retreat and the platform fade into the distance. "How much farther?"

Triad members poured onto the platform—three, five, nine, twelve, and still more. They seemed more intent on enjoying themselves than on rushing. Evan patted Kyle's back. The third Triad, perhaps their leader, quickly scanned the tracks and spotted them. He grinned, shouting something in Cantonese— something Evan would have understood mere minutes ago. But with his HUD refusing to cooperate, he was left to guess its meaning.

Several Triads opened fire on them, confirming Evan's suspicions. Bullets and tracers whizzed by. "Fucking move it!" he urged Kyle. Then, from behind Evan, in the direction they were heading, automatic fire retaliated against the Triads.

Triads dropped like flies, some tumbling from the platform onto the tracks, others fleeing or taking cover to return fire from safer positions. Evan couldn't see how many were dead or alive, as they had reached the end of the platform and entered the tunnel's darkness.

They passed a young Indian woman, kneeling and aiming a long-barrelled combination rifle at the platform—the same kind favoured by Special Forces for its versatility as both an assault and a quick-chambered sniper weapon. She continued firing until they were safely in the shadows, then stopped. Slipping her rifle over her shoulder, she walked after them.

"Put me down." Kyle obliged, and Evan patted him in appreciation. Standing on his own, he almost missed the opportunity to offer his hand to their guardian angel. When she walked past without a glance, he bit his lip and frowned.

That was rude, he thought.

The kid was far ahead of Kyle, too distant for Evan to see. Out of habit, he blinked for night-sight. "Shit."

"What's up?" Kyle stopped and faced him.

"I've got a problem."

They walked in silence for several steps before Kyle halted. His eye-shields glinted against the faint light from the platform. "What's up?"

"My HUD," Evan said, reaching toward his bump. "I took a hit to the head."

Kyle caught Evan's hand before her reached his wound. "Hang on," he said, moving around to examine the injury. Likely assessing the damage through his display.

Evan realised he had taken technology for granted. His generation was known for it, and there hadn't been a point in his life without computers. Until now.

Concentrating, he recalled the waiting room filled with parents and their eight-year-olds, awaiting chip implantation. That was before the law changed, before chips were surgically installed into foetuses during the second trimester, purportedly to help with pregnancy. Watch this space. The lobbyists are already pushing for the first trimester.

Kyle took Evan by the shoulders and spun him around. He grabbed Evan's arm and read the HAND display—now invisible to Evan. The only light came from behind them, and their path was pitch-black. He had to walk with his hand on Kyle's shoulder the entire time. He could have done with his night-vision augments, but they too were unavailable. He was scared. Not the panic he'd felt. This was concern that he'd done some serious damage to himself. All because of a scrambling idiot and a train track.

As Kyle continued to read, Evan stewed in his insecurities. He looked back over his shoulder to check on the Triads. They remained on the platform, not scavenging their dead or attending to their wounded. Why? Why were they holding back?

"Your chip's connection to the user interface is damaged, but the chip is still active and its housing is intact." Kyle's words offered some hope; perhaps the self-repairing device would resolve the issue. "Give it time to repair," he reassured Evan. "It's already healing your head wound. It won't get infected."

"Thanks."

"You're not having a good day," Kyle grinned, "are you?"

"Not my finest, no…" At least they were in good humour, he thought.

"Come on." Kyle placed his hand on Evan's shoulder and guided him into the darkness. He appreciated that.

"So. We finally got to meet the Triads. Can't say I liked them much."

"They've got bold."

"They kicked the SOP's arse."

"How many made it?" Evan asked.

Kyle looked at him. "To the tunnel?"

Evan nodded. He waited while Kyle scanned the blackness. "Sixty-three," was his answer.

His reply was a calm rendition of the facts, and Evan envied him. "From how many?" He couldn't hide behind the stats. He felt like a raw nerve.

Kyle looked up at the ceiling, reading the invisible information. "Too many."

"The Triads really live up to their reputation."

"It wasn't just them."

"What?"

"The Triads pushed through the SOPs, but the SOPs were already retreating down here. They cut down just as many to save themselves." The truth stung worse than the throbbing in his head. There would be no detachment for him there. No more hiding behind his HUD. He'd be exposed to everything and would have to deal with it.

Evan needed to know what came next, what the plan was, and how to move on. "What about the boy?"

"Harry Potter?"

"You going to call him that to his face?"

Evan waited a moment for Kyle to remember that he could not see whatever face he was pulling. "He's with his mother, six metres ahead."

"Good. We need some intel."

"Okay, let's swap over." Kyle dropped his hand from Evan's shoulder and placed Evan's on his. "Keep hold of my shoulder. I don't want to come back for you." He needn't remind him. Evan's hand clung firmly to his shoulder. Kyle picked up the pace and closed the gap to their contact—the kid and his presumed mother.

Evan squinted in the darkness, his eyes struggling to adapt to their shadowy surroundings. With each step forward, the blackness enveloped him, inviting him deeper into the gloom. Soon, he'd have to accept its invitation; soon, there would be no light to guide him. "Hey," Kyle called, "wait up."

They didn't. "Can't, they're only waiting for the flamethrowers." The kid's voice held such certainty that Evan couldn't dismiss it.

Evan didn't like his odds, stumbling through the dark, blind and helpless. "How far will they come in?" he asked.

"As far as the claymores."

PART TWO:

DROVE THROUGH GHOSTS TO GET HERE

CHAPTER SEVEN
THE POND

Jack Faraday, a minister who had earned the uninspired nickname 'Teflon' while clawing his way up the ranks of politics, was shrewd enough to avoid trouble. He kept his back against the wall, ingratiating himself with the right people, and intimidating the rest.

Joining the party came with two warnings: 'watch out for Oli Trench' and 'don't turn your back on Jack Faraday.' Had Oliver not been Chief Whip, Jack might have held the position. Neither were friends; people like them rarely had friends. They knew only those who could serve their interests. They shared a mutual respect for the game and each other's tactics. A shark recognises its own kind, after all.

Oliver had heard a rumour that Jack was sleeping with another minister's wife. However, it was just a rumour, and compared to other indiscretions within the party, it was a mere misdemeanour. Besides, Oliver wasn't exactly innocent himself. What mattered was keeping such indiscretions hidden. If discovered, you'd better have dirt on someone else or a proxy ready to take the fall.

That was how Jack had earned his nickname, because when you rise the ranks quickly in this business, you make more enemies than you do 'friends'. Jack's nickname served as a testament to his position; other ministers tried to tarnish his reputation, but everyone knew nothing stuck to 'Teflon.'.

Oliver hoped today's meeting would provide a different perspective from what he'd been led to believe. Faraday was not your average 'bencher, as he had popularity at the back. Having him as an ally would be much more advantageous than making him an enemy. Faraday loved to flaunt his influence, and Oliver just needed to give him enough room to do so. So, when he entered the lounge and saw Faraday at his usual table with Bartlett and Morgan, he didn't approach him.

Instead, he strode across the room, signalling the barman with his HUD to ensure a tulip-shaped glass of scotch awaited him at the bar. "Thanks, Charlie."

The Pond was one of twenty-seven licensed establishments in the Provisional Government buildings. Its name came from its view of a duck pond in the garden below. Classy and large, it accommodated Leadership and many backbenchers alike.

Yes, there were plenty of fish in the pond, and the biggest was Jack Faraday. This lounge, though not officially his, was dominated by his presence. He occupied the best table, and the most lucrative deals always went through him. That's why Oliver met him there, deliberately putting his back to the room. It gave everyone a chance to watch Faraday approach him.

Sipping from his glass, Oliver observed Jack approaching through the mirrored wall behind the bar. A tall, unappealing figure with red blotched cheeks and greying sideburns. He clutched a smoking cigar between lipless teeth as he sat beside Oliver. "You look like I need another drink."

Oliver allowed his lip to curl slightly. "Faraday."

Charlie, the barman, returned, sliding a glass of Disaronno on the rocks to his regular. "Charlie." Jack winked at him before tapping the ash into the provided tray. He wrapped his fingers around the crystal tumbler and savoured the sweet taste of distilled almonds. "You know," he said, eyeing Oliver's reflection, "I don't recall you ever visiting us down here."

"I've drained the Glenlivet dry everywhere else." Oliver sipped his scotch as Faraday snorted a laugh.

"Good to see you, Oliver," he said, drawing on his Davidoff and exhaling a blue cloud around them. "I've missed your humour."

"It can't be helped; you are human." Oliver's HUD activated the filter systems in his body, instantly easing the discomfort of breathing in both Faraday's repulsive odour and his cigar's smoke.

"Are you going to the Tate party this evening?" Jack asked.

Oliver recalled the invitation to the Tate's engagement party: black envelope, black card, gold-embossed typeface. He couldn't remember the date, but wondered why he had received it.

After all, Michael Tate was the First-Person Shooter World Champion. Specialising in hardcore free-for-all, his fiancée was another hardcore expert—adult fiction starlet Madison Fry. Their wedding was set to be the biggest since Kate and William.

Though he had never met Madison, he had encountered Michael once at a tech conference in Berlin three years prior. He assumed he had made less of an impression on the young man than the young man had made on him—which was minimal. "I wasn't planning to," he replied.

"Don't say that. It won't be a party without the whip." Faraday mockingly punched Oliver's arm, overstepping their relationship. Oliver, ignoring the punch more than the humour, swirled the glass in his hand and remained silent, prompting Faraday to continue. "Rough day at the office, sweets?"

"It's becoming a bit of a motif," Oliver admitted.

Jack fell silent, observing the man sharing his immediate space. Oliver had cultivated an aloofness, a distance between him and the ministers. Faraday was smart, but he doubted he could discern the exact reason for Oliver's presence at the Pond. Jack drew on his Davidoff again, eyeing Oliver curiously. "How's the old man?" he finally asked, resting his cigar in the ashtray.

"He's..." Oliver paused, using the tactic intentionally. He knew one of Faraday's key flaws was his impatience and insatiable lust for gossip. He only needed to give the impression he wasn't sure how to answer the question or suggest an internal debate over whether to be honest. Anything to pique Faraday's interest. "Persistent."

"Foolish more like," Jack scoffed. "Your entire office reeks of death."

It was a terrible joke; one Oliver detested acknowledging. "You're the funniest man on that stool." It was true, and Jack snorted again.

"Seriously Oli," Jack leaned in, "wolves are circling."

Oliver's ear perked up, his eyes slanting toward Faraday's reflection behind the bar. This wasn't a casual complaint against the Prime Minister; it was a warning, a threat against Jonathan and possibly Oliver too. "Care to clarify that?" he asked, restraining the urge to call Faraday a repugnant ass.

Jack shook his head, his hands flat against the bar and spread apart. "Tut tut, Oli." He shook his head again. "You know better than that. Besides, that's the least of your worries."

"Why? Are you flirting with me?"

Jack smiled. "I don't like the idea of being on the opposite side of you." It was a friendly, sincere warning, using a well-practiced tone of disarmament. Still, Oliver didn't relish the idea of Jack being his enemy, either. Not until he knew who was on his side.

"Jack, if you touch my leg, I will have to hurt you." Oliver smiled back at him.

"Now who's flirting?"

"I'm serious. I don't enjoy being teased." He dropped the smile. "I don't particularly want to go toe-to-toe with you, either. But unless you're offering something substantial..."

"Okay, but only because we're friends." Jack winked, leaning in closer. "I'll give you this for free. Reekes isn't entirely blameless for this morning's incident," he whispered into the Whip's ear.

Oliver stifled his sigh. He was here again, the tantalising hint of Lockhead. "I'm glad I didn't have to pay for that," he said.

"Droll, Oli." Faraday leaned back, reclaiming his cigar and inhaling deeply. Oliver watched the smouldering end flare red, then shut his eyes as the smoke drifted towards him. "If I elaborate, you'll come to the party tonight?"

Oliver broke the offer down. On one hand, he'd get the intel he craved, which he suspected concerned Project Lockhead. Faraday might not reveal everything, assuming he even knew it all. But there was also the slim chance that Faraday had caught wind of what Oliver had learned from Paul Anderson. In any case, Oliver found himself caught in Jack's snare rather than the other way around.

He'd have to attend the party Faraday had mentioned twice now. He knew little about the Tates beyond what he'd gleaned from the media, and he wouldn't call that reliable intel. Maybe Michael Tate was stepping back from the gaming scene, eyeing a run for Prime Minister. Odder things had happened, and he could speculate for hours. But that, he reminded himself, wouldn't get him any closer to the truth. "This better be worth it," he said.

Faraday flashed his wide, lipless grin and downed the last of his Disaronno. "I take it you've heard of Lockhead?"

Oliver managed to hide his surprise at Faraday's insight. "I have."

"That little operation set the Triads off this morning. And old Johnny boy green-lit it." Faraday lifted his cigar to his lips but paused just before taking a puff. "Might want to rethink how close you stand to him when the next polls roll around."

Faraday's warning would be valid if it held any truth. If Jonathan had authorised an operation that had caused civilian casualties, but Jonathan had claimed ignorance. "Is there any proof?"

Faraday's grin widened, aware that he had Oliver ensnared. "You don't want much, do you? For nothing."

"Can you tell me who brought it to him?" A name, something for Oliver to dig into.

"Who do you think?" Jack's smirk, emerging from the smoky haze, reminded Oliver of Alice's encounter with the Cheshire Cat. He'd given Oliver an evasive response because he'd posed a vague question.

Every military operation passed through the military and the MOD. "Harry Rockwood." He was the only other person Oliver knew who was as close to Jonathan. Harry spent considerable time with the Prime Minister, time Oliver wasn't always privy to because of his role. Oliver suddenly felt the stool on which he sat was awfully precarious. "Who's pulling his strings?"

"Bring me something sweet, and I'll think about it." Oliver hadn't expected Jack to reveal so much without something in return, but the smug tone in his voice made Oliver want to smash his face into the bar. He restrained himself, sparing Charlie cleaning up the mess, and opted to finish his Glenlivet instead. "Guess I'll see you tonight."

"Excellent news!" Jack grinned, tilting his tumbler. "One more for the road?" His triumph grated on Oliver's nerves—no one appreciates a braggart.

"I'll save myself for this evening," Oliver replied, sliding off the stool and smoothing his jacket, ignoring the gazes of those who had just witnessed their Chief Whip's defeat.

"Suit yourself," Faraday said, bidding Charlie closer for a top up.

2

Renner didn't turn around when Oliver entered his den. He was deeply immersed in mission control, literally connected to the communication systems supporting Bluebird and Fallout. But Oliver wasn't surprised when the man said, "You're making the rounds today."

Oliver approached the chair. Renner still hadn't turned to face him. As a tech expert, he preferred not to address his superiors directly. So, Oliver played along. "The rounds?"

"First the Pond, now here." Renner's right hand came up above his chair, his index finger wagging. "People will talk."

"People are talking," Oliver said. "That's why I'm here."

Renner swivelled in his chair like a starship captain, finally granting Oliver his attention. His expression bore the weight of a burden, a look Oliver rarely saw on Renner's face. He was, after all, somewhat eccentric in Oliver's view. "I was about to call you, anyway."

"Yes?" Oliver inquired.

Renner crossed his legs, gathering the trailing wires onto his lap and smoothing them out like a pet cat. "Uh-huh. You can go first if you like."

"How generous of you."

"That's the kind of guy I am."

"Okay." Oliver shut the door behind him. "It's a bit sensitive."

"Things normally are."

"Shall I get to it then?" Oliver asked, sensing the impatience between them.

Renner extended his hands, palms up, gesturing for Oliver to continue. It was one of many reasons Oliver preferred to avoid conversations with Renner. While respecting the man's intelligence and unrivalled computer skills, he found him to be an irritating individual who enjoyed teasing those around him. "I need everything you have on Jack Faraday."

The first sound Renner made was an eerie, musical 'woo' tone. "Spying on the party, are we?"

"He has something on the Prime Minister," Oliver admitted, anticipating this line of questioning. "I want to level the playing field."

Renner's eyebrows arched, and his bottom lip protruded—an exaggerated expression of interest. "Interesting. Very interesting. How did you come by it?"

"You have your ways, Renner. I have mine."

"Got a smoke?" Renner asked, the urgency in his voice catching Oliver off guard.

"I don't smoke," Oliver finally said.

"Neither do I," Renner admitted, swivelling his chair back around. "I've been thinking about starting, though."

Just one of Renner's many idiosyncrasies. "You really are odd."

"So everyone tells me."

Oliver allowed the silence to become uncomfortable. "Can you do it?"

"Doing it now. Do you want Faraday's personal files, too?"

"Nothing illegal. Please." At least, not yet.

"You're the boss."

"What did you want to tell me?"

"I've lost connection to the ground team."

Oliver restrained himself. "When?"

"Not long before you arrived. I had Kyle on and off for a bit, but now nothing."

"You don't sound worried."

"They got to the rendezvous. There was some static. They went underground."

"Nothing serious then?"

"The Triads attacked the station, but most of them didn't make it past the front gate. I don't think enough of them got in to concern Kyle." Oliver silently fumed over Renner's prioritisation methods for a moment, just long enough for the man to swivel his chair around to face him.

"What?"

The door chimed behind Oliver before he could unleash his thoughts, so Renner seized the opportunity. "Come in."

"Can you make lunch?"

Oliver recognised the voice and turned to see Antonia standing in the doorway. He was about to answer when he caught himself. Antonia hadn't asked if Oliver wanted to go for lunch since she wouldn't have expected to see him there. She was visiting Renner, a quirky, wired man half her age with whom Oliver doubted she had much in common. "Antonia?" He couldn't help himself.

"Oliver." The blush was as much a surprise to her as it was to both men in the room. "What are you doing here?"

"I'm following up on something," he said casually. "You?"

"I was hoping to pick up Renner for a spot of lunch," her eyes left Oliver for the man in the chair, "but he's probably too busy again?"

Renner held his hands up. "Sorry. I've got a stack on."

"It's okay." Her eyes moved back to Oliver. "How about you? Got time for some food?"

Oliver blinked up his schedule. "I have a meeting with Francesca Blake at one."

Antonia scrunched her face up. "From Whitby?"

"The one and only."

"Lucky you. Guess I'll be dining alone then." She gave him a wink, then waved to Renner. "I'll see you tonight."

"Yes, you will," he said, watching her intensely as she turned around and left the room.

"Wait!" Oliver said, calling after her. "I'll walk with you." He shot Renner a glare. "I want a report on the ground team."

"Before or after Faraday?"

"Before."

"You're the boss." Renner said, swivelling his chair back to his station.

Oliver stepped out of the room, catching Antonia as she waited in the corridor. He'd known her a long time, had dated her sister back when his hair still grew dark and he could get up the morning after an all-night bender without a mark on his soul. He had danced wildly with her, clapped for her at graduation. He had been present at her wedding, embraced her at her husband's funeral. Yet, he had never viewed her in a carnal light, not until this moment. "How long has this been going on?"

She grinned, her cheeks still flushed, but not from embarrassment. She radiated happiness, and Oliver noticed. "I do not know what you mean."

"Of course you do." He nudged her. "You goddamn cougar."

Her giggle morphed into laughter. Struggling to control herself, she momentarily covered her mouth with her hand.

"I knew it!" Oliver continued, "Sauntering in all doe-eyed, asking for a lunch date."

"Enough," she implored, tapping him on the back and proceeding down the hallway. "Please, no one knows."

"And it should stay that way. Who would've guessed... Renner?" he teased. "What the hell do you two even discuss?"

She shot him a glare as lethal as a bullet. "Three months, and he's a blast."

"Well, well," Oliver said. "I guess he must be."

"He is," she reaffirmed, but not to Oliver. She said it to herself and grinned in concurrence.

"It's good," Oliver confessed. "It's nice to see you happy." Politics hadn't become the idyllic dream they'd imagined as students. True, they'd experienced moments of joy, but Oliver increasingly felt his happiest days had slipped away. Witnessing his friends savour theirs was refreshing.

"I am!"

"Does he know?" Oliver knew that, like himself, Jonathan would welcome this revelation.

"No," she said. "And please don't tell him. Not yet."

In that instant, she evoked Oliver's initial encounter with her—youthful and optimistic. "Of course. As you wish."

"Have you seen him yet?" she asked.

"Jonathan?"

"Yes, since you called him earlier?"

"No, why?" he asked, suddenly attentive.

She hesitated, contemplating whether to proceed. "He wanted to speak to you in person. Not over the link." She paused for Oliver's nod. "It's about Pilger." She stopped again, and this time Oliver furrowed his brow in annoyance, but he caught her reasoning in his peripheral vision.

Walter Channing was walking toward them. "Oliver, Toni," he said with a broad smile that everyone knew but did not like.

"Walter," they said back in unison, waiting for him to pass before she continued.

"Pilger," she repeated, "got wind of something brewing. He camped at Heathrow all night, been there a few days, actually, connected to the orbital satellites."

"Someone had prior knowledge?" Oliver asked. "Someone knew what was going to happen?"

She nodded. "Perhaps not the exact event, but someone knew something would happen." She stressed the word 'something', indicating a probable cause for alarm. Conspiracy theories were rampant in politics. Hell, most seemed more plausible than the truth.

Oliver wished he'd heard this from Jonathan directly. They could've discussed the next steps, potential ramifications, and how it impacted them. If someone knew the Red Cross was entering London, then they also foresaw the explosion or played a part in orchestrating it. But the blast occurred in Triad territory, raising the question: who in the government had ties to the Triad?

Oliver pulled up Jonathan's schedule. Right now, he was in his office. The original meeting with the French Ambassador had been cancelled and replaced with an impromptu one that sent a chill down his back. "He has a meeting with Harry?"

"Yes."

Bits and pieces coalesced; some specifics remained hazy, but Harry was a significant component. Once Oliver removed himself from the equation and replaced himself with Harry Rockwood, a pattern emerged. A pattern of military conquest. A contingency plan, maybe? Something to appease the right-wing warmongers while the leadership pursued their pacifist strategy?

But to what extent had Jonathan compromised? What concessions had he made to maintain his position? Oliver required one more fragment, one more clue to grasp the pattern, and confront

Jonathan. "Thank you, Antonia," he said, "but I need to return to your younger counterpart."

"I thought you were meeting Francesca?"

He grinned, aware that he had the dubious honour of cancelling on her once again.

3

Oliver deactivated his link and strode into Lloyd's domain. Armed with the intel Renner had supplied, he dismissed the Prime Minister's Private Secretary, who gestured in protest. Oliver refused to be deterred. Not after confirming his suspicions or made his first steps in distancing himself. He convinced himself it was for the best. He was done adhering to others' schedules; the quicker everything came to light, the better for everyone.

He shoved open the door to Jonathan's office before Lloyd, the PM's secretary, reached the end of his desk, stammering, "No Oliver—"

Jonathan, seated behind his desk, had noticed the door opening and stared at Oliver as he barged into the room, with Lloyd shouting from the atrium. "No Oliver—" seemed to echo throughout the room. Oliver's fury was palpable. He was damned livid over being cut out. Yes, Jonathan held the title of Prime Minister, but Oliver functioned as the strategic mastermind.

Oliver had intended to barge in and give them both a piece of his mind. He had his question locked and loaded, ready to confront his friend: Were you going to tell me? But he didn't. Perhaps Lloyd's frantic calling gave him pause, or Jonathan's flushed face made him reconsider. Or maybe the brief interval it took to reach the PM allowed his anger to dissipate, realising that an aggressive approach was not only reckless but a terrible idea.

"Yes?" Jonathan asked.

The question hung in the room like a damp, mouldy sock. If Oliver answered truthfully, his intentions would be exposed. Rockwood, sitting opposite the Prime Minister, would realise Oliver had been digging independently and without Jonathan's knowledge—or was it with his approval? How long had these two power players been scheming? How deep was their alliance? Oliver knew Rockwood had presented Project Lockhead to Jonathan the previous year, and that Jonathan had approved it. He didn't know the reasons, or whether the approval had been unwitting. "Apologies, sir," he said. "I have urgent business that requires your attention."

Rockwood finally shifted, leaning over his left shoulder to examine the intruding Oliver. In a composed tone, he stated, "I should go, anyway."

Lloyd, flushed and flustered, squeezed into the room behind Oliver and waited patiently for the Prime Minister to direct him.

Oliver's attention, however, remained on Harry Rockwood, who returned the stare. It seemed he'd made the right choice. Harry's eyes were not those of someone in the dark; Oliver could plainly see he was one of the orchestrators, if not the orchestrator, and he had just interrupted a highly sensitive conversation. "If you're sure. I had no intention of intruding."

"But you did," Rockwood said, still seated. "And we're done." Harry had refocused on the Prime Minister, who also seemed to have lost interest in Oliver's entrance.

"Harry..." began Jonathan.

"It's fine," Rockwood interjected. "But you might want to rein in your whip. He's overstepping his duties." Did he know? Harry didn't turn around again; he was done addressing Oliver directly. "I'll update you when I know more."

"Thank you," said Jonathan.

"Prime Minister." Rockwood flickered, vanishing from the room.

Oliver lingered at the door with Lloyd, waiting for Jonathan to make the first move or say something other than stewing in silence. "Lloyd," he said, not looking away from Rockwood's vacant chair, "get out."

When Lloyd complied, Oliver felt as if he were a corpse in a sealed mausoleum, awaiting judgment for the sins committed in life. He remained by the door, just as Jonathan continued to stare at the spot Rockwood had occupied.

Oliver reminded himself it could be worse; he could have confronted them both. He might have labelled them liars and conspirators, securing himself a fate akin to Fawkes, Fraser, or Paine. Hell, even Edward Snowden. Deported, marked for rendition, and water-boarded at His Majesty's Pleasure.

"What was that?" asked Jonathan, finally looking at him.

"That was me, changing my mind," Oliver said.

"Is that supposed to be funny?"

"Fact."

"One that you're going to explain?"

Oliver indicated to the empty chair in front of the Prime Minister's desk. "May I?"

"You may not."

"Very well." Oliver sat down regardless, using the time to plan his next move. The opportunity to shout, "What the hell are you playing at?" had passed. Now he was on the defensive, with a rabid gorilla glaring at him. "I just bumped into Antonia."

"She told you I was dying?"

"No."

"Shame, I'd hope you'd disturb a confidential meeting for that."

"Quite," Oliver said, watching as Jonathan reached forward for the first of his oranges. Oliver was quick, his arm snapping forward to grasp the bowl. "Enough with the damned oranges," he growled, sliding the bowl out of the PM's reach.

Jonathan's eyes narrowed, and Oliver prepared himself for a childish retort. But when none came, Oliver thought perhaps he was getting through to him. "She told me someone tipped Pilger off. That someone knew the Red Cross was called into London this morning."

"Oh?" Jonathan said. "She told me some time ago."

"She told me that too," said Oliver, cautiously, "so I did a little checking. Following up on some leads, you know the ones. On Lockhead."

"What of it?"

"Well, it appears that one Harold Rockwood put it on your desk a little over a year ago," Oliver continued. "It also appears that you signed off on it. That you agreed to three tests. All of which were to be outside of the country."

"How did you get this information?" asked Jonathan.

"Does it matter?"

"Renner," the Prime Minister answered his own question.

"Is it correct?" asked Oliver, but the PM didn't answer. "Jon. Lockhead is connected to this morning's explosion. It's a military screw-up, a plan that has your signature," Their eyes locked as the words passed between them, "and Pilger was forewarned it would happen."

In Oliver's mind, it was clear. The plan was set up to fail. To set the Prime Minister up to fail. He hoped his counsel did not fall on deaf ears, that his friend could see what he saw.

"You think I don't know? That I don't understand? This is the last nail in my coffin?"

Oliver shifted into a more comfortable position, ready for the long argument. The PM was in one of his moods. "You need to tell me everything."

A second orange met its demise without reprieve. "Jon, please," Oliver said. "I can't help you if you don't tell me anything."

"I can't," Jonathan said. "You already know most of what I know. Three operational tests, signed off over a year ago. None of the tests were to be run inside British borders. The volunteers selected from searches out of China and Korea."

"What is it?" Oliver asked. Renner had confirmed all the rumours, but not the secured military files outlining the operation. "What is Lockhead?"

"I..." Jonathan trailed off, staring at his bowl of fruit.

"Damn it, Jon!" Oliver shot forward, grabbing an orange and hurling it against the wall with all his might. The skin burst; its juices sprayed over the white dado rail. He sat back down, expecting a nuclear explosion from across the desk. But nothing came. Not even a whimper. "You need to tell me. Because whoever tipped off the journalist put him in harm's way. It's not outside the realm of possibility they could have arranged for the Red Cross to be attacked."

Oliver pressed on. "We've heard nothing from the MOD. Not through official channels; they haven't spoken to Antonia. All the information we've had is from Special Branch and our friends. Of which, you don't have many. Rockwood, on the other hand, has been visiting you regularly and for reasons you've not divulged. On one hand, you bark and shout about paranoid theories, and on the other, you appear clueless.

"Well, Jon, this is real. Because if someone did tip off the journalist, and it looks very much like they did, then that person knew about Lockhead, what it is, and when it was to be used. Someone is working against you, and they're doing an excellent job." Oliver stopped, realising he, not Jonathan, had been the ticking time bomb.

Jonathan remained silent, breathing through his nose, his eyes staring dead into Oliver's throat.

"Say something," insisted the Chief Whip, unwilling to let his tirade go unanswered.

"No us?" Jonathan asked. "Someone is working against you." He thumbed his lapel in clarification. "Me. You said someone was working against me."

Oliver could have reviewed the conversation, but there was no need. He knew what he'd said, and Jonathan was right. "That's what you pick?" he shot back, "Out of everything I just said? You're gonna focus on that and get all worked up?"

The door burst open, and a gust from the outer room chilled Oliver's neck, making him turn. Antonia now stood where he'd halted during his own interruption. Behind her, the pathetic, sheepish Lloyd peered over her slender shoulder line, his gaze meeting the Prime Minister's. The man simply scowled at their intrusion. "Prime Minister," Antonia said. "Oliver. There's something—"

Jonathan raised his hand to silence her. "Lloyd," he snapped, "take the rest of the afternoon off before I have to sack you, there's a good chap."

"Yes, sir," Lloyd mumbled, slinking out the door. "Thanks."

Antonia slammed the door behind him and closed the distance to Jonathan's desk in a few strides. She swept her hand across the sleek onyx surface, activating the keyboard controls, and input the command without a word.

Behind her, the holographic fireplace flickered out, replaced by a massive wall-mounted screen displaying the news. Nadia Black, the BBC's fiercest political correspondent, took center stage, framed by images of Red Cross volunteers aiding in Sudan.

Oliver's eyes locked onto her. She pushed a stray strand of raven-black hair behind her ear, her gaze piercing the camera. "No, Richard. This is an investigation." Her deep, authoritative voice matched her towering, warrior-like presence, earning her the moniker 'Amazon.'

"Either way," Richard Billington's voice chimed in, the invisible anchor from her studio. "This can't be good for the government."

Jonathan shut his eyes, oblivious to Billington's silver-haired image materialising beside Nadia on the screen. Antonia hit mute, leaving Oliver to observe the Amazonian in silence. "They've got the reporter's details. The death toll, the chopper IDs, and claims that they were lured into London by a bogus SOS."

"Is that true?" Oliver inquired, pulling his gaze from Nadia.

"The SOS being fake?" Antonia questioned, to which Oliver nodded. "I don't know."

CHAPTER EIGHT
Ghosts And Boogie-Men

Two hours of darkness had passed—two hours of slow, silent movement, save for the occasional Claymore callout. At first, Evan thought he would crumble like he had at the shanty after the drive-by. He hadn't. The environment was so different, so alien to him, that he had to focus all his attention on surviving.

One misstep and he'd trip a laser wire. A Claymore would pop, showering them with high-velocity metal balls. The effect was not unlike a shotgun blast, except that two pounds of plastic explosives propelled the balls. So no, concerning himself with whether he was up to the task ahead came a far second to listening for the callouts. His chipset had not yet recovered, and it showed no sign of doing so. That left him without his computer assistant, TAP. Not a single blip in his eye-line. He couldn't see a goddamn thing. They hadn't brought flashlights. There'd been no need for them; they were extra weight and there were more relevant things to carry. The woman and the little one wore night-vision goggles. That was nice. They hadn't offered to share. He hadn't asked either. Was it stubbornness or embarrassment? Probably both, he admitted. It was an oversight; combat augments were shielded – Evan's chipset wasn't military but commercial, and someone, namely he, had failed. He could have brought night-vis or a torch, a candle, for fuck's sake.

Could-a, should-a, would-a.

Now he had no other option than to put himself under Kyle's complete control. Something he'd never done with anyone. Sure, he'd let the chip govern most his actions, doesn't everyone? But with a chip, there was always a level of control, always a way out. There wasn't one here. Not in the dark. If he dropped his hand from Kyle's shoulder, he'd be alone.

Over the course of the first half-hour, he'd adapted, accepting that each step could be his last. The SOPs had placed the Claymores as a cost-saving action. There's no need to guard a track entrance littered with landmines. No one would be idiotic enough to attack through a minefield, and if the SOPs had to retreat, they held the locations of each mine on their chips. No sense planting mines if there was a chance you'd step on one.

The journey grew somewhat easier after clearing the Claymores, their pace quickening as much as guiding a blind man allowed. The kid was eager to move ahead, but the woman reined him in, calming him down. It was simple to mistake them for mother and son, especially now, when Evan could only hear them and not see their physical differences. Not that he understood everything they said; they spoke in an

Indian dialect, which Kyle translated when he believed they weren't listening.

Evan couldn't determine their direction either. He had no map for reference. Kyle, with his endless patience, updated him as much as possible, but even he seemed uncertain. Since leaving Notting Hill, Kyle's chipset had acted strangely, too. His display and internal commands functioned well, and he could scan the immediate area, but his connection to Renner and the outside world was gone.

"Since when?" Evan asked.

"The station. I thought it was the SOPs blocking comms."

"Then we're too deep?"

"Possibly."

Evan suspected Kyle was withholding something, but he had stopped discussing it when the kid caught up to them, announcing it was time for a break. That had been about an hour in, and since then, the underground tunnels had twisted, ascended, and descended without giving Evan any sense of direction.

"Stop," said the woman.

Evan waited and waited some more. "What's happening?"

"The kid's checking the wall," replied Kyle, and Evan waited some more.

"What..." he started to ask when the sound of metal grating against concrete pierced his ears, "the fuck is that?"

"A door."

"This way," the woman ordered.

The door opened to stairs, which led to a short, flat walkway before a spiral staircase. Every stagnant pool they disturbed reeked of rotten eggs, and each step echoed like a drum roll. All was darkness, with

Kyle occasionally warning, "watch your step..." or "we're going up..." The tedious, blind task strained Evan's senses to the breaking point.

Evan stumbled more than once, steadied by Kyle's unyielding frame. A saving grace came in the form of a metal mesh on the inside of the spiral stairs, where Evan could weave his fingers, feeling the location of the next step.

At the top of the stairs, a faint light gleamed a short distance away, stirring a storm within Evan. Clinging to composure, he held back from embracing Kyle in gratitude. They'd made it.

He'd fucking made it.

They strolled at an easy pace along a dusty concrete path to another set of stairs; the light growing brighter as they neared the top. As his eyes adjusted to the light, his other senses dulled, and the putrid smells grew more tolerable. Realising they would soon reach the surface, Evan's hands trembled.

"Where are we?" Evan asked.

"Hell, if I know," Kyle replied.

"But we're nearing the surface. That is daylight?"

Kyle turned his head just enough for Evan to see his unimpressed frown. The light filtered through cobwebbed slats above them. "Yes, yes, it is."

"Of course." Evan felt foolish, but excited. No more darkness. They'd be out in the open. "Renner?" he asked tentatively.

"Nothing yet. Could be something in the structure."

They continued walking the rest of the stairwell in silence, pausing briefly at the top for the kid to push open a metal grilled door, which led out to a small tarmac apron enclosed by a mix of stone and rotten wood panels. Behind it stood a church. "How about now?" Evan asked, closing his eyes and letting the winter sun warm his face.

"Nothing."

"But we're out."

"I know," Kyle said, his tone laced with concern.

Evan glanced at the two walking in front of him. Neither seemed to pay any attention. Or at least, they hid it well. "Where are we?" he asked, hoping to spark a conversation. Silence lingered for five more steps before he turned to Kyle, puzzled.

The woman pressed herself against a black iron gate and pulled the latch. It clunked open satisfyingly. The boy climbed the wall and perched like a cat on top as she pushed the gate open, revealing the street beyond.

He dropped behind her, and they ventured out of the weedy yard, eyeing the large arched window-fronted church ahead. Beside it, a tarnished yellow sign barely displayed the words "hand" and "wash" beneath thick ivy.

"Clapham," Kyle blurted.

"No way! I remember Clapham—it's huge," Evan said.

"That's Clapham Junction. This is North." Kyle pointed to their left. "There's the subway entrance."

Evan glanced back at the small brick shed they'd left. "Then what's that?"

"Air raid tunnel."

"If we're south of the Thames," Evan mused, knowing most of Fletcher's time had been between Kensington and Notting Hill, "then we've no reports of the area."

He looked back to the wall, noticing the kid had moved on, joining the woman walking toward a bridge on their right. "We need some intel."

"Hold up!" Kyle shouted, but they paid no notice. "Hey!"

The woman turned first, but it was the kid who spoke. "Keep moving."

"We need to stop," Kyle pushed. "I need to check his chipset."

The kid glanced at Evan, then spoke to the woman in their Indian dialect. She assessed Evan, nodded, and hoisted her rifle off her shoulder. Within moments, she scaled the top of the bridge, keeping watch for anyone approaching.

The kid followed her, and Evan sensed it wasn't fear but a deep distrust for strangers. He didn't mind; it gave him time to catch up with Kyle. "Sit," Kyle instructed. Evan found a weathered wooden bench in the courtyard of a public house, its pink-framed menu standing out in stark contrast to the bleak winter landscape.

Ivy snaked through the bench, seemingly holding it together. Evan tested it with a foot and then a hand before sitting. It groaned under his weight. "Best not join me," he joked.

"Shush," said Kyle.

Evan winced as Kyle prodded. "Watch it!" he said, grateful for the banter after the unnerving silence in the tunnels.

"It's healing nicely," Kyle assured him. "Anything resembling a display?"

"Nothing."

"Don't worry too much. It'll probably sort itself out. And if not, Haines hasn't killed anyone in over five years."

Evan snorted. It was well known that the head surgeon at Special Branch faced a malpractice suit. Though Dr Haines had been cleared, the field staff maintained a dark sense of humour. Back in York, it would likely be Dr 'Hatchet' Haines patching him up.

He closed his eyes and inhaled the fresh air. "It's quiet around here."

"Nice and quiet," Kyle agreed.

"Any ideas why you can't get hold of Ren?" Evan asked in a low voice.

"One," Kyle answered. "You won't like it."

"Try me."

Kyle eyed the two guides. "I've got full functionality, other than sending and receiving."

"You don't trust them?"

"You do?"

"So, what? They're blocking us?"

Kyle nodded.

Evan pondered the possibility, giving Kyle's assessment the consideration it deserved. It was entirely plausible that they were being blocked. Window had equipment that baffled Special Branch and MI5. Either of them could carry a handheld device or have something subdermal. The question wasn't how, but why. "Maybe they're being cautious?"

"I'd appreciate being told. Not being dragged along without so much as a name."

A wood pigeon hooted. Evan turned, not having seen one since childhood. He'd been fooled—it was the kid, resting his knee at the edge of the bridge. Disappointed, he remarked, "he makes animal noises too."

"Maybe I'll call him Mowgli, instead of Potter," Kyle suggested.

"Both will go over his head." Evan doubted the kid had ever seen a film or read a book. What kind of life did he lead? He couldn't be over twelve. He had tattoos and guns—guns he knew how to use.

He was a thirteen-year-old man.

The kid stepped off the bridge, dropping to the road with the grace of an acrobat, landing effortlessly on his toes before padding over. "All good?" he asked.

"Yes, thanks," Evan answered.

"Then let's get moving." The kid looked up at Kyle. "We've got a lot of distance to cover." He stepped back, meeting the woman as she climbed down to their level.

Kyle helped Evan to his feet. "Of course, the other reason Renner's so quiet," Kyle said, "is that York could've been nuked." He gave Evan a firm pat on the back, ensuring he knew he was jesting.

"I'm more concerned about present company." Evan looked at their two companions walking away from them.

"Let me do the worrying."

"How far do you think we'll have to go?"

"We've gone a fair way in the tunnels and we passed several alternate exits. My guess? They want to keep us out of harm's way as long as possible. She especially doesn't like us all being out in the open." Evan raised an eyebrow, and Kyle took the hint. "Not far."

It was a reasonable assessment, but under different circumstances, Evan might have accepted it. For now, there were still too many variables. "Guesswork isn't really doing anything for me."

"Do you want me to do it?"

Thinking about it, Evan really did.

"Okay." Kyle said, then whistled. Not too loudly, just enough to pique their companions' interest, but short enough for any neighbours to suspect the wind. The kid turned around instantly, his face livid. The woman turned slower, checking the junction for movement before looking their way.

Kyle approached them. "We have some questions." Evan stepped up behind him. There was no answer before they arrived, and still no answer while they waited.

"Names would be a good place to start," Kyle added.

"You're Bluebird," the kid informed Evan, "and you're Fallout," he said, turning to Kyle.

The kid was amusing, if not annoying, Evan thought. Window had informed them of their operational names before they'd set out, a little piece of information he'd forgotten during the shootout in the subway.

"I meant your names," Kyle said, sounding annoyed.

The kid looked up to the woman, not seeking approval like a child, but as a soldier to a superior. She didn't reciprocate, instead she stared at Kyle. Her eyes were stony and unwavering. She wanted him to know she wasn't afraid. The kid looked down at her. The decision had been made. "Later. We need to keep moving."

"Now," Kyle insisted.

The woman stepped forward. She was older than Evan had first appraised. Out of the tunnels, in the sunlight, he guessed her to be nearing fifty. Regardless of age, her body remained lithe and her muscle tone put him to shame. Not an ounce of fat on her. Just like the kid, he realised. Neither of their companions sat around watching television.

She reminded Evan of Native American photos, skin leathered under the sun, eyes marked by pain he couldn't begin to understand. She could hold her own, wasn't afraid of Kyle, and didn't perceive him as a threat. But maybe she would listen to him. "We just want this to be friendly, assuming we all want the same thing."

Her dark brown eyes lingered on Kyle's for a couple of moments more, then curiosity got the better of her. She looked at Evan.

"We all want this relationship to work out," he continued, "don't we?"

"Nikki," she said, her voice surprisingly native to London, almost Cockney. She pointed to the kid. "Bo." She dragged the 'O' out to form an 'oh' sound. Nikki looked pensive and on edge, while Bo seemed ready to slit their throats for whistling.

Evan smiled. "Nice to meet you."

"We need to keep moving," she reiterated.

2

They travelled along the streets for hours, staying close to the buildings, close to cover. They ducked inside at the first sign of Triad or SOP patrols, maintaining distance as best they could. Kyle appeared to be right; Nikki wanted to keep them from harm's way, and she was doing a good job of it. He didn't see the enemy, only heard the sporadic, hideous cackle of machine gun fire echoing through the streets. Evan was content with that.

The street resembled a Picasso painting, with buildings rotted and twisted. Nikki kept them moving through the devastation that Evan was seeing for the first time through unfiltered eyes. No pop-ups, no heartbeats, no display features to distract him. He only saw what remained of London. Just as the sun began to set, Nikki stopped at a door, indistinguishable from the thousands of entrances they'd passed. She checked the street, surveyed the road and crossroads ahead, then back to the roundabout behind them. She beckoned to Bo with a swift tilt of the head. He nodded and entered.

Evan glanced at Kyle, wondering and full of expectation. "This it?" he asked her.

She looked at him. "Comfort stop." Evan felt Kyle tap him on the back before following Bo into the building. Nikki waited, impatience growing on her face. He followed Kyle through the doorway and up an uncarpeted staircase to the first floor. Whatever the building was, it wasn't a house. From the narrow passage and stairway, it opened up onto a large, open-plan floor. It could easily hold a football game.

Bo took a spot on the floor under a window that overlooked the street they'd just left. Kyle walked toward the opposite side of the building, and Evan followed. Outside, he could still hear gunfire echoing. He slowed his footsteps and turned, walking backward in Kyle's direction. He watched Nikki as she entered the floor; she looked his way but said nothing.

Nikki's clear dislike for him and Kyle grated on Evan's nerves. Her purposeful refusal to look at them and dodging their questions agitated him. If she didn't open up soon, the feeling would be mutual. At least Bo seemed curious, especially toward Kyle. He had caught him stealing glances more than once when he thought no one was watching.

Noticing Evan's gaze, Nikki turned away, spoke to Bo in what Evan now guessed was Punjabi, and disappeared through the fire exit at the east side of the floor.

"Anything?" he asked Kyle, stepping up behind him.

Kyle looked away from the window. "Nothing you'll want to see."

He looked anyway. Whatever had been happening, it was now nearly over. Seven SOPs ambled along the empty street in an almost elliptical formation. Between them crawled a wretched figure. Evan could just make out their taunts; occasionally, one of their laughs rang clear when the nearby gunfire ceased.

Kyle was right; Evan didn't want to see this.

But he couldn't tear his eyes away. One of the SOPs kicked the man in the side, sending him flailing like a turtle on its back, vulnerable and exposed. Another SOP slung his rifle over his shoulder and unzipped his other weapon. He urinated on the man as the victim raised his hands in a futile plea. From the first floor, Evan couldn't see his ethnicity. He was covered in mud and blood from his beating. He could hear his sobs, however, and recognised the dialect as Cantonese, even if he no longer understood it.

"Triad?" he asked.

"Probably not." Kyle was still watching, too. His face stone, like he'd seen this far too many times before.

"Then..." Evan started but stopped, unsure if he wanted to know.

"Why?" Kyle continued for him. "They're used to being in control. Today they realised they aren't."

Evan turned from the window, aware that if he kept watching, he'd feel compelled to intervene—an order Kyle would reject. Such action would compromise their safety and jeopardise the mission. Besides, he lacked the strength for another conflict, whether within their group or outside of it. Instead, he focused on the room, wishing he could block out the pleading Cantonese voice from outside. "Anything from Renner?" he asked, anticipating the answer.

Kyle remained silent, still observing the SOPs from the window. Evan wondered if Kyle wanted to stop the violence or join in, given the chance. Disliking the question as much as being held here with no information, he dealt with the easier issue.

"Hey, Bo?" Evan stepped away from the window, walking toward the kid. "Are you blocking us? We've had no signal since Notting Hill."

But Bo ignored him, engrossed in disassembling one of his shiny, pristine Desert Eagles.

"Hey, kid, stop playing with that!" Evan said, standing next to Bo.

"We're changing our travel plans," Nikki interrupted, drawing Evan's attention from the oblivious child.

"We have a travel plan?" Kyle's sarcasm was evident, but Evan agreed in principle.

"We wait here until nightfall and keep to the roofs as much as possible," she told Bo.

The kid looked up from his pistol, its components arrayed in a semicircle before him. "Deep?" he asked her.

She nodded.

"Okay," Evan said, feeling the conversation had ended as quickly as it started, and he still didn't know what was happening. Nikki seemed to have chosen English for them to hear but not understand.

"Deep?" he asked, "The Tooty Nung?" assuming an invitation.

Neither Bo nor Nikki acknowledged his question, and he felt his face redden with anger.

"Okay, this is fun and all," Kyle joined the group, "but you need to bring us up to speed."

Both Bo and Nikki noticed Kyle. "I just did," Nikki replied, "and that's all the information you need."

"That's not enough."

"Too bad," she ended her sentence in Punjabi.

So Kyle responded in Punjabi. Nikki wasn't surprised, but disappointed—disappointed that her secret conversations were no longer secret and never had been.

"In case you haven't noticed," Nikki switched back to English, "London is burning."

"About that," Evan interjected. "What exactly happened? We know the Triads are out for blood. That their Dragon King was killed last night?"

"You don't know?" Nikki's eyes widened, full of spite.

She glanced at him but kept her focus on Evan. She really doesn't like me, he thought.

"From the top?" she finally asked.

"Please," Kyle said.

Nikki removed her rifle's shoulder strap, leaned it against the wall, and placed her hands firmly on her hips. "The Triad believes the SOP killed Sin Lao. They've announced their vendetta, and everyone else is just trying to stay out of their way. You boys might as well wear SOP uniforms with your weapons and boots; you're more likely to get Bo and me killed transporting you than getting caught by Curb Bills."

Evan waited for her to finish, noticing her anger at having to babysit them. He knew the answer to his question from her first sentence: the SOPs were believed to have assassinated Sin Lao. She knew it wasn't them and possibly knew who had. "Who did kill Sin Lao?"

Nikki hesitated, debating whether she should tell them or wait for Window to do so. Kyle noticed her seething anger since they'd left the tunnel. Perhaps it wasn't just directed at Evan. "You know who did, don't you?" he pressed.

"Fletcher," she finally said.

Evan focused on the revelation. Fletcher. Dominic Fletcher? Not his fake identity, Dominic Blake. "How do you know that name?"

"This is bullshit!" Kyle interjected.

Nikki paused, realising her mistake. "Window will tell you everything you need to know."

While Evan wondered how Window would decide what he needed to know, Kyle stepped forward, pointing at Nikki. "Spill it!" he snarled. "You can't name drop without explanation. Tell me what the hell you did with him."

"You think I owe you something?" she spat back.

"I think your house is no longer in order, and Window may not be speaking for the whole southeast."

"Not in order? My house is smashed because of you and yours. And you need Window far more than we need you.

"Bitch," Kyle snapped. "The next thing out of your mouth..." His gaze dropped to the gun. Neither of them had seen Bo finish it or move, but there he was, standing close. Too close. The barrel of his DEagle pressed against Kyle's crotch.

Evan hadn't been paying attention. Something hadn't sat right with him when she'd said Fletcher's name. The subtle pitch change in her voice revealed anger, not toward him, but toward Fletch. It didn't matter whether Fletch had killed Sin Lao; what mattered was that she believed he did and blamed him for the death.

But there was more to it than that. Nikki wasn't just angry; she was scorned. Fletcher had betrayed her. Evan wasn't certain, but he was willing to bet on it. "He told you?" he asked, diffusing the situation as confusion rippled through the group. "Fletch told you his name, didn't he?"

The moment lingered, making Kyle uneasy. The pistol remained pressed firmly against his inner thigh, and Bo hadn't moved since planting it there. He stood like a sentinel, waiting for Nikki's order. It could end right there. They had said it; Evan needed them more than they needed him. Whatever that meant, they believed it—just as they believed Fletcher had toppled the Triad hierarchy and thrown London into anarchy.

Her eyes wavered, her hands slid from her hips. "Yes."

3

Nikki led the way in silence, speaking only to Bo and infrequently at that. She strode ahead of the group, occasionally dropping to one knee to confer with someone on her comms device. Evan couldn't get a good look at it, but Kyle said it resembled an old-style Bluetooth device clipped to her ear. Sometimes she called Bo to discuss, but mostly she took the calls alone.

Bo obeyed her without question. The perfect little soldier. He followed her directives without hesitation, trusting her judgment completely. They waited on one rooftop for twenty minutes while he scouted ahead and another ten when she scouted behind. He kept them moving and knew when they could speak in hushed tones or not at all.

Surprisingly, Bo no longer spoke at them, but with them. He didn't seem to resent them as much as Nikki did. When Evan asked him about it, Bo replied, "She wants it too much." She was anxious and wanted them out of harm's way just as much as Evan did.

They travelled across the rooftops, as planned. The path took them over loose slate and past crumbling chimney stacks. When they reached the end of a terrace, they found a workman's plank stretching to the next building. Occasionally, they encountered a scaffold-built bridge or a zip-line. Both Bo and Nikki had carabiners and cords tied to their harnesses. Evan had hastily chosen the kit before they left, not deeming climbing gear necessary. Fortunately, Nikki had two spares.

Evan hadn't zip-lined since basic training. He peered over the edge of the building, the alley below eight storeys down. Heights never bothered him, and the assault course was his favourite part of training. He fastened the clip to his harness, tossed his poncho front over his shoulder, and hooked onto the line. Grinning, he turned to Kyle. "I'm Batman!" and zipped across to the next building.

The wind intensified, and dark clouds filled the night sky. Evan sensed a storm brewing. He didn't relish crossing rooftops in foul weather but dreaded walking the streets even more, with the rifle crackling echoing around. Besides, the rooftop journey had its charm. He, Kyle, and Bo exchanged small talk, Bo participating more as the night wore on. The view was strangely captivating, devoid of gardens and upscale residences Fletcher had mentioned. "That's north of the river and some south; this area is in dispute. No one lives here," Bo explained.

"Disputed by whom?" Evan asked.

"Reapers, Kingz, and Tooty."

"I haven't heard of the Reapers."

Evan took Bo's pause as consideration on whether to answer. However, he replied in Punjabi, revealing that English wasn't his first language.

"Monsters," Kyle translated.

"Monsters?" Evan didn't like the way Bo suddenly looked at them, as if he were reading a menu.

"Yes," continued Bo. "They harvest tech. For the markets. They could," he paused, "retire on Fallout. He's worth a lot of cred."

Evan didn't want to know how much cred either of them were worth. "How powerful are they?" Unsure whether Bo meant figurative Monsters or actual ones.

Bo's eyes slanted, giving the impression he'd had personal experience against these Reapers. "Hardcore."

"And they're claiming this territory?"

Bo nodded, his eyes betraying something else. Loss.

"Where are they based?"

"The Dome."

The O2, the Millennium Dome. "No worries. We stay well away."

Despite the good news, Evan felt a nagging knot in his stomach. Fletch hadn't mentioned Reapers or the O2 in his report. The gangs had ceased fighting for a year, but Bo's tone implied something more sinister about these Reapers, altering his demeanour. They seemed more than mere street thugs. If so, why had Fletcher omitted them from his report? If he'd been close enough to Nikki to reveal his real identity, surely he would have learned about them.

Nikki's pigeon call from ahead interrupted his thoughts. Instantly, Bo left their side and scurried to her at the edge of the next roof.

"Boogie men," Kyle said. "They have them in Afghanistan. They scare locals into avoiding augmentation, keeping them au naturel to subdue any revolts more easily."

Evan glanced at the next roof, where Nikki kneeled, shielded from the wind by an air-conditioning vent, with Bo crouching beside her. "I'm not so sure," he said, observing Bo glance back at them while nodding at something Nikki was saying. "I think he's met them."

"Trust me on this," Kyle assured him. "Ghost stories and nothing more."

Evan wondered if Kyle was just trying to quell his panic. Was he such a coward that Kyle felt the need to protect him? And why did he trust a young teenager over a veteran serviceman?

"We have to drop." Evan hadn't noticed Bo return.

The steel mast, bolted to the floor and wrapped in leather, was sturdy. However, the zip line had been severed. Instead of a quick and safe route twelve storeys above the road, they'd have to use the fire escape at the side of the building, exit the alley, cross the four-lane street, and climb up to the neighbouring roof.

"Do they break often?" Evan asked.

"No," Nikki replied, "they get cut." She walked away from the pole, with Bo trailing behind. The natural questions would be 'by whom' and 'why.' Given they were being forced to the ground, Evan didn't like the answers his previous conversation suggested.

Evan was the last to reach the metal steps. Nikki led, Kyle climbed onto the railing, and Bo waited for him. The boy stood at the edge of the building, and Evan felt a parental urge to tell him to step back. The wind could topple the kid's slight frame off the roof. Remembering the boy had grown up here, Evan said, "It's a long drop," instead.

Bo didn't reply immediately, focusing on Nikki and Kyle, who were now on the next platform of the escape. Nikki stepped onto the next set of stairs. "Don't fall," Bo finally said, snapping his fingers and pointing to the escape.

Evan glanced at the dark clouds and the hidden moon before complying. The rickety fire escape shook and creaked as the wind blew through the alley, feeling too unsafe for all four of them. Eight storeys seemed an impossible task. By the time Evan reached the fourth, Nikki had dropped from the final platform to the ground, Kyle was about to follow her, and Bo waited for Evan to start down to the third. Then Bo said, "Stop." Evan complied, feeling the first raindrops on the back of his hand gripping the railing.

"What is it?" he asked.

"Shhh."

"I was until you said to stopped..." he muttered.

Bo whistled his pigeon call to Nikki on the ground, alerting her to the sound. She waved back and signalled Kyle to take cover. He crouched against the wall, while she ran to the alley's mouth, looking up the street at the approaching thrum. Evan pressed himself against the ladder, trying to flatten his body as much as possible. His thoughts raced toward the threat. A sound so apparent now, he couldn't believe he hadn't heard it before. Engines. Small and numerous. Motorbikes.

His thoughts raced to one thing. "Reapers?"

"Stay here," Bo said before stepping onto the railing and monkey-climbing head-first down the side of the fire escape. This really was his playground.

Evan observed from his fourth-floor perch as Bo joined Nikki at the alley's mouth. They exchanged a few words, and Bo darted into the street, disappearing from Evan's view. The sound of the bikes grew louder, so close he could almost taste the petrol in their engines. Some kind of patrol. A convoy of bikes, a number he couldn't count without his chipset. He knew Kyle had the information, but Kyle was on the ground, hidden in the alley. Evan grew acutely aware of his vulnerable position.

On the roof, Bo had mentioned the area was disputed. No one claimed it. It had to be one of the gangs: Tooty Nung, the Shadowkingz, or the Reapers. Evan wanted to avoid the latter the most, despite Kyle's assurance they were just boogeymen. At this point, he felt he could handle a fight, even being captured or killed. But the thought of having his body butchered and his tech sold on the black market made his stomach churn.

Nikki's whistle sliced through the mounting wind and rain. She stepped onto the road, her hand raised, stopping the approaching vehicles. They'd been instructed to wait, to remain hidden. Evan glanced down through the platform grills at Kyle, who still leaned against the wall, waiting. Evan would wait too.

The lead bike was a racer, decked in urban greys and red tags—the marks of the Tooty Nung. The rider wore dark leathers, his helmet embellished with red streaks and intricate patterns Evan couldn't decipher. Damn, he missed his chip. As the Nung removed his helmet, long braided locks tumbled heavily onto his shoulders. White nano-craft tattoos speckled his brown skin, flowing across his cheeks. Nine more bikes stopped behind him.

Nikki approached the lead rider, her stance casual and fearless. The rider shared her ease; none of the bikers aimed their weapons at her. From Evan's vantage point, no one seemed suspicious. They hadn't looked his way or down the alley. "They know you," he whispered to himself, "don't they?"

Evan's suspicions were confirmed as Bo joined them in the street. He'd probably found a prime vantage point for a crossfire, had they needed it. Bo fist-bumped several riders and chatted casually with one at the back while Nikki talked with the leader. Evan relaxed, assuming they were friendly. The conversation dragged on, feeling longer as the rain soaked him.

Eventually, the bikers donned their helmets, and Nikki and Bo stepped aside as they roared away.

Once the bikes turned a corner, Nikki and Bo signalled, and Evan scrambled down the wet fire escape. By the time he jumped to the ground, the others had taken shelter across the road in a gutted department store.

It was a department store or used to be. The front windows long gone, the interior sacked for all that was useful, leaving a dusty and windy space but at least it was dry.

"They were Nung," Nikki confirmed. "They're patrolling since the SOPs are distracted."

"Any news?" Evan asked.

"The Triad groups are competing," she replied.

Evan nodded, recalling his studies on Triad hierarchy.

"For what?" Kyle inquired.

"Their leader is gone. It's a power struggle. All the commanders are vying for dominance over the collective," Evan explained, earning an agreeing nod from Nikki.

"This morning, they targeted only SOPs. It was revenge." Nikki paused, hinting to Evan it wasn't the good news he'd hoped for. "This afternoon, they started attacking everyone. Whoever brings the most to the table gains the most leverage to become the next Dragon King."

"Who's been hit?" Kyle inquired.

"The Nung, north of the river. The south hasn't been attacked yet, but they expect it before tomorrow morning." She glanced at Bo. "Butcher is taking his troops to reinforce the Kingz."

Bo remained silent, betraying no knowledge of Butcher beyond his name.

Nikki continued, "We have a clear route to the boathouse. They left at sunset. Deep has the place secured, and we'll have somewhere to crash tonight."

"Staying on the ground?" Kyle asked.

"No, we're heading back to the roofs," she replied. "Just in case."

CHAPTER NINE
PARTY CRASHER

"Renner hasn't heard anything, has he?" Reekes' voice resonated inside Oliver's skull as he lounged in the back seat of his Mercedes Maybach.

"Nothing since Notting Hill," Oliver replied, glancing at his sterling silver Tag Heuer watch.

"How long has it been?"

Oliver thought about challenging him there and then, telling him it was needless to be concerned with the safety of the boys that he himself put in danger through his reckless signature signings. Instead, he settled on saying, "all afternoon. That's both Renner and Rockwood, unable to give us anything to go on."

"How much longer are we prepared to wait?"

"How long is a piece of string?" Longer than Oliver's patience, that much was certain. "Jonathan, I've arrived," he stated as the Maybach turned onto the gravel drive, weaving through the moonlit evergreen trees leading to the mansion.

"How long?" Jonathan repeated his question.

This time, Oliver knew he couldn't be flippant. "I don't think we have much of a choice, do you?"

Through the window, Oliver glimpsed the guiding peg lamps and the three-story house looming. "Short of sending in a strike force?" the Prime Minister said. "No, we don't."

The car halted, and a tantalisingly young concierge opened the door. Oliver slid out, smoothing the creases in his delicate silver suit, and marvelled at the grandiosity of the Tate stately home. Although Oliver came from wealth, his townhouse could have fit inside the mansion six times over. Not bad for a kid playing computer games.

"I'll call you later," Oliver said, approaching the main doors and nodding at the security guard.

"Call me in the morning," Jonathan replied. "I'm going to bed."

Oliver grinned, not at the gold-plated decor or the marble checkerboard flooring of the atrium, but at Jonathan. "Don't lie to me." He recognised his friend, the Prime Minister, had an insatiable itch, and he wasn't the only one who knew. Faraday had hinted at it, and if he knew, it was likely that whoever he worked for knew too.

"Good night, Oliver," Jonathan said, terminating the call.

It wasn't entirely Jonathan's fault, of course. Oliver understood that, which was why he had supported him all these years. In their youth, swept up in the romanticism of politics, Jonathan was a force to be reckoned with. Now, he was more like Boxer, waiting to be taken to the glue factory. That would make Oliver, Benjamin, he smirked.

Back then, they had planned to fix the country. The once-great nation had become a grim joke, much like themselves. Ill-conceived asylum laws, a recession, and greedy bankers had left their mark. Previous governments had tried to turn things around, but their legacy was a broken one, beyond repair—unless one considered slaughtering hundreds of thousands a solution. Oliver suspected Jonathan had secretly considered it during sleepless nights, despite his denials.

But Britain was not his itch.

For appearance's sake, Jonathan's family remained part of his life, but they were essentially estranged. As far as Oliver could tell, Jonathan hadn't seen or spoken to his wife, Maggie, for at least seven weeks. She stayed in Scotland with the children, whom Oliver hadn't seen in over 18 months. He missed the family and the respectable Prime Minister they once knew. Without them, Jonathan was diminished.

Jonathan had confided in Oliver that Maggie had asked him to quit. "Canada," he had said, sitting on the floor of his bedroom. "Just like William. Run away because it's too difficult, too hard to fix. Run away like some small child." While Oliver was a royalist at heart, he couldn't deny the public opinion that the King had abandoned his duty to the country by leaving.

"You could be with Kylie and Zoe," Oliver suggested, mentioning Jonathan's children, uncertain of what else to say. He didn't want him to leave, not before completing what they'd started. The family had just left York, and already Jonathan's resolve showed signs of strain. But Oliver offered him an out, knowing he didn't have one himself. He committed to seeing this through, regardless of the outcome.

Yet even before Jonathan answered, Oliver knew what he would say. Jonathan was also in this till the end, so his family wasn't the itch either.

"Who would keep you company?" Jonathan had asked. "When everything falls apart and the country can't be pieced back together, who will stand by your side?" He had smiled, reaching for the bottle he kept under his bed.

"You," Oliver said reluctantly. "You damned fool."

On nights like this, when the Prime Minister sat alone in his office, he would spike his morning oranges with Stoli from his locked desk, all under the watchful gaze of Winston Churchill's portrait. That old bastard still dominated the party long after his death. And that was the itch. No amount of alcohol could slake his thirst.

"Sir?" A teenage princess held out a tray of champagne flutes at Oliver.

He took one, smiled politely, and watched as she moved on to the next guest, wishing he were twenty years younger.

The atrium bustled with arrivals like himself, trading winter coats for drinks and canapés. Friends greeted each other as warmly as strangers meeting for the first time. The room overflowed with fake smiles and costly timepieces. Opulence was the theme of the evening, everyone decked in Beckham, Sies Marjan, Jay Z, or the more classical Coco Chanel.

Navigating a quick passage lined with mirrors, game consoles on podiums, and false idols, Oliver entered the main hall. Blue and gold-framed tables, mirrors, and paintings filled the room. Floating lamps hovered above the black-stained marble floor that seemed to span the entire house. The magnificence caught him off guard, and he barely registered the deep thrum of Blu3 Cr33p's music emanating from the corner.

This is what billions can buy, Oliver thought, sipping the crisp champagne. This is what Michael Tate, the undisputed FPS World Champion, eldest in the International League, and on the verge of retirement at twenty-two, had purchased with his winnings and franchised marketing deals. Soccer players of the past couldn't have dreamed of such luxury.

Tate could have had anyone in the world. That statement, like his title, is undisputed. Classy, slightly geeky, and with a working-class background, the ultimate working man's dream: play games, get anything, and he chose Madison Fry, the twenty-one-year-old adult simulation starlet boasting a flawless bronzed body and the most coveted HUDSkyn in the business.

Oliver didn't care for the trend of downloading another's appearance to overlay your own partner, still considering it cheating. Hell, he still remembered pornography being top shelf. But younger generations seemed to crave it. At least the taxes kept the NHS lights on.

Another waiter weaved through the crowd, bearing a tray of canapés. Oliver took one, tasting the salmon-filled puff just as he spotted the familiar face of Jack Faraday, impeccably dressed in his tailored Armani suit. Flirting with a stunning green-haired woman in blue silk, Faraday looked as sharp as any other multibillionaire in the room. "Faraday, you dog," Oliver said, slapping Jack on the shoulder. "How's the wife?" He knew this alluring woman was definitely not Mrs Faraday.

Jack held up his left hand, eagerly showing off his naked ring finger. "Dorothy, meet Oliver Trench," he said. "Oliver, this is Dorothy Fairfax."

"Of Fairfax Holdings?" Oliver offered his most charming smile. "A pleasure." He brought her hand to his lips, stopping just short of kissing it.

"You're the chief whip," she said, her smile as artificial as her chest.

"Indeed, I am, Ms Fairfax."

"I hear you keep a strict house."

"Okay, charmer," interrupted Faraday.

"I'll have him back in a minute," Oliver assured her. "I promise." He grabbed Jack's arm, leading him away from Dorothy and into the crowd.

"Hold on a second," Jack said, resisting Oliver's grip.

"Only a minute, I promise," Oliver repeated.

"Have you been drinking?"

Oliver glanced at his empty champagne flute. "Yes, but that's hardly the point. We're at a party."

"That's exactly the point." Faraday said. "What's the rush?"

"You promised me names." They halted among the crowd. "I've come to collect."

Faraday shifted uncomfortably; this wasn't the Oliver he had bested at the Pond earlier. "This isn't how we play the game, Oliver."

"Oh, I've brought you something." *Courtesy of Renner, you repugnant ass.*

Jack's smirk didn't fool Oliver. He didn't enjoy this side of Oliver—the one who relished in watching politicians squirm like dying fish on a deck. "Something sweet, I trust?" Jack asked, still playing the game.

"Insider trading," said Oliver.

"Always a crowd pleaser."

"Last year, a group of benchers bought a bundle of stocks in Asuka Corp." The memory flickered in Faraday's eyes. "A week before the legislation deemed their augmentations safe by EU standards." Blood drained from Jack's face. "They used aliases, of course, offshore bank accounts, the usual. But Special Branch works wonders, don't you agree, Jack?"

"I..." he stuttered. "I wasn't part of the legislation." Faraday wasn't lying, but Oliver was far from finished.

"Wonders, Jack." Oliver grabbed the man's forearm, displaying the blue HAND Logo and connecting their chips. He transferred a gigabyte of files to him. "You see, Minister Bartlett was part of the legislation." Jack's HUD lit up with photograph after photograph. "And you're still fucking his wife."

Jack stared at the photos in silence, then the documents. The incriminating paper trail that Oliver had found connected him to fraudulent share manipulation. His cheerful facade crumbled; it was over. Oliver had found the skeleton in his closet, and he knew it.

"It's your turn," the whip added.

Jack mustered his remaining wit and fired back. "You're a cunt."

"So Mother is fond of telling." Oliver snatched Faraday's champagne from his hand triumphantly. "Now, out with it."

Jack glared at him a moment longer, watching Oliver drink what had once been his before conceding defeat. "You already know about Harry Rockwood."

"Indeed, I do."

"Percy..."

"...Browne?" Oliver's eyes widened; he had assumed Percy to be nothing more than a whelp. "You're serious?"

Jack nodded. "He and Harry are the ringleaders."

"How many in total?"

"Oliver, some of these guys—"

"I don't care. They've made their choices." He twisted Jack's forearm, illuminating the HAND Logo. "I want them all." He needed them all; Percy was popular—very popular on the benches—but he didn't have the guts for something like this.

Jack finally gave in, transferring the list of names to Oliver. "Why'd you rush me like that?"

"Both you and my mother have covered that."

"We were going to offer you a slice of the pie." Jack was borderline sulking, but even in defeat, he piqued Oliver's interest further.

"Were we?" The invitation made sense now; they wanted him here to make a deal. A deal that, judging by Faraday's eyes, might be taken off the table. Faraday, Percy, and Rockwood—all with their hats in the ring, but none of them seemed like puppeteers.

Jack nodded, his eyes drifting from Oliver.

"They're both here, then?"

"Percy is."

Oliver followed his gaze to the grand piano, currently serving as a discarded flute table. Percy rested an elbow on it, chatting with a group of men—all of whom were focused on another pair. A strikingly suave man with shockingly white hair, as well as the party's host, Michael Tate.

"Who's he with?" Oliver asked, looking at Mr Suave.

"Private Sector." He turned back to Faraday, wanting more. "No one you want to tangle with."

Oliver recognised the tone in Faraday's voice and called it. "You're scared."

"Leave off, Oli. It's just a piece of advice."

"Am I likely to find myself outmatched?" asked Oliver, looking back at Mr Suave.

Then came a different tone from Faraday—one that Oliver recognised, too. Not fear or casual political misdirection, but simple truth: "You're likely to find yourself dead."

The statement halted Oliver's pursuit. He had the back of the man's head in his sights, but his HUD couldn't identify him. Yet, even without the information displayed, Oliver had the distinct feeling he knew the person. Jack's warning was as clear as they came, and Oliver was sure of that much. But Percy and Rockwood must have had a backer—someone outside the party, someone with money.

The fear in Faraday's voice lent Oliver the idea that this man was that backer. So his interest persisted; he needed to know. "Does Private Sector have a name?" He waited for his chipset to provide facial recognition.

As soon as Faraday uttered the name "Felix," Oliver knew.

"Fray." Felix Fray, "Heir to Fray International?" The question lingered, but he didn't need an answer. He didn't need to see Faraday nodding to know he was right. Fray International built everything from small arms to computers, robots to cuddly toys. It produced the platform HAND still used. But among all Fray International did, Oliver would bet his soul it was the private security army being sold here tonight.

"Well," Oliver returned his attention to Faraday, "introduce me."

Oliver observed Felix listening intently to the conversation as he followed Jack to the piano. He was exactly as he'd imagined someone like him—beautiful platinum hair, crystal blue eyes, and a suit Oliver guessed cost more than his yearly earnings.

As he approached the group, he felt his stomach knotting. Faraday's words echoed in his ears: "Likely to find yourself dead." Jack Faraday hadn't used the words lightly; his warning was sincere, and Oliver didn't relish the thought of being dead.

"Faraday," said Felix, making room in the group for the two newcomers.

"Mr Fray," Faraday said, but Felix already ignored him as he turned to the Chief Whip.

"And you must be Oliver Trench."

"Mr Fray," Oliver accepted his hand, shaking it.

"Call me Felix," the man practically oozed charisma. "Please." Oliver could have mistaken him for one of his own.

"Michael," the Tate boy held out his hand next.

"I know," said Oliver, "I saw you at last year's FPS Championship." Oliver followed the games as much as he filled the gap between football premierships. He knew some names, enough to carry himself in polite conversation. "An inspired final."

Michael seemed taken aback by the interest. "You follow FPS?"

"Avidly. Congratulations on the engagement—you've upset a lot of men." Oliver smiled, shook the young man's hand, and was introduced to the others in the group, one by one. All of them private sector, all of them hangers-on. Eager to be seen with the host and increase their share margins with popular culture kids.

The conversation revolved around this, as Michael reluctantly neared his retirement. Sponsorships were moving abroad, heading to Korean and Japanese teams. "Perhaps a funding grant?" one of the suits suggested. The group laughed, and Oliver remembered why he disliked attending these events.

He didn't, however, give them any idea other than he was enjoying their company. He laughed with them, pandering to the incredulous nagging of tax cuts that happened wherever he appeared socially.

This was not to be polite. Felix, like Faraday, was switched on. Oliver couldn't tell for sure, not without further conversation, but he could sense that Faraday's warning was justified.

Felix sipped his drink, never dominating the conversation but always listening. He consistently drew out others' views without revealing his own. The game had begun before Oliver joined them, with Felix and Percy skilfully guiding the group through topics like China, lazy politics, and lack of funding—all challenging subjects that put Oliver on the defensive. He deflected, evaded, and countered with ease, but his patience, like all things, eventually wore thin. "So, what are my options?" he asked, directing the question to Felix.

The man smiled. "Somewhere you'd rather be?"

"I warned you," said Percy, sipping his drink.

There was a nod of agreement between them. "You did." Then, for the first time since Oliver had met him, Felix's attention drifted away from the conversation and across the room.

Oliver followed his gaze until they were both looking at her. He wondered how he hadn't noticed her before now. Madison was as gorgeous as her HUDSkyn sales suggested; it was hard to believe that every man at this party wouldn't be downloading her that evening. Those who didn't probably already had. Either way, she worked the room in a slinky blood-red dress, her face framed by her perfectly long, brown, tumbling curls.

"Mike, your fiancée beckons you," said Felix.

"Then I best not keep her waiting." Michael glanced over his shoulder, spotted her, and raised his glass before turning to say his farewells. "Gentlemen."

"Great to finally meet you, Michael," Oliver said.

"A pleasure, Mr Trench." He nodded to the others and left the group, making his way to his captivating partner.

"Remarkable manners for someone so young," said Felix. "Don't you agree?" Somehow, he had a fresh flute of champagne. "Now, gentlemen, I'm sure the stimulating conversations at the buffet table are more to your liking."

The group, including Percy and Faraday, dispersed, leaving Oliver staring at his empty champagne flute. "Top-up, Oliver?" asked Felix, summoning the nearest waiter. "You don't mind me calling you Oliver?"

Oliver couldn't think of a reason to object, so he shook his head politely. "Go right ahead." He exchanged his empty flute for a full one.

"Excellent," Felix beamed. "And since we're being so friendly, I hope you don't mind me being candid?"

"I'd prefer it," Oliver said.

"Good." Felix took a moment to size up Oliver as if he were a fresh dish at a banquet. "Then you won't mind if I say Reekes is out of control. Secret meetings... the man's paranoid with only two friends: you and that voluptuous cougar running the Home Office," he said, pausing briefly. "He's past his prime, and the opposition is laughing at all three of you."

Oliver had to admit Felix had an impressive grasp on the situation. "But you already know this. That's why, Oliver, you tipped off the press."

Oliver remained silent. It was the second time in one day he'd found himself face-to-face with an adversary who had him exactly where they wanted. He had tipped off the press; he'd needed to shake Jonathan up and distance himself from the PM's office in case his investigations proved accurate. However, now standing before the puppet master, he wasn't about to admit that he had been pulling strings himself. "I'm quite sure I have no idea what you're suggesting." The lie slipped as smoothly through his lips as the champagne he sipped.

"Oliver," said Felix, "please don't embarrass yourself."

CHAPTER TEN
THE BOATHOUSE

Evan leaned against a broken wall, peering out from their building, a derelict on the corner. He didn't know the street name; he hadn't seen a sign for miles and hadn't attempted to access his chip for any information in just as long. The back of his head still throbbed, and all he craved in that moment was to rest for the night and start a new tomorrow.

Nikki leaned against the same wall. They were three meters apart, and between them, the wall had a man-sized hole punched through it. Rain poured through, just enough to prevent them from getting comfortable, but at least the wall shielded them from the wind. She observed the street with a monocular equipped with numerous dials and buttons. Evan presumed they designed it for more than just night use. He'd seen similar ocular devices in museums. He toyed with the idea of mentioning how she hadn't offered him her night-vision tool back in the tunnels, but decided against it.

"They're taking too long," she said, not looking up from the device.

"How long have they been?"

She checked her watch. "Twelve minutes."

They were taking too long. The boathouse was run by Nikki's friend Deep, who was supposed to supply them with a boat to cross the Thames. That would be in the morning after some promised hospitality— food, fresh water, and beds. Evan imagined those beds again, the soft mattress and plump pillow, and the good night's sleep he was going to get.

Twelve minutes was definitely too long. Too long because they would have been called over if their friends were still there.

"Wait." She peered through the scope again. "I can see them. They're alone." Her voice grew more defeated with each word, as if she was being beaten with a stick between each syllable.

Evan peeked over the top of the wall. The weather was atrocious. The rain pummelled the ground so hard that it would be difficult to hear a car engine drive past. It took him a while to spot them. Visibility was minimal, meaning he could barely make out shapes in the dark. He caught sight of them as lightning flashed in the sky above; Kyle sticking close to a building across the way while Bo jogged across the road toward them.

Bo slipped through the hole in the wall and shook the rain from his frame. "You're right," his voice was grim, looking at Nikki.

She cursed under her breath and kicked the ground. "Triad?" she asked.

"SOP," Kyle said, ducking through the hole. He took his poncho from Evan and wiped the night from his face and hair. "Nine of them."

"Any sign of Deep?" she asked Bo.

"Just the SOPs. The boats are still tied."

Kyle crouched next to Evan. "They haven't fortified the building. I think they're lying low, hiding from the Triads. I saw a burned-out APC further down the road and some bodies around it. No sign of the Triads, though."

Evan wanted to smile, as that was supposed to be good news. It was for Kyle. Not for Nikki, who had fallen silent. She hadn't mentioned how close she was to the people living there, how close she was to Deep. By her actions, she no longer needed to. She stood up, walked away from the three, disappearing into the darkness and further into the building.

"This isn't Triad territory," said Bo, "it's ours."

"I thought this was Tooty Nung—" Evan started.

"It is. It's also ours."

"But I thought you were part of Window's clan?" asked Evan, puzzled.

"We are."

"So Window is Nung?"

Bo rolled his eyes. "No." He shook his head and walked after Nikki.

Evan wanted to ask further, but he knew he wouldn't get anywhere. The conversation was over.

"They still don't like me," he said to Kyle.

"You are kind of a dick."

"Fuck you."

"Exactly." Kyle sat down next to him. "Cut them some slack; they've just lost their friends, and they look exactly like the enemy right now." Kyle was right; he had boiled down the situation to simple reasoning.

"They're not—?"

"Going to kill us? No," Kyle grinned, "not me, anyway. I'm not so sure about you."

Evan stifled a laugh just as the wind kicked around. It blew a wash of water through the hole, nearly soaking him. "Shitting hell!" he complained, moving further inside.

"Complaining you're wet now?"

Evan was about to retort when he saw Kyle was still soaked himself. "No. I was about to say so much for an easy ferry."

"It still could be."

It only took Evan a few seconds to catch up. "We have papers." They'd need to connect with mission control, but they could get onto a boat without going toe-to-toe with the SOPs. If they weren't too shot up to check before shooting at them and if they believed that Bo and Nikki were their guides or captives. "There's a lot of ifs."

"But it can work."

Evan felt the idea taking root in his mind. "If we can hack them, Renner can alter the papers, and we can get a boat from them." He turned to the darkness behind him. "Nikki!" he called, then back to Kyle. "This can work. You're a genius."

"What?" she asked, standing next to Evan.

"We can hack the SOP commander, hack all of them, and they'll let us take a boat. No questions asked."

"No."

Kyle understood her objection and countered, "You can block me again once the hack is done."

Nikki spat something back at him in Punjabi that Evan couldn't follow. "English," he said, silencing her. "Please?"

Her eyes narrowed into her all-too-familiar glare. "I was just telling your friend here how convenient it is that your guys took the one way across the river. And your magic solution is calling for backup."

"You think the SOPs took this base because of us?"

"Why not?"

"Because if they knew enough to block our path, do you think they need us linked up with base?" Evan glowered. "Besides, you think I want the SOPs in my way? You think I'm happy with all the killing? I'm trying to meet your boss. I'm here because I want to stop the killing." He took a breath. "Jesus – we have to trust each other at some point."

"I'm not starting that trust by betraying Window."

He bit the inside of his cheek, defeated. She wouldn't budge, and he didn't want to ruin what little they had by pushing further. "Okay then," he changed course. "We can still try it. We have legal papers; we can bluff you through as guides or prisoners."

Evan heard Bo laugh at 'prisoners,' and asked, "Are they likely to fall for that? Given that they're hiding out, the rest of their squad dead on the road outside?"

"What happens when they don't fall for it?" Nikki added.

Evan didn't want to answer.

"They shoot," Kyle answered for him. "Then we shoot back."

It was the answer Evan had avoided. He didn't want SOP blood on his hands. They were just doing their job. There had to be another way. "How far until the next crossing?"

"I already said this is the only way across," Bo replied.

"It can't be," Evan insisted, looking at Nikki.

"Why?" she shot back. "Why can't it be? You blew most of the fucking bridges up in twenty-one, and your SOP pals control what's left."

"They're not our pals." Evan knew he'd been baited as the words left his mouth.

"So let's kill them and take a boat," Bo said, his voice dripping with cold indifference.

"You can't be serious," Evan said, looking at Nikki. Not that he thought Bo was joking, but he couldn't believe Nikki would take the kid seriously.

"This is the only way across," she pointed out, glancing at Kyle. "You heard what he said. They haven't fortified, and most of them are asleep."

Evan looked at Kyle for support but found him staring out the hole, silent. "What if we steal a boat?"

"They'll be all over us when we start the engine," Bo said.

Evan squinted. "In this storm?"

"They have diesel engines; we'd be lucky if the storm would suppress the sound enough to avoid alerting everyone in the area," Kyle said. He understood their argument and the urgency of the mission. The longer they stayed in one place, the more danger they faced. The longer they moved through London openly, the higher the chance of ending up dead. They needed to get to Window quickly and safely. The mission was above them all, but Evan refused to give up his humanity. "We're not killing them."

"He doesn't have a problem killing," Kyle indicated.

The kid didn't understand. "That was different; we were under fire," Evan said, hoping it would be enough.

"But he ploughed through them," Bo persisted. "How many SOPs did you kill?"

Evan was about to correct him, but felt his mouth go dry. SOPs. They'd been following them ever since the M4, and they'd continued to follow them until they met at Notting Hill, the SOP station. They'd been separated. Kyle had shot someone, someone who was about to kill Evan as he tumbled from the platform. Someone Evan hadn't seen. He'd hit his head, not thought about the attack. He'd assumed Kyle would have had to kill some Triads since they were the ones chasing them into the tunnel.

Had Kyle said something, mentioned that the SOPs were defending the stairways? Stairways Bo had circumvented using the ducts. It was Evan's mission to speak with Window, to deliver the Prime Minister's message. It was Kyle's mission to ensure Evan got there in one piece. How many SOPs had Kyle killed to get back to Evan?

Evan looked at his silent partner, now the devil's advocate, gazing out through the rain with his augmented eyes—his killer eyes.

"You're running out of time," Nikki reminded Evan. "This is the way across."

Evan felt cornered, running out of ideas and grasping at straws. He needed to keep the body count down. "Can we at least keep the sleepers out of it? Drop gas in or something to keep them asleep?"

"If we had gas, we'd knock the entire building out." She was right, of course.

"I can kill all of them before they wake up." Bo's detached reasoning terrified Evan. In his eyes, the kid was worse than Kyle's thought process. At least Kyle's actions could be explained by duty. The kid, however, lacked something fundamental. He wanted to kill these men.

Evan surveyed the group and found himself outnumbered. "We're not killing anyone," he said to Nikki.

"I'm right here." Bo seemed to dislike being excluded as much as Evan hated discussing plans with a murderous child.

Evan needed an idea—one that would keep them safe and get them across the river. If he could devise such a plan, they'd go for it; he was sure. The boathouse might have smaller boats with oars. They'd have to wait out the storm, but it was an option, provided they had them.

Six of the SOPs were asleep. He turned to Kyle. "Where are the sleepers?"

"Top floor," Bo answered.

Evan waited for Kyle's response. "What he said," Kyle confirmed.

Bo glared at him, but Evan ignored it. "The drones have gas." Both Kyle and Evan carried one FRP drone each. A lightweight disc, with two vector thrust propellers. Inactive, they were small enough to fit in a hand or attach to a belt. They were remotely operated but required an active link connection they didn't have. They were also programmable; users could input a plan, and the onboard AI would navigate obstacles to achieve the desired result.

"Not in this weather," Kyle stated. "If we set them off inside the building, maybe. But they're small, enough to knock out one man apiece."

The lightweight frames would be useless in the storm, but they could release them inside the boathouse. That was doable. His plan could work, potentially saving two lives, but the group had already moved on.

"We could draw them out, catch them in crossfire," Nikki suggested, calculating the risk to the group and looking for the quickest way through the building. Like Bo, she had no problem killing the SOPs. They were obstacles that needed removal. Unless Evan thought of something else, every soldier in the boathouse would die.

"I got this," Kyle said, "if you can get the boat ready." He was looking at Nikki. She nodded.

"Got what, exactly?" Evan asked.

"I'll break into the top floor, make sure the sleepers can't interrupt anything. Then knock out the three on the ground floor."

Evan tried to read Kyle's stony face but failed. "Lethal?"

"No."

"You're risking us all by leaving them alive," Bo said. "They can alert another group or come after us."

"They're not in any shape to come after us," Kyle argued with the kid. "And if they could alert another group, they wouldn't be hiding in your boathouse."

"And you're sure you can take them all out without alerting the rest?" Nikki asked.

Kyle just smiled. He flexed his muscles and switched into combat mode. His systems were limited to local commands and sensor information, but he was no less lethal in close quarters than if he'd been connected. His eye shields slipped down from his brow, his skin tinted an urban camouflage grey, and Bo's eyes lit up, exclaiming something wondrous in Punjabi that caught Kyle's attention. "Damn right," he said with a confident smirk.

2

In twenty-one seconds, fifty meters of road vanished beneath Kyle's feet without him breaking a sweat. His limbs could do more, but he wanted to remain invisible. The boathouse, a sturdy three-story building with a bottomless sub-level holding awnings, had its own weed-ridden parking lot and a sixteen-foot-tall stone perimeter wall.

Kyle was at the top of it with one kick off.

Squatting, he surveyed the lot, unchanged since he had left. A bullet-riddled APC parked against the wall was hidden from the road. No one patrolled the grounds, and no lights shone from inside the building. The SOPs were definitely hiding.

Another APC had been hit further up the road, its crew murdered and left roadside. Confirmation to all that they were dead—no point searching for dead men.

Bo had scouted the boats, leaving Kyle the perimeter. Kyle hadn't mentioned to the group what he'd seen: the slipway piled with Tooty Nung bodies. Not when Deep was supposed to be their friend. They were looking forward to the rest and the company. If Kyle had told them what he'd seen, that the slipway was piled with Tooty Nung bodies, well, he'd have had a hard time convincing everyone not to run in, guns blazing. Kyle knew he had to earn their trust. He just wished there was another way to do it than to lie to Evan.

In Kyle's view, the SOPs had driven in, requesting help or another building to hide in when the Tooty Nung turned them away. Afraid and with nowhere else to go, they couldn't face being thrown back into the preserve during open season on SOPs. He doubted they took that news lightly.

There had been more of them then. Among the Tooty Nung, he counted six SOPs. They faced twenty-six Nungs—bad odds—but had few other options. Their APC had a damaged fuel tank, limiting their mobility. They would've had to walk through hostile territory with limited ammunition, without airlift support because of the weather.

The survivors dropped the bodies by the river, which would claim the corpses when the tide came in. They had no choice but to rest. Nine men split into three groups with a staggered sleep rotation. Three-hour watch, six hours sleep, until morning.

Kyle would have done the same if his augments required rest.

He assumed the group on the ground floor was on the first watch. He could see their hearts beating through the boathouse walls. All three in one location, in the front with a window to watch the entrance and grounds. It wasn't what Kyle would have done—it left them vulnerable to people like him.

Silent under the storm's noise, Kyle dropped to the tarmac and sprinted to the house. Three entrances were on the ground floor: one double door at the front, a large gate at the back opening onto a gangway and pier, and a single side door next to the fire escape that led upward, stopping at each floor.

Kyle chose the fire escape, its old steel creaking and scraping against its joints no louder than the wind. Satisfied it wouldn't compromise his position, he continued to the second floor and halted. He could see his team's heartbeats flashing white as they moved towards him. They weren't needed until he had finished. No heartbeats emanated from nearby buildings; the only threat lay in this house.

He moved along the escape to the next set of stairs, pausing at the window. Its glass had been replaced with tarpaulin. Kyle pulled a knife from his boot sheath and cut his way in. The storm tried to follow him, drenching his feet and brow. He missed only three things from his time in Afghanistan: the spicy Kabuli Pulao, the women, and the weather. Soldiers usually found it too hot, but Kyle preferred it to the rain back home.

Crouching in the shadow beneath the window, he smelled stale gunpowder and spilt blood from earlier events. Six men slept above him, while only two hearts beat below. He snapped his head to the end of the hall; the third guard was climbing the stairs.

As the guard stepped into the corridor, Kyle vanished into an unlatched door, leaving the tarpaulin flapping and wet footprints behind. He watched the heartbeat continue, hearing footsteps approaching the window and his hiding place. He gripped his knife, blade aligned with his forearm, and silently stepped to the side of the door, preparing to strike.

He wouldn't be able to see him through the wall. Kyle's body camouflaged him from curious eyes, even if they were augmented. The guard would have to come through that door. He would push it with the muzzle of his pistol, check the corner if he had any sense, or walk straight in if not. Either way, it didn't matter. Kyle would grab the guard's wrist and pull him forward, unbalancing him, and bring the knife across his throat.

It didn't happen.

The guard rushed into the adjacent room instead. Kyle breathed easier and stepped back into the corridor, grateful for their sloppiness. Checking the next door, he found a stick-man symbol for a male toilet.

He considered interrupting the guard in his moment of vulnerability, but couldn't bring himself to do it. Instead, he pulled a small, round, charcoal-coloured device from his harness: a knock-knock. Simple and effective, it was one of his favourite tools.

Pressing the knock-knock against the door, he flattened his thumb on its surface until the rim flashed twice. He removed his thumb, leaving the device fixed to the stick-man's head. One down, eight to go.

He stepped back, ensuring the guard was still occupied. Satisfied, he looked down through the floor at the two heartbeats below. Still there. He glanced up and counted six sleeping heartbeats, averaging

64 beats per minute. He un-slung his rifle and approached the stairwell.

Four meters of straight staircase with rubber pads and a handrail greeted him. He wedged his rifle through the gap, angled towards the top. With his network feed down, he checked the scope's view for accuracy. Blinking a command, he received a "Sentry Activated" response. Seven down.

His timer showed he was on schedule, despite his brief hideout. He spotted the rest of the team in the courtyard. All according to plan. He released his Browning sidearm and rested his aim across his knife-hand. It was time to take down the last two.

The hearts were still together. Close, just over a metre apart. Both of them were sitting, or were a little short to be real troopers. He flipped his visual to heat signature. They were sitting opposite each other at a table, playing cards in the dark. He'd take them inside the room.

He closed on the door, stopping outside. Behind it, he heard a gruff, defeated voice. "Go fucking fish." The rest of the room was bathed in reds and blues. It looked to him like a kitchen, and he was pretty sure the blue mass on the right was a sink. He waited some more. He waited for the distraction. It would be one of three. Either would give Kyle the advantage he needed.

He looked to his feet, the awning underneath. In the basement, three heat signatures were busy preparing the boat. He looked upward. One heat signature had stood up and walked to the sink and was washing its hands. Further up, the remaining six heat signatures were still in dreamland. One of two then. He looked through the door at the card players; he could hear one complaining to the other. He'd give him something to complain about in three. Two. One.

The floor shook beneath him as the sound of the engine filled the boathouse. He kicked open the door and fired. The first shot entered the throat of the man on the right. It was a clean and practised shot that sprayed and disorientated his friend with blood. Kyle snapped his aim to the left, the second bullet piercing the eye socket of the second man before tearing out the back of his skull. Kyle snapped his aim back to the right. The man on the right clutched his throat, trying to stem the flow of blood. The third bullet entered his chest, piercing his heart and killing him.

He looked upwards; the SOP rushed to the door and opened it. In their simple design, knock-knocks flash twice on arming. They record the surrounding distance. Then when the distance changes, say when a door is opened, they explode. There was a flash of brilliant white on his infrared field. Three of the nine were dead. Soon, those nine would be dead too.

Kyle checked the bodies for spare ammunition. He couldn't use their weapons, but could use the bullets if they were the same calibre. He tapped the cargo pants pocket and struck lucky. Forty calibre softs. He placed them in his own pocket as the sound of his rifle started. One short burst. He looked up through the ceiling and found it a mess of red and yellow. The gent's toilet was on fire. He blinked back to the heart sensor just in time to see one die.

The remaining five hesitated, expecting someone at the foot of the stairs. Kyle's rifle would pick them off, but if it ran dry, or they got lucky, they'd have one last surprise. He holstered his Browning and knife, then left the kitchen, leaving the dead SOPs to bleed over their card game.

Kyle walked at a pace, following the narrow corridor to its end where he met a hardwood door painted black with iron fixings. It was locked. He shouldered it once. It shuddered at the force but held. The resistance came from the mid-section, an iron bar perhaps. He pulled back his fist and fired a punch at the door. His arm travelled through it to his shoulder. Behind it, he heard the splintered wood rattle to the ground. Above him, his rifle rattled at the next poor SOP to attempt the descent.

Three remained. He blinked a request to his rifle, remembering the comms block when the bullet count failed to appear. The three didn't concern him, but he had expected to be on the boat before the rifle exhausted its ammo. It was an old building and there was no guarantee his surprise might bring the house down.

Kyle quickened his pace, nearly jogging towards the boat. Once the rifle's standard ammunition depleted, it would switch to the undercarriage grenade launcher. Without communication with the weapon, he had no way of knowing when that would happen. Taking no chances, he hurried.

Reaching the jetty, he leaped onto the tugboat. An explosion erupted above them. All six undercarriage grenades had detonated. The building trembled, concrete dust rained down, filling the air with a thick grey haze. Kyle exhaled in relief as the structure remained standing.

Evan waited for him, leaning against the port-side rail, eyes fixed on Kyle. He seemed poised to scold Kyle for disobeying orders not to kill. But Evan hesitated, weighing every factor before reacting to Kyle's actions. Was the engine turned on too early? Had something gone wrong? Or had Kyle planned it all?

Kyle hoped Evan's silence indicated he knew, deep down, that the killings were necessary. Evan didn't want to sacrifice nine lives for the mission, but Kyle would. It was a trade-off he stood by, having earned the trust of the two leading them—the ones close to Window. They believed SOP lives held no more value than those in London. Oliver wouldn't have chosen Kyle to accompany Evan if he'd wanted a different outcome. This world wasn't meant for people like Evan. Kyle would get him where he belonged, but first, they had to navigate this treacherous landscape—a place for killers.

CHAPTER ELEVEN
HOW TO MAKE FRIENDS AND INFLUENCE PEOPLE

Oliver departed the Tate mansion just after three in the morning. The party had drained him, and his meeting with Felix had stirred more concern than he'd anticipated. He was troubled, having expected Faraday to name political rivals—individuals he wouldn't hesitate to crush. The private sector's involvement, especially from someone as calculating as Felix, hadn't crossed his mind.

Politicians always faced issues with the private sector. Capitalist society relied on business, and business interests only aligned with constituents as long as they spent money. Lobbyists were incessant nuisances, akin to nagging housewives Oliver preferred to avoid.

Felix, however, was a rare breed—a dangerous kingmaker. Oliver couldn't fathom Percy Browne as Prime Minister. The man was a fool. The alliance baffled Oliver, persisting in his thoughts into the early hours. On paper, Percy had merit as the Foreign Secretary, but off paper, he was a self-serving imbecile.

Nonetheless, Felix had given Oliver vital information. He faced a formidable opponent with a stronger hand. Bluffing would fail, as Felix already knew about Oliver's tip to the press. Oliver needed to gamble on a new hand. While waiting for his car outside the Tate Mansion, he sent messages to two likely slumbering individuals.

The sleek, black Maybach rolled over the gravel driveway, stopping before him. With no concierge in sight, Oliver opened the door and slid into the back seat. "Market Street, please, Joe." The driver raised his gloved thumb, as always, and started the engine without a word.

"Jonathan," Oliver thought, awaiting a response.

"Oliver?" Reekes replied, voice distant and groggy.

"Sorry to disturb you."

"Who is it then?"

"Percy, Rockwood, and Felix Fray."

A lengthy pause followed, which Oliver used to confirm his next meeting and send Reekes the most recent publications on Felix. "You sure?"

"I just met with Percy and Felix."

"They said Harry was involved?"

"Yes." He hesitated before adding, "They invited me to join them."

After a long pause, allowing Oliver time to analyse his earlier conversation and evaluate his decision, Jonathan finally asked, "Have you?"

"I'm considering my options," Oliver replied. "Jon," he paused, weighed down by uncertainty, "they intend to kill you."

2

Market Street lay deserted at 3:15 a.m. Street lamps glowed dimly, brightening as the Maybach approached and fading once it passed. "Here is fine," Oliver said, waiting for Joe to pull over before opening the door. "I shan't be long," he advised, stepping out of the parked vehicle.

He smoothed the creases in his suit and ignored the cold nipping at his skin, raising goosebumps beneath his shirt. He didn't have far to walk—just enough time to run through the plan in his head one last time.

He had to tread carefully. If he appeared too eager, they would grow greedy and decline his offer. He couldn't let them know how desperately he needed them; how vital it was to build a strong enough hand against Felix. Percy had significant support in the party; without him and Faraday, Oliver's options were limited. He had no choice but to turn to the opposition. He needed a coalition.

They awaited him, as he knew they would. Seated at the back of the coffee shop with two steaming mugs, they sat alone. He didn't acknowledge them yet. Instead, he ordered his espresso and watched the robotic servant, adorned with green and black branding, prepare his drink. Only then did Oliver join the two patrons. The woman was Julia Greaves, shadow treasury and confidante of the second; Justin Fox – the shadow Prime Minister.

"Oliver," said Justin, waiting impatiently as Oliver removed his blazer and hung it on the back of his chair.

"Ministers," he finally acknowledged, sitting down and unfastening his collar and tie. "I hope you don't mind, but as neither of you dressed for the occasion..."

Fox scoffed at the comment, his unkempt red hair and unshaven face unimpressed by Oliver's bravado. Julia, however, had put effort into her appearance. "It's gone three in the morning," she said.

Oliver smiled. "Indeed it has."

"Well?" Julia wasn't known for her patience.

"Good party, was it?" Fox interjected.

Oliver replied with a nod, wondering if it were a slight since he hadn't been invited, and blew the steam from the surface of his espresso. "I have an offer for you." It was an obvious answer; he'd dragged them out at three in the morning to meet at a Starbucks, of all places. He wasn't about to discuss the Swans smashing Liverpool earlier that evening. Still, he needed to let them know who was doing them a favour.

"Why the cloak and dagger?" Fox asked, clearly the more cunning of the two.

Oliver checked the mirror on the back wall, which was large enough to see the front door while covering the serving area, including the robotic servant. He blinked a command to his chip; should his peripheral catch something he shouldn't see; his HUD would alert him. "We have some..." How should he put it? "In-party issues."

"So, you've come to the opposition for advice?" Julia's words held a distinct tone of gloating.

"If it's that sorry excuse for a health—" Fox began, but Oliver interrupted, "We're not meeting over legislation."

"Then why are we here?" Julia asked, as blunt as they come.

Oliver mulled over her words, wanting to give her the benefit of the doubt. She needed her beauty sleep, after all. But no more than he needed her help. If he had the choice, he would have met with Justin alone, but he didn't have the luxury. Like Laurel and Hardy, they came as a pair.

Both ministers had given Jonathan trouble on over five pieces of legislation in the past year, not to mention catching the PM off guard with the foreign aid to Africa debacle last month. He expected more from them. If they were sharp enough to cause him problems in the House, they should be switched on at 3:23 a.m.

He began to wonder if he was wasting his time when Fox blurted, "You're moving on Reekes. That's it, isn't it? You're going after the seat." There was some hope, after all.

"I'm not moving on him," Oliver clarified. "Percy is."

"Does he know?" asked Julia, presumably meaning Jonathan.

"He's up to speed on things," Oliver confirmed.

"What about us? Does he know we're meeting?"

Oliver looked her in the eye, finally appreciating her thought process. "That's between us. For now."

"Percy has a lot of support; he won't leave you with much of a leadership if he calls Reekes out," she said, blunt, astute, and altogether incorrect.

Percy had no intention of calling him out.

PART THREE:
IMAGINE

CHAPTER TWELVE
PERCY BROWNE

Percy had graduated third from the top of his class in Corporate Law and Political Science. His best friend Carl had grabbed him around the shoulder and told him it didn't matter if he'd broken the record or just scraped by; a solicitor he would become. His father, perpetually dissatisfied with Percy's achievements, had punched him in the stomach so hard that he'd stopped breathing.

When he awoke on the tiled kitchen floor, he wiped vomit from his lips and lifted his shirt to discover the early blooming of a bruise. His father sat watching television in the next room. Clearly, he'd said his piece, so Percy stood in the doorway for an uncomfortable minute, attempting in vain to gain his mother's absent affection. After the minute, he retreated to his bedroom, alone, knowing that it would have been less painful if he'd come second and not at all if he'd been first. He might have even received a smile.

Percy, along with all his immediate family, had been a party member for as long as he could remember. He still recalled vivid memories of dressing up with the rest of the Browne clan, attending the club, and watching his father knock back shot after shot of whiskey while he and his brothers drank carbonated syrup and ate a plethora of flavoured crisps provided by Walkers.

He had endured school, college, and university without so much as a drink, fearing the repetition of his father's persona. The drool-filled maw, flared nostrils, and red eyes—everything about his father that he despised was mirrored in Jonathan Reekes.

"You're a cad, Percy!" Even the Prime Minister's vocabulary reminded him of his father. "God only knows what decrepit, vomitus hovel spat you out." His cheeks burned, and his sunken eyes glowered with a fury he had yet to experience up close. "You swore an allegiance to the king–to me!"

"If the Prime Minister would hear me out," Percy blurted, giving himself a second in pause. The old man seemed tired and rabid; Reekes looked so feral that Percy feared he might take a bite out of him if he got any closer. However, behind the explosion of condescending wit, Percy noticed that this dressing down came closely after Oliver had learned of his recent extracurricular scheming.

Percy couldn't comprehend how this thing still held the title of Prime Minister. The PM had become an awful, drunken cretin steering the government into jagged rocks. That creature now sat poised to leap at him, engorged on bad food and alcohol, glaring at Percy as if he were some common street punk who had offended him.

Long gone were the days when Percy had respected the man, when he had voted for him. Staring at Reekes now, Percy struggled to remember why he had ever done so. He harboured no ill will toward the man, but as Reekes had stopped listening to anyone other than himself, Percy saw no other option but to put his plan into action.

Jonathan Reekes, consumed by an obsession to fix the country with all the king's horses and All the King's Men, was a damned fool. He ignored the European PM's warnings; Jaeger was a reasonable man, but his lack of tolerance for Jonathan's idiosyncrasies was well documented. Jonathan disregarded France, frequently antagonised Spain, and seemed satisfied to merely suckle on the American teat. But even the Americans were showing concern.

Reekes was oblivious, unable, or unwilling to comprehend that the planet was at a tipping point. In less than twenty months, the world would run out of oil. "With the U.S. and China distracted by the remaining oil supplies, Europe—"

But Reekes cut him off. "Please tell me you're not going to hide behind one of your think tank's tales?"

Percy shrank as Reekes shouted again, just as he expected. Jonathan never liked that projection date. He refused to listen to the mere suggestion that America's preoccupation with China would feed interest in Europe. The idea of the rest of the world turning to coal when the largest countries fought over the remaining oil seemed ludicrous to him. And thanks to Thatcher, Britain had vast coal supplies. "MI6—" Percy tried again.

"Would tell you Hitler had crawled up from hell and was raining Nazi zombies on us if it meant getting them a bigger budget." Reekes lifted his bulk from his chair, lumbering toward Percy like an ogre.

For a moment, Percy thought about how that statement would play out if he had said it in the House, in front of the entire party and its opposition. "If one would allow me to finish a sentence, perhaps one could use all the facts to scold me?"

There was a pause. No retort, not even a snort of disdain from the Prime Minister as he closed in on Percy, close enough for him to smell the sweet citrus on his breath. Percy's lips quivered, his nostrils flaring at the revolting creature that loomed in front of him. Still, at least Reekes had let him finish his sentence.

The PM creature squinted, unsure of its next move. "Then skip to the end," it said.

"The world is collapsing," Percy continued. "You're neglecting your duties to the state. There's more to the Kingdom than London."

"There is no Kingdom without London!"

Percy lifted his hand, shielding himself from the spittle. It was clear his approach wasn't working, so he tried another. "Prime Minister, my strategy—"

"Murders millions of British citizens."

Percy didn't debate the semantics; most people living beyond the fence weren't British. A new generation of squatters dwelled there now. No, Percy was more intrigued by Jonathan's awareness of the strategy, his new strategy. He had Oliver Trench to thank for that.

"Both London and the South-East are irreparably savage," he said. "Every study conducted in the last ten years has concluded the same thing. They won't submit to conventional, civilised law. They won't allow chipsets to be implanted, and even if they agreed, we can't afford it."

He had never yelled at the Prime Minister before, but this was something he believed in. Jonathan Reekes needed to recognise his folly, or the country would fall prey to Europe's greedy gaze. The knives were already being sharpened.

They had to act now.

He had to act now, and no one, not even this ogre, would stand in his way.

Without chipsets, London's populace would be unemployable. Unable to access bank accounts, they wouldn't be able to buy anything—not even bread or water. They couldn't assimilate into the consumer market and were, therefore, undesirable to society.

If they could transform the south into a profit, corporations would come to their aid. To achieve this, they had to cull the herd, efficiently police the borders, reclaim the land inch by inch, sell it off to private firms, restore the treasury, and start repaying the country's debts before anyone came to collect. "We bleed soldiers and lose public support daily. Implementing a private security force—"

Percy's head snapped to the right. His father's face blurred in his vision as his jaw warmed to the skin before he realised the loud cracking sound was Reekes' backhand across his face. Blood filled his mouth, coating his throat and teeth. He clenched his hands into fists, ready to retaliate, but he didn't. This wasn't the time.

"You went behind my back." Reekes was shouting again. "My back! And for what? To destabilise an already tenuous peace—" He raised his hand to Percy's unflinching face and closed his index finger to thumb. "I am this close to fixing it."

Percy had heard this argument time and time again. The same refrain, repeated like a terrible dance track for eight years: ever since Reekes had taken power. If Jonathan could fix it, he would have. There would have been progress on something. There hadn't been. And for him to deny responsibility when he had signed the authorisation for Lockhead in the first place, he was nothing but a hypocrite.

Instead, Reekes only had himself to show for his efforts—a drunken, violent fool whom Percy had no intention of allowing to bleed this country any longer. "There's a chance for a peaceful resolution, and I'm taking it," said the creature, leaning back onto his desk. "I won't join the ranks of Hitler and Stalin. I won't be remembered as a butcher."

Percy tested the loose incisor with his tongue before looking the PM in the eye. "You won't be."

CHAPTER THIRTEEN
A KINGDOM UNITED

Since the boathouse, the tug crew hadn't spoken with Evan, and he preferred it that way, allowing him time to ponder recent events. His three companions had revealed their true nature, and he found himself isolated. They were killers; he was not.

He sat on an overturned lobster cage, gripping the aft wall as the boat sliced through rough water. Nikki stayed in the cabin, steering the vessel, while Kyle leaned against the port side and Bo moved between the two.

In the silence, Evan repeated one question internally: had he known? Had he known Kyle would kill the SOPs? No. He hadn't thought Kyle would or could disobey his order, but had he explicitly ordered him not to? Instead of replaying the previous conversation on his HUD, he bit his lower lip. Relying on memory rather than a backup was unsettling.

His gut told him he'd made it abundantly clear the SOPs shouldn't be killed. Yet, they were all dead, killed by the one person he needed to trust. Doubt bred, like rising damp crawling through his veins. He observed Bo, who had gravitated toward Kyle since the boathouse. They sat close, laughing at each other's jokes, and Kyle happily displayed his many augmentations.

Even Nikki showed him some respect—why not? He'd done what she wanted, exacted the revenge she sought, and earned their trust in the process. A cold logic accompanied that thought, leaving a bitter taste in Evan's mouth.

The rain had ceased by the time the morning sun revealed its brilliance. It rose over London with such awe-inspiring radiance that Evan almost forgot the city's dangers. Only when he saw the Millennium Dome's reflection in the river did he recall Bo's stories—Reapers lived there.

He glanced down the boat's length; Bo was showing Kyle his brace of pistols, his most magnificent and deadly toys. It was easy to think the country was too far gone, too indifferent to be fixed. Now the Triad had disrupted the delicate balance. Could Window deliver on his promises? It seemed an insurmountable task, considering London's infrastructure alone would take years to rebuild. Then there were the neighbours: Reading, Dover, Cornwall, and the rest of England.

Bo darted into the cabin and momentarily reappeared at the door, beckoning Kyle with one of his DEagles. Evan almost stood and followed, but stayed seated, watching Kyle enter the cabin and speak with Nikki. They looked so damned cosy, such good friends now, probably laughing about the men who wouldn't return to their families.

When the boat lurched, Evan's grip loosened, but he maintained his position on the lobster cage. He swallowed a mouthful of icy Thames water as a wave crashed over him and onto the deck. "Jesus!" he shouted, resisting the urge to release the rail and stand in shock. The wind stung the cold across his face, forcing him to close his eyes. He was lucky; a second wave slapped against him, almost knocking him from his seat.

He stood this time, his body screaming, and stamped the pain onto the deck through his boots. "Bastards, that's cold," he said, as the first shivers took hold. He couldn't remember ever being that cold.

Then the Thames calmed, and the boat returned to its usual bounce. The waves splashed against the sides but didn't flood over. He gripped the rail and glanced back towards the cabin.

All three remained inside, Bo and Kyle observing him from the cabin's comfort. Fuckers. He gazed at the passing dome and the small group of people watching from the dock. From this distance, he couldn't discern them well—ominous shapes that evoked scarecrows in his mind. They stood together, more a sinister entity than individuals. These were the Reapers; Evan had no doubt. Fortunately, they made no move to interfere with their journey.

"Spray is pretty heavy." Kyle had settled next to him, unnoticed by Evan's preoccupation.

"Sorry?" he asked.

"You're wet."

"No shit."

"You know why I did it."

Evan knew, but he didn't respond, too focused on their observers.

"I had to gain their trust."

"Then you must be happy with yourself, all warm and cosy in the cabin," Evan snapped.

"Jesus Christ, you're a child. I got us on the boat, kept you safe, and scored points with the team."

"Are we going bowling or something?"

"Something."

Evan couldn't take his eyes off him. "Something?"

"I reported in to base; they know we're good. Renner says hi, by the way."

Evan smiled involuntarily; the news was positive, and for a moment, he forgot its cost. "Anything else?"

"He confirmed Sin Lao and that the Triad hit almost every SOP base in London."

Evan nodded. "Any instructions?"

"Get it done ASAP." Kyle grinned.

"Yeah, right?"

"I don't think we're the only ones in the middle of a shitstorm." A wave crashed against the boat, spraying them both.

"Yeah, well, at least their showers are hot," Evan said through chattering teeth. "Did you see a coat or anything in the cabin?"

"I'll check with Bo."

"Not Mowgli?"

"I said it worked." Kyle's attention slipped from the conversation to behind Evan's back. "Wow."

When Evan turned, he saw the silhouette of Westminster sprawled on the embankment and instantly remembered Sky NEWS broadcasting the attack in glorious 1080i worldwide, two days after the British Government had fled London. It took a single mob of faceless thugs armed with Molotov cocktails and pipe bombs only nine hours to destroy what had taken over 34 years to build.

At its apex, the clock tower still stood—two and a half sides anyway, the rest crushed under the bell they'd named Ben. Cut free, it had crashed down and out of the west-facing wall. "I never thought I'd see it," Evan declared.

"You still haven't, but you and I are the first steps to fixing that."

"I get the feeling we're too late."

Bo strutted along the deck, looking a little too cocky in his one-sided smile, a little too confident in this stride.

"Put these on." He threw a couple of burlap sacks to their feet.

"Seriously?" Kyle looked as surprised as Evan felt. They'd travelled half of London with them. "Why now?"

"I thought we were all best buds?" asked Evan.

"Just put them on." Bo didn't enjoy repeating himself, or maybe he felt uncertain. He'd shown Kyle nothing but admiration since the boathouse. Now he was giving orders, perhaps realising that by getting closer to Kyle, he'd removed some barriers—barriers he could no longer hide behind. He looked less than a man, with the sun rising behind him. He resembled a teenage boy ordering an adult, and Evan, thankfully, stifled his laughter.

He reached down, picked up the bundle, handed one to Kyle, and placed the other over his head. There was no point arguing at this point.

"You too, Fallout," Bo added.

"You're not tying our hands?" Kyle inquired as he donned his own sack.

"That would be pointless," Bo retorted.

"And this isn't?"

Bo didn't respond; instead, he fastened the sacks with their pull ties.

"I can see you, Bo," Kyle remarked.

But Bo had left them, walking back toward the front of the boat.

"I can see him, I can see him in goddamn infrared walking to the cabin."

2

Evan rested a hand on Kyle's shoulder, shuffling along the small plank, and recalled their first tentative steps back in the tunnels under Notting Hill. He followed each of Kyle's steps until they reached the jetty. Both of them could see the burlap webbed across their eyes, but they could still make out shapes and see the light shining through.

"Keep straight," an unfamiliar voice advised from ahead, "There're no lifeguards stationed here, and I ain't jumpin' in after you."

"Dunstun," Nikki's voice emerged from behind Evan, followed by the unstable floor bobbing as she bounced past.

"You didn't have favourable odds."

"I expect half of what you won."

"What makes you think I bet on you to make it?"

"You better had," they chuckled.

Evan tried to count how many friends they'd just made. Dunstun stood close enough to block some of the morning light, while Nikki positioned herself ahead. He couldn't hear Bo, but he assumed the kid was nearby. There was a sense of more people, but any shapes he discerned through the sack were too alien and obscure to identify.

He kept his hand on Kyle's shoulder, walking and stopping as they received frequent orders to do one or the other—sometimes from Dunstun, other times from Nikki, and once from a voice up high. When told to stop, they waited. They heard a mechanical noise—a winch, perhaps, or a wheel in need of oiling. He counted the time between the order to stop and move, always between fifteen and twenty-seven seconds.

Though he couldn't see anything beyond black shapes through the sack's material, it was easy to sense they were being herded. Shepherded through a series of gates. He counted his steps from the jetty, intent on knowing the distance back to the river if things went south. After the third gate, he realised that running for the river might not be the best escape. Hearing Dunstun say, "Get in," followed by the familiar sound of a fist banging on a car door, he knew the river was a no-go.

He climbed into the vehicle. It had a footstep, and he had to reach up to the roof before clambering in. He imagined a 4x4, something like a Range Rover, perhaps. The seat was less than comfortable, the harsh fabric of an old, folded blanket thrown over it.

"You okay?" Kyle inquired.

He paused before answering, waiting for the door to close after him. "Yes." He could barely hear Nikki and Dunstun chatting outside the vehicle. "You?"

"Could you see any of that?"

"Some shapes. Gathered we moved through some gates?"

"And then some. They have guard towers, snipers, machine-gun nests. I'm pretty sure I saw an X4 parked up in the distance."

Serious firepower.

The X4 was an American-designed, Australian-manufactured anti-riot robot—a couple of tonnes of armoured steel, a tank-sized spider. Typically deployed with water cannons, it could be fitted with any number of armaments. "How did they get their hands on that?" The question was rhetorical, but it needed to be out there.

The front doors of the vehicle opened, and people jumped in. "Not much further," Bo said.

"Thanks," Evan replied.

"That's cute." Another voice, a woman's, chimed in just before the engine started.

It was an old fuel engine, its vibration unmistakable. Evan remembered his father taking him to school in one, before they switched to electric. "This petrol?" he asked.

The vehicle pulled away, but no one answered. Maybe Bo didn't know, or perhaps he was still that child Evan saw ordering Kyle to wear the burlap. Either way, it seemed the driver controlled the flow of information in the car.

"It feels like petrol," Evan continued.

"Could be diesel..." Kyle filled the dead air that followed Evan's statement.

"Where do you get the fuel from?" America and China were on the brink of war over the last oil reserves, and here they were, riding in a combustion engine in a Third World state. No answer. Fine, Evan thought. He had enough to ponder. These people were better equipped than he'd expected.

Everything had surprised him. First, they'd hidden Window's message in an archaic radio signal. Second, they'd blocked contact with the base and remained invisible to their own sensor equipment. They'd held the boathouse until the SOPs took it from them. They had an impressive defence system in place from the river, including the pricey military hardware, the X4. Who were these people, and why, with all that tech, were they travelling in an old Range Rover?

Evan mulled over these apparent questions. Questions that, in his eyes, should have been at the forefront of Fletcher's reports. Dominic Fletcher wouldn't have made these mistakes. That left two options: either they'd hidden it from Fletcher, in which case—why were they so matter-of-fact now? Or he'd deliberately excluded them from his reports. Although he didn't like it, the latter seemed more believable. So the next question was, had Fletcher been coerced, or had he chosen to do it himself?

3

The rover travelled for ten, maybe fifteen minutes. Preoccupied with his thoughts, Evan lost track of time. He wasn't worried, knowing Kyle was counting every second with his chipset.

When they stopped, the driver and Bo exited first. Their doors slammed shut, and Evan heard the driver speaking with someone before his door opened. "Out," she said. He swung his legs over to his side, held the roof's lip to steady himself, and stepped down from the vehicle, waiting for his next instruction.

The ground was soft, not sinking soft, but soft nonetheless. Cold morning mud, perhaps. No one was talking. It was a hostile and untrusting scene he found himself in. The light had dimmed, and the shapes through his burlap sack were darker here. He no longer distinguished people or buildings.

"This way," a man's voice said, followed by a small hand resting on his shoulder and nudging him to the left.

The procedure resembled that at the jetty. They walked for a while, then stopped briefly. People talked to each other but not with each other. He knew Kyle could see him—the red blob in his heat vision would vibrate with each pulse his tracker sent out—but he couldn't see Kyle. "Fallout?"

"Yeah?" Kyle's voice was behind him and close.

"Just checking."

No one else spoke. No one told them not to speak. They didn't care. Evan and Kyle could have conversed throughout the route, he guessed. But they had nothing to say to each other, not when both knew the other was alright. They wanted it to be over. They wanted to reach the end of the rabbit hole—to meet the elusive Window.

"Wait." A woman's voice, Nikki. She must have been with them the whole time. Evan didn't think she'd ridden in the car with them, so there must have been a convoy.

Evan shifted his weight from foot to foot, feeling the now hardened and uneven cobbles.

"Okay, bring them up." Nikki again.

The cobbles disappeared, replaced by a concrete step, and then carpet. He expected to reach their destination once inside. But wherever they were, it was vast. Corridor after corridor, door after door. So much so, Evan contemplated if they were moving in circles.

"Wait," Nikki ordered again. This time, Evan heard her close a door. The change in pace and procedure led him to believe they'd reached their destination.

He was wrong. "Okay," she said, returning.

Evan felt the slight hand on his shoulder push gently, and he appreciated their relatively fair treatment. Herded further forward, the woman behind him warned, "Mind your step." Recognising her voice as the driver of his Rover, he felt around with the tip of his boot, hitting a raised border.

"Thanks," he said, stepping over it. The carpet ended, and he walked on a metal grid, perhaps a gangway. He wondered where the hell they were— deepest, darkest crap, it felt like. The floor sloped subtly, but he could tell. He was heading down.

That wasn't all. The air was thinner, processed through air-conditioning. Adding up the clues, Evan deduced he was inside a large building with many rooms. No stairs, no elevators, yet he walked downward into an air-conditioned area. A faint hum filled the air—not the air conditioning, but the sound of strip lamps. The clues led to fruitless theories.

"I prayed for you," a woman's voice said. An older woman, her words strong and weighty. "For you all," she added.

The driver's hand pulled gently on Evan's shoulder. Time to stop again. He wondered if the woman had included him in her prayers. "How are you, my boy?" she asked, but not for Evan or Kyle.

"Clean," Bo replied, standing just in front.

Four words repeated inside Evan's skull like an old cartoon comedy reel: Are. We. There. Yet?

Around him, the group shuffled about, their boots distinctive on the metal flooring. They moved around and behind them, back the way they had come. They'd stopped before, but never left alone. "Fallout?"

"Just us," Kyle said.

"Can you see anything?"

"I could see the whole trip," he sounded exasperated. "We're underneath Whitehall. Well, I'm pretty sure we are. Six people walked us down here, all armed. Four people were waiting in here. They locked the door behind us."

Evan pulled the sack off his head. The room was unimpressive—about ten metres square, all steel plate, a bulkhead door in each wall, and an oval red rug in the centre.

"Could you see who they were?" Evan asked. "The new ones. I could hear Bo and Nikki; our driver was here too."

"Just heat signatures."

"Seems strange," Evan said, considering their situation. "Eerie."

Kyle stepped into the room's centre and rubbed his foot on the rug. "No red curtains. That's a plus in my book."

Evan recalled a childhood memory of fear and fascination. "I didn't take you for a Lynch fan."

Kyle crouched down and ran his hand through the rug. "I'm full of surprises."

The door on the far side, opposite the one they'd entered through, squeaked. The circular handle spun—slow at first, then faster, until a loud clunk filled the small room. The door opened, and a man walked through. His head was shaved, his face unshaven. He wore plain green cargo pants and a black t-shirt with a white fist printed on the front, its middle finger extended into a birdie.

The man quickly glanced at them, then turned and closed the door behind him. "Which one of you is Bluebird?" he asked, his voice overtly familiar.

"I am," Evan replied.

The man looked from Evan to Kyle. "You his caddy?" But Kyle was too busy appraising him to react to the question. It seemed to upset him. "You shy, boy?"

The man's voice was devoid of any accent—a trained voice. Familiar, yet Evan couldn't place it or didn't want to. The man in the small metal room with them was someone who spoke publicly on the radio. Evan was sure of it. "Window?"

The man, presumed to be Window, stood face to face with Kyle. His jaw bounced up and down, chewing gum fervently. He didn't react to Evan's observation. Not at first. He was too busy trying to rile Kyle up. "You shy, boy?" Evan added candidly.

The man stood back but didn't drop his gaze. Wired to explode, his eyes were dry and shaky. He needed to blink. He didn't. "Fallout," he clicked his fingers and pointed at Kyle. "That's you."

"Are you Window?" Evan repeated.

The man stared back at him, then looked again at Kyle. Anticipation dripped from his brow as he held his gaze. He looked back at Evan, smiled, and extended his hand for a shake. "Yes."

Evan accepted Window's hand, gravely disappointed. This gangly fool was the leader of Free London—the man with the impossible challenge of putting London back together after the Triads had torn down all his work.

"Follow me, please," Window said, turning to the door he'd entered through. He swung it open and stepped out.

Evan looked at Kyle, who grinned, extended his arm, and bowed. "After you."

"Fuck off."

They followed Window along a tight corridor of steel. Strip lighting hung above them, and Evan mentally congratulated himself for recognising the sound of their neon buzz. They passed a cross-section, a junction in the corridor, and continued straight. They turned left at the next intersection before reaching another bulkhead. Window opened it and stepped through.

Inside was another room, similar in style but far larger than the previous one—twice the height and length. The floor was carpeted, and the room furnished with mismatched leather sofas and chairs. A cluster of tables huddled around the room's centre, forming a large conference table surrounded by twenty chairs.

Other than Window, Evan saw Bo and Nikki in the room, along with nine others dressed in similar attire—brown leather and khaki. Whatever conversations had been going on stopped as soon as they entered the room.

Evan felt like he'd stepped into the OK Corral.

Window shattered the silence with a booming question, "Who's making the coffee?"

One of the young men pointed to the central table, where several jugs and a collection of cups and mugs stood. "Right there, D."

"You expect me to make it?" Window asked. "After what I just did?"

Evan suppressed the urge to challenge his insult—the man was beyond obnoxious. Was that even an introduction?

"I'll do it," one of the other men offered, in a voice Evan recognised from earlier. Dunstun.

"Good man," said Window. He spun on his feet and faced Evan. "You like coffee?"

Evan and Kyle nodded, neither looking nor feeling impressed by the man before them. "You are Window?" Evan asked again, incredulous.

He stopped waving his hands about. "Yes. I'm fucking Window. Are you simple or what?" The man turned his back on them and walked toward the cobbled-together table. "Get simples and his silent partner a coffee, too. They can add their own milk and sugar. The Hilton, this is not."

He leaned against the table while people bustled behind him. "You have it?" The question targeted Evan, who carried a message from Jonathan Reekes for Window's eyes only—the same message Dominic Fletcher had been delivered.

Evan nodded and reached around his back. Attached to his belt line was a small cylinder. It unclasped with a simple clip-slide. He threw it forward, Window catching it easily. He examined it, ran his finger along its length, and thumbed the end, searching for an entrance. When he found the screw cap, he paused. "This won't explode in my face. Will it?"

Evan wished it would. "It's quite safe," he reassured Window, staring back at him, refusing to give any satisfaction.

Window spun the tube in his hand, scrutinising Evan's expression while mulling it over. "Do me the honour." He stopped the cylinder and tossed it back to Evan, who caught it, unscrewed the cap, and tapped out its contents: a single piece of rolled paper.

Evan placed the tube on the table, holding the paper out in Window's direction. "It's safe."

"Can't be too careful." Window grimaced, stepping forward and snatching the paper from Evan's hand. He unrolled it and began reading.

They waited while Window grunted and snorted his way through the document, graciously accepting their mugs of coffee. Evan especially needed it; his last drink had been the bottles of beer at Notting Hill.

"You know what's on this?" Window looked at Evan impatiently. "Have you read this?"

He hadn't. "No."

"But you know what's on this?"

"Yes."

"Then Bluebird, I must ask this: are you taking the fucking piss?

CHAPTER FOURTEEN
POLITICS AND SAUSAGES

The new House of Commons in York, far from the historic Houses of Parliament, mimicked its predecessor but lacked the heritage of the original location. The purpose-built room functioned as an assembly, with the two largest parties sitting from left to middle, the smaller parties on the right, and all facing the Speaker at the front.

Dark wood and green leather gave way to sheet glass and stage lamps, all designed to put the government on television, enabling the country to watch them in vivid high-definition hologram as they fixed problems, righted wrongs, and improved lives. In fact, one could very well say they stole its architectural design from Berlins' Bundestag.

Despite the rumour mill threatening Reekes' administration, there had been much discussion on issues and legislation. The Opposition, eager to fling mud at the Prime Minister, surprisingly refrained that morning.

From his seat, Oliver observed Percy during the session, occasionally checking if any confidants shared the Foreign Secretary's quizzical expression. The Liberals, with Fox at the helm, goaded the Prime Minister into discussing the National Health Service an hour into the session.

Outwardly, it seemed like a heated argument. In reality, it was more akin to World Wrestling Entertainment—a scripted spectacle. Oliver sat back, enjoying his handiwork. The icing on the cake? He was a mere nine chairs away from Percy, whose simmering rage warmed the chilly room. Oliver's broad smile forced him to cover his mouth to avoid drawing attention.

Percy had annoyed Oliver not because of any conspiracy, but because his perceived ineptitude had allowed him to catch Oliver off-guard. Although Fray was an adversary, Oliver would battle. Percy was a tiresome obstacle he would simply walk over. The morning's humiliation, courtesy of the Prime Minister, was only the beginning. Oliver chuckled, hand still covering his mouth. One didn't want to be caught sneering at the words "A dire need to save our NHS" echoing from the Speaker of the House.

Percy must have been inwardly cursing, utterly confused by the NHS resurfacing without even a page to read in the morning's cabinet meeting. He would suspect Oliver, of course. Percy wasn't entirely useless, despite appearances. No doubt, he was preparing his rebuttal for a confrontation in the hall.

After the session ended, Oliver exited the room through the towering double doors with everyone else, positioning himself at the opposite wall and waiting. He waved to Jonathan, who headed straight back to his office as usual, likely for some well-deserved vitamin C.

"What the fuck are you playing at?" Percy's approach went unnoticed.

Unruffled, Oliver replied, "Language, Percy. We're in the house. Besides, I don't know what you're talking about." He offered a disarming smile, hoping to rile Percy up further.

It worked. "This farce," Percy jabbed again, targeting the soft tissue under Oliver's collarbone, "with Fox."

"Are you referring to the NHS?"

"Of course I am!" Oliver thought he saw a blood vessel burst in Percy's left eye. "We haven't mentioned the NHS in the Cabinet for months. Why the hell is he doing it now?" The mark left by Jonathan's ring on his lip was visible.

"Contrary to popular myth, I'm not privy to all of his dealings," said Oliver.

"Yet he seems privy to yours." Percy's suspicion didn't throw Oliver off balance.

"You're fond of speaking in riddles, aren't you?" Oliver remarked.

"Don't give me that. Don't give me your nonchalant superiority!" Percy snapped. "You know, he summoned me." When Oliver remained silent, he continued, "You expect me to believe he reprimanded me for no reason other than being me?"

"You think he needs more?"

"You told him where you were last night; that's why he—" Oliver grabbed Percy's arm before he could finish the sentence, dragging him along the corridor.

Oliver hadn't expected this level of confrontation or blatant accusation, especially in the house and in front of people. Percy must have had more support or had more riding on his deal with Fray than Oliver realised. He mentally noted to run a fresh whip count of their supporters later—better to be cautious than finding oneself drowning without a lifeline.

He led Percy through the fire exit on the right, entering a stark, unpainted brick stairwell frequently used by MPs for private conversations. "Percy," he said, releasing him. "Jonathan is a cantankerous bastard who believes you're nothing but a vapid grin, wedged into his cabinet by your excessively wealthy family." He wanted to continue, but needed to end this conversation. "He doesn't need any other reason to put you down.

"Now, if you're pissed at him, woo hoo for you – so is the rest of the bloody country. But if you come at me again like some rabid dog, I will put you down." Oliver paused, inhaling calmness, and stared at Percy with malicious intent, half-hoping he'd retort.

He didn't. Instead, Percy stared back, frustration seeping into his eyes. But he remained silent.

Oliver smirked, a cheap but well-deserved gloat.

"Fuck you!" Percy barked, spinning on his heels like a soap opera cast member, and stormed back into the corridor, away from the Chief Whip.

Oliver caught the fire door before it slammed shut, pressed it open, and followed Percy into the corridor. He relished the sight of his defeated opponent returning to his place.

"What was that about?" Oliver recognised Antonia's voice but didn't look her way.

"I was heading to the lounge," he said, watching Percy hurry past Fox and his friends at the House's entrance. "If you don't mind hearing about it over a drink?"

"What is it?"

This time, he faced Antonia, noticing her deep brown eyes in a way he hadn't before. "Come on." He raised his elbow, allowing her to slip her arm through its crook. "He thinks I'm playing both sides," was all he said.

"Are you?"

He planned to laugh it off and change the subject, employing his usual deflection tactics. But for some reason, he confided in her, answering, "Absolutely."

2

The argument was going poorly. Window, or Danny—Dee to most of his group—was a pompous, arrogant ass. Whenever he spoke, his hands waved as if he were conducting his argument like a concerto. The piece of paper Evan brought with him was the man's point of contention—the entire thing.

He mocked the Prime Minister's polite opening, soured his sentiments for peace, and outright refused the offer to open negotiations.

"He's a fucking idiot!" Window opined. "He's ignoring what I've been saying or has completely missed the point." In the half-hour of his rant, several people left or were excused. Evan guessed those remaining were Window's core group, some hanging on his every word. Others, like old woman Craven, offered a suggestion now and then. He listened to no one, only allowing Nikki to finish a sentence.

Bo sprawled over the couch, hands resting under his head, looking utterly bored. Kyle appeared ready to put a bullet between Window's eyes, and Evan couldn't believe he'd risked his life to meet this fool. He tried explaining the Prime Minister's position several times, but Window knew better.

From Evan's perspective, Fletcher had met some of Window's group's outer members, and negotiations were progressing well. The next step was for Dominic to be where Evan was now, providing Window the opportunity to meet with Jonathan Reekes and negotiate terms for Southern and Northern England's peaceful reintegration.

Evan couldn't understand how Danny expected any different. After all, Fletcher had been negotiating this on the lower levels before vanishing. Growing tired and worn thin by Window's incessant rant, Evan finally snapped, "What were you expecting?"

It broke Window's stride, causing him to stumble over the rest of his sentence and hang his head in defeat. Then he looked up at the ceiling. "Jesus suffering fuck, give me strength."

Craven's attention was caught by the blasphemous remark. "Daniel, please," she said, her eyes matching his scowl.

He didn't reply to her, but nodded an apology and focused on Evan. "Who did Fletcher report to?"

Evan eyed him carefully, noting Window's past tense when referring to Dominic. "What?"

"Do you report to the same person?" A follow-up question, again to Evan, assuming he was more an equal to Fletcher than anything else, although Evan had given no indication.

"He reports to me."

"You're shitting me."

"That's funny, coming from the guy who's spent the last half-hour bullshitting to the choir." Evan heard Kyle snigger at his remark. "And why are you referring to him in the past tense? What do you know that I don't?"

Window watched him from over the rim of his coffee mug. "Because he's dead."

Evan glared at the man, disliking what he heard, but not shocked to learn Fletcher's fate. Nikki's attitude during their conversations about Fletcher had raised suspicions.

"And for you to claim he reported to you when you know nothing about this operation or Fletcher is fucking lu—"

"Daniel!" Nikki interrupted.

He didn't look at her, but stopped talking momentarily. "I didn't believe you; I'm sorry." He gestured with his mug apologetically.

"They should know," she said.

"Know what?" Evan asked.

Window appeared disappointed. "He really reported to you?"

"Yes." Evan knew he'd missed something. Fletcher had filed no reports on Bo or Nikki, and both claimed to have known him personally. The way Window carried on, it seemed much was missing from Fletcher's reports. There was a reason Window didn't want to deal with them. "So, for the tenth time, Fletcher reported to me. Now please, for the love of God, start explaining, and maybe we can work something out instead of wasting each other's time."

They stared at each other for three excruciating seconds. Just as Window looked to be turning his back on Evan, he placed his mug on the table instead. "Window isn't one person," he started, "it's several. The broadcasts result from, not the reason for the gangs working together."

"You have a working government?" Evan asked.

"Yes," Window smiled. "Of sorts." His energy from the belligerent filibuster refocused. "It was your fault, you know, your SOPs. They kept us fighting each other for years, not that it took much at first. But then we got wise. When we started sharing information, we learned."

"When you say 'we'?"

"What you call gangs, all of us. The Tooty Nung and the Shadow Kingz were the first; they'd been formed to protect their neighbourhoods. It was the next step in protecting each other, so the other groups followed. Once it became clear that most of our problems came from the SOPs, the Triad were the last to join." He stopped, remembering something. "Sin Lao was a good man; he didn't deserve..."

Window paused again. Whatever had transpired, he was close to it. It was etched into his heavy brow. Evan had received more information than he had in a while, some resembling what Fletcher had provided, but he knew there was more. He had to coax it out of Window. "And you're the voice of the gangs?"

Window blinked. He said nothing, just stared at Evan. Did he know what Evan was doing? Was it obvious Evan was pumping him for information? Or was there more to him than Evan had initially judged? He was wired, passionate, and arrogant, but not a fool.

"You could say that," Window said finally, his gaze shifting to Kyle.

"So the message isn't for you." Evan brought Window's eyes back to his.

"I am Window."

"But we understood Window was in charge down here." Evan glanced around the patchwork table at the mostly empty seats. He saw tolerance slipping from Window's face; he was reaching his limit. However, Evan needed more information—everything he'd believed before coming to London was being dismantled by this one man. If he wasn't Window, he needed to speak with whoever was, regardless of their numbers. "Where's everyone else?"

"This is everyone else," Nikki said, "everyone who will meet with you."

Evan's heart pounded in his ears – what the hell did that mean? Kyle grabbed his wrist, but he couldn't help himself. "Sorry?"

"This is what you're getting," Window replied.

"That's it? I've been shot, hit on the head, and walked through Hell to get here, to meet with the leader of this shithole hoping to fix this fucking country, and all I get is an audience with a madman hiding behind the curtain?"

Silence ensued. No one knew how to react, least of all Evan. He had unleashed his thoughts. All he had left was the time between his words and the room's reaction.

Beside him, Kyle released his wrist and braced himself. For what, Evan wasn't sure. But he felt it too. Someone would retaliate. The only question was who. Window was already primed, Nikki appeared ready to lunge across the table and throttle him. Bo sat upright, prepared for action. Dunstun and the others were less likely, but he suspected they'd join in once someone else started something.

"This shithole," Window broke the tension, "this hell, as you so eloquently put it, is my home." He jabbed Evan's shoulder with his iron-like index finger, "And you're only here because Dominic Fletcher and Lao went off the rails. He started a fucking war! That's why no one came to meet you."

"This is a waste of time," Kyle's voice caught Danny off guard, and he glanced at the soldier.

Window gave an enormous clap and said, "That, Caddie-shack, we can agree on."

Evan agreed as well, but remained silent. He felt like a raw nerve when Window spoke. He needed time to digest the information, time away from the madness to absorb everything. Instead of wanting to rip off a table leg and beat the caffeine addict to death.

Around and around they went. Fletcher was an assassin, sent to kill Sin Lao and ignite a war. Sin Lao's death had been unfortunate and devastating to London's harmony. The Triad, the largest gang, had unleashed a swift and brutal retaliation over their leader's death. Like a tsunami of violence, they'd annihilated everything in their path.

But Evan couldn't accept Fletcher had started it. It made no sense. Sin Lao's death was as detrimental to Jonathan Reekes' plans as it was to London. Why couldn't Window see that? Why couldn't he understand that by killing Lao, Fletcher wouldn't be able to complete his mission? A mission he firmly believed in.

"Fletch could have killed all of us," Bo spoke up. He hadn't been as disinterested as Evan had thought. "Easily." Window glanced over his shoulder.

"Bo," Nikki said, "take them to the mess."

He was standing before Evan could think. Good little soldier.

"Wait," said Evan, "what will you be doing?"

"Talking about you." She stared at him until he gave up.

Bo stopped next to Kyle and waited for them both to stand up before saying, "This way."

3

The room remained silent until the door closed behind them.

Then the only sound was of Window slurping from his mug. Nikki knew he could sense her gaze, waiting for him to make eye contact. He didn't. "Don't look at me like that."

"You're taking it out on them," Nikki said.

"They know nothing."

"Exactly."

"That's no reason not to take it out on them."

Dunstun leaned into the table. "They're not here for us."

"That's right." Window waved his hand. "Bluebird was all about meeting everyone else. Just because they weren't here for me, doesn't mean they weren't here for anyone else."

Nikki fumed silently for a moment. "We expected this before Bo and I left to meet them."

"Not to this extent," Window clarified.

"They blew up Lao," Dunstun added. "Years of work have gone straight to Hell."

Nikki shuffled in her seat and brushed her hair back. "I don't think they're responsible."

"What's stopping us?" the old crone Craven asked, silencing the table as easily as flicking off a light switch.

"Baiser!" Window screamed the French obscenity, launching his coffee mug across the table. It twisted in mid-air, spilling its contents before smashing into the wall. Ceramic shards sprayed outward and clattered over the floor. His head dropped, too heavy for him to bother holding any further, and his arms splayed outward over the tabletop.

Nikki reached toward Window and put her hands over his shoulder. "The Triad will have a new King soon, then we can—"

"That new King will be Grekko," Dunstun interrupted. His nominated leader stirred the remaining members of the room. "You all know it will be. Then watch this city burn – the Triad under his leadership will not bow to the rule of the Kingdom."

Nikki watched as Dunstun roused the room against her. Grekko was a vile psychopath, a wild dog leashed by Sin Lao. He'd turned into a savage lieutenant who had escaped the blast that killed his master. If he took control of the Triad, then Dunstun was right. "Then all the more reason to go."

"That's madness!" Dunstun argued.

"Is it?" Nikki asked. "If what you say is right and Grekko takes control of the Triad, we would lose a large portion of the city. But we could win if we had help from the other groups and—"

"The SOPs?" Window finished her sentence. He had slowly lifted his head during Nikki's argument and was staring right at her with his lopsided smile.

"They'll never go for that," said Dunstun. "The other groups wouldn't go for that. They'll offer nothing more than martial law."

"He has a point," Window said to Nikki.

"This is the first time we've had any kind of cooperation between the gangs," she replied. "And the first time a Prime Minister has wanted to talk."

"You saw their faces, just as I did." He twisted his arms and took hold of both her wrists. "You've spent more time with them. More time with Fletcher. He was here for months. He knew you, me, Dunstun, Craven, even Bo by name. They knew nothing. If Fletcher wasn't reporting to Bluebird, then who was he reporting back to? Reekes? I don't think so. Someone is pulling the strings out there and it isn't the government."

Nikki saw the truth and fear in Window's eyes. It was the reason he hadn't snapped up the chance to meet with the Prime Minister. Fletcher had turned on them and their friendships, for reasons they couldn't comprehend. If the Prime Minister they wanted to speak with was not in control, it would be a waste of time and a dangerous one at that. They had an unseen enemy out there, an insidious mind playing a deadly game.

A game that, if won, would unite the country like before. It would end the poverty, the violence, and the life they all shared. It was their dream. If they ever wanted to live in a United Kingdom again, they had to take this chance, even if it meant dying. Nikki could see the reluctance in Window's eyes, which she mistook for fear: Danny was afraid of dying. "You can take me with you."

"No," he smiled. "Not with Lao gone. Dunstun is right, Grekko will become the next Dragon King, and when that happens, we're going to need all of you here."

4

Evan chewed on his turkey. He enjoyed watching his companions eat, but felt alienated. He'd been preoccupied with his food and hadn't paid attention to the conversation. Bo and Kyle were speaking Punjabi, which he couldn't understand. As he neared his fill of lunch, he became more aware of not being included.

"I'm right here," he reminded them, immediately feeling like a sourpuss.

Kyle had sauce on his lip when he smiled. "Bo says I'm badass."

"Cute," said Evan. "Wipe your mouth and try saying that again."

Bo pointed and laughed at the red juice escaping down Kyle's mouth. It was a pleasant picture, a normal picture. They were getting along, and even the nanocraft Raven on Bo's skull was pacified.

Kyle said something to Bo in Punjabi, and Bo nearly coughed up a mouthful of food when he laughed.

"What?" Evan slapped a grin over his insecurity. "What's so funny?"

They both looked at him from across the table. Bo bit his lip, trying not to laugh any further. Kyle appeared like he was about to apologise. "I asked Bo," he said, "whether he thought you were badass too."

That was it. Bo was laughing tears. Kyle was chuckling. So was Evan.

"You're a pair of bastards," he said, failing to stop his laugh, his stomach clenching and his chest bouncing, "but you're not wrong."

They laughed some more, and Evan felt the remaining stress fall from his body. When they stopped laughing, he caught his breath and slaked his thirst with a glass of iced water. It was the best water he'd ever tasted. Then Bo asked Evan a question that caught him off guard. "Do you think we're worth the trouble?"

"Coming here?"

Bo nodded.

It was an honest question, one with an expansive answer, and Evan would have been more than happy to discuss it over the course of an entire evening. But the kid wasn't looking for that; he was looking for resolution. He could see the anticipation foaming at the boy's mouth. "More than anything."

Bo washed a mouthful of turkey down with his glass of water. "Danny does too."

The sound of his name raised every hair on Evan's neck. "Is he always so—" he searched for a diplomatic word, "charming?"

"We think it's the coffee," came the reply. He caught himself before he could snigger; it wasn't meant as a joke. He was grateful he caught himself because Bo's follow-up arrived on a more serious note. "He has a point."

It had been a long-arsed rant, so Evan quizzically asked, "Which one?" not knowing which of Window's points Bo referred to.

"Fletcher was here a long time before Danny trusted him. He worked the streets, got to know Nikki first. That's the only reason Danny took any notice of him. Nikki doesn't trust anyone." Evan believed him. "Fletcher was the first person outside of the groups to find out about us. The first person any of them believed in. Now he's dead, and our home is in flames."

Evan had noticed that Bo was talking about everyone but himself. "What about you? What do you think?"

The kid avoided his eyes, the table being far more interesting. Perhaps. "It's different for the others," he said, not looking higher than Evan's chin. "They didn't grow up here. They want something that used to be. Something that I don't understand..." he trailed off.

"It doesn't have to be," Kyle said.

"That's what Nikki says," Bo continued. "People shouldn't have to die except for old age. That's her favourite." He played with his turkey, forking the meat robotically without paying much attention. "She wanted it too much, and now she's sad. Now all of them are sad. They're dreaming. Dreams are for children."

Evan felt disgusted. Not at Bo directly, but that the kid could say it. "I'm a dreamer," Evan said, hoping he wasn't the only one left.

"Everyone," Craven startled all three of them by the silent approach and loud voice. "I have some good news."

CHAPTER FIFTEEN
EXTRACTION

Dunstun piped up. "Give it a moment," he said, but he couldn't understand. He'd never been chipped, had never been connected. Evan had been on both counts and could taste the anticipation of returning.

Dunstun crouched under the unit. For some strange reason, the designer of the communications systems had placed the keyboard on the floor. There was a small monitor there, too. "This was here when you found it?" Evan asked impatiently.

"All of it," came Dunstun's reply from under the desk. "We've brought in some other stuff, but there's only so much you can do without ripping it out, and it was only supposed to operate for twelve months."

Just like the kitchen. This had to be one of the fallout bunkers under Whitehall. It explained how they had the technology to hide the transmissions. But it was an explanation up to a point. There was the matter of certain upgrades, but it was no longer in the realms of impossibility. There was no longer any mysticism attached to Window's work, or Window himself.

"Okay, you've got your link." Dunstun stood up and pulled the creases out of his tunic. "Make your call, Mr Bluebird."

Evan leaned into the table, pressed the circular button with the microphone pictured next to it. "Renner?"

Nothing. Not a peep. He tried again. Still. He tried another three times, and one more for luck. Again, nothing.

"Maybe they've given up on you?" Dunstun's snide remark wasn't helping.

Evan didn't give him the satisfaction of reacting. He had been considering calling for Kyle: they had opted against using his personal communications in favour of their shielded one. But that was before he found this piece of crap wasn't working. He pressed the button again. "Renner?" Nothing. He tried another six times before he closed his eyes and prayed for Renner not to be sleeping. Or worse.

Then, distantly, he heard his familiar voice. "Bluebird?"

"Copy that," Evan said, smiling. "It's good to hear your voice, old buddy."

"You too, Bluebird. Where in hell are you?"

"I don't know for certain," Evan bleated, tapping his fingers against the tabletop in excitement. "I need to speak with Dickens."

"Copy that."

He disappeared for a few moments, then returned. "Patching in."

"Bluebird, this is Dickens." It was the Gorilla's voice, Jonathan Reekes, using his designated codename.

"Good to hear your voice, sir."

"Yours too, my boy. Good news." He paused for a few seconds. "I hope?"

"I am requesting an airlift for myself, Fallout and VIPs. As soon as you can." Evan didn't have to imagine the Prime Minister's beaming smile on the other end of the radio. He heard it in his voice.

"Consider it done."

"There's a pulse package attached to this transmission. It's coded for Renner to access." There was a pause while they checked and conferred.

"Yes, we have it. Coordinates?" Reekes asked.

"That's it. We're heading there directly, so as soon as you can."

"We have a Lex on standby. It will be in the air within five minutes."

"Thank you, sir."

"No. The thanks belong to you. We know what's been going on down there. I'm glad you're alright."

2

On the other end of the transmission line, Oliver sat on Jonathan's desk, pulling on his cuffs and watching the Prime Minister. He was elated, rubbing his hands together and scratching the back of his head feverishly. Why not? Oliver thought to himself; this was what they were working towards. He deserved it. They all deserved it.

It could even change things. All their dreams might soon be answered. Jonathan Reekes could be remembered as the Prime Minister who put the country together again when all the King's horses and All the King's Men could not.

"Amazing news!" Reekes spun around and yelled as the transmission ended. Christmas had come early to the Prime Minister's office.

"I'll alert the Cabinet," Antonia announced. To business then: always to business. Oliver grinned. She was so much like himself.

Jonathan raised his hand at Antonia, stopping her in her tracks. "Wait until it's absolutely necessary," he said. "I don't want to give anyone enough time to mess this up."

3

In London, they didn't wait long. The transport was ready and waiting at Heathrow. The coordinates were for King James' Park. The grounds used to be a tourist attraction, with acres of lush green grass and plump tree foliage. Now, it was a frozen wasteland made of broken mud and sod framed by a bare tree line.

"What's that?" Evan pointed to the large white bubble tents behind the trees.

"Weed." Nikki pinched her thumb and index together, making the universal gesture for smoking.

"Yours?"

She grinned but didn't answer. She looked up at the sky. The design of the Lexington GT6 enabled stealth engines; not that they ran silently, as that was next to impossible. Only the Japanese were rumoured to have created such an engine. Instead, the VTOL aircraft redirected its sound, flipping it directly above or directly below, depending on altitude and the pilot's tactical preference.

They hadn't heard its arrival because you could only hear the engine above the craft. Its visual camouflage allowed a similar invisibility, a technology known as shifting. Developed by a combined research project between Britain and the United States in 2025, you could only see the craft when it fired its weapons or by proximity, but its appearance was transparent once it was over forty metres away.

"They're here," Evan confirmed, marvelling at the VTOL as it settled quietly just north of his position and precisely on the coordinates provided by Dunstun.

It measured twenty-six metres from nose to tail, had six vector-thrust engines, a craning neck, and enough firepower to give a Chinese Juggernaut pause. The British government had five of them, while the Yanks had kept another thirty-two for themselves.

Kyle led Window and Bo towards it as soon as the landing struts touched the ground. It left Evan standing next to Nikki, Dunstun, and Craven, all of whom had come with them to say goodbye. It had been a tense farewell. Dunstun, in particular, voiced his discontent with the decision for Window and Bo to go. Evan could understand it, as this had never been done before. Window and Bo were doing just the thing that he and Kyle had done: leaving their home to enter a hostile environment. All they could do was hope it would work out...

Nikki caught his eye before he stepped away; his intention had been to leave with no further conversation. They had said their goodbyes earlier, before the transport arrived. But now he saw the worry on her face. She was losing them: Window was old enough to understand the consequences of the action. He wondered if she thought, like he did, that Bo didn't. "He doesn't have to come."

"Daniel needs him." She had stopped looking at Evan, instead focusing on Bo entering the Lexington.

"Is he yours?" Realising he'd not asked before.

She smiled. "Yes." She paused. "No," her eyes dropped to the floor. "I found him in Covent Garden when he was six." She smiled at the memory. "Eating fresh dog, he'd made the shiv himself."

Evan failed to see the happiness in the memory, but he realised she regarded that meeting highly. "He'll be fine."

She nodded plainly. "He knows how to survive." There was a sadness in her eyes.

"I should thank you," he said, not knowing what else to say.

She blinked away a tear before it fully formed. "Take this." She handed him a small glass-like tube, no bigger than a cigarette filter.

He rolled it in the palm of his hand. It was possibly a quantum drive, but a design he'd never seen before. "This a pen drive?"

"Trust has to start somewhere," she reminded him of his own statement. "Right?"

He looked her in the eye quizzically and nodded. "Thanks," he said, pocketing the device; evidence that would help the cause, he was certain. "For everything," he continued, smiling, then turned toward the Lexington.

"Bring them back to me," she said simply.

He stopped instantly, and at seven minutes past one in the afternoon on December thirteenth in King James' Park, he made his promise. "On my life," he smiled, saluted Nikki, and ran to the transport.

CHAPTER SIXTEEN
THERE'S NO PLACE LIKE HOME

Kyle looked out of the side of the transport and announced, "We're back."

Evan pressed his nose against the window and smiled. "For a moment there, I wasn't sure we were going to make it."

Kyle stared at him. "For a moment?"

Evan punched him in the shoulder. "Thanks. For everything."

"Don't mention it."

The landing pad, one of nine, had been reserved, flanked by military personnel. Evan counted thirteen in total, including the standard ground staff.

"They've brought a welcoming committee," noted Window.

"You're almost royalty," Evan conceded.

Bo peered out of the side, looking on with an intense scrutiny reserved for snipers. When the Lexington banked to its left, only Bo remained glued to the side.

Once landed, Bo and Danny separated instantly. Officers with wide shoulders took their guests' objections in stride. "We're to take you directly to your quarters. The Prime Minister is preparing the cabinet to receive you. If you would like refreshments, I can take your order." Evan and Kyle, however, found themselves standing on the landing pad, with nothing to do but smell the engine fuel. "Don't think I've ever enjoyed this smell before," Kyle said.

"It does smell particularly like roses today."

"Sir." The faceless officer appeared from nowhere. "Mr Trench would like to meet with you."

"Okay," Evan said.

"Sorry, sir. I was addressing Commander Ross."

"Oh," Evan blushed, "That's you, I guess."

"That's me," Kyle said.

"Sir, he's waiting for you in the House."

"The House?" Kyle asked, following the officer from the landing pad, wondering if he'd misheard. The House was not where he'd expected to be debriefed. "Of Commons?"

"Yes, sir."

Kyle didn't move.

"Sir, he's expecting you."

"I'm sure he'll understand me making sure a friend gets to Doctor Haines."

2

"Good to see you back in one piece," Oliver said, his remark sincere. He'd been friends with Desmond,

Kyle's father, until lung cancer took him six years ago, and still invited Kyle and his mother to his family barbecue each summer, as tradition dictated.

As Kyle walked toward him, weaving between the rows of seating, it was hard not to see his father's likeness in him—the broad shoulders, the confident stride. "Evan took a few knocks." He even sounded like him.

"I know," Oliver replied. "Haines already has him?"

"He's probably sharpening his scalpel right about now."

"The Hatchet?" Oliver smirked. "He's been sharpening them all morning." Noticing that Kyle didn't share his humour, he added, "How are you?"

Kyle sat before he answered. "It's done."

"I didn't ask that."

"I'm fine." He was exactly like his father.

"Your father would be proud," Oliver said, knowing it to be true. His son had made a crucial first step in putting their country back together again. Desmond himself had spent much of his own life rebuilding Sierra Leone during and after the nineteen-nineties.

That had been where he had met Kyle's mother, Olayinka, from Freetown. She had accused him of being an arrogant, greedy western opportunist. He admitted to being arrogant and insisted they argue the rest over dinner that evening. It was a story he loved to tell. Much of it, Oliver suspected, was liberal with facts and fancies, but he missed his old friend's retelling of it. "You brought back the elusive window," said Oliver.

"It's done," he repeated, his eyes looking at the floor.

"What happened down there?"

"I kept him alive." The syllables cracked against Oliver's skull like a gavel, letting him know Kyle did not care to continue the conversation, that he had completed his mission and decided he'd not fully reconciled himself with. Kyle wasn't normally one for reflection, and his silence was as surprising as it was disturbing.

"Hey." Oliver put a hand on Kyle's shoulder. "It's only London," he said, catching the look in Kyle's eyes and instantly regretting his words.

"What about the Prime Minister?" Kyle asked. Oliver released Kyle's shoulder. It was a question worthy of debate, but he wasn't sure he could answer. How does one tell a friend he was plotting against another friend? "He's flirting with the good old days." Kyle's face remained quizzical. "Not good," Oliver offered.

"He better step up quick. This Window guy has caffeine for blood."

Oliver thought of the oranges on Jonathan's desk. "Jon has a similar disposition."

Kyle's head tilted slightly. "Yup." He didn't ask for any expansion. He was the man charged with jumping in front of a bullet for Reekes. He knew every subtle failing that Jonathan had, just like Oliver, which made his concerns even more pertinent.

"Look," Oliver said, blinking a command message to the Prime Minister, "take a couple of days off. Get some rest."

"I don't need rest."

"Not yet. But another forty hours and you'll be needing a good day's recharge."

"I'll take it then."

"You've done us a great service; you'll get a medal for sure. Evan too, for that matter, and one you'll be able to wear. Take the night off, come back to mine if you don't want to bunk here. The spare room is always there should you want it." Oliver's HUD blinked a return message from the Prime Minister. He read it. "The Prime Minister insists you take time off. He's asked Gillespie to continue managing his protection."

Kyle didn't look at him, just nodded in agreement. "I could do with a couple of drinks."

"Good!" Oliver's teeth shone shiny and white. "File your report, and I'll meet you at the barracks. I have a few items to deal with before leaving."

3

"No one knows who they are." As always, Nadia Black captured her audience with her trademark sultry voice, "But a source close to the Prime Minister is saying that today, after twenty years of hostile rejection, peace negotiations with London have been going on for most of the afternoon.

"This comes as fortunate news after yesterday when it was announced that an investigation—"

Bo waved his hand, changing the channel. Nadia Black vanished, replaced by a tropical landscape with salt-white beaches and hotels standing in crystal waters. Yours for just ten thousand pounds a week. He waved the image away, bored with the pictures but entertained by the seemingly magical gestures.

After the trip, they had escorted him and Danny to this room. The door was locked, and guards were posted outside. They had argued over that. Danny, condescending to Bo, telling him it was fine, nothing to worry about. It was temporary, just like they had kept Bluebird and Fallout hooded.

Bo understood; he just didn't like being controlled.

For a little while, they had some fun. Bo had never felt a fully downed bed before and discovered the joy of bed jumping. Laughing until his stomach hurt. But it wasn't long before the man in the suit turned up. "Come with me," he said. "Not you," he indicated when Bo started walking towards the door.

"It's okay," reassured Danny, clicking his fingers and reactivating the wall. "Watch some TV until I get back."

Left with nothing but the tube, he had waved his way through four hours of inane imagery before Danny returned. Opening the door, slamming it shut, and spat. "Merde!" He grabbed the nearest thing to him—a statue of King Henry riding a horse in full armour—and threw it.

It smashed over the faces of Michael and Madison Tate.

"Good meeting?" asked Bo, looking at the fresh dent in the wall behind the image. The ranting tirade ran for fifteen minutes straight. Round and round the insults went, so much so that Bo counted twenty-three 'idiots', fifteen 'ignorants', and he couldn't have counted how many times he'd heard the word deaf. He laughed when he heard "bulbous ass," but for the rest, he remained silent.

"—and the smugness!" Danny continued. "How can they think we'd want to go back to that?" Bo knew what was coming. It was the impossible wall, the Jerusalem factor, as Danny explained it. Jews and Palestinians would never agree on anything until they came to an agreement on Jerusalem, and neither of them would ever agree to relinquish or share it.

Jonathan Reekes aimed to repopulate Southern England and reinstate the pre-existing laws. His laws. Enforced by his forces. But to Danny, this seemed impossible. London and the South had moved on; they were an emerging country. They weren't squatters, and they weren't about to submit to the same laws and banking institutions that had landed them in this mess.

Bo flipped through the channels as Danny repeated his arguments. It was best to let Danny rant. Like a dog chasing its tail, he would eventually lie down.

"Every time I'm getting somewhere, one of his ankle biters pipes up, 'but sir'." Bo assumed Danny's impression of the politicians was more comical than accurate unless the man sounded like Terry the Gun Merchant, who only spoke with half his mouth because of a stroke.

Bo didn't laugh this time. The next channel caught his attention. He'd never seen a naked woman before, not like this one. Surrounded by measurements and information that told Bo she was flawlessly designed, she stood at five feet and nine inches. A thirty-six-inch chest, eighteen inches on the waist, and twenty-two inches on the hips. She had twenty per cent body fat and weighed 110 pounds. She never needed to eat, would never talk back, and would do whatever Bo told her to do. She was the perfect companion, the perfect trophy, and Bo believed he deserved her.

"She's a doll," Daniel said, finally off his subject.

Bo's cheeks flushed red. "She's beautiful."

"She's not real. You won't find a woman who looks remotely like that unless she's come off a production line." Bo sometimes forgot that Danny hadn't been born in London. He knew things about the outside world.

He considered Danny wise without fully understanding the concept and trusted whatever he said. But gazing at the unblemished skin and inviting eyes, Bo couldn't believe him—she looked too real.

The image changed as Danny waved to the next channel. A gardening show, one that Bo had flipped past hours ago. He tilted his head to object. "You can't afford her," Danny said.

Bo returned to the gardening, uninterested, insulted, and red-faced.

"You know what my dad called democracy?" Danny asked.

Bo continued to watch the gardening with disinterest. He'd heard it before, but Danny must have mistaken his silence for an invitation. "It's two wolves and a sheep deciding what's for dinner."

Bo knew the quote wasn't Danny's dad's—he was a parking attendant. The quote belonged to Ben something, but he didn't care. Normally, he'd switch off at this point. Danny would turn to Craven or Nikki or Jonas to chat when Bo didn't listen. But they weren't here, and there was no avoiding it. There was nothing left but to play along. "So, what about the people?"

"People?" The ruse worked. "They're apathetic at best. That's why they voted Johnny Reekes in."

Danny hadn't been voted in, not by traditional methods, anyway. He had fallen into the right group at the right time. A natural leader who had stumbled onto the bunker network, he had risen above the norm, especially when he offered similar bunkers to the group leaders.

Craven often told Danny, "I would vote for you." Bo liked the sentiment more than he understood it. He also knew that when the fighting stopped, when it genuinely stopped, there would be a vote, and Danny would win.

"Besides—" Bo usually despised this part. Danny believed in it so fervently that he'd die to protect it. Today, however, Bo enjoyed listening. "What's the point of using your freedom of speech if you're only reminded you're lucky to live in a country where you can speak up? 'Hey buddy, this country is awesome, shut up! You could be stoned for what you're saying in Iraq!' What's the point in saying you're not happy with something if you're just ignored? What's the point? Unless someone listens?"

The warrior in Bo would never let that end in such a defeatist approach. He would stick a knife in the person until they listened. "That's the people's fault."

"You know what happens when they stand up?" Danny said, reminding Bo of New London's history. How the people had stood up, they'd shouted their beliefs to their leaders. And here they were, twenty-two years later.

"I need," Danny stared at the garden on the wall, "I need Reekes to understand that we've evolved. That we want and can build our own future."

Bo mulled over Danny's rant, smirked at 'bulbous ass' again, and arrived at a simple, yet effective solution. "Could you speak to Reekes alone?"

CHAPTER SEVENTEEN
FOR KING AND BLOODY COUNTRY

Fixing Evan's chip was supposed to be a simple procedure, or so Dr Haines had explained before putting him under. "Ah yes," he'd said, "a common fault with commercial chips, especially in the sports." Evan had a commercial chip. Only field agents received military-grade chips; the rest of the Branch made do with software upgrades and a pat on the back. "We'll just swap this out and harden the interface. Two hours tops."

Two hours under the knife, and not just anyone's knife—Dr Hatchet Haines' knife. A small price to pay for a sharp knock to the head, it was not. It had shorted out the wiring connecting his retina projectors. Evan's current chip had repaired itself, but the wiring between the systems had gone unattended. He didn't need a new chip, but the upgrade was free, so why not?

He woke up three hours later. His head felt as if someone had opened it up and played with his brain. Through the plexiglass window of the operating theatre, he could see Dr Haines, reading one of nine holographic panels—the important one, the one that told him whether the operation had been successful. "All good, doc?" His palate was dry, and the words grated his throat on the way out.

Haines gave him the thumbs up from behind the window. "The new chipset is nesting favourably." He swiped a hand over the report. "Try a command."

Evan blinked, his HUD appearing promptly. Glowing red and blue lines depicted his medical report, specifically his brain and the nested chipset deep inside the fleshy tissue. He summoned messages, emails, missed call data, and news feeds. Anything he could get his hands on, he'd read them all at the same time—be damned if he couldn't.

"Take it easy for the next hour," said Haines. "This chip is faster than your previous one. It will take your brain some time to adapt to the processing speed."

He wasn't wrong. Evan was pulling information to his HUD faster than he could think. Documents, images, video feeds, audio files all piled on top of each other. It was incredible. He checked his official report once more; it had been passed out to the relevant people, the Prime Minister being one of them. He hadn't opened the file, but he checked the time. It flashed on the bottom left of his HUD. The default setting, he moved it across to the bottom right and saved it.

It had been almost four hours since the Lexington had landed. "They know I'm up, Doc?"

"Uh-uh."

"Any visitors?"

"Only the one you asked for."

Evan left the gurney in search of his clothes. "How long ago?"

The reply didn't come right away. Dr Hatchet Haines was checking his HUD. "An hour ago. They're behind you."

Evan looked to the window. Haines was pointing over to the other side of the room. On a side cupboard, neatly folded, was a government-branded sweat suit: joggers, hoodie, and trainers. "Thanks, Doc."

He dressed hastily, leaving the room after pressing an open palm against the plexiglass wall. "Thanks again." He traded the empty infirmary for a silent corridor and hurried as fast as decorum would allow in the halls of the Parliament building.

An hour, he told himself, was long enough.

2

"I hear you came to visit," Evan said, barging into the Control Room.

"You should knock." Renner spun his chair around. "I could have been watching porn."

"You needed to watch porn after seeing me in a surgical gown?" He raised his arms wide for his approaching friend, hugging and breaking apart, laughing.

"Your humour didn't survive the procedure, then?"

"I asked Hatchet to put it in a jar for me."

"Best place for it. It never worked properly." Renner punched Evan in the arm. "Glad to have you back, man."

"Careful, or I'll have to tell your wife that you have a man crush on me."

"She's not the wife."

"She is, though," Evan winked.

"Not at all, my friend. We like to keep it mysterious."

"That's funny; I heard it was kinky." It was a practised routine of two friends blowing off the stress gained over the last couple of days. It was good to be home. "I heard you dress up as Winnie the Pooh and chase after her honey pot."

"Sweetest honey in the building."

"It must be if it has you crawling back to her every night."

Renner hooked Evan's arm and pulled him back in, giving him a big bear hug. "Good to have you back, you petulant little shit!" He released him and pointed to the only chair in the room, his control chair. "Take a seat. You want a drink or something?"

"Some water or something fizzy if you have it." Evan relaxed in the leather recliner. "Did you get it?"

Renner passed him an empty glass as he crouched down beside the chair. There was a mini fridge built in its base. He handed up a can of lager.

"Do you have anything soft?"

The look Renner produced was a cross between dismay and devastating concern. "You were shot on your first field mission. Hit your head with enough force to smash a watermelon apart, and you don't want a drink?" He checked the door to the control room and lock it. "Don't listen to that little cricket on your shoulder; listen to your old friend Renner and drink." He clicked his finger, and the room was bathed in a red hue. "I guarantee you'll be needing something harder soon enough."

The red hue signified that the room was locked down. In one simple gesture, it no longer appeared on the building's security recordings, so no eyes or ears could pry into what was happening between these four walls. Evan had been here more times than he could recall, but not once had Renner locked it down. It had to be something to do with the small glass tube. "Something up?"

Renner nodded. "It's a quantum drive."

"I thought it might have been, but I didn't recognise the model."

"I'm not surprised." Renner stood behind him now, connecting the hardwire to the port on Evan's wrist like a UV.

"Why?"

"It's DGSE."

He flinched as the hardwire's tip clamped around his port and injected the inner cable into his arm. "It's French?"

"Oui, oui!" The DGSE or Directorate-General for External Security was France's outside intelligence agency. What in the hell was Nikki doing with it? "It was also holding something so sensitive that you, my fine friend, are about to be the second person in the building to find out what's on it. As long as you didn't show it to anyone else before me?"

Evan was too stunned to answer. How did they have French intelligence technology?

"Shall I take your silence as a no?"

"Sorry, yes... I mean no. No one else knows about it. Not even Kyle."

"Well, in that case, I feel quite privileged."

Evan could tell he was more nervous than he was letting on. "What's on it?"

"Fletcher."

"Come again?"

"It's a recording of his chipset." Renner held up the glass tube. "At least the last three months of it. I don't think it could fit any more on here. It's not that big. We designed one last year that can hold three times—"

"Ren..." Evan glared at him, willing him to get to the point.

"Yes. Three months of raw footage, recorded from a transmitted feed, sent from Dominic Fletcher's chipset." Renner slipped the drive into his chair and stepped back. "The last recording is dated two days ago."

"He stopped transmitting a week ago." He knew Renner also knew this; he was mission controller and had been responsible for catching all of Fletcher's transmissions. "You told me. You were the one who told me we'd lost him a week ago."

"We did. I did," he corrected himself. "However, he was still transmitting. It wasn't to us, but he was transmitting to the MOD. To MI5 and your savage friends. They were piggybacking the signal. They saw everything, too."

"So what?" Evan was doubled up with confusion. Dominic had transferred from MI5 to Special Branch under instruction from the Prime Minister. He knew him, or at least, thought he had known him. "Are you saying Fletcher was a double agent?"

"I don't want to make assumptions about our late friend; I've only had the data for just over an hour. I'll need a couple of days at least to run it through my systems before I can make that kind of judgement." His eyes were off to his right, no doubt searching his brain for some way of speeding up the timeframe. Then he flicked back to Evan. "At least a couple of days, okay, maybe a week. Did I say there were three months on here?

"I checked the data streams – if the savages hacked the transmission, then they're better than I am. I'd be more inclined to say he gave them the codes to piggyback."

"He allowed them to watch?"

"Maybe he was lonely, or maybe he went Colonel Kurtz out there. I don't know. I might never know. I don't want to promise anything. What I will say is that we may be in luck. Whether or not they hacked it, if it's in the last three months, I'll find it."

"Because the data is raw." It was unabridged. Whatever Fletcher saw, said, heard, or felt, they would learn.

"Yes, my young Padawan, that is correct." He bit his bottom lip, forming a grimace. "And there's something else."

Evan hardly believed there was more to come, but then he remembered the thing that Nikki and Window had told him. "He killed Sin Lao."

Renner's shoulders slouched. Evan could see him working it out in his head. "They told you?"

"I didn't believe them."

"They tell you about Lockhead?"

"Lockheed?"

"No. Lock and Head together, Lockhead."

Evan shook his head. "What is it?"

"It's an operational codename, one that's been about the corridors over the last couple of days. Oliver asked me to check into it for him. He's been like a ferret after a snake – you probably had it easier down London than some guys that happened to be in his way." Renner recognised the face of impatience in Evan. "Well, strap in. I think I found it."

Renner moved to a holographical interface at the rear of the chair. "Tap twice when you've had enough and try not to puke over the chair," he said as Evan's vision diluted into the fade. A dead-zone waiting to be filled with Dominic Fletcher's raw data file.

"Boot me."

3

His left eyelid tore open, and sleep's fresh scab rolled down his cheek into the pit. The pitch darkness was as expansive as it was cold, cold enough to freeze the balls off a brass monkey, his father would say. No, not his father, Evan corrected himself. Dominic's father. This was Dominic's experience. Evan was reliving his thoughts, his entire digital being, and Dominic was exhausted. He stuck his tongue out of his mouth and licked his dry, cracked lips. He had no memory of drinking recently, no memory of arriving at this shared present.

"Where am I?" he asked with his own mouth, not Dominic's.

"Shall I just tell you how it ends?" Renner's voice sounded off. It wasn't in the same place as Dominic. It was elsewhere, bodiless.

"No." He wanted to see it for himself. He needed to see how it had ended, what Nikki had intended him to watch. How Dominic had taken out Sin Lao. "It's disorientating."

"That's the mix of you watching the raw feed and Dominic's anxiety levels. I'll plug you with a mild sedative – that should counter the effects."

He tried to move his arms but found them locked tight at the wrists. He looked up and saw why. Iron manacles held them in place above his head, and he could feel the strain in Dominic's shoulders. The pain was numbed. He must have been hanging there for some time. Whoever had him had held him for days like this, and whatever their purpose, Dominic had grown to love these chains, this archaic feat of engineering that bound him in place. They were both his keeper and his saviour.

Without them, he'd fall into the pit, where they waited for him. The chattering demons. He didn't know how many there were. Dominic had never counted them. But he feared them. They were to Dominic a precise depiction of a masochist's wet dream and his own nightmare. He loved his chains for keeping him from them.

Evan still felt the tug of reality, a notion not unlike the fourth beer of the night. Everyone, at some time or other, has tried it raw. There are plenty of people who deny it, who say things like "I've watched it on a screen." But it's all just a way of saying they didn't inhale. It's the taboo. It's the dirty little secret like the sex tapes of the thirties. Why wouldn't you want to see what it was like being someone else? It's not watching what they saw; it's experiencing every sense they experienced. Touch, excitement, smell, euphoria, taste, ecstasy, sound, despair, sight – everything.

Porn starlets like Madison Fry make millions every year from allowing her fans to experience her. These experiences are not raw. They are edited, to convey the good, the positive Government-approved feelings. Everyone has tried it, in some fashion or other. Evan had done so; he had more than one such experience saved on his server and plenty of his own memories he could and would relive. Less popular, but still available, were the bad ones. The illegal ones. The ones that deal with the other side of life, the drug taking, the rape, the murder, and the snuff. All the ones good people pretended weren't out there.

The danger with them is losing oneself, getting trapped in the past, or someone else's past. It's easy to believe one reality over the other when you want to. When the one you're choosing to experience is, for lack of a better description, better than the one you live. That's why they're banned. That's why Evan couldn't be sure whether he was the one controlling Dominic's motion now, as he swayed back and forth, or whether he was just along for the ride. It was all too real.

Evan had undergone the training; all Government personnel did. All political figures underwent that particular training too. Ever since Didenko, the Russian Ambassador to Korea, had been kidnapped and broken, torturers had found a new toy in breaking a person by destroying their reality. He remembered that. The first lesson in hardening oneself against such methods— "Do not rely on your technology, for that will be the first thing they turn against you." Professor Hendrickson of the Foundation had a flair for the dramatic, but Evan remembered his lessons well.

He knew he could no more manipulate his surroundings than a brick could control the weather. However, his mind alone understood the experience's simple truth. Every sense of his being denied him that truth; to all intents and purposes, he was, in that moment, Dominic Fletcher. He could smell the rancid damp from the wooden beams above him and the cold draught running across his back. Most of all, he desperately wanted to scratch the itch on his left ankle.

In the room above, he heard the door creak, followed by shards of light shooting down between the floorboards. They had returned; Evan didn't know who. Not yet, but Dominic did. It must be time for breakfast, Dominic mused. Or supper. Or torture. Whatever it was, they were back and in numbers. Both Evan and Dominic counted at least five sets of feet walking above him.

The light fractured his cell into twisted, nightmarish shapes. Dominic blinked furiously to defend himself against the horrors. Each blink brought more focus to his dungeon. He couldn't gauge how far from the floor he hung, only that it was high enough. The smell of rotting flesh and faeces was too close for comfort, as were the chattering demon dogs. He was high enough. The fear Evan felt led him to believe this hadn't always been the case.

Voices drew his attention upward. Mandarin. Triad. They were loud and coarse enough for him to hear. They didn't care if he was asleep. This was their way, Evan knew. They would speak above him, letting Dominic know they were preparing for him. They moved about, their shadows blocking out the beams of light from his ceiling like a cheap disco system.

The group holding him captive had chosen to call him Dingo. The name was as good as any. He wouldn't give them any other name to use. They assured him that if he didn't give them anything, they would take everything. He hadn't been keeping score, but he was sure they were winning.

The footsteps above were just the grunts. They weren't his footsteps. He wasn't here yet. They weren't ready to bring him up. Evan stared at the ceiling regardless. It would happen soon. In a slash of light across his arms, he saw the caked blood on his flesh. What had they done to him? What had they done to Fletcher? Then he felt the pang, a frozen fist crushing his innards. A memory so powerful Evan felt the tear run down his own cheek as well as Dominic's.

Patricia and Michael—Dominic's wife and son—haunted his thoughts. Patricia, the ash-blonde dancer who had introduced him to ballet and her world, was a jewel. And young Michael, only three, had just begun his life. Dominic remembered Michael padding from his cot and into his arms the day he'd left for London. The memory, locked away in his chipset but inaccessible, remained safe in his mind, untouchable and more potent than any digital reconstruction.

He clenched his fists and felt his fingertips reach his palms. Surprisingly strong, they inspired him to try again. He grasped the manacles and pulled with his remaining strength. His arteries bulged, feeding his muscles with oxygen as he raised his body. He held the manacles behind his head for four agonizing seconds, thoughts of Patricia and Michael fuelling his determination, before his strength failed him.

As he dropped, his shoulders wrenched from their sockets, sending waves of pain through his body. A child-like yelp escaped his lips, and the barks and snarls of anticipation below spurred him on. He breathed deeply, focusing on Michael, counting to ten, and finding his breaths easier as he continued. He had to escape this hell, to keep fit, to endure the pain. His family would see him through this, and he would reunite with them. The pain receded, granting him a brief reprieve.

But then, a small white flashing oblong appeared at the bottom right of his vision. He couldn't ignore the tiny, flashing sprite—a simple cursor. Blink, blink. It moved to the right, further away, like a speck of dust on his eye. Blink, blink. Both Evan and Dominic recognised it simultaneously.

The cursor flashed, darted to its left, leaving letters in its wake: 'Rebooting system'. It vanished, replaced by a blinking '0%'. The number climbed rapidly, reaching '100%' in under fifteen seconds. Dominic's chip completed the booting process, and his HUD activated.

A pale blue hue illuminated his display, framing the nightmarish scene with familiar comfort. He could now determine the length of his ordeal: six days, feeling more like a month. Evan accessed Dominic's medical report, instinctively aligning with

Dominic's thoughts. A three-dimensional representation of his body materialised, and Dominic's smile faded as the grim details unfolded.

His medical system had halted the bleeding in his right eye-socket. The optic nerve was sealed, but proper medical attention was necessary. The eye was gone. He almost remembered the rusted spoon plunging into soft flesh, feeling the eye burst. The silver lining: his skull remained mostly intact, save for a fracture on the rear side and grazing from the eye-gouging.

Both arms bore lacerations and bruises, but muscles and bones were unharmed. Dominic suspected his captors wanted him hanging for an extended time. Evan concurred; the rest of Dom's body had suffered worse. Three cracked ribs, nine fractures, innumerable lacerations and punctures marred his upper torso. His chipset had passively treated all the damage.

Although in dire condition, Dominic's chip had managed the major issues, offering hope. He might see Michael again, welcoming the toddler's excited embrace as he had the day he'd left. But the display revealed a memory he'd suppressed, one he wasn't prepared to confront. Dom's 3D image showed no knees, ending midway down the thighs. Evan felt bile rise in Dominic's stomach, tasting the foulness. Blood loss hadn't killed him, and no infection had set in. But Dominic Fletcher would never walk on his own two feet again.

The barks tormented him, and he recalled being lowered into the pit among the pack of dogs dwelling there. Another tear escaped, one for his son Michael, who he doubted he'd see again.

Unless... He blinked his command and waited, an eternity seemingly passing. Deep down, he expected the answer. But he had hope, his display, and a medical report showing he could be saved. With proper care, he could live a normal life, as a father and husband. To hell with the army. He needed his chip to connect, to call Renner and summon the cavalry.

He watched the cursor flash, wondering if it would ever deliver a message. Then came the disheartening news he expected: "Unable to connect." Computer says no.

The demon dogs below stirred, now fully awake and alert. He raised his phantom feet from their jaws, remembering. He blocked out their barks and yelps, listening for what had roused them. Above, distinctive footfalls announced his arrival. One step fell lightly, the other heavy, like an elephant. He entered the room, moving toward Dominic.

Dominic had dubbed him Igor. A name tag materialised around his neck whenever Dom looked at him. It provided scant comfort during the beatings, but it was enough to help him endure. He had labelled all his captors this way, finding it entertaining until they ripped out his eyeball and short-circuited his chipset.

He tracked Igor's steps to a point directly above him. After a pause, a smouldering ember drifted through the chain hole and bounced off Dom's cheek. Hot, but not enough to burn or make him flinch. The cigarette cherry descended toward the dogs below. Instead of their barks, Dominic listened for the footfalls of another—a newcomer, neither soldier nor monster like Igor. These steps were softer, exuding confidence and power.

The plate cover above him lifted, and Dom jerked upward with the force of a helicopter turbine. He closed his eye until his chipset adjusted to the contrast in lighting. He stopped as abruptly as always, the manacles clashing against the loop and swinging his naked body until a Triad grabbed the back of his thigh, steadying him.

The room loomed large and barren, Evan observed for the first time. Sixty metres long, wooden planks with metal joinery—an old warehouse, most likely. Six men were present; Dominic had seen five before, all wearing his assigned dog tags.

Hubert, a lanky African with animated nanocraft tattoos tallying his victims. He'd already shown Dominic where he'd end up. "Right here, pretty boy." He'd grabbed his crotch beneath his jeans. "Right at the tip, where you belong."

George, a Chinese mercenary, had cracked Dom's first and third ribs.

Bill and Ben, both Chinese, rarely strayed from the stack of ceramic flowerpots at the room's far end. They enjoyed watching but seldom commented and never participated in the torture.

Igor—Chinese as well, but Evan needed no pseudonym or introduction. He'd seen files on this man, Grekko, Sin Lao's chief psychopath. Interpol knew him as a ruthless Lao family foot soldier, wanted for human trafficking, drugs, executions, and more. No vile job seemed beneath him. A file in Brussels even hinted at Grekko's involvement in Thomas George's assassination, Britain's Ambassador to Germany, the previous year.

His artificial black eyes unnerved even soldiers, but his left arm left the most lasting impression. Composed of steel, spot welds, and pistons, it allegedly came from the very tank that had crushed his birth-given limb. The gruesome sight lent credibility to the rumour.

Grekko shuffled like a cave dweller, his armoured limb weighing down his left shoulder. Pistons and wheels whirred as its fingers guided the arm with each clumsy step. Evan agreed with Dominic in a split second: Grekko's four-fingered claw could burst his head like a water balloon.

The newcomer, clad in a pinstripe suit, stood behind Grekko. His hair slicked with oil, his face seemingly greased too. He halted Grekko mid-stride, speaking in hushed Mandarin tones. Dom strained to hear, his HUD failing to translate the conversation.

The newcomer's face contorted, eyes narrowing into slits as he spat out words. Something about the situation irked him, and he vented his displeasure with barked orders. Grekko nodded, his head tilted submissively. His soft response contrasted with his hulking, violent frame. This time, Dom's chip caught the Mandarin and translated, "It is safe. Watch."

Dominic braced himself, anticipating the agony to come. He expected Grekko to step up and unleash his armoured fist, as he had done countless times before. But he didn't. Instead, the Newbie raised his hand. "No," he said in English, stepping up to Dominic. He seemed too clean to dirty his own hands, Evan thought. Yet, he wasn't too cocky to confront Dominic.

A wire mesh frame flickered over Newbie's face. Had either Dominic or Evan blinked, they'd have missed it. Neither did. No further information appeared. "What was that?" Evan asked. "Did Dom just scan someone?"

Renner's hand rested on his shoulder. "Clever boy—just keep watching," he whispered.

"Can he hear me?" Newbie asked in flawless English, complete with an Oxford accent.

"There's nothing wrong with his ears," Grekko replied, and both moved closer.

Newbie nodded, his eyes never leaving Dominic's face, scrutinising him with surgical precision. "Why are you here?" Dominic smelled onions on his breath.

"He brought me." Dominic glanced at Grekko, bracing for the blow. He expected Newbie to throw the punch himself, but Grekko's human hand caught Newbie's wrist at the last moment. Grekko's other hand delivered a crushing blow to Dominic's gut. He swung like a slab of meat, gritting his teeth but refusing to scream.

Hands grabbed Dominic from behind, steadying him. Newbie smiled, licking his lips like a true sadist. Dominic closed his eye, knowing Grekko's second punch would be harder. The metallic fist slammed into his ribcage, and his HUD flashed with updates. To Evan's surprise, Dominic held firm, jaw clenched, denying them satisfaction.

"He thinks he's a tough guy," Newbie mused. "Maybe Bruce Willis, eh?"

Dominic disagreed; no dead actor could compare. He pooled blood in his mouth and spat it at Newbie, splattering his face and collar, allowing himself a brief smile of triumph.

Grekko's retribution came swiftly, his mechanical arm backhanding Dominic's face. Tissue and muscle tore apart, making Evan cry out. The right side of Dominic's jaw dangled, sinew and saliva spilling. It took Dominic longer to catch his breath than it did for Newbie to retrieve a handkerchief and clean himself.

Dominic's breaths were shallow and rapid, blood pooling in his throat, bubbling with each exhale as he struggled to swallow. All he managed was a painful wince. His eye locked on his torturer, the goblin-like figure delighting in the nightmare he'd unleashed.

Newbie, however, fumed. "You fucking idiot!" he yelled. "How can he tell us anything now?" He glanced at Dominic's mangled face. "Get the car ready. Tell Lao I'll be down directly."

Grekko glared at Newbie before acquiescing. "Understood."

Newbie lingered, but said nothing. He left acknowledging no one, following Grekko to the door.

Hubert, who had been waiting on the sidelines, stepped forward. He watched Newbie leave before approaching Dominic. He raised his oil-stained finger to his crotch. "Soon, my boy," he said in English, grinning menacingly. Evan shuddered at the sight.

His greasy hand moved from his groin to Dominic's, fingers spreading to grab a fistful. Dominic's nostrils flared, his eye locked on Hubert's. The lanky African squeezed tightly, and pain shot through Dominic's body. He shook in his restraints, helpless. Blood gushed from his jaw, splattering his chest and Hubert's fingers as they slithered up to his throat. "Maybe it's safe now?" Hubert taunted. "To fuck your mouth, no?"

Dominic's eye blazed, but he couldn't retort. His jaw just flapped uselessly.

"What's that, baby?" Hubert mocked. "Not quite safe?" His hand tightened around the remnants of Dominic's jaw.

No.

Dominic's agonised scream drowned out the sound of his jaw muscle tearing and Hubert's laughter. The room spun, lights blurred into lines, and everything else became a dizzying haze. He didn't see Hubert toss his jaw through the hole in the floor like trash. He didn't hear the dogs' frenzy below.

As the room kept spinning, bile erupted from Dominic's throat. Evan felt his own stomach churn. If Hubert hadn't caught Dominic's thigh, he would've vomited on himself. How much footage was left?

A well-dressed Chinese man entered the room. Newbie and the rest turned and bowed. Another flash, another mesh webbing, appeared over his face. Dominic was too far gone, his neck limp. But Evan saw and recognised him. He'd seen many photos and knew the end was near. Whatever would happen would happen soon, because Sin Lao, the Dragon King, had just arrived.

Then it clicked. Newbie, with his oily features, resembled his father. Newbie was Kaedyn. But why had Sin Lao come for Dominic? Why was Dominic so important?

'Requesting go order...' flashed on Dom's HUD. Was he so lost in his thoughts and memories that he hadn't noticed his chip transmitting? Or had it intentionally concealed the fact? Dominic frantically accessed his files, searching transmissions and discovering his feed had been sent to York all along— to someone other than Evan. The piggyback he'd placed kicked in the moment his systems rebooted, now feeding to London, to the savages, as Renner had said.

Whoever watched had left him at the torturers' mercy for six days, making him believe he was alone and hopeless. They had kept Evan in the dark, unable to mount a rescue. They'd gone to extraordinary lengths to convince Dominic and the Triad that he was isolated.

The Triad would think they had the upper hand. If they couldn't force Dominic to talk, they could rip out his chip. Their delay in doing so was worrisome. It would have been more efficient, but perhaps they lacked the facility. Window might have it. Had Window handed Dominic to the Triad? If not, why hadn't he attempted a rescue? He knew Dominic's location.

Sin Lau approached, his gaze never leaving Dominic even as his son, Kaedyn, spoke to him. Evan read the subtitles that underlined their disdain for Fletcher. "He is an assassin. You should have stayed in the car."

The Dragon King ignored the warning, even when Fletcher's remaining iris flickered white; Lao approached him.

'Primary target confirmed' flashed Dom's HUD. Evan's stomach twisted, realising they'd betrayed Dominic.

'Proceed.' Dom read his HUD's second message. Proceed with what? How could he proceed? There was nothing left of him?! Dom's chip executed the order in one second. The Save Our Souls message transmitted on all signals, as per protocol. Dominic swallowed drying blood, his one eye wide and terrified, fixed solely on Lao.

His chip identified Sin Lau as the target, sending the 'Go Command' to Dominic's internal explosive device. In three seconds, counted down by his flashing iris, Dom's skull would burst, becoming a fireball engulfing the building. He craved more time to curse the bastards who put him here, who had implanted a bomb in his head and allowed this to happen.

But time was nonexistent. He closed his eye, thought of Michael and Patricia, and wished he had his jaw to spit his regiment's words, "For King, and bloody country."

Evan leaped from the chair. His feet slid on the floor, and his legs buckled. He collapsed, drenched in sweat, gasping for breath. "What the fuck, Ren! You could've fucking warned me."

"No way. If I had to sit through that, so did you." Renner crouched, waiting with a glass of whiskey.

Evan grabbed it, gulping it down. "Suicide bomb?"

"I wouldn't go as far as suicide, but the result's much the same."

"That's Lockhead?"

"It appears so." Renner retrieved the glass, placing it back on the side table.

Fletcher was an unwitting assassin; he hadn't known. "They put hoods on us." It made sense now. "On Kyle and me, it made little sense at the time, but they wanted to ensure we weren't walking bombs, too." Nikki and Window had been right. The Prime Minister wasn't in control; his government and military worked against him. Or worse, he was in on it. But Evan dismissed the thought. Killing Sin Lao made it harder to bring Window in, and they'd tracked Fletcher the entire time. Bo nailed it—Fletcher could have killed Window at any moment.

And he had led them here, straight to the viper's nest. "Where are they?"

Part Four:
Burn it Down

CHAPTER EIGHTEEN
COUP D'ÉTAT

Evan hurried down the corridor, clad in his Special Branch issue tracksuit. The meeting with Renner still seared in his mind. He'd believed it was over—bring back Window, job done. He'd expected negotiations, but nothing requiring his involvement. Instead, he'd found himself embroiled in a tense situation, and knighthoods were the furthest thing from his mind.

"Kyle," he sent the message, but received no answer. "Kyle, call me as soon as you get this."

He couldn't afford to chase after him. It might be better not to involve Kyle, who followed orders, not instincts. If the higher-ups orchestrated this mess, Kyle could end up on the wrong side. Evan pushed the thought aside, focusing on the situation at hand.

He slowed his pace, realising rushing would draw attention. In the PPB, cameras and ears monitored everything, except for some personal quarters.

Two suits approached— Mark from IT and an unfamiliar auburn-haired woman with freckles. "Ah, Evan," Mark said, stepping into the corridor, blocking Evan's path.

"Sorry, Mark, I've got urgent business."

"Just wanted to introduce you to Jodie."

Forcing politeness, Evan shook hands with Jodie, admiring her green eyes. If life were simpler...

"I'm really sorry, but I have to go."

Mark didn't budge. "That Cat 12 you asked for—"

Evan didn't listen, slipping past. Mark tried to block him, but Evan stepped over, brushing against him. Caught off-guard by the contact, Mark retreated.

"I'll catch you for a drink," Evan called, leaving them behind.

The rest of Evan's journey passed without incident, and he offered the guard a smile and a wave before knocking on Danny's door.

"Come," Danny said from inside.

Evan entered, finding Danny sitting on the bed, engrossed in the news about the Tate engagement. Nursing a Coors, Danny barely acknowledged Evan's presence. "What are you doing here?"

"I came to apologise." Evan studied Danny, waiting for a response.

After a moment, Danny winked. "I love the personal touch." Evan's irritation flared, remembering their tense first encounter. An image of his hands around Danny's throat flashed through his mind, but he forced his attention to the news. Madison Fry, clad in a figure-hugging green sequin dress, held his gaze.

"What are you watching?" Evan asked.

"Some rich kids are getting married. When did porn become acceptable?" Danny inquired, genuinely curious.

"It's always been acceptable," Evan replied, eyes still on Madison.

"No, it hasn't," Danny argued. "I wasn't born in London, and it wasn't acceptable when I was growing up."

Evan realised he'd been side-tracked. He'd come to discuss the memory stick Nikki gave him, to admit he believed Danny and thought they were in danger. But where was Bo? Scanning the room, Evan noticed the open window. "Where's Bo?"

"He's taking a bath," Danny said, but Evan had already found the empty bathroom.

"He's not." Panic gripped Evan, and the room seemed to spin. He grabbed the doorframe for support. "Where is he?" he demanded, his mind racing.

Danny remained composed, eyebrows raised. Evan closed the distance in three strides, grabbing Danny's shoulders and lifting him off the bed. The beer bottle bounced away as Evan slammed Danny against the wall. "Don't fuck me about!"

Danny's cool façade crumbled, his jaw slackening and eyes widening. Evan tightened his grip and slammed him against the wall repeatedly. "Where—" and again, "is—" and again, "he?"

"Okay, okay," Danny gasped, unaccustomed to the physical onslaught. "He's gone to arrange a meeting."

Evan knew who with before Danny said the name. Dumb bastards. When Bo got caught, they'd be arrested or shot—likely shot. Evan halted before sending a message through his chip; his body-man would intercept it and alert the guards to Bo's approach.

With the Prime Minister's residence on the building's opposite side, Evan had to move fast. He slammed Danny against the wall one last time and sprinted down the corridor. If Bo got to Reekes first or triggered an alarm, Evan would fail Nikki, and the hope of a free London would die with Bo and Danny.

In his haste, Evan barely noticed the slim, shaven-headed man in a suit approaching. Their shoulders collided, and Evan hurriedly apologised before continuing.

2

The slim man, unfazed, strode toward Danny's door. "Jimmy," he said, stopping at the entrance.

"I didn't think you'd turn up," the guard replied.

"I had additional orders. They haven't caused you any trouble?"

"None, and you just met their only visitor."

The man glanced over his shoulder. "Yes, he was in a hurry."

"Well, if you don't mind," Jimmy said, stepping away. "I need to take a leak."

"Knock yourself out." The slim man waited for Jimmy to leave before knocking on Danny's door.

"Fuck off!" Danny yelled.

Ignoring him, the man entered, silenced Walther aimed at Window. Danny's face revealed his understanding of the situation. He scrambled to his feet just as two bullets hit his chest, propelling him off the bed and into the wall with enough force to crack his neck. He slid down, leaving a crimson trail on the curtain.

With casual grace, the slim man circled the bed, eyes locked on Danny. A professional, he wouldn't make hasty judgments. Even when he saw the saviour of Free London was dead, he shot him in the face—just to be sure.

3

Against his better judgement, Oliver decided to give Jonathan another chance. He had read the transcript of the meeting with Window and met several attendees, including Antonia. All said it was futile to pursue. If he could persuade Jonathan to drop this, he could achieve the impossible, part the Red Sea, and, God willing, save Jonathan's life.

Oliver found Reekes slumped against his desk in his private residence. Collar undone, tie askew, and stinking of vodka. Oliver snatched the bottle and dropped it into the paper bin near the window. He filled and switched on the kettle before the Prime Minister stirred.

"Who's there?" Jonathan slurred, eyes unfocused.

"It's me," Oliver replied. The room felt stuffy. The fireplace roared, making it hard to tell if heat or alcohol had knocked the PM out. He opened the window.

"What are you doing?" Reekes called. "It's fucking December!" The window hissed open, and Oliver breathed the brisk air.

"You said you'd given up," Oliver said. When Jonathan didn't reply, Oliver checked if he was awake. "What? No retort?"

Reekes stared at him through yellow-stained eyes. "Come on, you lump." Oliver hoisted him back into his chair, recalling a time when Jonathan had been lighter.

He dropped him into the chair and tried to fix his collar, but Reekes slapped his hands away. Oliver stared at him. "I spoke with Antonia," he finally said.

"It'll work." Whatever dullness held his wit vanished, replaced with the madness of obsession.

"She didn't seem to share your optimism."

"It will!" Oliver tried to remember the fresh-faced Jonathan Reekes, full of genuine optimism. But now, he could only see the desperate Mr Hyde in place of the long-lost Dr Jekyll.

"You're a disgrace," Oliver said, hoping his words would penetrate Jonathan's thick hide.

"Thank you, mother," Jonathan retorted, wiping his mouth and brow.

Oliver turned his attention to the kettle's click. "I mean it, Jon." He walked over to the kettle and prepared a mug of coffee. "Sort yourself out. Go see Percy. Tell him you've changed your mind. Side with him, start the process, step down, and leave for Edinburgh with dignity."

"It's because he's not from here." Jonathan had ignored him completely—he spoke of Window. "I think he may be foreign. German, maybe French. It's as if he's purposely making requests he knows I cannot grant."

"I doubt that, Jon." He handed him a mug of coffee. "Everyone else thinks he's a lunatic."

"I will make the fucking deal. I must. I can't. I won't be used anymore."

"Drink it," Oliver said, pointing to the mug in Jonathan's hands, "or I'll have Haines' flush that shit out of you." He considered doing it anyway. Haines was still in the building. "Jon," he said, "I want you to tell Percy that you're on board."

But the Prime Minister was ignoring him, drinking his coffee.

"Even if it's delaying him." Oliver snapped his fingers in front of Jonathan's face. "Please Jon. I need more time."

"Oli," Jonathan said, "I forgive you."

"For what?"

"For leaking the helicopter story." Oliver knew he couldn't deny it, Jonathan had caught his tell before he could gloss it over. "I know you had an affair with Nadia. It made good politics. You distanced yourself, positioned well for a seat in the new regime." He set the mug down. "You should accept it."

Oliver was stunned.

"It's alright," said Jonathan. "Honestly, Oliver, I know it's my fault. I'll do what I can to help—"

"Don't!" Oliver cut in. "You're a fucking idiot if you think I'll accept this."

"TTFF," he said, and Oliver smiled. He hadn't heard Tough Titty Fish Face in a long, long time.

"What about Maggie? The kids?" Oliver asked.

"She's gone for good. Months ago, we kept up appearances to avoid scandal, but..." A tear rolled down his face.

"You can still fight," Oliver said.

"I have nothing left." And with that, Oliver knew he had nothing left to do here.

4

The hunter's patience was limitless, lying flat on the roof. He observed Reekes gesturing wildly, face reddening. He waited, motionless in the darkness, as the other man opened the window, biding his time.

He waited for the man to leave.

He stood, calculating his trajectory. In three steps, he'd reach the roof's edge; one jump, he'd land on the roof above the Prime Minister's window. One step back, and he'd descend onto the balcony. From there, he'd enter the residence. He intertwined his fingers, cracked his knuckles, inhaled, and sprinted.

The manoeuvre was flawless.

Bo crawled into the residence like a feline, sticking to the shadows cast by the fireplace. He paused when Reekes' wandering eyes glanced his way, allowing darkness to conceal him. The drunken gaze shifted, searching for the cup on the desk.

Jonathan grasped his coffee and blew into it. He didn't drink. He didn't move, the mug resting on his stomach as it gently rose and fell. Bo emerged from the shadows, inch by inch.

He reached the desk undetected and climbed onto it. Squatting in front of Reekes, Bo cleared his throat.

Reekes snorted, almost snoring, but the coffee mug slipped from his grasp, spilling onto him. "Jesus!" he cursed. He flung the mug, eyes shut, not seeing the child warrior.

Bo coughed again.

This time, the Prime Minister opened an eye, peering through his drunken haze. He blinked his second eye open and focused on Bo. He didn't look surprised or scared—just old and weary. He wondered how this drunkard could wield the power to command a country. "He wants to talk to you." Bo delivered Danny's message. "Alone."

"I can't," Reekes replied.

The answer was too quick. "You want peace?" Bo countered.

Reekes nodded. Although unspoken, Bo recognised the desire for peace in the man's eyes. "That's how you get it."

"I can't—" Bo raised a hand, silencing the Prime Minister. He had heard it: three silenced gunshots and the unmistakable sound of a victim collapsing.

With the guard outside the room, Bo assessed his options. The window was open; he could flee before they entered. But why hadn't an alarm sounded? Why had someone taken out the Prime Minister's guard? Glancing around the room, he chose his weapon.

"What?" Reekes asked, but Bo had vanished back into the shadows.

The door opened just right, neither slow nor fast. A suit—one of the PPB's security staff—entered, blond hair cropped, nothing distinguishable. "Can I help you?" Reekes asked as the man shut the door, not noticing the silenced Walther in his hand.

"Just making the rounds," Blond said.

"Sir," Reekes corrected.

Blond smirked, stepping in and raising his pistol.

Bo saw his future crumbling with the Prime Minister's death. If he escaped now, he'd return to Danny as a failure. Witnesses didn't survive long, and Reekes was the only negotiator. Gripping the vodka bottle by its neck, he smashed it against the fireplace and screamed.

Too late. Blond fired two shots into the Prime Minister's chest. Danny was right—the Prime Minister was weak. But this was meant to be a civilised society, not like home. He glanced at Jonathan's understanding face, knowing there was no difference between his world or this one.

Kill or be killed was the only true law.

Blond spun, eyes widening as Bo charged. He fired, his aim too high, the bullets hitting the shadows. A fatal error that all too many had made in the child's past. Bo slashed at Blond's gun arm, making him stumble and drop the Walther.

Bo vanished into shadow again, leaving the disoriented Blond standing in the room's centre, blood dripping from his torn forearm. He didn't whimper, earning Bo's respect.

Crouched at the side of a dark wood cabinet, he watched Blond scour the room with his eyes, slowly turning around on his feet. Then with his back toward him, Blond raised his hands and clapped once—a loud, echoing sound. Bo's heart sank as the room's dim lighting flared up around him, leaving him no place left to hide.

He sprinted, bottle ready. The broken, bloodied glass aimed for Blond's kidney, but the man turned. Surprise was no longer an option. Blond blocked the attack, punching Bo's unprotected face.

The counter threw Bo back, crashing into the cabinet. He shook his head, ignoring the throbbing pain in his jaw and back. He focused on wiping that smug grin off Blond's face.

His glass weapon lost, he chose another. He kicked a teapot at Blond's skull and charged. Blond swatted it away, realising too late he'd been distracted. Bo's foot slammed into Blond's knee, then his throat. He unleashed a relentless barrage—punches, kicks, targeting kidneys, throat, and groin. Screaming like a savage until Blond's iron grip caught his leg. He spun, flinging Bo at the fireplace.

Bo slammed against the mantle before hitting the floor, winded. He was lucky—Blond's throw had been panicked, not calculated. Otherwise, he'd have a broken back. Instead, he was allowed a couple of breaths, but he refused them. He wasn't about to allow Blond an advantage.

Bo found his bottle and was on his feet before Blond reached his pistol. He sprinted, low, bottleneck tight in hand. "Yo!" he yelled, spinning Blond around before sliding between his legs and jabbing upward. Blond's scream signalled a direct hit.

Bleeding, Blond ripped the bottleneck from his groin. "I'm going to fucking kill you!"

Unfazed, Bo held Blond's Walther, aimed. "Good fight," he said, pulling the trigger. Nothing. He tried again. Nothing. Checking the safety, he pulled back the slide.

Blond, still holding the blooded bottle, waved it toward Bo. "Peasant."

He pulled the trigger again—still nothing.

Blond charged at him, swiping the bottle at Bo's face—Bo released the pistol grip, spinning it by the trigger guard and catching it by the muzzle. His arm whipped Blond's head. BANG! Blond dropped just before the pistol connected.

"Not the boy!" Reekes shouted, causing Bo to step back from Blond's impotent swing and turn around to see Evan holding a smoking pistol...

5

Evan stood over a dead Parliament Security Officer, armed with a stolen pistol, accompanied by a child terrorist and a shot to shit Prime Minister. In times like this, there was nothing else to do but run with it. "You okay, sir?" he asked, kneeling next to the Prime Minister.

"Fine," replied Reekes, not convincing anyone.

"How about you?"

Bo looked fine, physically, just annoyed that he had just been saved more than anything. "Good," he said, fiddling with the discarded, non-functioning pistol.

The room was smashed, for lack of a better description. Bo had put up a hell of a fight against the PSO, one that could have gone either way if not for the Walther. "Not bad."

"The gun jammed." Evan knew Bo was self-sufficient, but the kid had likely counted on the pistol working. Unknown to Bo, all parliamentary weapons were coded to government officials.

"I hit the panic button," Reekes said, propping himself against the desk, his face ashen and his shirt crimson.

"That you did," Evan said. "Now sit, sir." Checking the Prime Minister's medical feed, he added, "You're in shock." He helped Jonathan sit. "I'm surprised you're talking." Catching a whiff of Reekes' breath, he continued, "The drink's probably helping."

"The building is on silent alert," said Jonathan. He was grasping at something in front of him. Presumably something he could see in his HUD, but Evan had the feeling the blood loss was more likely to blame. He was right, however: the building was on silent alert. Evan could read the same feed on his display, except the details were wrong. According to security, the London delegation had killed the Prime Minister over five minutes ago.

"It's that cretin Percy," Jonathan said.

"He's killed you?"

Jonathan nodded, his hand resting on Evan's arm. "Don't rebuke it. They don't know what's happened yet, or that you're here."

"They know I'm here," Evan countered.

Jonathan huffed. "Trust me."

Though Evan remained sceptical, no one had burst through the door yet, not even the medical team. "The medical team will be here soon."

Jonathan smiled. "It doesn't matter. Percy will delay them as long as he can. He's got Rockwood—my old friend, Harry the bastard Rockwood. I think he's got Oliver too, but he may yet surprise me." He laughed, coughing up blood.

Evan scrutinised Reekes' eyes, struggling to accept the truth. Everything had gone to hell. He knew of Percy and Rockwood, but Oliver was different. Over the last year, Evan had reported to him, respected him. "Oliver couldn't betray you."

Jonathan laughed, covering his mouth to prevent another bloody spray. "You don't know him."

Evan wanted to argue, but his peripheral feed showed security heading their way. Parliament was locking down, and guards were converging. If Reekes was right, they wouldn't hesitate to use force.

"I know. I don't understand how a prick like Percy has done it either," Reekes said.

"How many enemies do you have, sir?" Evan asked, readying to leave, pistol in hand.

"He saved my life."

"Mine too," Evan agreed. Jonathan gripped his hands. "They'll be after him, and the crazy one. Get them out of here. Back to London."

Easier said than done. They were on the sixth floor of England's most fortified public building, and an army was amassing outside. "Piece of cake," Evan murmured, though time was running out. This might be his last conversation with Jonathan Reekes. "You need to tell me about Fletcher."

"Get them back to London," Jonathan repeated. Evan thought he'd evade the question, but Reekes finally relented. "I didn't know. They were randomly selected, three test subjects meant for use outside the Kingdom. Fletcher was to be sent to China, but you changed his orders. I guess Rockwood changed his orders too. I didn't know, I couldn't..." He trailed off, lost in his guilt.

"So, what now?" Bo asked.

"We get the hell out of Dodge." Evan unlocked his pistol for free use and handed it to the kid. "Swap."

Bo scowled, offering the Walther. "It don't work."

"It will for me."

"Find Oliver; he'll help you," Reekes suggested, but Evan ignored his contradictions.

"What the hell are you waiting for?" Renner's voice invaded his head.

"We're just leaving," Evan said.

"Leave! They're on your floor."

The peripheral feed confirmed security forces were closing in. There was nothing on the floor but private quarters, a lift lobby, and a fire escape. If they left through the door, they'd face a firefight. If they stayed, they'd bottleneck the attack but have nowhere to run.

Evan nodded at Bo. "How did you get in here?"

6

Evan was second through the window. Bo was already crouched next to Danny, still lying dead on the floor. His feet rested up on the bed in an entirely comedic pose, a scene from the morning after. If the carpet wasn't flooded with his blood, Evan could have mistaken him for being comatose.

"Window is dead." Renner was watching, but Evan advised him anyway. It wasn't a surprise as much as it was a disappointment.

"Don't put the kettle on," Renner said. "I'm masking you, but they're running door to door."

Bo said his goodbyes while Evan assessed the scene. Two bullets in the chest, one close-range to the face. Coordinated attacks on both rooms. They'd intended to blame the Prime Minister's assassination on Bo and Danny, but they hadn't counted on Bo's unchipped presence. An oversight Gillespie would no doubt pay for in the morning.

Capitalising on small miracles, Evan switched to thermal vision. The guard posted outside was gone, and the corridor was empty. For how long?

"Where is everyone?" he asked Renner.

"Gathered around the PM's quarters and fanning out. You've got two at the scanners; pass them for a clear route to the elevator or stairs."

"If we hurry?"

"If you hurry."

"Bo," Evan whispered urgently. "We have to go."

The kid acknowledged him, raising his hand and asking for a minute with his index finger. His raven flapped its wings and squawked silently at Evan. He looked through the door again, but there was still no sign of movement. Time was running out. "Bo, we have to go." The kid cocked his head, rage simmering beneath his grimace.

Bo turned back to Window, placing his hand on the man's face.

"Eh... Evan..."

"What is it, Ren?"

"I've been pulled in to help security find you."

"That's good, right?" Evan thought it was perfect; Renner could misdirect them.

"Yes and no. I can't keep flipping comms. Gillespie's no fool; he'll suspect I'm speaking with you. I'll have to go silent, but I'll do what I can. I can't see the kid on the systems, so keep hold of him."

"Understood."

He checked for Bo and found him in the same place. His hand on Window's face, his head bowed as if in prayer. He gave him another five seconds before calling his name again. This time, Bo ignored him. He ran his hand down from Window's face and planted it on the wet carpet. After wiping Window's blood on his own face, Bo stood, the raven's wings casting shadows across his face, transforming him into a devilish figure.

7

Outside the Parliamentary grounds, the air was biting. Oliver walked behind Kyle, wrapped in a scarf. The alarm was silent, appearing only on staff HUDs, while the world outside was none the wiser. They walked in silence, each pondering their decisions. The last words spoken were from Kyle. "You're the boss," he'd said, not agreeing with Oliver's decision to leave.

Oliver didn't mind the silence. Quite the reverse, he needed time to compartmentalise. His decisions in the past twenty-four hours would bear a substantial weight over the coming months and years. Of that, he was certain. They were the best choices on offer. Of that, he was also certain. Whether he could live with his decisions was altogether uncertain.

They walked along the hedge-framed road, passing the give way sign that warned them of the impending intersection and then continued walking for quarter of a mile. There, in a village train station car park, Oliver had left his Maybach. When he had left it there that morning, he'd told himself it was because he needed the air. He had, after all, given himself a slight hangover from the previous evening's festivities.

But now, as he walked towards the vehicle, he wasn't sure whether he hadn't already decided to let Jonathan go when he'd driven in this morning. He beeped the alarm and the doors unlocked. Kyle climbed into the driver's seat, and Oliver settled in the back, ignoring the flashing message on his HUD.

"Am I taking you home?" Kyle asked for the second time.

"No." Oliver's house wouldn't be safe tonight. "Into town we go."

Kyle started the car and pulled out of the car park, taking the most direct route to the town centre, as indicated by his own GPS system. He didn't further the conversation, leaving Oliver to stare out the window and contemplate his unread message from Jon.

He knew it would be from Jon. He knew exactly what it would be. Jonathan may have given up, but he wouldn't miss a chance to stick it to Percy. To help Oliver, and that was where Oliver felt the most guilt. He'd allowed the circling wolves to take his friend, and that was something Jonathan would never have done to him.

In his message, Oliver would discover the means to win this thing. This thing he'd not started, but he'd manoeuvred himself away from Jonathan with the full intention of surviving. Like the old joke, the roar of a lion wakes two men camping in Africa. One man is quick to put his trainers on and the other says, 'You can't outrun a lion!'

"No, but I can outrun you," Oliver muttered, staring at his reflection in the car window.

"What's that?" asked Kyle, not taking his eyes off the road.

"Nothing," replied Oliver, blinking the command to open the video message. The vitreous image leapt from the inbox and grew until it filled Oliver's eyes, replacing his immediate surroundings with those of Jonathan's private study. A skewed angle; presumably where he'd left the Prime Minister. Doctor Haines' face was intimately close. A quick look at Jonathan's vitals revealed the bullet wounds the good Doctor worked on. Behind him, two suits were standing at the door.

Oliver's guilt twisted his guts, and he urged himself to send a message in return, but this wasn't a live broadcast. It was a recording, time-stamped forty minutes previously. Whatever the Prime Minister intended him to see had already happened.

One suit moved into the room, allowing three newcomers to enter. Another two suits, presumably Special Branch – ones Oliver failed to recognise, and the third was Percy. His foppish strut gave him away before Oliver saw his vapid expression. "Dear God!" he said. "Are you alright?" He stood on the other side of Jonathan's desk, wearing a rehearsed look of concern.

"Disappointed?" Jon asked.

"Concerned," Percy corrected. "When I heard, I feared the worst."

"That I'm still breathing?"

"What? I thank God you are."

"Christ, Percy!" Jon snapped. "Your bloody assassin is right there!" He pointed to the blonde-haired corpse on the floor.

"I don't—" Percy started.

"Don't you insult me. I've two bastard bullets in my gut!"

Percy's demeanour changed. His charade fell, discarded to the floor like a cheap coat. He waved a hand, a signal to his accompanying guards. They took out the two suits guarding the PM's door first. Hatchet Haines fell next. As Percy leaned into the desk, "Then," he said, "perhaps you should take the hint."

His guards turned their pistols on the Prime Minister, their bullets ending Jonathan's recording along with his life.

Oliver wiped the tear from his cheek as easy as he'd wiped his friend from his life. There was no time for sentiment, no time for regret or indecision. The course was set, there was nothing to do but proceed.

8

Whatever Renner was doing, it was working. With his guidance, Evan had led them down two floors with no resistance. If their luck held, they'd escape the building. Everything was going smoothly, except for Bo. The kid grew increasingly agitated with each detour, itching for confrontation.

Evan leaned against the corridor wall, waiting for Bo to catch up. They were on the Government administrative floor, near the main office where five armed individuals were searching. They needed to get past them and choose between the elevator or stairs—both monitored by CCTV. Renner's trickery masked Evan's signature and heart, making him invisible to local scanners, just like Bo. Fooling CCTV into ignoring someone was almost as hard as fooling the cybernetic eye. 'It can be done, but I'll need a couple of hours' Renner had said, so Evan's plan was to avoid both by prying open the elevator shaft and heading straight to the first floor. From there they could exit through the kitchens with minimal casualties.

He hadn't told Bo, who was wound tight and eager to fight. Evan didn't blame him, but their current situation didn't allow for it. And he wasn't sure he could stop Bo if the kid tried.

"What's the holdup?" the kid asked on cue, almost slavering with anticipation of a potential problem.

"Just checking the security systems." Evan tapped his head, hoping to quell Bo's curiosity. He searched for a route around the office, aiming to avoid the armed men. Exiting quickly and cleanly was crucial; leaving a trail of bodies would only make it harder.

"We're wasting time."

"This way." Evan nodded, moving along the wall – shoulders loose, his pistol gripped tight. The open-plan office was coming up on his right; he could see the corridor branching off toward it and he slowed. He raised a finger to his lips and passed the corridor, counting the red blips on his HUD.

"What is it?" Bo asked.

"Nothing."

"Then why are we avoiding it?"

"It's just offices and not the way we want to go."

"You're lying," Bo said.

"We don't need to engage the security forces," Evan admitted. "If we can leave unnoticed, we'll have a better chance of escaping the city. This route circles around them."

"The longer we're in the building, the higher the risk of being discovered," Bo argued.

Evan couldn't believe he was debating with a teenager. "Fighting our way through guards will only give us away."

"Then don't leave any witnesses."

"They share data, kid." Bo's nostrils flared at the word. "They're all connected," Evan continued, pointing to his eye. "If one spots us, they all do. There are five of them in that office. We can't take them all out without being noticed. It's too risky."

"This is like the boathouse," Bo said. "You're afraid to kill."

"I don't want to kill, not unless I have to, and right now we don't. We can go around." Evan pointed down the passage, but Bo kept looking towards the office. "Bo, they're just patrolling."

"They've got orders to kill me on sight, right?"

"Don't be a smartass."

"If you're not smart, you're dead. And don't think you're exempt. If you're helping me, they'll probably kill you on sight too." Bo was likely right. His raven paused, sharing Bo's expression. They seemed deep in thought before Bo spoke again. The Raven leaned toward his ear and opened its beak. "How many guards are downstairs?"

Evan checked his map. Over thirty guards were at the front entrance, with groups of ten or twelve near the other doors.

"If we take out these five," Bo's face lit up, eyes wide. "How would the other guards react? Would they come up here or stay downstairs?"

Bo's twisted logic focused on numbers. "They'd likely split," Evan conceded. If there was a confirmed sighting on an upper floor, guards would converge. "They'd have to leave some at the entrances in case we slipped through."

"Then let's take these out. We keep the death count low. Happy?"

"I'd prefer no deaths at all."

"You counted over fifty guards downstairs. I can't handle that many."

"We don't need to handle them at all."

"You said if one sees us, they all do. We should use that to our advantage."

Evan felt cornered by the ruthless kid. "I promised Nikki I'd get you home," he said, hand on Bo's shoulder.

"Then stay close." Bo winked, slipping away and heading towards the office.

Evan wanted to shout 'wait', but Bo was too far. Muttering, "Damn it," he chambered a round in his pistol and followed.

They approached the target: a door with a glass slit revealing five guards searching the office and nearby rooms. Through his thermal vision, Evan saw two chatting on a desk, oblivious. The other three inspected adjoining rooms—two together, one alone.

Evan relayed their positions. The two on the desk carried automatic Glocks, the others, Browning pistols. The pistols had range and stopping power, but they could manage. The Glocks, however, were a different story. They'd unleash a hail of bullets once the fighting started.

Bo pressed against the door, peeking through the slit. "Can they see us like you see them?"

"Unlikely." Evan guessed—they wore vision enhancer goggles, but not activated. Augmentations were expensive, and the government was... frugal. Plus, since they hadn't reacted to their presence, they probably couldn't see them.

"I'll take the automatics," Bo said, gripping the door handle.

"Wait." Evan halted Bo. "No deaths." Bo slipped through the door. Evan delayed, stopping the door latch from striking closed, held his hand in place as he readied himself. Bo could and would take out the automatics in the centre of the room. That left him with a two and a one. The two were checking the officers to the right of the door, the remaining one was checking rooms to the left.

Crouched, he eased through the door, remaining low and silent. Bo crawled under desks towards the centre. The automatic-wielders chatted inaudibly—mental conversations. Evan snuck along, stopping at the desks' gap. He rolled into the open, settling against the next row. Bo neared his targets, taking a hidden route behind them.

A faint noise caught Evan's attention: a potted plant leaf hitting an office window. One guard must have knocked it. He crept towards the room; the two red blots still inside. He needed to neutralise them there, buying precious seconds. No luck: one guard exited, standing by the door and looking his way.

Shit.

Evan sank lower, underneath the pod of desks and crawled toward his target. If they both entered the next room, things might stay clean. He searched for Bo but couldn't see him.

Time was running out.

Evan had reached the edge of the desk, the furthest point he could travel without being seen. The PSO still stood in the doorway. His second target was still in the room. Too far apart. If he took one out, then the other would have time to respond. If he saw the first go down, he reminded himself. But if he waited any longer, Bo would make his move and all hell would break loose. He shifted right for a non-lethal shot, positioning for the second guard through the partitioned wall.

Still on his knees, Evan slid his pistol up the carpet, willing every muscle to silence as he flattened prone under the desk. With the pistol firmly in his grip and rolled up on his right shoulder; he closed one eye and let his TAP guide his aim. He breathed in, checking the second heartbeat in the room. He didn't have the shots he wanted. Exhaling slow, Evan tapped the trigger guard, and came to his decision. He would wait until Bo made his move. It wouldn't be neat, but he could take the two of them out with as many shots.

Evan's arm trembled, Bo was taking too long. Supporting his elbow, he repositioned his finger before the trigger. Come on. The target neared, a metre away.

Holding his breath, Evan followed TAPs realignment. Then the boots shifted, turning around and heading back into the room to join his companion. Evan rolled from under the desk, crouched and followed him as far as the doorway. He leant against the frame, keeping track of the heartbeat.

"Shit!" a voice cried, followed by grunts and yelps.

Evan entered the room, confronting the first PSO's shock. "Sorry," Evan said, slamming his pistol against the man's head.

The soft crack of metal against skull signalled his body to drop and Evan advanced, as the second PSO raised his pistol. Evan fired, hitting the searcher's shoulder. The PSO dropped his weapon.

Evan charged, colliding with the PSO. They tumbled, shots ringing out in the main office. Evan slammed the PSO's head against the floor. The guard's knee struck Evan, tears filled his eyes, and his grip loosened.

The PSO grabbed Evan's collar, kneeing him in the stomach and hurling him onto his back. Gasping for air, Evan heard the hammer cock.

Smirking, the PSO said, "Sorry."

The gunshot pounded in Evan's ears, the PSOs throat exploding outward, showering him with blood before the body staggered away and finally dropped, revealing Bo standing behind him. "How did you get so old?"

Evan grimaced, he was clenching his teeth. Adrenaline flowing through him. Chest tight, nostrils flared and couldn't understand the remark. "What?"

"Unlock these," Bo demanded, holding up two sub-machine guns. Evan agreed, using a table for support.

Evan unlocked them while scanning his security feed, confirming Bo's plan worked. Reinforcements approached quickly. He informed Bo, regretting it when the kid spoke. "Told you," Bo said.

They sprinted, smashing doors open en route to the lift lobby. The scrolling feed showed troops closing in. Stairwells, fire escapes, and elevators swarmed with security. "Hurry," Evan urged, needing to reach the lobby before the lifts.

He collided with the elevator door, HUD flashing the blips surrounding his position; they were out of time. Slipping his hands between the smooth metal, he forced the right panel open enough to wedge his boot between the doors. Moving his body between the doors he pushed hard, his muscles screaming in acid before the doors opened.

"Move!" Evan yelled as the elevator cab neared. Bo leapt onto the cable, sliding into darkness.

Evan reached across, the sound of the approaching elevator cab buzzing all around him. His fingers touched the wire, stroked, and clasped it. Holding tight, he half pulled, half jumped to the cable. The door slid shut behind him and above him, the cab's brakes screeched. Evan was gone, sliding fast down the cable. Heat burned between his thighs, skin reddened, splitting his palms.

His feet slapped the concrete bottom of the shaft, followed by his arse a second later. He splayed out on the cold flooring, breathing hard but thankful to be doing so. Bo waited for him to recover before asking, "are you okay?"

Evan laughed, hands bloodied, legs scorched. "Good, thanks. You?"

"Good." The kid felt neither pain nor fear. "Did it work?"

Evan switched to thermal imaging to find the answer. Dozens searched the upper floors. He tapped the feed's link for more information, 'targets on fifth, administration'. And not to make it too easy, there were still plenty of guards waiting by the exits. "It worked."

"Then let's go." Bo's eagerness bordered on uncontrollable.

There were six men in the kitchen and fifteen in the foyer at the front of the house, plus another five.

Maybe.

His thermal sight couldn't quite make out the exterior of the building. "What are we waiting for?"

"I'm thinking."

"About what?"

The kid's eyes were yellow smudges, his head a blurred red in Evan's thermal sight. If he offered him the choice, they would go through the front. Fifteen people to slaughter and his ledger would still have room for more, of that Evan was sure. But if Evan argued to go through the kitchen and the six men that stood in their way. Then, when they ran outside to the wall, they would have twenty men chasing them instead of eleven. Bo may be young, Evan thought, but he was also a warrior. He was reckless, but not suicidal. Reluctantly, Evan brought the kid into the fold. "Numbers."

"Tell me."

He did. All of it. His reservations and all the information on the outside of the building. Where the aircraft were kept, how they couldn't risk stealing one. They wouldn't get as far as York's walls before getting shot down. They'd have to run into the city and find a place to recoup. He kept it as brief as he could, they didn't have time for him to cover the tourist information. When he was done, he asked, "What do you think?"

He stared at the kid's yellow smudges, unblinking hellish eyes in the darkness of the elevator shaft, and waited while Bo mulled it over. "The front of the house aims east? To the wall?"

It did not come as a surprise. "Yes."

"Then we take the fifteen. We'll have surprise on our side. If we go through the kitchen, then we still have to make our way around and we'll probably run straight into them, anyway. Better to kill them first."

"I—" He was going to fight him again, but he knew it was useless. They had to do this Bo's way or they would end up dead.

"Stop it," Bo said. "I'm not a child."

"I didn't say anything."

"You were going to."

Evan shook the remark off. "Straight run from the elevator to the door. Wait for the shooting."

"What'll you do?"

"I'll head up, get onto the mezzanine, and draw attention so you can get in the middle of them."

Bo smiled. "Plan!" he said, holding fist out for a bump. Evan reluctantly bumped.

9

The foyer resembled French Château architecture. Stairs arched down from the mezzanine, hugging walls, curving inward to face each other. Paintings of prime Ministers and royals decorated the walls. The double doors, or the main doors to the Parliament building, were three inches of iron, clad in carved mahogany. Designed and built to withstand a siege. They were, in one word, magnificent.

Evan lay flat on the ground, shuffling towards the banisters on his elbows. Below him, fifteen men and women, people he worked with, said good morning to and goodnight to. Men he'd sent Christmas emails. For some of them, he even knew their children's names. Tonight, they stood in his way. Stood in the way of values he couldn't allow to be trodden on.

He wondered if it were possible for Renner to overload their chipsets and knock them all out before the bullets started flying. It had been done before, he'd read a paper on it at some point or another. Renner would save their lives, but he would also put himself smack in the middle of Gillespie's crosshairs. His heartbeat with the rhythm of the devil's blacksmith, hammering the chains of guilt which would forever burden his soul. But there was no other option, not tonight.

He peered through the banister. Bo was waiting, as he said he would.

Six men stood by the doors, three either side, with the rest mingling in the middle. Restless and waiting for orders.

He rolled back onto his belly, extended his Walther and his recently claimed Browning, it was time to put his new and improved chipset to work. He picked his targets and fired. They dropped, two clean throat shots. He fired again, another two shots. The third bullet sank into another throat. The fourth embedded itself into the mahogany cladding. He pulled his hands from the rails and rolled clear of the responding hail of bullets.

He watched Bo dispatch the larger group with gruesome ease, rolling up close and firing kill shots into chests or maiming them with a shot to the crotch, then finishing them with a second to the face as they dropped. Clearly these were his favourite moves; tried, practised, and perfected. Bo flipped backwards and forwards, rebounding off the floor as easy as he did the walls and his attackers. He danced among the fevered group, ducking and weaving from their attacks like a psychotic ballerina.

Evan braved further vantage on the chaos. No one was firing at him, not when this demon child was amongst them. They scrambled around, looking for cover, looking for the perfect shot. They didn't get it. He knew where all of them were, knew where to draw one in close to prevent another from firing, taking both out in quick succession. He wasn't so much as killing them, but teaching them a lesson in chess.

Evan picked another off from the perimeter, alerting no one to his position. The bullet struck the guard in the heart, sucker punching him to the ground. He moved to his next target and dropped him too. Soon, the last shot was fired from Bo's pistol. His automatics already empty, slung to the ground several deaths previously. The guard clutched at his throat as his heart pumped thick red jets out from between his fingers.

Bo stopped still, listening to the man's life pour from him and for the sound of any retaliation. When there was none, he looked up, straight into Evan's eyes and smiled. Evan doubted he'd ever looked so happy and the image turned Evan's blood to ice, the devil's hammer struck the anvil.

He joined Bo at the bottom of the stairs. The kid was already searching for a way through the door, of which he could find none. "How do we get out?"

Evan put his hand against the onyx plate at the side of the double doors, allowed it read his hand. He hoped the door to open. It didn't. "Shit..."

Evan looked around the room, the two doors they'd entered through were the only ones. If they got caught in here by the force undoubtedly heading towards them... "I need a bigger gun," Bo said, searching the closest bodies.

It had happened and being cut from the security feed was the start of it. Evan was locked out: they must have identified him back upstairs. "Shit..." he repeated.

"I passed the toilets on the way from the elevator." Bo smiled, holding an assault rifle in his hands, one with an undercarriage.

"Yes."

"I was joking."

"No," Evan waved Bo's words away with his hand as he approached him—he meant yes to the choice of weapon. "The undercarriage – they designed these doors against an external attack." The grenade launcher should do nicely. "Are there any more of these?"

Bo was beaming. "Three."

"We only need one each."

"Oh," he said, deflated.

He ran the numbers in his head again. "Okay, let's give all four a go."

"Boom!" The kid's reaction was accurate if nothing else.

Evan unlocked the guns, passed them along and took a rifle in each hand. Four launchers aimed toward the door. "Aim for the centre." He smiled with Bo. "On my mark... fire!"

CHAPTER NINETEEN
HIDING OUT

Oliver spoke first. "You dumped the car?"

"Far enough away," Kyle replied, shutting the door.

The hallway showcased photos of celebrities alongside Nadia Black. She stood shoulder to shoulder with world leaders, shook hands with businessmen and embraced Oscar winners. This was her house—a haven for tonight.

"I'll put the kettle on," Oliver said, leading Kyle into the kitchen. He kicked at the Yorkshire Terrier that circled his legs. It fizzled and faded but remained persistent in bothering him as he walked the length of the room.

Damned holographic pets.

He grabbed a cup, poured a tea, and slid the china to Kyle while reaching for a glass of cognac.

On the wall screen, Nadia appeared with a clear photo of Bo, standing outside the PPB and aiming an automatic rifle at the camera. "The Assassin, 'Gunboy', has murdered approximately twenty people inside the Parliament Building. He would have killed us too, if his rifle hadn't jammed before he ran into the night," she said.

"Is that true?" asked Kyle.

"It's the news. What do you think?" Oliver replied, sipping his cognac.

Percy appeared behind Nadia, walking up to an exterior podium flanked by spotlights, "Here comes the Foreign Secretary," from around Nadia, dozens of reporters rushed to their spots in front of the podium.

"This should be good," said Oliver.

"Good morning," said Percy. "Thank you for coming at such short notice. Jonathan Reekes, our Prime Minister..." he paused, looking over all the lenses aimed at him, "has been murdered by the London delegation.

"Both terrorists have escaped into the city on foot."

Kyle pulled a chair out from under the table and sat with Oliver. Percy continued. "For public safety, martial law has been authorised with immediate effect. Thank you. That is all I have to say at the moment." Percy turned and stepped away from the podium amongst a torrent of camera flashes and questions.

"That was poetic," Kyle said.

"He's always had a way with words," agreed Oliver.

He then mouthed the words in sync with Nadia. "Will there be a retaliation?" she asked.

Percy hesitated. "An emergency cabinet meeting is gathering as I speak." He took the bait, opening himself up for an onslaught.

"Is this an act of war?" A reporter asked, followed by a barrage of questions. Percy's shoulders slumped, his face revealing confusion. Oliver felt his facial muscles tense, resisting the urge to grin.

"Thank you," Percy said. "That is all." The camera refocused on Nadia. Oliver tapped the table, muting the screen.

"What's going on?" Kyle asked, forcing Oliver to consider and to realise that it wasn't just a smile that he wasn't quite ready to do.

He wasn't ready to speak the truth.

"Percy just made a buffoon of himself," Oliver said, watching Nadia's silent image.

"What's going on with you?" Kyle pressed.

He considered telling him that Jonathan Reekes was a hero over anything he'd ever done. That act alone had elevated the Prime Minister from drunkard to a pedestal, while dropping Oliver to the dung heap. Their colours revealed. Jon had met his fate with defiance, while Oliver received a thick strip up his back, as bright and yellow as the sun. "We need to destabilise any standing that little shit has on claiming the party."

"You're dodging the question."

He eyed Kyle. "Maybe it's because I don't understand your question?"

"Tell me what went on tonight. What happened with Jonathan? What do you know about it? Why you're not concerned about someone kicking the fucking door down?"

Oliver glanced at the front of the house through the kitchen door. He was right. He had earned his answers. "What Percy said is only half-truth. Jonathan was murdered, but not by the kid. It was Percy who gave the order and Jonathan..." Oliver stopped, remembering his hero, "was expecting it."

"He sent me his own snuff file," he continued. "I'm not saying it's the reason I'm confident no one is looking for us. In all honesty, I'm not sure they know it exists. They'll probably suspect something...

"And in answer to your last question, Renner activated our Level Four Protocols." They were concealed from the normal searches: level four was intended for hostile invasion, ensuring government official could escape. To all intents and purposes, they were invisible.

There was a point within the growing silence when Oliver considered whether he'd muted the kitchen and the wall. It was almost ten seconds since his confession when Kyle next spoke. "I'm going to check the house."

Oliver shook his head. He hadn't expected a hug or a pat on the back.

"You'll be wanting to back that file up," added Kyle, standing.

"Yes," Oliver agreed. Yes, he would.

2

At four in the morning, Nadia wearily inserted her key into the front door, not noticing the shadow inside. She received a weapon pointed at her face as a reward. "Jesus, Kyle!" she exclaimed, sidestepping him.

"Sorry," he said, scanning the road behind her before closing the door.

"Where is he?" she asked, hanging her bag on the banister.

"Kitchen."

Nadia nodded and walked down the dark hall. Opening the door, she found Oliver at the kitchen table, surrounded by a nearly empty bottle of cognac, a glass, and two mugs. "Made yourself at home, then?" she remarked with a hint of jest.

Oliver stood, disarming her with a smile. "I didn't have time to shower."

She surprised herself when she slapped him, standing there in silence, watching his cheek redden.

"I'm sure I deserved that?" he said.

"I was outside when Gunboy blew the door open, narrowly missing me. Then the kid nearly shot me. And Special Branch confiscated the fucking footage." Oliver knew the loss of her scoop hurt the most. "What the hell is happening? Why did you send me into that mess?"

"Nad..." he said, settling his hands on her hips as he did when he wanted to dance. "We're in a bit of a bind."

"A bit..." she couldn't believe his words. "...Of a bind? Are you crazy?"

His hands found her neck and cheeks. "I'm sorry." Damn him. His finger traced the contour of her lips. "But I need you." He curled his hand beneath her chin and brought his lips to hers. It had been too long since they'd shared any intimacy, and she welcomed it as the knowledge she was safe in his arms.

"Jesus, Nad," he said, feeling her second slap.

"The kid is Bo, the one we brought from London," said Kyle.

"Was he alone?" Kyle asked.

"No. He was with someone, a guy."

"Can you show me?"

"No—aren't you listening?" she said. "Special Branch confiscated the footage, took the data from my chip and Clive's. All we got was the kid's photo they issued to the press." She glared at Oliver. "It was my scoop," she said, noticing the absence of a special little Terrier. "Where's Tikka?"

"I'll put the kettle on," Kyle offered.

"I'll have a scotch," she said, staring at Oliver.

"I switched her off," Oliver admitted. "She's annoying."

"You know she doesn't like that."

"She's a hologram."

"Ice in the scotch?" interrupted Kyle, holding the bottle and a glass.

"Two fingers scotch, one finger water," Oliver replied.

"At least you get that right," Nadia said, slipping off her shoes. "I take it you're both staying the night? Sorry, morning?" The night was almost over.

"If you don't mind," Oliver said.

She wondered what he'd say if she declined. "It's rude to leave a woman in the middle of the night."

"Thanks," Oliver said, reaching for his empty glass.

"Well, you both seem remarkably calm," Nadia remarked, "considering."

"I have some leverage," Oliver offered.

"Is it about that kid?" she asked, accepting the glass of scotch from Kyle.

"Maybe."

"Shot at, remember?" she sipped her drink.

"I have Percy executing Jonathan."

"Shut the front door."

"Seriously," Oliver added, sipping his empty glass. "Kyle, would you mind?"

"Well, I just thought of a way you can make tonight up to me," she said.

"I'm sure you have, but..."

She grabbed Kyle's arm as he reached for Oliver's glass. "Kyle, you shouldn't do everything he asks of you."

"I don't like being idle," he replied. "And I don't have the stomach for politics."

"Few do," she agreed. "But I think Oli needs to remember to do things himself once in a while."

"I've missed you," said Oliver.

"Yet you find it easy to stay away," Nadia retorted through an insincere smile. "You're giving me an exclusive on the footage. Don't think you're leaving here before that." She knew he wouldn't. He'd pretend it would make sense to leave a copy behind should the worst happen. "How deep does this go?" she asked, before he started lying.

He was warning her. "That's sweet, but I'm a big girl."

"The guy," Kyle asked, "with the kid?"

"Yes?"

"Was he a scruffy, wired-looking man in his thirties?"

"No," she replied. "He was younger, twenties maybe? Wearing those awful jogging suits you all have."

"Evan?" suggested Kyle.

"What does it matter?" Oliver asked.

"If they're together, then maybe—" Kyle started.

"They're not worth the risk," Oliver cut him dead.

"There are only three of us." Nadia had also been counting.

Oliver raised his hand. "I understand where you're both coming from. Evan, I agree, could be of some use. Possibly. But the boy is a cooked hand grenade. You've branded him as what? Gunboy? The London Assassin? We can't associate with him now."

"I can retract it," Nadia lied. "Tell the people the truth, maybe?"

Oliver's face flushed crimson. "Are you schooling me?"

"I'm offering a suggestion," she said.

Oliver stared at her with fierce, round eyes. "No," he said. "Any move we make will increase our chances of being found." He looked at Kyle. "We can't afford that. We can't reach out to anyone. Not our friends, not Renner, not Evan, and certainly not Gunboy."

She'd seen him concerned before, seen him angry, but this was new. She'd never seen him scared before. Yet she was always impressed by how he kept his composure. Oliver's hands never trembled, and neither did his words. "We're on our own."

CHAPTER TWENTY
A Bridge Too Far

They'd been running for hours, pursued by dogs, men, and searchlights, scanning the ground from the clouds above. He'd led them into the city, hoping to shake off their pursuers in the alleys, streets, and non-land-mined Underground. They avoided major roads and cameras, aiming for residential areas with no surveillance. Be smart, don't be dead. Steer clear of commercial zones.

Currently, they hid in an alley behind a Chinese restaurant, the evening's cooking stench wafting from black garbage bags. Bo watched the street while Evan slumped against a dumpster. "Come on, Renner. Get back in the game," he said, talking to himself, exhausted and longing for his bed.

As Evan couldn't reproduce the sound of a wood pigeon, Bo whistled the sharp, short signal they'd agreed upon: one for trouble, two for clear. He hesitated, his pistol at the ready as he waited for the response. When it came, he relaxed long enough for his body to realise it was time to move. They were nearly at the park—an unlit field of trees with no CCTV—where they could recuperate.

He joined Bo on the opposite corner, eyeing the next stage of their escape: a recently cleaned street, well-lit by harsh white LEDs, illuminating the roads and pavements, acting as protectors from the night. The bus stop was a little distance away, but the advertising panel was unmissable. They'd seen more than a few during their dash through the city, not just on bus stops. Shop windows, taxis, buses, junction screens above the road, and likely on every household screen in York—all shared the same image.

It had taken Evan by surprise—God knows what it had done to Bo. He didn't look happy, but he didn't look angry either. The kid's first taste of the modern media machine pitted against him. Some of his animated pictures cascaded down the sides of buildings, for Christ's sake, all of them the same angry, confused image. Bo, the child warrior, Gunboy.

Aiming his rifle at anyone who looked at the image, his face distorted, painted with blood and smothered by a raven's wings. All contained the same repeated message: 'Gunboy. Armed and extremely dangerous. Stay at home. Call this number.' Introduced to the world as a brand image, he'd be a household name by breakfast: the boy who killed a nation.

Evan caught Bo staring at his own image. In any other circumstance, a thirteen-year-old becoming a celebrity would call for celebration, but not for Bo, and Evan didn't know how to comfort him. "We'll be out of the city by sunrise." They had to be, because when the city woke, Bo would have millions of unwitting chipsets searching for him as York's commuter population went to work. MI5 would use everyone and anyone to find him without their knowledge or consent. Both of them, Evan mentally corrected himself.

Percy must know he was involved, too. Bo's face plastered everywhere for all to see, striking fear into the city: Watch out, the bogeyman is about! He could only guess, but it was probable he was left out of the media, as they already had enough scandal without bringing in inside help. Percy would want to avoid an investigation as much as Bo was avoiding conversation.

"How much ammo do you have?" Evan asked.

"Full mag on the pistol, ten left in the SMG," said Bo, not needing to check.

Evan carried a little more: a rifle with an undercarriage slung across his back, one grenade, and a handful of rounds. His pistol was half-full.

"After the park, we'll cross the bridge — we'll take the engineer's platform under the main road."

"What's the plan?"

"After the road?"

"No, the plan. The big plan."

Evan scratched the tip of his nose. "I'm taking you home. You know that."

"You said that," Bo said, sounding tired and flippant. "So, what's the fucking plan?"

"I'm not sure what you're looking for, Bo, but that's it. I'm taking you home."

Evan didn't know what the kid wanted from him. They'd already discussed their immediate plan: get out of the commercial zone, steal a car, and leave the city. Evan hadn't considered how he'd return, if that was even possible. Would he ever see his family again? His course of action was to get to London, where he'd likely stay until Percy brought war upon them.

Percy would. That's what Jonathan Reekes had wanted to avoid at all costs and what Percy wanted to push forward. Cull London's population, retake control of the land, make it profitable for the country. Eliminate black markets and illegal offshore interests.

He was taking Bo home to Nikki, but there wouldn't be a home. Of course, Percy would need public support first, but he'd have it in spades after Reekes' supposed assassination. It could take months, maybe a year, but it would happen. Tanks, walkers, drones, and mechs for good measure. Be damned all who stands in our way. This here is our land.

"We have to get out of the city," he repeated, hoping that would suffice.

"What about the guys who killed Danny?"

Evan faced the cold killer, and revenge was all this killer demanded. "Bo, we can't go back."

Bo chambered a bullet in his SMG.

"They have too many men, too many guns. By now, they'll have tactical squads, artillery, and combat droids swarming the estate. We'd need an army, or a great fucking bomb." Evan spread his palms to emphasise his statement, but Bo remained unimpressed and muttered something under his breath. "Come again?"

Contempt burned in the boy's eyes. "Coward."

Evan had heard it the first time, of course. Well, he'd read it. It was too low for his ears, so his chipset had processed the word and displayed it on his HUD. He'd never been called a coward before, but he'd felt like one. He'd felt like one not long ago, on his knees in a shantytown, bullets raining down on him. But he'd never believed he was one. "Do you know what they'll have waiting for us?"

"Nothing I can't cut through."

"You haven't the faintest idea. They'll have X4's patrolling the perimeter. Portable pill-boxes bolted into the ground. One hundred and fifty soldiers from the military base on patrol. Not because they expect you to come back, but to make everyone think you're a threat. In reality, if you go, you'll be a smudge on the tarmac in seconds."

"I should have been rescued by Fallout." Bo's remark cut him worse than the first.

"He'd tell you the same thing. We can't get back into that building."

"You can't, maybe."

Evan watched as Bo's raven arched its neck, staring at him with the same mocking expression. "Neither can you."

Evan reached for Bo's arm, but the boy snaked away from his grasp. It was a mistake, and Evan didn't see it coming. The jab struck his kidney, and in that shattering surge of pain, he thought it had exploded. He placed one hand on the ground to balance himself, the other to hold his gut while Bo bolted.

The kid ran back the way they'd come, towards the search pattern that was in full force, looking for them. Evan mouthed the word, "Stop!" but he had no breath to speak. He put his efforts into standing next, which worked out a little better. Aside from a little stagger, he was on his feet. He took a lungful through his nose and began running after Bo. He worked off the partial stitch across his gullet before putting in the speed.

He ran hard, but even with all the money spent on his muscles and cardio, it wasn't enough. Bo was making ground with each step. "Wait!" he called, but

Bo raced out into the street, crossing it without checking. Evan couldn't help but think how stupid it was, how in four hours, he would have been hit by commuter traffic.

Evan scanned the road as he left the alley. He didn't slow; he had to keep up. He dashed across the road and into the next alley, skipping over the bin lids in his way. Ahead of him, Bo ran to his left and kicked off the wall, careening across the alley to the opposite wall just to kick off that one as well. He repeated the process from right to left, and right to left. Each time he moved forward and up, up until he sailed over the top of the right-hand side wall.

"You got to be kidding me," Evan blurted into the night. There was no way he was going to do that. He clambered over the wall, his trainers scratching the stone and concrete until he toppled over to the other side. Panting, he looked across the back garden only to see Bo dropping from the top of the next wall and into the next yard. He rolled his eyes and continued his pursuit.

Bo slowed enough to taunt him, but never enough for Evan to reach him. He wanted Evan to follow, leading them back to the PPB. Perhaps Bo knew he couldn't do it himself or convince Evan to join him. But he knew Evan would keep his word to Nikki. The kid might not favour Evan's prowess in combat, but he trusted his loyalty. He'd come back for him when no one else would.

They travelled along the same route back, albeit more on Bo's terms than Evan's. They were definitely on track to the PPB. Bo didn't know the city layout, meaning he would take the exact route they'd used previously. He might have been faster, more dextrous than Evan, but the older man had the advantage now. He knew the city. So when Bo turned left, Evan continued straight ahead. Bo's path would intersect with the boy's and would take him longer to get there. Evan had a straight run. It was out in the open, but it was the only way he could see him catching Bo before reaching his destination.

He sprinted through the streets, cursing the cameras. As he passed an empty bus stop, Bo's face distracted him from the black SUV parked at the end of the street. He turned right, descending the stairs and leaping four, five steps at a time before reaching the bottom.

He glanced upward, momentarily forgetting he couldn't see Bo's heartbeat. Following the department store's windows, he felt the acid in his muscles burn and his breath tighten. His HUD responded, flooding his mouth with the metallic taste of adrenaline.

Bo shot out of the alley ahead. "Jesus!"

It hadn't worked.

The kid was too fast.

Evan gave chase again, knowing they'd likely encounter the search patrol soon. Headlights ahead confirmed his prediction. He needed more time.

Bo skidded to a halt, disorienting Evan for a second. Unable to see what Bo saw, he watched the kid aim his pistol and fire at the approaching SUV. Bullets ricocheted off the black armour and bulletproof glass. The grille snarled as it raced towards them.

Evan slid into Bo, grabbing his arm and yanking him out of the way. "This way!" He tapped Bo's shoulder, steering them off the main road and onto a side street.

A second SUV skidded around the corner, stopping just in time for Evan to slam into its grille. He spun against the front before continuing to run, while Bo vaulted the bonnet and joined him. "There!"

Evan pointed toward the shopping arcade, knowing their pursuers would have to follow on foot.

The first SUV stopped, bumper to bumper with its companion. Violently, the roof panel retracted, revealing four open-top cylinders that pointed skyward. In unison, they popped, prompting Evan to glance back, expecting a cannon. But he saw something far worse.

Combat drones popped from four cylinders and took flight. Silver footballs encased in flat disk weapons platforms; they were known as the Saturn. The disc whirred clockwise around the ball, producing a distinct screaming noise that gave them their unofficial name, the Screaming Saturn, which still haunted survivors of the '30 Paris riots.

Evan recognised them instantly. "Don't stop!" he yelled over the approaching turbines, "Not for anything." They entered the arcade, running on cobbled stones between glass storefronts. Four Saturns. Why couldn't there have been only two? Don't be a wuss, you coward.

The first drone entered the arcade, maintaining a distance behind them. Evan spotted its reflection in the glass signage above and realised they had no cover. They needed to run another twenty meters before reaching the next street. Unless...

"Left!" he yelled, aimed his pistol, and fired into the plate glass of a shop front. The window shattered into a spiderweb of cracked glass. He fired again, causing the window to crash downward, littering the arcade with shards as the shop alarm blared. As if anticipating their escape, the drone opened fire, tracers streaked past, tearing up the ground and hurling broken glass into the air, blocking their exit.

The Saturn pursued them relentlessly, matching their pace but never exceeding it. "What's it waiting for?" Bo asked.

"Shit!" Evan realised. The drone had cut them off from turning into the shop while continuing the chase.

This one drone, one of four, was herding them.

Nearing the exit to the next street, Evan shouted, "Watch your sky!" He fired aimlessly at the drone behind them, knowing his bullets would likely be ineffective but hoping to distract it.

Bo burst from the arcade, sliding under the waiting drones while emptying his SMG's ammunition. Evan followed, crushing a discarded glass vial underfoot and barrelling through the first man he encountered.

He eyed the man's nondescript black suit, the kind you don't want to see when the government is after you. Yet something didn't fit. The SUVs were plausible, but the Saturns?

No time to ponder.

Following Bo, Evan recognised the street. "Turn right!" he instructed, but Bo had already veered left towards the bridge.

Evan glanced up and behind. The drones had vanished, save for the one on their tail. It was too quick for his amateur aim, but it had a weakness: high winds. He grabbed his rifle, dropped to his knees, and slid forward. Rolling, he steadied himself and aimed at the approaching Saturn.

His finger hovered over the trigger, doubt creeping in. The once-solid plan now seemed insane. The drone wasn't a cheap online buy; it was military-grade, armoured, and racing towards him.

He fired.

The grenade launched, arcing over the Saturn, and exploded behind it. The drone wobbled mid-air but stayed on course. The blast propelled it forward, its disc angled down to slow its approach, but not enough. Evan had time to stand, grip the stock, countdown, and swing the rifle like a bat.

The impact sent the drone careening into a storefront, shattering glass and triggering another alarm. His rifle clattered to the ground, broken. Evan's arms shot up in triumph, grinning at his improbable success. He shook his head and resumed his pursuit of Bo.

The suspension bridge's tall masts loomed ahead. Evan's HUD displayed three options: left to the park, useless with Saturns on their tail; right towards the city centre; or straight ahead to the bridge, which was once an escape plan but now promised death.

Evan raced down the road, urging Bo to turn right into the awakening city. If they could find a hiding spot and survive until tomorrow night... Bo glanced back, then veered right away from the bridge. "Come on, you beauty," Evan whispered to himself, following Bo into the city's depths.

Bo's turn was taking him to the dead centre of the turn off and into the path of the first missing drone. He saw it, ducked under it... It spun on its axis and have chase. Following as Bo closed on the front of a department store.

Evan fumbled for his pistol, too far away for any other options. He aimed and watched as Bo sprinted towards the glass-fronted shop, using it to launch a backflip over the drone. The kid grabbed the spinning disc, and his weight, combined with gravity, fought the drone's engines until inertia sent it crashing into the pavement.

Bo rolled away from the sparking wreckage and rested, letting Evan catch up. "Did you see that?" Bo asked, revelling in his victory.

Evan grinned, catching his breath and checking his HUD. "That's two down," he said, both of them smiling. "Two more to go, and the SUV is close." Evan clapped. "Let's hustle."

"Bluebird," Bo said as he stood. "You know I didn't... you're alright."

Evan found it endearing. "Don't worry about it, little britches."

"Little britches?"

"Jungle—never mind. We need to go."

"Which way?"

Evan hesitated. "The bridge might not be the best idea anymore."

"Standing in the street is?"

"Come on," Evan said, nudging Bo as they started towards the city centre. "There's a car park a few streets over." With luck, they'd find a couple of cars left overnight.

As they rounded a corner, Evan's HUD blipped with an approaching SUV, its headlights flooding the street. Above it, he spotted the metallic glint of another drone, likely targeting them. There wasn't enough cover to close the distance safely; they'd be shot before they could inflict any damage.

"The bridge," Bo suggested, eyeing the patient headlights.

"If they have support on the other side, we'll be cut off," Evan countered. "I think they're herding us towards it."

Bo scanned the area, then the bridge. "Whatever happens, it ends on the bridge."

Evan marvelled at Bo's resolve. "If it gets too hairy, jump into the river."

Bo grimaced. "Seriously?"

"It's not like the Thames."

The SUV revved its engine. "They're impatient," Bo observed.

"They're wondering what we're doing," Evan said, scanning for the remaining drone and SUV. "I don't think they have much support. They'd have cut us off from all angles by now. They want us on the bridge before they make their move."

Bo heard the drone's engine first. "You're wrong." He pointed towards the Saturn and sprinted for the bridge. Evan saw a glass vial shatter on the pavement just past where Bo had stood, then felt a sting in his neck. He ran, yanking the needle out as he went.

Evan's chip indicated the toxin was diluting on the left side of his display; it wouldn't affect him. They wanted him alive and underestimated his augmentation. They didn't know he had blood cleaners. These captors definitely weren't Gillespie's men; otherwise, they would have used a different tactic and toxin.

They reached the bridge surprisingly easily, but crossing the River Ouse changed everything. Evan heard the Saturn drones screaming in stereo, pursuing him, while the SUV's engines and tyres screeched as it turned onto the bridge.

Darts shattered between Evan and Bo, unnoticed by Bo. More followed, getting closer to him. Evan zigzagged, taking a dart in his back. His HUD neutralised the toxin, but Bo wouldn't have that luxury—then it dawned on Evan.

They weren't after him.

A massive sound loomed overhead, drowning out everything else, followed by a spotlight that blanketed the bridge and blinded Evan. He blinked, reducing the glare instantly. Bo shielded his eyes, but didn't slow down.

The VTOL tracked them from above, and Evan knew he couldn't protect Bo from the drones much longer. The VTOL and SUV likely carried similar ammunition. They were out of options. "Jump!" he shouted.

The call was futile. They ran beneath four engines generating over 160 decibels and Bo was too far ahead. He was at full sprint and distancing himself every second. Evan checked his six, overlaying his HUD to lock on the drones if he didn't see them in his snapshot glance. He needn't have bothered.

A Saturn curled beneath him, its stabilising ring cutting into his leg before shooting upward. It struck him in the soft area around his bruised kidney, and the thrusters engaged. As Evan's breath left him, the drone lifted him off the ground. His fingers scrambled for a grip on the orb, but it slipped through his sweaty palms.

The ring burned across Evan's stomach after cutting through his hoodie. He wanted to scream again, to shout 'jump,' but the VTOL's engines drowned him out, and he had no breath. The drone carried him away, leaving Bo alone. The iron railing clipped his heel, and the Saturn took him over the edge of the bridge.

Over the water, the drone's engine buckled, sputtering beneath him. They dropped, Evan's stomach lurching upward, clawing at his throat, before the engine flared again. They hung in the air for a second, the drop to the Ouse looming. Evan wanted to smash the machine, but it was pointless. Whoever 'they' were, they'd won, and he'd broken his promise. The Saturn's engine failed once more, and they fell.

2

On the bridge, the moment he fell from sight, Bo glanced around. Evan was nowhere to be seen. He was, as he had somehow always expected to be, alone. Without hesitation or contemplation, he continued. Damn them all, he thought, and ran.

The VTOL accelerated, flying overhead before banking and lowering its nose to the left of the bridge. As it descended, the side door opened, and three riflemen hooked themselves onto the safety rail. Three laser dots appeared on Bo's chest as he sprinted towards them.

He aimed his pistol at the middle gunman and kept running. When he fired, a needle struck him in the back of the neck. He watched his target falter and fall forward, a comrade grabbing him and holding tight. The VTOL veered to the right.

No, it didn't. The bridge did. Or so Bo thought. He found himself on the ground, face pressed against the tarmac. He didn't feel pain or fear; his breathing slowed, and all he wanted to do was curl up and sleep on the surprisingly warm and comfortable surface.

He closed his eyes, oblivious to the woman's voice. "Call it in," she said.

CHAPTER TWENTY-ONE
THE MORNING AFTER THE NIGHT BEFORE

Kyle poured fresh coffee into two mugs as she entered the kitchen. He must have heard me moving around upstairs, she thought.

"Cuppa?" he asked in his perfectly sexy voice from his perfectly formed mouth. If only she'd met him first...

"What time?" Oliver spoke on the phone.

"I should keep you around," she said, half meaning it.

Kyle smiled. "Did you sleep well?"

She stifled a laugh, not considering half an hour as actual sleep. "As well as." Nadia noticed again how perfect Kyle looked, his eyes bright and alert, his skin rich with colour. She was jealous. "Tell me your secret," she said.

"Huh?"

"You haven't slept a wink all night, and you look ready for the catwalk."

"I don't need to sleep." He smiled again. "Perks of the job." As if it would answer all her follow-up questions.

"Okay, I'll be ready." Oliver's conversation continued at the kitchen table. When she glanced over at him, she noticed Kyle watching her. Not in the way she had hoped. It was then she noticed he stood between them; was that on purpose? He wasn't obstructing her route, but he turned his shoulder into her path, slightly facing her. Was he protecting Oliver? And if so, was she a threat?

Oliver disconnected the call, his hand flattened against the kitchen table, copying and uploading the conversation to his server. "Don't forget my exclusive," Nadia said under her breath, knowing Kyle had heard her.

He didn't look so cute at that moment. She hadn't thought he was anything like Oliver, and oh, how Oliver loved his paranoid games. She allowed it, of course, not because Kyle would enforce it, but because she didn't expect any of them to make it to brunch alive. So she played along. "Who was that?"

Oliver didn't turn around immediately, even though she knew he had heard her that time. He often delayed his responses for dramatic effect or to control the conversation. She watched him lift his palm from the table and stand. "The Anti-Christ," he said, and she grinned inwardly at his dramatic effect.

He took his coffee from Kyle and blew on the surface. "We have to get ready," he said to Kyle. "There's a car on the way." He drank from his mug.

"Where to?" asked Kyle. She knew Oliver wouldn't say, he wouldn't want her to know. No matter how much she wanted to know. He would guard the information, telling her it was for her own protection.

That knowing too much would put her in greater harm's way.

What a steaming pile of shit that would be to hear, so she wouldn't ask. The truth was he didn't trust her. She was a reporter, and he would use her to report what he wanted reported just as he had last night, but he would never confide in her. It wasn't personal towards her, either. He'd never trusted anyone, except maybe Kyle.

So when he said, "I'll fill you in on the way," she didn't look surprised or upset. She didn't question. She'd remember the times he'd done the same and said the contrary and knew this would be the last time she'd think of him as a lover.

He was just a great man, but obsessed with winning. She wouldn't show her momentary weakness, for he didn't deserve it. She would simply let go. She would not let his paranoid games take their toll on her any longer.

They made small talk in the twenty minutes they waited for the car to arrive. She walked them to the door and kissed him on the cheek before they opened it. He would need that, she thought. He'd need it when he met with the Anti-Christ, when he needed to remind himself that he was still a good man.

She didn't stand in the open doorway, as there might be cameras out there looking for a glimpse of her. She told herself this as she stood behind the door and said her goodbye. But in the mirror next to the door, the tears welling in her eyes revealed the truth. When she closed the door, she closed it for good.

2

It was ten minutes past six when Renner found him. He nearly missed him too; that's what all-nighters do to a person. Kills their attention. But his previous incarnation, the alert version of Renner that made the adjustments to Evan's chipset, made it impossible for this exhausted version of Renner to mess it up.

Antonia had fallen asleep on Renner's living room couch a couple of hours earlier. In excitement, he yelped and called, but when she didn't respond, he did the only thing he could. He threw an empty can of BullPhett at her head. It was her turn to yelp, but not from excitement. "What the hell, Joe?" she said, sitting up.

"I've got Evan."

"You threw a can at me?"

"I didn't have anything else."

"You could have walked over to the couch."

"Yeah... sorry 'bout that." The thought hadn't crossed his mind. "If you're making a cuppa, I'll have a coffee."

"Where is he?" she asked. No coffee then...

"Bank of the Ouse." He had found both Evan and Bo on the city cameras hours earlier. They were running through the streets, pursued by SUVs and a swarm of drones. He had watched Bo being taken in an unmarked VTOL but lost Evan when he had dived into the river. He had checked the embankments up and down twice, and now, thankfully, Evan had washed up on the mud a couple of miles downriver.

Being the man who had set up Evan's firmware, it took him little time to hack the man's system. He then provided Evan with a gentle electrical jolt that bolted him upright. "Sorry for the slap, buddy, but we've wasted all the time we had looking for you."

Evan's own view floated on Renner's left while an image from the reconfigured CCTV camera feed, watching him from across the road, floated on the right. "Where am I?" he asked, looking around the riverbank.

"About three clicks from where you fell."

"I jumped."

"And I was going to give you a seven." Renner grinned. "Listen. I need you back in play. You ready for a pickup?"

"Good to go."

"I'm sending some trusted peeps to you, and by trusted, I mean me. Don't move from your location. I've scrubbed you from every system known to man. It was hard enough finding you before; now it will be next to impossible."

"Say again?"

Renner brought him up to speed on the information he had gathered while searching for Evan; how Gillespie had supplied a fake recording of Bo, now the assassin at large, murdering the Prime Minister. Evan, his plucky sidekick helping him escape the Parliament Building, was being kept in-house. But as Evan had guessed, it hadn't stopped them from looking for him. Renner continued to explain he had removed Evan from every database in the world. "No facial recognition system in the world will know it's you."

"Is Kyle with you?"

"No," said Renner. "There have been some... developments."

"Commander," Antonia cut him off. "This is Antonia Fairchild."

"Ma'am."

"So far, we've only found you," she continued. "We'll debrief you fully once you come in; the channel is encrypted, but I don't want this conversation continuing over the net. I trust you understand?"

"I understand," Evan concurred. "One more thing?"

Antonia looked at Renner, her eyebrow lifting in the way she did when she wanted his approval on something. He couldn't see any problem with them continuing the conversation to its conclusion; after all, it was his encryption algorithm. He nodded in the affirmative.

"Go ahead," she said.

"Do you know where the kid is?"

Now it was Renner's turn to look at Antonia for approval. She made him wait a moment, considering before complying. "We lost him in the back of an SUV."

"They were contractors."

"Are you sure?" Antonia asked, but Renner had already guessed.

"Public Service doesn't pay for the tech they were carrying, ma'am."

CHAPTER TWENTY-TWO
Mount Olympus

When the driver closed the door, Oliver had been awake for forty-seven hours. His chip advised the best remedy was actual sleep, but with no opportunity, he ordered another caffeine booster. That, along with the real coffee he had just drunk, would keep him going for another couple of hours.

Most of the cognac had left his system; any trace amounts lingering would be gone by the time they landed. He had to be at the top of his game, and he knew he wasn't anywhere near it. All he had was a pair of twos and maybe an ace with Jonathan's recording. He was going up against Fray with nothing but vanity and wit.

The limo lifted within seconds of the driver seating himself. Oliver watched Nadia's home grow smaller as they rose into the clouds, and for a moment, he was glad she would be safer without him.

Once the limo reached the required altitude, Oliver felt the g-force push him into his seat as it sped up along its route. It was as quiet as it was peaceful in the sky. If he didn't know better, he'd allow himself to fantasise everything was as it should be, and that when he got to work, Jonathan would be there to abuse him.

He didn't explain things in the car as he said he would, nor did he send a silent, secret message to Kyle informing him of the plan or their destination. He suspected they were being monitored, as he knew Kyle also suspected. He proved this by not asking for the information. Still, he could have been sulking.

After ten minutes, the limo banked to the left. Oliver instinctively checked out of the window and was rewarded by the sight of the colossal steel and glass cigar that was the home of Fray International Headquarters. He had seen it before, as it was always visible from the PPB's third building. It stood tall enough to be seen from much of York on a clear day, like today.

He recalled the promo films, running on most channels during its seven-year construction. A building large enough to be considered a city—an exaggeration, but not far off. The skyscraper was self-sufficient and housed all its employees, as well as its more elaborate expenses, such as its rainforest.

And why not? The Fray family had made its fortune in Britain. HAND was their brainchild; the Honour Thy Enemy FPS series was also theirs. From those platforms, they had secured a legacy lasting thirty years. Why couldn't they show off a little?

Arrogant arseholes, Oliver conceded.

Francis, Felix's father, had made it his business to predict the future and made it extremely lucrative. His company was based in York but had offices in both Dubai and Nevada. They had to move to Nevada after the Californian construction was destroyed in the quake of '24. Digital communication and fantasy were the tools with which he had made his fortune. Only in later years, when the world grew jealous of his triumphs, did he turn his head toward weapons and munitions.

Felix senior dined with Rockefeller and sat in on the Bilderberg meetings. He was one of the world's most revered and feared men, and Oliver was about to explain to his son why he didn't follow the plan. Oliver, who was nothing more than an ant compared to the political power that was the Fray family. This was the closest Oliver had ever felt to making a terrible decision.

The limo touched down on one of the many petal-shaped landing pads midway up the cigar, and soon after, Oliver's door opened. "This way, please," the driver said, standing outside. Oliver stepped out, feeling the cold fresh air slap his unshielded face.

"How far up are we?" he asked the driver while Kyle joined him on the platform.

"You don't want to be jumping off," the driver pointed toward a railed gangway. "Follow that to the main reception."

"Thank you."

The driver paused, perhaps unfamiliar with the polite comment. "Any time, sir."

Oliver pulled his jacket closed tight around his neck. The wind was bracing and fast. They moved swiftly along the connecting platform to the circular portal in the cigar's side.

He glanced upward but failed to see its top. It was, as they say, a large stack. They passed through the portal and were greeted with air-conditioned warmth. The atrium was vast and impressive, its floor paved in marble, appearing to dance under the mottled light from the ceiling – which was the bottom of a giant fish tank.

Oliver watched the tropical species and then their shadows as he followed the pulsing red line floating ahead of him in his HUD, directed to one of several reception desks. The young man sat pleasantly behind it. "Welcome to Fray International."

"I have an appointment with Mr Fray," Oliver said, still admiring the atrium's beauty.

"Which one?" the young man replied, catching Oliver off-guard. He hadn't considered both of them would be available, or that his arrival hadn't been expected.

"Felix," he answered, trying not to notice the armed guards blending into the walls. He trusted Kyle had already accounted for all of them and so focused, waiting for the beautiful young man to finish blinking at his invisible display. When he did, he looked to his left, and Oliver followed his eye-line to the rust-haired man approaching.

Kyle remained statuesque, while the newcomer smiled and offered his hand. "Oliver Trench?"

"Yes." It was a good vigorous shake, and Oliver knew in that instant he was not one of the grunts filling the building's corridors.

"I'm Greg Fielding, Chief of Security," the man said with a friendly sincerity. "I'm afraid your colleague won't be able to join you."

Oliver nodded at Kyle, who reciprocated. "I'll wait here."

"I'm afraid that's not acceptable either," said Fielding. "We don't allow weapons in the building, and while you're not carrying any... per se... it's quite clear that you're augmented." He paused, reading the information from his HUD's scan of Kyle. "And heavily."

"I won't send him away," said Oliver.

"You won't have to; we have a lounge area. I'd just prefer he wasn't in reception."

"Scaring away the friendly folk?" messaged Kyle. "I'm sure that will be fine, Mr Fielding."

"Very good," said Fielding, lifting his hand high to beckon one of the unobtrusive guards over. "James here will look after you."

Oliver watched James lead Kyle away, feeling suddenly naked and alone. He settled his feet flat on the floor, took a breath, and turned his attention to his chaperone.

"This way, if you please, Mr Trench." Greg led him in almost the opposite direction to the way James was taking Kyle. Oliver stopped dwelling on it; he had to put it out of his mind before he met with Fray, or it would be all over. Fear did nothing but dull one's wits. If he intended to succeed, he'd need to be better than this.

He followed Greg and his forced casual stride to the nest of elevators along the east wall. Once inside, the Chief of Security blinked a command, and the door closed with a rolling hiss. Oliver felt a tug in his knees as the cab ripped upward. He followed the display on his left, racing up the floors of the building in bright holographic numbers.

There were several floors for administrative offices, several for earth and ground support for the rainforest above it, and then through the canopy into the commercial zone. Adverts for various restaurants appeared in his peripheral, bouncing on the spot, all fighting for Oliver's attention. He blinked them away as they raced through the domiciles, where the cab slowed.

When it stopped, it had travelled over three hundred floors. He had been in the elevator for less than a minute. The doors opened into a long white corridor that instantly looked familiar to Oliver. "Mr.

Fray is waiting for you on the veranda." Greg pointed to the corridor's end, where a glass door stood.

"Thank you," Oliver replied, stepping out of the elevator. The door slid shut behind him, and he found himself alone in the opulent surroundings. He walked towards the glass door, unhurried yet purposeful. Each step brought further familiarity to him. Doorways led to stunning rooms adorned with gold-flecked chairs and oil paintings of seventeenth-century France, but it was the hallway that gave it away—a classical beauty he distinctly remembered walking through before.

Mirrors. From floor to ceiling, the corridor was encased in mirror. Oliver's reflections flanked him the length of the corridor, his face tired, his stride broken. This was not the image he needed to present. He'd left his friend to die, coerced his brother into helping him, kept Nadia at arm's length, and refused to help those who needed him most.

But it was all for the country. The country needed strong leadership—Jonathan was no longer that strength, and Percy was no replacement. Felix claimed to be the potency, albeit a non-elected power, and he would need to be kept in check; Percy was no wrangler either. Is this what has become of you? Are you really only here because Percy isn't right for the job? Or is Felix right—have you wanted this all along?

He found himself standing still in the corridor, his reflection staring back at him with disdain. "I'm sorry," he said, tightening his Windsor knot and pulling on his cufflinks. He ran his hand through his hair and saw his old self smiling back at him. Giving himself a wink, he continued down the corridor, increasingly impressed with the detail and enhancements. The lights responded to his presence by illuminating him as he walked. No doubt the building would offer more invisible technology to its guests, should they require it.

When he reached the end of the corridor, a seven-foot sterling silver robot opened the door for him. It didn't quite have a face, but beneath its transparent head casing, it displayed an expression by dancing blue lights. On its chest, it proudly bore the Mercedes Benz logo. "Welcome, Mr Trench," it said with a disarming tone. "I am Vernon."

"Hello," Oliver replied, continuing to be impressed.

"Please, follow me."

Once out on the veranda, Oliver took in the lush gardens surrounding him. Rows of tulips and shrubs extended to the building's edge, and although he was three hundred floors higher than the gangway he had crossed, he felt neither the cold nor the wind he had endured during his walk from the limo.

The edge of the building must have been fitted with air cannons, firing directly up to create an invisible wall, shielding those on the rooftop paradise from the winds and keeping the heat produced by the disguised heaters in the trees. "Thanks for coming," Felix called from his thatched patio chair.

Oliver waved to him, not judging the man for enjoying the sun in his shades and casual lounge wear. "Felix," he said, walking over.

"Have you had breakfast?" asked Felix. "I can recommend the eggs. Vernon is an excellent chef."

"Please, sir. You'll make me blush," the disarming voice commented from behind Oliver.

"Just a coffee, please," Oliver replied.

"Excellent, Mr Trench," said Vernon. "Would you prefer: Affogato, Antoccino, Black Eye, Black Tie, Breve, Cafe Americano—"

Oliver was sure Vernon was about to list every type of coffee under the sun. "Just a latte, please."

The blue lights curled into an enormous smile. "As you wish, Mr Trench. Mr Fray, would you care for anything else?"

"Nothing, thank you, Vernon."

Oliver sat on the available straw chair and waited. He thought Felix would start the conversation promptly, but he seemed more intent on finishing reading whatever was on his data paper. Waiting, he looked at the gardens again and then around the building when it fell into place. "The Porcelain Trianon," Oliver smiled triumphantly.

"Almost. It's a replica, but I had it decorated with my favourite parts of Versailles." Felix lowered his paper.

"Where did you get the marble?" Oliver asked. "Or is that fake too?"

"Feeling guilty?" Changing the subject, Felix seemed intent on toying with him.

"I'm surprised by how well you think you know me," Oliver countered.

"I know," Felix flashed his perfect teeth, and Oliver hesitated. He didn't want to fight with this man. This man was the key to beating Percy.

"Jonathan died years ago," Oliver said. "All I did was stand aside while Percy buried him."

Felix placed his paper on the table, sinking back into his chair. "I couldn't have put it better myself. You stood aside."

"My being there wouldn't have changed anything."

"True," Felix conceded. "But it also would have proved you to be a team player. I know that your friend's death isn't an easy pill to swallow, and I discussed my concerns the other night."

It reminded Oliver of the conversation at the Tate party, how Felix had sweet-talked him, explaining where he saw Oliver in the new world order. "I didn't like where the plan led."

"You could have just said." Felix held his hands open. "You could have called, said, 'Hey Felix. I'm not quite right on the details. Could we discuss them further?'"

"Quite," Oliver said. "But pardon me for saying, I don't trust you."

"Of that, Oliver, you've made yourself abundantly clear." Felix leaned forward in his chair. "You have a recording?"

Oliver was not surprised. "Of Jonathan's death."

"I'm interested in knowing what you intend to do with it."

Oliver relaxed a millimetre; they both wanted to deal. "That depends."

"You have questions?" Felix exhaled. "New ones? Or are you looking for different answers to the ones you've already asked?"

Oliver ran his tongue between his teeth; he had so many questions, he barely knew where to start. He could understand why Fletcher had been used. Destabilising the Southerner's hierarchy made Fray's deal for security look even more promising.

He'd jumped into bed with Percy to lock down that deal. Promised Percy the job of Prime Minister, but what he couldn't understand was, "Why kill Window?"

"Opportunity," Felix offered.

"Not good enough." Oliver raised an eyebrow. "Sorry."

"He was DGSE."

"Bollocks," Oliver scoffed. "That lunatic was not French Intelligence."

"Would you prefer me to say that he was an idealist; a man who wanted a free state, a free London?"

"It would be more believable."

Felix offered his hand. "See for yourself."

He didn't want to. He didn't want to believe this radical notion was possible, let alone the truth. The French? He was on good terms with most of their cabinet, had shared gifts with Adreanna, played squash with Ninon. It couldn't be true. It wouldn't be true. What would this mean for him if it were? Felix would be right. Everything that he and Jonathan had worked for was nothing but a precarious house of cards.

"Oliver." Felix beckoned, furthering his reach.

He relented, accepting Felix's hand. The blue Fray-designed hologram appeared between them. In it, a stack of digital files, all pertaining to Daniel Payne, aka WINDOW. Oliver scanned the first couple of pages as Vernon returned with his beverage. The machine waited patiently until Felix waved him away. Oliver hadn't noticed; he had bitten hard on the bait and found Fray's hook. "He's not DGSE anymore?" he finally asked, minimising the document on his HUD.

"Not for several years," Felix said. "My intelligence points toward a corporate employer. I have suspicions but haven't been able to ascertain for certain."

"You appear to have a substantial account on him. More than Special Branch could find."

"It's all authentic."

"Then you appear to have the advantage."

"I always do," Felix pointed to the garden table, on which sat Oliver's drink.

He claimed the tall glass cup and stirred, blending the coffee with the milk while craning his neck around until he found Vernon. "Thank you."

"You are quite welcome, Mr Trench."

"He was trying to argue for a free south," Felix continued with their previous conversation. "No doubt a staging ground for European conglomerates."

Oliver drank from his cup and found it amusing how Felix's plan to profit from the South did not differ from his competitors. "He wouldn't have got it," he said.

"It doesn't matter."

"Of course it does." Oliver bit hard; it had to matter.

Felix dropped his facade. His entire body tightened. "I'm not going ten rounds with you, Oliver," he snarled. "I won't pretend to be your father; you know how this works. So, you can either stand against me or listen to my offer."

Oliver had worked in the business long enough to know that Felix believed himself to be right. Saddam Hussein had been an idealist; one they'd tried to control and failed. Through Felix's eyes, Oliver could see Window would only stand in his way. Felix didn't want a free south. Felix wasn't looking to fix the problem; he was looking to profit from its perpetuation.

Oliver needed to convince Felix that uniting the Kingdom could also be profitable. He had to convince him he and Jonathan were right. "There is another way."

"There really isn't." Felix was quick to dismiss him. "Europe wants our oil and coal reserves." Oliver felt his lip tighten; he'd heard this before. Fictions aimed at increasing the annual budget spending and consultation fees, the fear tactic. "Sceptical, Oliver?

Take it from someone whose business is international. I sit with these people. I know what France has been doing to force Germany's hand. Trust me when I say the world has not forgotten the British Empire and has no love for it.

"While you've been playing the small game, Europe has been deciding on how best to divide up our little island. They're just waiting for an excuse. We've been an embarrassment for over fifty years. The Second World War bankrupted us, and we've been living on a name ever since, that and living in the shadow of our big brother the U S of A.

"But that is all changing, Oliver. Big brother is looking elsewhere. China is going to make its move soon, and the entire global political stage is going to shift."

Oliver had heard this too, but the news from the European Union had shown no indication it was true, and no British spy had confirmed it. It was always from the think tanks, the privately backed think tanks. This wasn't a political takeover; this was a business one. The corporations were taking over. "For the good of the country?" Oliver asked.

"And a substantial fortune, I must admit, one that I'm prepared to share." Felix winked at him, confident in his sales pitch.

"Not if it means going to war with London." Oliver stood his ground.

Felix didn't reply right away; Oliver wondered if he was surprised or just indignant over his latest remark. "I already have a Prime Minister willing to work with me on those terms."

"Not if I release the footage," Oliver reminded him.

"Yes." Felix admitted. "There is that."

"I also have a majority in the house—"

"No, you have a coalition with the Democrats," Felix corrected him. "Percy has the majority."

Now it was Oliver's turn to pause. He hadn't expected Felix to know about the coalition. "None of that matters if Percy goes to jail."

"Then I'll put Rockwood on the throne," Felix said, grinning. "Or Faraday. It really doesn't matter who."

Oliver's blood boiled in his veins. Felix had found his breaking point; the thought of Faraday as Prime Minister was enough to send him over the edge. "I..."

"Work with me, Oliver," Felix told him. "I'd be lying if I said that I prefer any of those imbeciles in your stead. Rockwood, yes, I can work with him. But he's military; I'd have to groom him, spend time gaining political allies; I'll be happier with him running the security side of things. You're a perfect candidate— you've outsmarted everyone you've competed against."

Oliver gritted his teeth. Competed against—as if this were some interview to be Felix Fray's caddy.

"I want you to be my Prime Minister," Felix continued. "If we don't show we can make a profit from the South in eighteen months. France is going to invade, and you can kiss your United Kingdom goodbye. Not because France is superior in every which way, but because our country is nothing except for a name alluding to some distant past."

"How do you know I won't publish this conversation to the courts?" Oliver asked.

"Oliver," Felix replied. "Don't embarrass yourself."

CHAPTER TWENTY-THREE

STRANGE BEDFELLOWS

Renner spoke. "Okay, I don't want to brag," he said, knowing he was going to, anyway. "But with no small effort," Renner continued, and Evan smiled. "I've cracked the national network. You're now invisible to everything except the naked eye. That includes everyone with augmented eyes or wearing display glasses."

"That's everyone then," Evan replied, sitting outside a quaint coffee shop. Nothing special, just one of a hundred million located in York. This one was close to where he needed to be, and the coffee was good. His glass cup was nearing the end, and he tapped his index against its side as if counting down the remaining seconds he would sit there.

No longer in his government-issue sweat suit, he was freshly washed, shaven, and dressed in a plain pale blue workingman's shirt. Sturdy denim jeans and Caterpillar boots completed the new look. They were Renner's clothes—he couldn't go back home, and they'd had too little time to go shopping. "Antonia checked in?" She'd been there most of the night, leaving to find out more about Oliver's whereabouts.

"Nope."

"Do you want to check on her?"

"Listen, Ev, if there's one thing I know about Toni, it's that you never rush the girl."

"But she should have checked in by now?"

"She's gone to work; she can't drop a message to us without bringing Gillespie down on top of her."

"I thought you said you were in the clear."

"Having no evidence against me differs from not knowing I was involved. Gillespie may be a company boy, but a fool he is not."

That was true, but if Gillespie knew Renner was involved, then it stood to reason that anyone in his circle of friends would be under suspicion. "They know you two are an item?"

"Best kept secret in government."

Evan smiled at the remark and sipped his latte. "You hope so."

"I know so."

Evan finished his drink in silence, his eyes now on the street and, more importantly, the bus stop on the corner. It was pleasant, sitting there in the morning sun. It was cold, but it was fresh, and he didn't have guns firing at him. If he closed his eyes, he could almost imagine none of this had happened. But he couldn't give in entirely, with Bo never being too far from his thoughts.

A cheeky damned fly came in on a breeze and landed on his hand, scrambled across his knuckles, and took flight again as Evans flicked his wrists.

"Don't swat it," Renner warned.

"Be quicker with your introductions."

He watched Renner's robotic fly land on his table and patter close to his hand as the bus turned the corner onto his street. "That the one?"

"Indeed, it is."

Evan left the table. He tapped his pocket, ensuring his new toy was still there before heading toward the bus stop. The fly followed him. He read the bus route displayed above the front window; it was the one he'd been waiting for. He stepped up the pace as the bus approached, but it wasn't slowing.

He hadn't seen the old lady with her wheeled bag sitting there. When she stood and waved the bus down, it allowed him to slow down. He could have made it if he ran, but he didn't want to draw attention to himself. While being technically invisible, it really only meant that people's chipsets wouldn't register him unless they looked directly at him, set off any alarms, or remember seeing anything but a blur. Besides, if he missed this bus, there was always another.

The bus, like all others in York, was a dull blue colour. It seated a maximum of fifty people, and this one looked full. Evan could see several passengers standing behind the driver, who was still human. One of the few cities left in the world that still had them. He wondered for a moment why the taxi service had swapped to AI, until the vehicle stopped a second later.

The door slid open with a hiss, and the elderly woman stood patiently as three passengers disembarked. Evan strolled past, close enough that his arm rubbed against the side of the bus. In his head, he counted: one, two, sliding a palm-sized magnet down his sleeve, three, four. He pressed it against the side of the bus, five and six.

Behind him, the fly inspected his handiwork. "Looking good," Renner said. The fly landed on the device. "Activating in three, two, one." The fly abandoned the magnet as the bus pulled away. It continued to hover near the device, now a metallic blister on the side of the bus.

"Come on, little fella, don't be scared," Renner continued.

The blister vibrated, splitting open for six legs which clinked against the side of the vehicle. "There we go," Renner said again. "Get a move on, little guy." The small robotic spider scurried beneath the transport.

"You realise it doesn't understand you," Evan said, paying too much attention to Renner's idiocy and not where he was going. He bumped into a man in his forties, a bulging gullet in a pin-striped suit. "Woowah!" the man exclaimed, staring at Evan in disbelief.

"Sorry," said Evan. The gullet turned tail and ran, taking Evan a second longer to realise that the man had been staring through him, his augmented reality lenses refusing to acknowledge Evan, just some crazy featureless apparition. He had to be a little more careful.

"If you spent more time listening to me instead of trying to get one up on me..."

"Shut up, Ren."

He cut across the road and through the park, the one that he and Bo had headed to last night before it had all gone to hell. I'm doing something about it, he reminded himself, while avoiding the dog walkers on the grass. On the other side of the park was a multi-storey car park. He entered through the pedestrian stairway and climbed the seven flights until he reached the roof.

The roof was nearly empty, save for four consumer VTOLs and Renner's mobile command post, the Buzzard. Evan climbed the metal rungs, entered through the hatch, and found Renner in the cramped main bay. "Where is it?" he asked, closing the hatch behind him.

Renner pointed to the largest projected screen around him. "Nearly there," he said, excited. Evan sat on a pull-down shelf and observed the camera feed, showing the streets of York from the small fly Renner controlled. "Looking good," Evan commented.

"This is what I do, young Padawan." Renner's toothy grin reflected the orange glare of the holograms. "Now be a darling and pass us a BullPhet." He gestured with his hand, mimicking Alec Guiness's rendition of Obi Wan Kenobi, who was a favourite of his.

He grabbed two cans from the fridge near the cockpit hatch and returned to his shelf. "Catch."

Renner caught the can and cracked it open without uttering a word. His concentration was on the screens, on the minute fluctuations in air speed and direction. Controlling a fly didn't appear easy. "Here we go." He gulped from his can. "Let's mix this up a bit." He swiped his hand across his panel of screens, causing them to ripple and change. The smaller views minimised, dropping to his lap and making room for the 'Fly Cam'.

The bus on the screen struggled, smoke billowing from its engine, until it stopped precisely where Renner intended. "Perfect," Evan said. The bus now blocked both ramps in and out of Fray International's underground parking lot. Renner moved the fly to the roof of the bus, facing the security box at the entrance to the Fray building.

"They don't wait long, do they?" Evan noticed a robotic guard emerging from the security door, waving its hand. "That's not good," Renner frowned.

Evan smirked. "Not the droid you were looking for?"

Renner rolled his eyes. "I need a human, smart ass."

They watched the entertainment unfold. The droid, manufactured by Mercedes, was polished black with chrome highlights. "Do you have sound?"

"Of course."

Evan continued to wait while Renner watched. "Can I hear it too?"

Renner pulled an ugly face usually reserved for mocking the mentally challenged. Then the sound feed accompanied the video feed through the buzzard's systems.

"I can't," said the pot-bellied bus driver. "She ain't moving."

"You cannot leave your vehicle here," replied the guard with its tinny voice.

"You offering a push, buddy?"

The droid stayed silent amidst honking cars queueing behind the bus.

"He's calling for a supervisor," Renner stated the obvious. Droids never made decisions or thought independently.

The bus driver flipped off the droid, then re-entered his cab and the guard moved to the rear of the bus to direct traffic past the vehicle.

"Here we go." Renner pointed to the security door opening again, revealing a short, well-groomed man in a crisp uniform. He rushed to the guard, ran his hand over his hair, and pursed his lips.

The 'Fly Cam' lifted from the bus roof and pitched to its left, causing Renner to curse in frustration.

"Damn this wind." He levelled the camera out and flew it around the scene, watching the bus driver coming back out of his cab.

"There's an engineering team on its way," he explained to the human security guard.

"How long will they be?" asked the human guard.

"Not long."

The fly moved in on the security officer, landing on the back of his collar and climbed up to his neck. It immediately fired a microscopic dart into the man's skin. The guard flinched and brought his hand hard across the back of his neck, killing the fly and destroying the camera.

They both stared in silence at the blank screen. "Did you get it?" asked Evan.

Renner didn't answer. He was still looking at the blank screen, his top lip curled up and flashing his whites, but that was about it. He sat in silence, looking at nothing but the dead projection. Evan didn't know if this was normal, or if there would be a delay, or whether Renner was putting together an apology. "Renner?" he nudged his shoulder.

"Shush!" Renner replied. He wasn't waiting; he was working through his HUD, images Evan couldn't see. Suddenly, the displays changed, and the internal security network for Fray International's UK Headquarters filled the workstation. "We're good," he continued. "Just give me a minute."

2

Forty minutes passed while Renner worked indefatigably to break the necessary code barriers of Fray International. If he were successful, he'd have what the law enforcement industry called 'an orgy of evidence.' He'd also have the bragging rights of hacking a fortune one-hundred company.

Meanwhile, Evan moved the buzzard to Nottingham Forest, not wanting to be near Fray International on the change Renner failed. Intrusion Countermeasures Electronics, or ICE, would pop Renner's skull like a metal box in a microwave and Evan would have several squads on him quicker than he could say—

"Jesus suffering Christ," Renner said.

The words came from Renner, not what he had expected or wanted after forty minutes of silence. The buzzard was parked in Nottingham Forest. It seemed poignant to Evan when he was looking for opportunities. Crawling back to the vehicle's main bay, he found Renner still seated, drooling, but otherwise intact.

"What have you got?" Evan asked.

"Oh my God, oh my God, oh my God!" It was like he was making sweet love. "I'm in!"

He was, and he was in deep. Within the next minute he'd confirmed that Oliver and Kyle had checked in at the front desk earlier that morning. "I'm not sure where they are now." He had one foot in the conversation and the other in the matrix. "They're still there." Commenting in small concise bites as and when he discovered them. "Oliver's had lunch—with the big Bossman."

"Fray?" asked Evan.

"Felix," he said, pausing. "Kyle went to R and D. Can't see him anywhere. Either of them."

"Anything on Bo?"

Silence fell again. Seconds stretched to minutes while Renner searched Fray's computer systems, sifting through emails and digital memos for anything with Bo's name or which could be related to Bo. "I think—Yes, Fray sent Special Operatives to look for two people matching your and Bo's descriptions last night," Renner revealed. "You're dead, amigo."

"At the bridge?"

"Indeedy. If it makes you feel any better, they would have preferred to take you alive, but the kid was the primary target." He held his hand out open. "Can please."

"You're lucky I need you."

"Just get me the can and stop your whining."

Evan obliged him while Renner continued to discover more information. When he returned and dropped the can in his hand, Renner was no longer smiling.

"Look at this," he pointed at the nearest screen to Evan. It was a straightforward list of code-named files. "It's his Tech Lab menu. And it's enormous."

"Feeling a little insecure, Ren?"

"Yeah right, but seriously..." Renner entered one file. A mass of blueprints and three-dimensional images appeared for a long-barrelled assault rifle. "Fifty rounds a second."

"Ouch."

"I know, right?" Renner was salivating even more now. "I knew they had some military contracts, but they're branded as cutting edge in social media and computer processing."

"They're adapting," said Evan.

"For what?"

Oil was running out, that American's negotiations with China had stagnated. "The end of the world."

The designs vanished, and the screen had returned to the list. He scrolled down another file, another weapon. This time a two-legged weapons platform, a crowd control robot the size of a transit van on stilt legs.

"Are any of these in production?" asked Evan.

"Just prototypes."

"No sales references?"

"Why would that mat..." Renner trailed off as he grasped Evan's question. "Clever... clever." He fell silent, searching for sales references or inquiries, but found none. "If he's selling them, it's not in this database. I can try other areas later, but for now, I'd say you're right. He's making them for himself."

Evan didn't like being right. Fray, notorious in the business world, had made lucrative deals and built the modern communications network spanning the globe. A world on the brink of collapse, and Fray was creating weapons for himself. More sinister was Kyle and Oliver's involvement. Kyle was a weapon himself, seemingly Oliver's enforcer. Oliver, on the other hand, could become Prime Minister—a government leader in Fray's pocket. "We need something concrete."

"Already on it," Renner replied.

Evan nodded, returning to the cockpit. "And find Bo."

"I haven't forgotten."

He climbed back into the cramped cockpit to update Antonia. "Angel, this is Bluebird. Please come in."

Antonia's face appeared on the view-port. "Bluebird, this is Angel. Line secure. Please report."

Evan noted her aptitude for military protocol. "All parties are where we presumed," he said.

When she didn't reply, he knew she was contemplating their next move or deciphering Renner's odd noises—sniggers, whoops, and obscenities.

"Can we ascertain Oliver's allegiance?" she asked. Evan thought for a moment.

"No confirmation either way. Just some dinner arrangements," he added. "All parties are still at the location."

He knew she'd want more, all angles covered and eventualities assessed. That was the smart approach, one Evan would've considered in his past. Now, he focused on keeping his promise. "Private has a catalogue of weapons, an arsenal ready for production." 'Private' was their code for Fray.

Antonia's face scrunched. "Private is shortlisted for the southern security contract."

"That makes sense. Groom our friend for king, get the security contract." Evan convinced himself. "By making it look like the south assassinated Dickens, he'll gain public support to replace the regime." He waited for her reply in the tense silence.

"Find out more," she said, calm and resolute.

"Wait." He stopped her. "I'm going to get him out."

"No, that's out of the question. All we have now are suppositions. We need evidence."

"You have the catalogue of weapons, and I know where he is. I can do this."

"It's not enough. The child's public enemy number one. You'll need an army to breach Private's fortress, and even then, can you imagine the headlines?"

She didn't understand. Bo was his responsibility. "I have to get him back."

"And I'll help you, but lawfully." She paused. "First, we need to know if our friend is compromised."

Despite his urge to save Bo, Evan knew charging into Fray's fortress would be fatal. "We'll do more digging."

"Good," Antonia replied, satisfied.

"And if an opportunity presents itself?"

"Call me back. This is chess, not Yahtzee." She vanished.

He saw she was playing the long game, something he hadn't since waking up in the mud. Evan hadn't considered the 'why' factor. A loud whoop from Renner brought him back. More information meant they could defeat their enemies. They would have everything Antonia needed to bring down Oliver and secure her position as Party Leader.

Returning to Renner, Evan felt better with a plan. It might take time, but it would work. He'd take that holiday to New Zealand, he'd promised himself.

He peered at Renner's screens, hoping for something comprehensible, but they only confused him.

"I have him!" Renner shouted, making Evan jump.

"I'm right here, you idiot."

"It's Bo."

"What?" Evan didn't like Renner's expression. "What about him?"

"They've upgraded him. They're going to use him to assassinate Percy tonight at the PPB—" Renner was lost in the system. Information overload. "Holy shit, they put a fucking bomb in his head."

3

Felix Fray never stopped selling himself. He constantly spouted information, likely from his HUD. Oliver had been with him all day, and they hadn't spoken to anyone else, besides Vernon, who trailed them like a well-trained dog. Felix must have run his business through his HUD while giving Oliver a tour of the building.

While that impressed Oliver, he still didn't trust him and that, it seemed, worked both ways. Even with Oliver agreeing to be part of the grand scheme, he'd been kept at arm's length. Felix was smart, smarter than Oliver wanted to credit him for. Not unlike an abusive lover, Felix had separated him from his support networks. Keeping him from Antonia, away from Renner. "Only for now," was his favourite restraint for Oliver. "They'll only get in the way. There's nothing for them to do. Can't have you running off again, can we?" were some of his others.

He was sure Felix would divulge more, just not today.

To cement his position in Parliament, he'd agreed to Percy's execution. Felix was not one for loose ends. He liked precise surgical cuts. There was no love lost between Oliver and Percy, but the context in which Felix wanted Oliver's commitment was a tad hard to swallow. In Felix's eyes, by leaving the PPB prematurely, Oliver had sealed Percy's fate and the fop's ephemeral position as party leader.

"You scattered the game pieces," Felix had said. "It took me all night to reacquire them."

Felix wasn't crude enough to put a gun in Oliver's hand and have him pull the trigger. He at least had some respect for him, above Percy anyhow. "The best way to deal with a loose rope is to bring all the parts back together and burn them into one again."

Oliver could have argued it would only work with nylon rope, but knew better than to interrupt Felix. "Not only will it keep it clean, but it will be believable. The media will lap it up. I'm sure you could put a good word in for us, too."

He's referring to Nadia, Oliver thought, and remembered how she had said goodbye and her warm lips on his cheek, but he needed to remain focused on the country. Even if it cost him everything, he would still be able to have influence in policy. He would be the country's voice. If Felix was right. "How do you know he'll go for it?"

"The kid?" asked Felix.

Oliver nodded yes. Who else?

"We'll tell him Percy killed Window." Felix was fond of looking out over the city from his high-rise windows, and this conversation was no different.

Not only would the plan keep it clean, keep it believable, it would fortify Parliament's new stance on Southern England. London would be regarded as a clear and present threat to the country. It would need reminding of its place.

The plan would keep it clean and believable while fortifying Parliament's stance on Southern England. London would be seen as a threat, requiring control. The child had come to York to protect Window and had inadvertently become the linchpin holding the country's peace. If he killed Percy, Oliver would become Prime Minister. Felix would win the security contract and move south. Emulating the Chinese capitalist model, Felix would profit enough to appease their neighbours and prevent an invasion.

"Think of it as a new Dubai," Felix said. "But instead of burying a potential workforce under the car parks, we'll put them to good use."

"Slave labour?" Oliver asked.

"I'm not a monster, they'll have a liveable wage."

As well as business, Felix guided Oliver through his headquarters, moving down the building at a far more leisurely pace than on his ride up the elevator that morning. They discussed the processes of the building, how the rainforest was open to all staff as a relaxation hub as well as producing the oxygen for the building and the waterfall that generated some of the building's electrical capacity, with the wind turbines fitted to the exterior doing the rest.

"All three Fray towers follow the same basic design, each with improvements on the last," he explained. "Dubai draws energy from heat pockets beneath the earth, and we're supplying thirty per cent of the city's power at no charge."

By the time they reached the tech labs, Oliver decided Felix was not the Anti-Christ, but a man who understood the world and made hard choices. His disassociation to human empathy was quite shocking. However, once you looked past his cold logic, you could come to understand his reasoning.

"The kid should be ready soon," Felix said. "We had to introduce a lot of physical architecture since he didn't have any tech in him. That tattoo, though— beautiful nano-craft." Felix continued talking, but Oliver couldn't hear him, overwhelmed by an incessant ringing.

He didn't notice the thin, pale lady until she handed Felix a small metal briefcase, eliciting a broad smile. "Is that what I think it is?" asked Felix. She nodded and left. "He's going to love these."

Oliver knew Felix meant the boy, not Kyle. The boy whose name he couldn't bring himself to say, and here was Felix giving him a present.

"Oliver." He turned to see Kyle walking towards them and his heart sank to his boots. "You look whiter than usual," Kyle said.

"Very droll, Kyle," replied Oliver.

They both looked as awkward as Oliver felt. "Would you two like a moment?" Felix was not one for leaving dead air. "Bo has a couple more minutes before we can see him. I don't mind if you want to catch-up or compare notes." Oliver caught the subtle wink from Felix and wanted to punch him for it.

"Thanks," Oliver said, leading Kyle to the nearest window. They were high up, a couple of floors above the landing pads. "You okay?"

"Never better." He watched the entire floor while speaking. "You?"

"I've made a deal."

"That's what you came here for," Kyle said, intuitive as ever. "No surprises?"

Oliver hesitated a moment, then replied, "It's not the deal I wanted."

"We're not dead," Kyle offered. "That's a good thing."

Oliver found replying to that phrase harder than anything he'd ever done. "Indeed, very good."

"Fallout!" Both turned at the sound of the kid's voice. There he was, sprinting from the glass door, a surgical gown billowing like a superhero's cape. He hugged Kyle tightly, his raven flapping its wings excitedly.

"Hey kiddo, how you doing?" Kyle asked, crouching down to meet him eye to eye.

Bo stepped back, grinning. With a quick blink, his body hummed with electronics. Gum guards filled his mouth, muscles contorted under his skin as the nano-armour worked itself into place, and his eye-shields slid into position. When he answered, he did so in Russian. "Badass."

He raised his fist, and Kyle bumped it with his own, both chuckling. "You are a badass motherfucker," Kyle said before launching the first of many playful punches.

"He'll be combat-ready in ninety minutes," Felix whispered to Oliver, startling him.

"He looks ready now," Oliver said.

"There are some operating programmes downloading."

Oliver watched Bo and Kyle play. It was the first time he'd seen the boy, and the plan became all too real. "Will it work?"

"Please," Felix sounded insulted.

Oliver pressed on, unconcerned. "How many will go with him?"

"Just him," Felix answered.

No more witnesses than necessary. "You think that's a good idea?" Oliver questioned.

"It needs to be authentic. Percy has security. If anyone clocks anyone other than Bo, they'll know he had help from the outside."

"You can scrub the footage," Oliver said, aware they'd already scrubbed Jonathan's footage.

"True," Felix agreed. "But this is cleaner, authentic, and not just for now, but a hundred years in the future. It won't do us any good to have a British Zapruder film. Having one altered piece of footage is going to be tough enough. We'll have to alter it periodically as technology gets better. Having the real McCoy—that's priceless."

Oliver wasn't sure it had been Felix's point, but he backed down. It was an agreeable argument. The later, unaltered footage would support the first by default.

"At least send Kyle as backup." Oliver suggested.

"I'll think on it." Felix must have taken Oliver's silence as an end to their conversation because he sauntered over to Bo and Kyle. "Hi there," he said to the child, who turned and stuck out his chest.

"Hi." His raven shifted uneasily, eyeing Felix with suspicion.

Unfazed, Felix knelt and offered his hand. "I'm Felix." Bo hesitantly accepted, and Felix revealed the silver briefcase. "A little bird tells me these are your favourite brand."

Oliver looked away, disgusted by Felix's charm and his own complicity in the plan.

"Sweet!" Bo lifted the two Desert Eagles from the case. "DEagles!"

"They're yours," Felix said, like a doting father.

"Mine?" Bo's mirrored eyes looked on Felix's sincerity for a flash-fire moment before they returned to the sharp, elegant contours of his new weapons. These gorgeous creations were unlike anything he could have salvaged back home, as each one had been specifically crafted for him. Gleaming reflections instead of scratched imperfections, etched Ravens cut into ivory grips. They were perfect, and he grinned so.

Oliver seethed, taking part in a repugnant plan he'd once judged Jonathan for. He hadn't understood how it could be allowed, how it could be justified. Now, he'd permitted the same thing to happen again, and his involvement made it even worse.

"How would you like to kill the guy who murdered Danny?" Felix asked.

Bo spun the pistols on his fingers like a miniature cyborg cowboy. "Hell yes."

PART FIVE:

PROFIT IN PEACE

CHAPTER TWENTY-FOUR
TALINGWORTH ROAD

Renner declared over his steaming mug of coffee, "Well, as you've surmised, folks, this will be anything but easy, but it marks the end." He paused for dramatic tension. "One way or another."

"Does she know?" Evan inquired, keeping thoughts of the imminent future at bay.

"Toni?"

"How many other women do you know?"

Renner's middle finger extended for the fourth time that hour. Of course, she knew. Renner didn't keep secrets from his woman. Evan was aware of that; he was simply thankful he didn't have to argue with her about the necessity of their plan. Renner had stayed out of the conversation, as expected. "She knows."

"Did she say anything?"

"Lots of things. None you'd find useful or polite."

"You in the doghouse?"

Renner hesitated, his lips touching the rim of his mug. "If we could do it her way, we would. You know that."

"I know. I just want you to know I appreciate you taking the flak over me."

"Don't worry, buddy. She doesn't blame either of us. This is out of our hands, and she knows it. She just wants more time."

Evan glanced at his bootlace, untied it, and curled up on his toes. Don't we all, he pondered. They'd acted when Renner discovered the bomb inside Bo's head. A similar device to what Fletcher had had installed in his cranium: an unwitting suicide bomber.

He'd argued as much to Antonia, discussing the political fallout if they 'rescued' him. She couldn't afford to take sides, waiting until the music stopped before choosing her chair. Both Evan and Renner were already in the grey area; Renner was under suspicion when he'd allowed them to escape the PPB, and Evan was dead.

So reluctantly, Antonia agreed. But she refused to participate. Renner slept for an hour, then spent several hours inside Fray International's computer systems, sifting through anything related to Lockhead, Oliver, Percy, government contracts, London, and Bo. To the best of their knowledge, he had successfully gathered information and remained anonymous.

Everything seemed fine until Renner woke him up an hour ago. "Change of plan."

Evan assumed it was a change to their plan. Have him climb over the east wall instead of the west one. "Yeah?"

"Percy will not be at the PBB."

"Does Fray know?" If he didn't, Bo would be sent into Parliament, regardless.

"That's how I know," Renner said.

"It's not a red herring?"

"Seriously, Evan, I'm getting more than a little pissed off when you belittle my skills."

"It was just a question."

"A question would be along the lines of, how does this change things?"

"Have I done something wrong?"

"Yeah, you belittled my skills. I was quite clear on that."

Evan closed his eyes, rubbing the sleep away with his index and thumb. He'd worked long hours with Renner before, but not under so much stress, and he'd also had the benefit of being able to call it a night. No such luck now. He gave himself a couple of seconds before asking, "How does this change things?"

"I'm glad you asked." Renner grinned again.

"Just tell me."

"Percy is staying at home tonight." There was a pause. "Don't worry," Renner said, reading Evan's expression. "His family won't be. The plan is to drop Bo into the street and have him work his way to Percy before exploding all over Talingworth Road."

"Talingworth?"

"Percy's address. I thought you were smart?" He winked at him. "All residential, four-storey brownstones complete with middle-class tenants. Both sides of the road have facing buildings, three steps leading up to the front door and five front-facing windows. Terraced with pitched roofs. Slim paved front yards with iron railings and gates."

Evan held up his hand. "Can't you show me a picture or something?"

"My description is not good enough for you, cowboy?"

"Wouldn't it be faster?"

"It would be if there were pictures. There's not even a Google Map of this place. It's fenced at each end. Many political figures live there and value their privacy."

Defeated, Evan nodded. "Please, continue."

"Why thank you. Percy has replaced his family with SB."

Evan's heart sank like a pair of concrete boots. Percy was using Special Branch to protect him from Bo.

"Thought you'd like that," Renner said. "Twenty of them and FYI, Carl and Louise are heading up the teams."

He knew both of them, both good people. Good commanders and good friends. Carl played a mean game of rugby and could eat his weight in burgers without gaining any weight. Louise had let Evan use her father's time-share apartment in Portugal last year. Now they'd be standing between Percy and Bo. They didn't stand a chance. "Can we get them out? Tell them to stand down?"

"Gillespie's locked me out. I'm pretty sure I'm out of a job." If he was upset, Renner didn't show it. He could quadruple his wage in the private sector anyhow. "That leads me to the downside of our venture. The street is tight, and there's no CCTV, so I'll have to rely on comm chatter. As I can't listen to SB chatter, I'm left with the cops. At least ten will be stationed outside the house." After he stopped talking, his face turned ashen and his eyes dulled.

Evan had seen that face before, in the mirror on the night he'd left for London.

"I'm not sure we can pull this off," Renner admitted.

Evan placed his hand on his friend's shoulder and told him not to be a wuss. Renner's eyes lightened a tad, enough for Evan to continue. "What's next?"

Renner smiled. It was a fake one, but Evan appreciated the fact he tried.

"We're going to have to be fluid," said Renner. "If we go in rigid with one plan of attack, the moment something goes wrong, we'll be in the crapper. We need to approach this like water, find the cracks."

He had hoped his face would explain his reaction to Renner's new and enthused contribution. It didn't. "You've lost me."

Renner arched an eyebrow. "We don't know how Bo will attack the house. We don't know if Kyle will be there." He paused, grimacing. "Kyle will kick your ass."

"Not if you're quick about things."

"If you get close enough to touch him, then maybe. It depends on whether Fray has played with him as well as Bo."

"Let's cross that bridge if we come to it," said Evan.

"Yup," replied Renner. His eye twitched, and a thought blurted out. "We'll fit your Exo with optical camouflage and non-lethal rounds."

"I thought optics were useless against personnel."

"You're nervous and not thinking straight. Of course, the ground crew will see you, but just a blur, and only if they look directly at you. If the cops decide to pay some overtime to a chopper pilot, at least you won't have to worry about being picked off from the air. Consider all eventualities."

Evan's head hurt. They'd been at this all afternoon, and they were going nowhere. After an hour considering all eventualities, they were still nowhere, except Renner had made himself a hot chocolate, and Evan had suited up.

All black, standard-issue Special Operations clothing: 'check'. Combat harness: 'check'. One Browning high-powered, semi-automatic pistol, non-lethal with spare magazines: 'check'. One army standard Exo frame: 'check'. When he had fastened his bootlaces, he grabbed a black beanie and pulled it onto his head: 'check'.

"You look gorgeous," remarked Renner. "You sure you don't want the camouflage?"

"Cops haven't said they're using a chopper." He had enough to concern himself with, without having an optical camouflage cloak flapping around him. He was going to zip-line down from the buzzard. Battle his way through the police, as Renner had put it, and then a house full of SB to save not only Bo but Percy, too. If he got that far—there was still a good chance Kyle would be there, and if Evan was ever scared of Bo, he was terrified of going toe-to-toe with Kyle.

This time, Renner read his face. "I'd come down with you if I thought I could help."

He smiled in return. "You will be."

"Just remember, the Exo will put you pretty much on par with his strength, but he's going to have speed on you, and he's trained. So, you're better off letting your HUD and suit do the macho stuff."

"Is this supposed to be a pep talk?"

"Just remember to trust in the suit."

"I've had basic training."

"You'll do fine," Renner smirked. "Want to go over it again?"

"There's nothing to go over. I'll just have to be fluid."

"Be the water," Renner added, holding his fist ready for a bump that didn't come.

"You know there's something wrong with you, don't you?"

Renner's smile split his face in half. "I'm a freak on a leash, baby."

2

High above Talingworth Road, Evan counted his breaths at the open hatch of the Buzzard. Ten seconds away from readying his zip-line, he prepared to begin his descent when Renner blurted out an obscenity. "What is it?" he asked, voice lost between the wind and turbines.

"Every light in a six-mile radius just went out."

The national grid was next to impossible to hack into, let alone control. You'd have a better chance of breaking into Wall Street. Six unlit miles in which to hide the true target. No power to Percy's house and no power to his security systems.

There was no point in guessing who had turned the lights off. Fray International had the guts and means to do it. But they wouldn't waste it; they would time it precisely. Renner hadn't spoken above his personal rumblings while he climbed, and Evan hadn't wanted the distraction, either.

"I can use this," Evan said. Steadying himself on the edge of the ramp, he blinked up the dwindling red blips of the police force. "They're not wasting any time."

"Neither should you."

Evan peered over the edge, noting it was a long way down to the road. So far, he didn't want to guess the distance. He pulled a hook from the spool of high-tensile wire and clasped it to his suit. If he thought about it, he'd be there all night. So, he didn't.

The air rushed against him as he fell headfirst into battle. The street, too dark to make out in the blackout, was painted with light blue contours depicting the townhouses, the road, and cars parked along it, several of which had been placed as barricades on either side of Percy's house. Presuming they were police, Evan painted an additional yellow star on their bonnets.

The red blips darted amongst the cars in uncoordinated chaos. "Bo's on the street."

"Chatter has something attacking them, but they haven't been able to ID it." No surprise, they're running like a bunch of idiots. "There's a sniper too."

"Kyle?"

"Don't know, somewhere on the roofs."

The road raced towards him. Another thirty seconds and he'd be unfastening the cord. "Slowing descent." He made a final count of the red blips; there were only four left. Too late for most of them, and by the time he reached the ground, there might not be a police force left. Then a crazy idea hit him; he would let his HUD and Exo suit handle the macho stuff.

Evan reached behind him, pulled his Browning free, aimed at the nearest red blip, and fired. The shot went wide, and the force from the shot swung him backward. He aimed again, firing the pistol, this time clipping the target in the shoulder. "What in hell are you doing?"

"Being the water." He pitched forward, feet held high with the ground racing towards him. "Shit!" Shielding his head with his hands and arms, he hit the ground, spraying sparks as the metal of his Exo scraped against the tarmac.

The following seconds slowed to a crawl as he blinked the command, vaporising the zip wire in a flash of white. He staggered to his feet with his suit's assisted hydraulics and, licking blood from his gums, aimed for his next target and fired. The shot hit the red blip dead centre, knocking it to the floor – better to stun them than let Bo kill them.

The kick came from nowhere. Staggering backward, he stumbled, feet slipping on the red-slicked tarmac. He steadied himself, simultaneously scanning the blue cars. Nothing. "I think you just found Bo," said Renner.

"Or he found me," Evan corrected, waiting for the gunshot. Nothing. "Bo?"

The patter of feet was heard too late; the swipe connected too fast at the back of his ankles, and Evan was down on the ground – Bo on top of him, black mirrored devil eyes reflecting Evan's dazed expression. "Bo, wait!" Two pistol muzzles stared down at him.

"Grab him," Renner called in Evan's ear, and Evan complied. He reached for the kid's ankle but found only air. Bo was gone, and Evan was alone on the road. He clambered to his knees, searching the blue outlines for a heartbeat.

Bo must have recognised him. He had said nothing, but there was no way he had mistaken him for someone else. Unless Fray had replaced his brain with a computer.

Evan stood, chambered his next round while keeping his eyes on the road. Then to the roofs; was he out there? "Kyle!?"

"You've got movement on your six," warned Renner.

Evan spun around, left hand supporting his right's aim. "I don't see anything." Or did he? "Wait." Standing on top of a police car, a foot on either side of its strip lights, was Kyle, aiming an assault rifle straight at him. "Kyle?"

"You're dead," came his heart-stopping reply.

"Kyle, wait." But he was waiting; his words weren't a threat – they were a statement.

"I can't do anything unless you touch him," said Renner.

"Hey, I'm working here."

Kyle remained silent, continuing to aim his rifle at Evan's heart. "You don't have to do this." He stepped forward; Kyle's aim dropped and fired, the bullet ricocheting an inch away from Evan's foot.

"Don't move."

Two words communicated a vital fact to Evan: Kyle had no desire to kill him. He counted the half-second it took for Kyle to aim the rifle back at his heart and waited another two seconds. "You're being deceived," he said, stepping forward. Kyle's aim faltered, and they both fired. Trusting the suit, Evan's initial shot struck the rifle, disrupting Kyle's aim further and revealing his chest, where Evan planted his second and third shots.

As Kyle tumbled from the car roof, Evan raced towards him. He vaulted over the car with ease, skidding to a halt beside his target and seizing his outstretched arm. "Got him," he said, only for Kyle to slip from his grasp and deliver a punch to his gut.

"Didn't get him," Renner said. "Need a couple of seconds."

"uring the "nslaught of belly p"nches, Evan held firm, dropp"ng his knees onto Kyle's shoulders and immobilising him. He pressed his open palm against Kyle's face and counted to two. "Now?" At three, Kyle's head attempted to pull away; at four, his legs thrashed. "Renner?"

With a mechanical hiss, Kyle's legs snaked up behind Evan, wrapping around his head and securing their grip. Evan's suit-enhanced spine strained under the force of Kyle's legs. Five, six. "Renner!" Ultimately, the legs triumphed, flipping Evan backward and smashing him into the police car he'd just cleared.

"I'm in."

"Fantastic," Evan grumbled, extricating himself from the dent and standing up.

Kyle's knee slammed under Evan's jaw with such force that it shattered three teeth. Pain ricocheted around his face in an instant. Once more, Evan found himself on the ground. Glancing up, he saw Kyle standing nearby, dusting off his sleeves. "Ren?"

"Give me a couple of seconds."

"One, two," Evan said, rising to his feet, never taking his eyes off Kyle. "Can we?"

Kyle's gut punch landed with impossible speed and force, robbing Evan of breath and sending him crashing to the ground for the third time. Coughing up red phlegm, he realised he had little chance of winning a direct fight with Kyle. Nevertheless, he'd hoped to last longer. He raised his hands in a desperate plea, but he didn't see Kyle's foot rise. It came down hard, crashing into the back of his Exo Suit and flattening him. "You think a time-out will save you?" Kyle taunted.

"What..." Evan spat blood from his mouth. "What's it like?" He looked up at Kyle. "Being Fray's lapdog?" His mocking smile caught Kyle's boot, and the ground vanished beneath him, his head colliding with the squad car.

Kyle's hand closed around Evan's throat, lifting him off the car. "What's it like being mine?"

Kyle's grip drained Evan of any hope of success. He shut his eyes, watching his HUD flicker out. He didn't need it. "Renner."

He heard nothing and felt his strength ebbing away. Darkness encroached. In a few seconds, he'd pass out, and it would all be over. But then, deep in his mind, five words resonated with a meaning more profound than any he'd known before: It can't end like this.

Evan mustered his remaining strength and kicked hard, driving his boot into Kyle's crotch. The grip on his throat weakened momentarily, and that was all he needed. He inhaled a deep, life-giving breath, his eyes fixing on Kyle's distracted expression. He launched a punch aimed at Kyle's throat.

The punch fell short, only grazing Kyle's cheek. Evan's fleeting advantage wasted on a feeble blow. Kyle tightened his grip again, taunting Evan. "Look at yourself!" he sneered, his arm remaining steady, as though Evan weighed no more than a bag of sugar. "Give up."

Evan fought to maintain focus between strained breaths. He thought, five seconds my ass. If he survived this, he'd have some choice words for Renner. "Hurry," he said, almost without realising.

"Hurry?" Kyle echoed, casually pointing his pistol at Evan's head. Then, with less certainty, "You in here, Renner?" Kyle's eye shields retracted, revealing his black eyes and silver pupils locked onto Evan's. "I can't let you go after him. You don't know the full story."

Evan didn't care about the full story; nothing could justify planting a bomb inside a child, having him massacre an entire police squad, and endanger countless others. "Leave the kid to finish his mission," Kyle urged, gradually lowering Evan back to his feet. It seemed like a gesture of peace, as if he expected Evan to comply. "When he's done," Kyle's hand released his throat, and Evan gasped for air, "we'll go for pizza, my treat."

Evan rubbed his sore throat, grateful for the reprieve. Kyle's words took a moment to register, overshadowed by the relief of breathing freely again. 'Leave the kid to finish... When he's done, we'll go for pizza, my treat.' Evan stared at Kyle, dumbfounded. Was it possible? He tried to speak, wanting to ask,

"You don't know?" but the words refused to come out.

"He doesn't know," Renner answered for him.

"Know what?" Kyle demanded. "What don't I know, Renner?"

Evan raised a slow hand to Kyle's shoulder and patted it. He forced out the words, "Going in," his voice rough and strained, and stepped past him, only to be halted by Kyle's iron grip on his wrist.

"Stay," Kyle commanded.

"The kid has a bomb in him," Renner revealed.

"The hell he does."

"It's true, man. Look," Renner showed him. "He's rigged to explode when he sees Percy."

Evan caught a flicker of belief in Kyle's face—a subtle exhalation of one thought, a fresh breath with another—then his eyes met Evan's again, searching for a reason to doubt. "I'm sorry," Evan said, placing his other hand on Kyle's and effortlessly releasing the grip. He walked away.

Kyle didn't move; he just stared at the spot where Evan had stood.

"I can disarm it," Renner offered.

Evan kept walking, heading for Percy's front door. "Wait."

Evan slowed. Good, he thought.

"I'm coming with you." Kyle joined Evan at the steps, and they entered the house together.

As Evan forced the front door open, it pushed back, revealing the first of the Special Branch bodies propped up behind it like a macabre Halloween draft stopper. The tiled floor, as well as the entire hallway, was covered with crimson stains, fresh evidence of Bo and his Desert Eagles' rampage. Another fallen agent lay at the end of the hall, caught off-guard as he rushed out of the kitchen. "How lethal did you guys make him?" Evan inquired just before gunshots echoed through the halls above them.

Kyle slid past Evan and gripped the banister. "Eagles, he's upstairs."

They discovered bodies three and four on the stairs, positioned so precariously that when Kyle brushed past the first, it slid down, forcing Evan to sidestep. Evan noticed his Browning was missing, so he picked up a standard-issue weapon dropped by the Special Branch and readied it. "Where is he?"

"Hurry," Renner responded tersely.

"Can you patch me into him?" Kyle asked.

"He's heading to the third floor. Move it!"

"Bo!" Evan called out, reaching the next landing and discovering even more devastation. Agents were draped over the banisters or piled on top of one another, their torsos riddled with gaping holes or skulls missing altogether. The high-calibre bullets Bo used had done their job. "Bo!" Evan yelled again, hoping to catch the boy's attention. His heads-up display counted the bodies; this had been their last stand, the last line of defence. They were running out of time. "Bo!"

In a matter of seconds, Bo's chip would identify Percy's well-documented face. The confirmation from his augmented eyes would trigger a request to the base, followed by an affirmative response and an almighty explosion. Evan shook off the thought as he stepped over a fallen body. "You grab him," said Kyle. "I'll take..."

Gunshots rang out from the floor above them. "Bo!" Evan shouted, but received no reply. The unmistakable sound of twin reports from Bo's weapons of choice filled the hallways. He was on the next floor up, and according to the schematic and the cluster of heartbeats, so was Percy. The endgame was near, and Evan could sense the impending judgment.

"No killing," Evan warned, his hand sliding up the rail.

"Hurry!" Renner urged.

The muzzle flash was as deafening as the gunshot, casting a white light on the floor before engulfing it in blood and darkness. Evan reached the top of the stairs first, spotting Bo at the end of the corridor. A freshly killed agent fell to the ground, joining several others.

Behind Bo, a large floor-to-ceiling window allowed the moonlight to illuminate the surrounding carnage. Bo fired his pistol through a doorway, the flashes briefly lighting the landing and revealing arterial sprays on the dull magnolia wallpaper.

The boy was almost unrecognisable to Evan. His body was encased in unbranded armour, absorbing the light from his muzzle flashes, making him appear as a shadow even in the brightest light. His body seemed completely alien, but his face was all the confirmation Evan needed. It was the bird, the mad raven with wings flapping frantically as the boy emptied his magazine that sealed it.

"Bo!" Kyle shouted, causing the boy to turn his head. Bo swung one of the Desert Eagles towards Evan, who didn't wait for the trigger to be pulled before moving. He pushed away from the banister and found himself against the magnolia wall, running alongside it towards Bo.

"Stand down!" Kyle shouted from behind him, giving the boy a moment's pause. It was enough for Evan to gain an advantage – he dropped his shoulder, crashed into Bo, lifted him off the ground, and spun around, putting his back to the large window, hitting it with the full force of his Exo-enhanced leap.

The window emitted an unsatisfying thud before throwing them back to the floor. I've been to Percy's house and all I have is this lousy t-shirt. Epic fail, Evan, well done. But it wasn't over; he rolled on top of the boy. "Stand down!" he yelled at Bo and the agent peering through the doorway.

"Get off me!" Bo demanded, though Evan had no illusion of containing him for much longer.

"Mr Wizard, do your thing fast," Evan prayed. Then, to Bo, "He tricked you."

"Get off me! He's a dead man!" the boy snarled.

"Don't make me break my promise, kid..." Evan said.

Kyle double-tapped the agent in the chest with his pistol just as a second appeared in the doorway. "I said stand down, dammit!" Evan shouted at Kyle.

Using the distraction, Bo found Evan's elbow gimbal in his Exo and pulled. His new robotic limbs made quick work of the hardware, and Evan soon felt his left arm go limp. Bo was out from under him shortly after, stopping short of Kyle. "Fallout?"

"Hey, kid," Kyle fired a couple of shots into the doorframe to scare off the agent and took Evan's place as Bo's restraint.

"What the fu..." Bo's struggling was futile. "Let me go!" he said, dropping his Desert Eagles in favour of escape, which proved equally futile.

"Finish it."

Evan heard Kyle's voice in his head as the two agents snaked through the door, both their sidearms trained on Bo and Kyle. Neither of them was concerned with Evan. He wasn't the threat. "We're leaving," he said.

The nearest guard, a tall, powerful figure with a freshly torn nostril and cheek, sniggered. "I don't think so." Evan recognised the voice, then the disfigured face: Carl, poker player extraordinaire.

He knew Carl, knew he would prioritise Percy's safety above all else. He would wait, assess the situation further. After all, Evan and Kyle were unexpected pieces on the chessboard. "Please?" asked Evan.

"Shut it!" the other suit said, one that Evan didn't know.

"Sir, we have them," Carl said.

"Carl, it's me – Evan."

"He said, shut it!" Carl reinforced his colleague's earlier order, aiming at Kyle. "Get on the floor."

"Get him out of there!" Renner said.

"You think?" replied Evan, needing a delay tactic. "Percy! Fray betrayed you. The boy is a bomb."

"I said, get on the bloody floor!" Carl's voice fell on top of another's. Someone else had said something, something small but concise. Evan separated the second voice from the first in his display and replayed it. It was there; someone had said, 'Wait'.

"Guys, Bo's chip just went haywire. It's linked to Percy's voice, too." Renner, the harbinger of doom, had returned.

"I won't ask again..." Carl said, stepping closer to Kyle. "On the floor. Now!"

Kyle dropped to his knees, firing his pistol from his hip and hitting Carl in the knees. The agent screamed as he fell to the floor, grazing Bo's back and Kyle's arm with return fire on his way down. Kyle spun around, presenting his back, intending to shield the boy, but losing his grip and setting Bo free.

It was over. Evan saw the future unfolding: Bo retrieving his twin Desert Eagles, shooting Carl in the back as he leapt over him, and killing the last agent before entering the room and seeing Percy. This would be it for all of them.

Evan moved before his train of thought ended. Scrambling forward, he retrieved his fallen pistol. To his left, Bo aimed his Desert Eagle, its muzzle lined up too close for Evan's comfort. When it fired, the warmth from the flash washed over his cheek, but the bullet wasn't meant for him. Instead, it found its mark in the agent standing inside the room, knocking him to the floor with a burst of red.

Neck and neck with Bo, Evan extended his right leg, pushing into the boy, hoping to knock him off balance or, at the very least, give him a moment to question his surroundings and grant Evan the upper hand. Not counting Carl writhing on the floor behind them, only Percy remained. Evan screamed – a powerful, barbaric yawp, laced with anger and the will to live.

There was no more time for conversation, letting Percy off with a warning. He needed to get to him first before Bo killed them all. He fired into the dark room, revealing Percy in the muzzle flash before firing twice more. The first hit his chest, the second his face – but not before he called out, "Please, no!"

Evan halted a metre into the room, took his shots, and stopped dead, waiting for the explosion.

"That was close," Renner said. "You don't want to know how close."

Evan turned around, expecting Bo to be right behind him, aiming his gun at him for stealing his kill. He was nowhere near; Kyle must have grabbed him shortly after he'd taken out the agent because he was struggling under Kyle's arms in the corridor. Lowering his pistol, Evan saluted him in thanks.

It was then he saw Carl and remembered the gunshot just before he shot Percy. The man's head was spilling out on the landing, a tragic witness to the crime of the century, but he needn't have died. All of them, none of Percy's bodyguards, and even

Percy himself, could have survived this night. To hell with them and their politics.

"What now?" asked Kyle.

"I don't know about you," Evan said, "but I intend to keep my promise."

CHAPTER TWENTY-FIVE
FRAYED RELATIONS

Oliver listlessly prodded his meal. Monkfish, arrayed on a bed of spinach with a cheese and wine sauce, and crushed nuts sprinkled atop. It bore a fancy name and had been cooked in some elaborate way, but Oliver couldn't recall what Vernon had said when he'd presented the dish, and he didn't care to search his recent memories. To him, it was simply an unappetising mass.

Meanwhile, Felix devoured his food with gusto. Seated across the marble banquet table, he was almost finished. He animatedly described the cooking process while wearing a constant smile, despite not having cooked the dish himself. "You have to make sure the pan is hot and don't leave it in there over four minutes, or you may as well bin it."

Oliver nodded, feigning interest, and swirled his fork in the sauce. "Oliver," Felix said. "You've hardly touched it."

"Yes," Oliver admitted.

"You're not one of those people, are you?" Felix skewered a piece of the tender fish with his fork, holding it up between them. "That thinks this is the poor man's lobster?" He brought the fish close to his mouth, paused, and asked, "You're not a snob, are you, Oliver?" He popped the fish into his mouth, sniggering as he chewed.

Oliver longed to tell him the truth, to make a rude gesture and blow Felix a mocking kiss. Instead, he asked, "What's wrong with being a snob?"

"Everything—they're worse than the plebs. They're the posh plebs." He speared some spinach, twirling it around his fork. "They're the posh sheep," he sniggered, "following popular opinion and buying whatever's fashionable. Still, I wouldn't be here without them."

"Quite," said Oliver, envisioning Jonathan's face in his dish.

"Don't look so glum."

Oliver glanced up from his plate and reached for his wineglass. Unlike his food, his appetite for the Sancerre grape remained unquenched. "It's happening right now," he said, raising the glass to his lips. "People are dying right now."

Felix swallowed. "It's happened. Percy and the boy are dead." He grasped his own glass and lifted it. "To victory."

Oliver set his wine back on the table. "I won't toast to murder."

"Spoilsport!" Felix drank a mouthful and returned his glass to the table before picking up his fork again. "It's over, Oliver. You may not like it, but it needed to be done. I admire you feel the need to be guilty about it, but when you're Prime Minister, you'll soon understand that guilt is merely a distraction. You'll still be required to function; the sooner you make peace with your decisions, the quicker you can move on."

Oliver stared at his wineglass.

"Oliver?" Felix queried, prompting Oliver to look up. "You've done the right thing. And if you disagree, consider this – Jonathan had to go." Oliver's attention was now fully on Felix. "We could have worked something out for Percy, but I wanted him gone to prove a point." Oliver fought the rising bile in his throat. "Do I need to explain further?" For an uncertain stretch of time, Oliver stared at Felix before shaking his head, allowing Felix to resume eating with a smug satisfaction.

Oliver surrendered to his guilt, letting it envelop him, finding a sense of security and humanity within its embrace. Tomorrow, he would take the first public step towards power, signing the Fray Security deal and keeping Britain out of foreign hands for a while longer. "All the King's soldiers and all the King's Men..."

"Will put the kingdom back together again," Felix completed the rhyme before Oliver even realised he'd begun it. "We two will be remembered as the men who restored sovereignty to Buckingham Palace."

Oliver drained the last of his Sancerre, and as he placed the glass back on the table, Vernon appeared at his side. The perfect butler, silent and ever-vigilant. He'd remained in the background all evening, serving and clearing their plates, refilling their glasses as needed. Vernon's silver-coated mechanics tipped the bottle, pouring wine into Oliver's glass.

The blue tint was immediately noticeable. Although not a connoisseur, Oliver knew wine came in red, pink, or white — never blue. His eyes flickered towards the curtain, illuminated by the changing external light, shifting from blue to red, then back to blue. "Are you expecting anyone?"

"No," Felix replied. "Vernon, tell them to come back during business hours. Would you please?"

"Of course, sir." Vernon replaced the bottle in the ice bucket as he left the room.

"Sit back down, please," Felix urged, but Oliver had already crossed the room, peering into the garden.

Immediately, he spotted it hovering over the building's edge. Its siren was silent, but its beams and light-strip flashed persistently, alternating between red and blue. It wasn't unusual for police to fly directly to a penthouse during an emergency, bypassing any unwanted red tape. However, their silent presence without communication was peculiar. "Have they pinged you?"

Oliver hadn't noticed Felix's approach. "No," he replied, standing beside him.

Vernon walked out into the garden, waving at the uninvited guest.

"I don't like this," Oliver remarked.

"It is a tad concerning," Felix admitted, sipping from his glass.

"Percy?" Oliver suggested.

"Everyone's dead," Felix confirmed. "I received the report. All dead." He then looked over to Vernon. "Anything?"

From the window, Oliver watched as Vernon's head swivelled at an impossible angle for any human to achieve.

"Nothing," Felix answered Oliver's unspoken query.

The police car tilted, its right headlight dipping while its back end straightened. "What's it doing?" Oliver inquired.

As the car's front end dipped and the engines propelled it forward, it followed a trajectory like a dart striking a bullseye. It crashed its grille into Vernon, and both car and robot vanished from sight.

Oliver recoiled as the window trembled violently. "Jesus!"

"Has nothing to do with this." Felix dropped his glass and stormed away from the window. The lights around the building flickered and faded, while Oliver's nose detected the acrid scent of burning fuel. "He's hit the damned house!" Felix roared, leaving the room.

Oliver trailed Felix from the dining room into the hallway. To his right, smoke billowed through the open veranda doors. Flames clawed at the glass, charring the white paint black.

Felix froze in the centre of the hall, and Oliver instantly understood why. Amidst the smoke, a dark, unmistakable shadow emerged.

"Kyle?" Felix inquired.

In response, Kyle forcefully raised his pistol. The bullet tore through Felix's stomach, dropping him to his knees. Fray clung to his dignity, refusing to whimper. "Wait!" he gasped, pressing his palm flat on the marble floor to steady himself.

Two more bullets struck Felix, one on his raised knee and another grazing his thigh. This time, he couldn't stifle a cry, squirming in the blood pooling around him. Oliver remained rooted to the spot, unable to act or speak, witnessing Felix's agony.

Kyle holstered his sidearm but kept something in his right hand as he approached his prey.

"Wait," Felix pleaded.

"Wait," Oliver echoed. Surprised by his own voice, he hadn't expected Kyle would halt out of curiosity rather than submission. Kyle stopped, Felix's blood lapping at his feet, and waited. But Oliver was unsure of what to say next. His throat felt dry and empty.

Felix coughed up a mouthful of crimson fluid, losing the last vestiges of his dignity. Desperate and terrified, he retched and writhed on the floor, babbling incoherently, punctuated by the occasional "Please."

Seeing Felix stripped of his eloquence and reduced to such impotence provided Oliver with an answer to his question. Am I like Felix? "Don't kill him," he said.

"Why?" Kyle shot back.

Oliver could tell his friend he didn't want to be a killer, that there was already too much blood on his hands. But Kyle wouldn't understand. Oliver had made his choice and should face the consequences.

"Why?" Oliver hadn't seen Kyle draw his pistol again, but staring down its barrel was no less terrifying.

"I need him," Oliver confessed, unable to meet Kyle's gaze. It was partly true; he could try to fix the country without Felix Fray, but he'd fail. He needed Felix more than Felix needed him.

"Him?" Kyle redirected the gun to Felix. "You need this piece of shit?"

"I do," Oliver acknowledged, looking at Felix, bleeding out on the floor. "God help me, Kyle, I need him."

Oliver's and Felix's eyes locked as Kyle's voice burned with fury. "You know what he did?" Oliver followed the pistol's aim, focused on Felix. "What this bastard did? He killed the kid. He killed Evan."

"Evan?" Oliver hadn't expected to hear his name. The man was already dead.

Oliver averted his gaze from Felix, spotted the elevator and the dial on its frame—the numbers rapidly approaching them.

"I did..." Felix screamed, "what was necessary—"

"Don't talk," Kyle growled.

Oliver stepped forward, his hands raised defensively. "I knew about the boy." Kyle's attention shifted back to him. "Kyle, I knew." He moved between the two men. "I didn't know Evan would be there. We all thought he was dead, but what Felix says is true, he deserves to die, and so do I, but right now we're the only thing standing in the way of invasion." He stepped closer, his voice hushed. "Security is on their way."

"They won't save you."

Oliver wasn't sure which of them Kyle was referring to, or if he meant both. "If you kill him, you won't be able to hide anywhere. His father will use all his resources to find you."

"And you need him," Kyle added.

"And I need him."

Oliver didn't immediately feel pain, only a vague warning triggered by the sound of Kyle's pistol firing. Breathing became difficult, as if the room's oxygen had been depleted. The room spun. He didn't hear Felix's hysterical laughter or the elevator's chime. He focused on his next breath.

Kyle stepped back, having primed and tossed a grenade over Oliver's shoulder. Oliver thought he heard distant screams—agonised prayers consumed by a fiery tidal wave that knocked him off his feet. As his knees cracked against the marble, he felt the tightness in his gut. He looked down at his hands, cradling his blood-soaked shirt and the bullet hole in his abdomen.

As he stared at the wound, he couldn't comprehend he'd been shot. Being in the line of fire had been unimaginable, being shot even more so. Oliver's medical report flashed on his HUD—beckoning, 'Read me.' I can't die like this.

Kyle crouched before him, pressing his pistol against Oliver's cheek. He looked into Kyle's armoured eyes and saw his own ghostly reflection. "Oliver." He watched Kyle's lips move, unable to hear his words. "I won't kill you, but you're doing this on your own."

Kyle stood, forcing Oliver's head against his thigh and granting him a perfect view of the destruction down the corridor: a blazing elevator, warped mirrored walls, and Felix, drenched in his own blood, crawling toward the dining-room door. Kyle fired twice, both shots hitting Felix's shoulder blades, halting his escape. The third and final shot shattered the man's skull.

Kyle's leg support vanished, and Oliver, unable to control his limbs, crumpled to the floor, his blood mingling with Felix's. There he rested, waiting for the encroaching darkness to claim him.

CHAPTER TWENTY-SIX
NEW YEAR'S RESOLUTIONS

He reclined on the bed, scrutinising his medical progress reports projected onto his closed eyelids. The bullet had threaded through his stomach, narrowly missing his spine by less than an inch. Surgery had been performed at Fray International, but for recovery, he'd been transferred to Clifton Park and was slated to resume work in another three days.

But that hadn't stopped the office coming to him.

"Bartlett and Morgan have jumped the fence on the test ban treaty," Antonia announced, sauntering in with a punnet of strawberries.

Oliver opened his eyes. "Is it two already?"

"Almost three," Antonia retorted, settling into the chair beside his bed. "I see you're still savouring the drugs."

He smiled. "Indeed."

"I preferred your old room."

Oliver hadn't. That room was shared, whereas this one had just enough space for his bed, one or two chairs, and his monitoring equipment—a compact bedside table with a touchscreen surface. It also boasted a window overlooking the car park. "The view is superior."

"Strawberry?" she proffered the punnet. "They're good."

Oliver plucked a plump one by its stalk. "Already sampled them?"

"Two for one. I've got an empty tub in the car."

He grinned, savouring the fruit. His sense of taste was gradually returning, but fully appreciating delectable flavours like strawberries would take time. "That makes five?" he asked, referring to her initial statement.

"Six. I still think Gardner is holding out on us."

"It'll pass." Oliver selected another strawberry. At least it was juicy.

"If Faraday stays on course," she remarked.

"He will."

"You sound confident."

"I am," Oliver affirmed. "Anything on the nomination?"

She swiped a strawberry just as his fingers reached the tub. "We'll announce you when you're discharged."

"No contenders?"

"I considered it, but the job's mortality rate is utterly unappealing."

"So it seems," he replied.

"Besides, you're a hero now. Who would dare challenge the man who survived the Gunboy?"

He smiled, well aware it hadn't been the kid who had shot him. That honour had fallen to Kyle, who had done so to save his life. By shooting him, he had cast doubt on his relationship with the traitor. He'd made his point and reminded the gods they were mortal.

"I know you don't want to discuss it. But you are getting the job, so you need to fill vacancies," said Antonia, snatching another strawberry.

"Who do you think?"

"Well, given your newfound faith in Faraday, I think he'd make a good Whip."

"So do I."

"As for the Foreign Secretary position, I'm not sure."

"I know who I want for Foreign," Oliver said, touching her hand. "I need suggestions for Home Secretary."

She blushed. Not a full crimson face blush, but a subtle pink tint to her cheeks that only a close friend would recognise. "You don't want to keep it open for one of Fox's lot?"

Oliver shook his head. "I want someone I can trust."

She nodded, grabbing another strawberry. "About that..." she trailed off in a way that could only mean a question was about to follow.

"Go on," said Oliver.

"What happened? I mean, I've read the report, but it all seems far-fetched."

"Have you not seen my footage?"

"The Branch locked it down."

"Don't tell me Renner allowed Gillespie to stop him," he said, noticing her blush replaced by a look of sadness. "What is it?"

"He's gone," she said. "The same night you were shot."

"I didn't know," he blurted. "I'm sorry."

"Don't be daft." She looked down at his hand, still holding hers.

So Renner had vanished too: he must have been working with Evan. And then helped Kyle, or vice versa. Either way, two confidantes were now gone. He swallowed at his mistake. How quickly he had forgotten him. "When is Jonathan's funeral?"

"Wednesday."

He nodded; he would be out of hospital by then. "And Percy's?"

"Possibly Friday. There was talk of Wednesday, for expediency, but they were concerned about elevating him above his station."

Oliver chuckled. "He was almost Prime Minister."

"I'm sure they'll decide soon enough." She took another strawberry. "Last one, I promise."

He laughed again. "Help yourself."

"The Fray funeral won't be until next week. They're waiting for his sister to arrive."

There it was: Felix's name. The man he'd shielded from a gun. It sickened Oliver to think he'd done that when he'd chosen to step aside as a gun was pointed at his friend. The icy grip of guilt reached up at him from beneath the bed, and like a chain, he felt it encircling his neck. Until he recalled Felix's words.

He touched Antonia's elbow. "What's next?"

2

The fresh morning sun warmed Evan's night-chilled face, his fingers brushing the surface of the Thames. His arm dangled over the canoe's side, drifting in silence. His legs rested on the bow's seat, elevated as he lay flat on the boat's bottom.

Bo crouched on the bow deck in his familiar predatory manner. They had travelled mainly in silence, sharing a few moments of strategy discussion and occasional small talk. Not wanting to draw attention was the excuse they gave themselves. The real reason was not having anything to say to each other.

Evan didn't blame him. Bo had been wronged in a way Evan could only attempt to empathise with. Being violated was the closest comparison he could muster. Fray had manipulated Bo for purposes far beyond his understanding, and if that wasn't enough, Evan had robbed him of his revenge. Perhaps Evan was projecting his own guilt onto the situation, or maybe not. But Bo's coldness, his distant persona, left Evan to confront his own demons.

Or maybe it was Evan's reluctance to consider his decisions that led him to ponder Bo. He had killed Percy Browne, an unarmed man, in cold blood—an act he'd thought himself incapable of. After a night of restless sleep, he knew it would take time to come to terms with that choice, which placed him on the wrong side of the law and, ultimately, the wrong side of the fence. He couldn't say if he'd see his father again or if he'd want to. He didn't want to think about his mother's reaction to his death being broadcast globally with that dreadful label: terrorist. He disliked the idea of his entire existence reduced to that single, fear-inducing word.

All because he'd chosen to prioritise an innocent life over corruption. As a result, he'd live as an outcast, his friends and family believing him to be a dead terrorist. But no matter how much he'd lost, the gain was far greater. Bo would live and soon return to his family and Nikki, the woman to whom he'd made his promise.

Bo leaned back, taking a paddle, dipping it into the water, and steering the canoe slightly to port.

Evan raised his head above the gunwale; they were finally there. When Bo told him their destination, Evan had thought it fitting. Now, seeing the entrance approaching, he couldn't help but think how life tended to mock itself. The place was the Tower. The entrance of choice, Traitor's Gate.

He didn't know if he'd stay with them or if he'd even be welcome. For the first time in his life, his future was uncertain. Yet Evan remembered his father's advice: 'Don't be a wuss.' And with that memory, he finally smiled.

The End.

Acknowledgments

I would like to express my deepest gratitude to the individuals who contributed to the development and success of this book.

First and foremost, I extend my heartfelt thanks to Siobhan Marshal-Jones and Gary Compton at Tickety Boo Press. Their invaluable support and belief in my work transformed this project from an editing commission into a published novel.

I am also immensely grateful to the Nanowrimo community, whose collective enthusiasm and encouragement played a vital role in the completion of this book.

Last but certainly not least, I must extend my profound appreciation to my wife, Tereza. Without her unwavering support, this story might have remained an unpublished screenplay gathering dust on a shelf. Her motivation and persistence have been instrumental in bringing this project to fruition, and for that, I am eternally thankful. Thanks for kicking my ass.

Find out more

ABOUT LEIGHTON DEAN BY VISITING HIS:

WEBSITE: WWW.LEIGHTONDEAN.CO.UK
FACEBOOK: LEIGHTON.DEAN.AUTHOR

THEWRITEDEAN

Printed in Great Britain
by Amazon